I0760869

THE MYTHS OF MIDWINTER

THE HOUSE OF CRIMSON & CLOVER VOLUME VIII

SARAH M. CRADIT

Cover Design by Sarah M. Cradit

First Edition
ISBN-10: 1517657806
ISBN-13: 978-1517657802

Publisher Contact:
sarah@sarahmcradit.com
www.sarahmcradit.com

ALSO BY SARAH M. CRADIT

KINGDOM OF THE WHITE SEA

Kingdom of the White Sea Trilogy

The Kingless Crown

The Broken Realm

The Hidden Kingdom

The Book of All Things

The Raven and the Rush

The Sylvan and the Sand

The Altruist and the Assassin

The Melody and the Master

The Claw and the Crowned

THE SAGA OF CRIMSON & CLOVER

The House of Crimson and Clover Series

The Storm and the Darkness

Shattered

The Illusions of Eventide

Bound

Midnight Dynasty

Asunder

Empire of Shadows

Myths of Midwinter

The Hinterland Veil

The Secrets Amongst the Cypress

Within the Garden of Twilight

House of Dusk, House of Dawn

Midnight Dynasty Series

A Tempest of Discovery

A Storm of Revelations

A Torrent of Deceit

The Seven Series

1970

1972

1973

1974

1975

1976

1980

Vampires of the Merovingi Series

The Island

and more

The Dusk Trilogy

St. Charles at Dusk: The Story of Oz and Adrienne

Flourish: The Story of Anne Fontaine

Banshee: The Story of Giselle Deschanel

Crimson & Clover Stories

Surrender: The Story of Oz and Ana

Shame: The Story of Jonathan St. Andrews

Fire & Ice: The Story of Remy & Fleur

Dark Blessing: The Landry Triplets

Pandora's Box: The Story of Jasper & Pandora

The Menagerie: Oriana's Den of Iniquities

A Band of Heather: The Story of Colleen and Noah

The Ephemeral: The Story of Autumn & Gabriel

Bayou's Edge: The Landry Triplets

For more information, and exciting bonus material, visit www.sarahmcradit.com

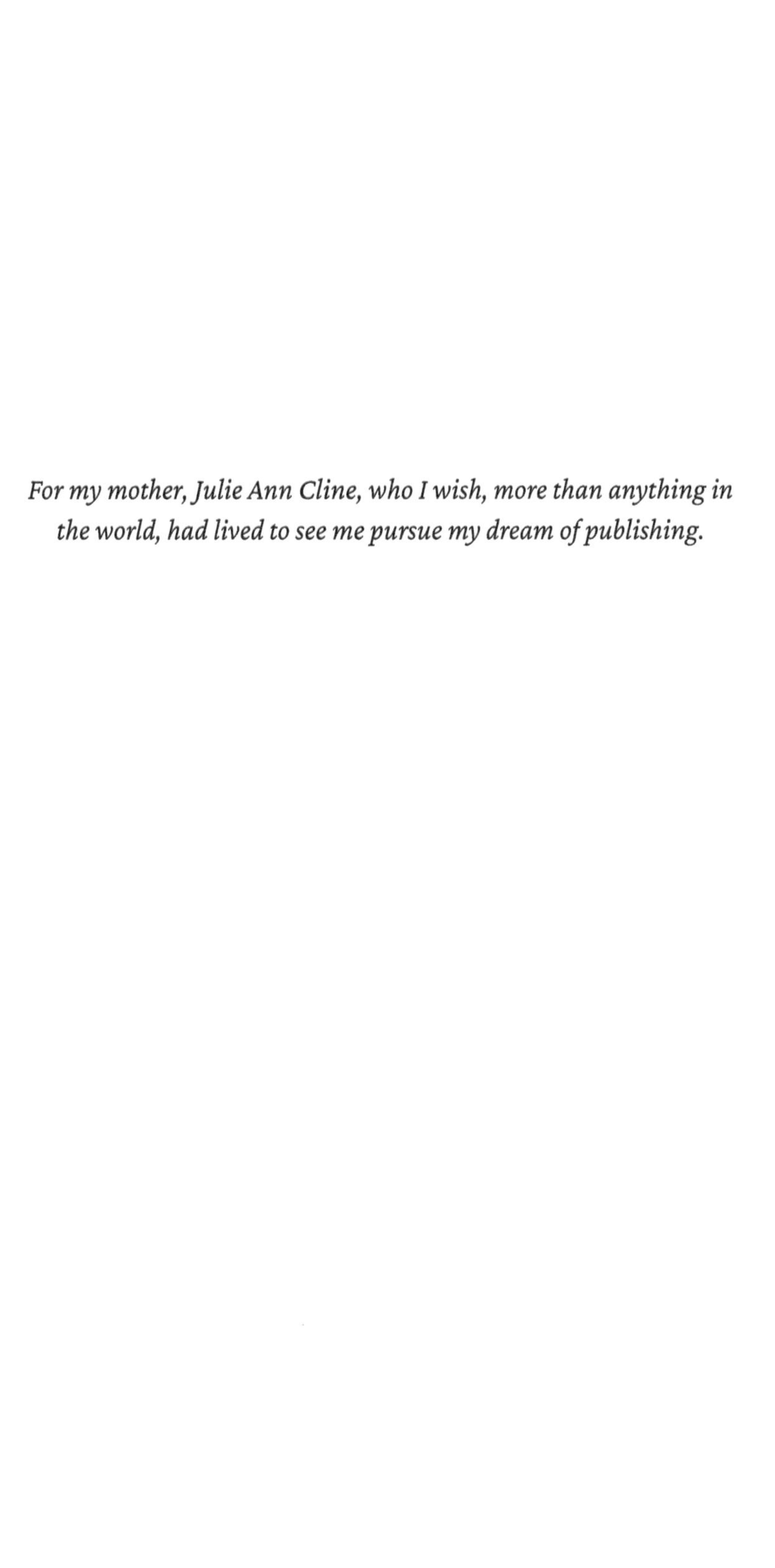

For my mother, Julie Ann Cline, who I wish, more than anything in the world, had lived to see me pursue my dream of publishing.

"Beware, lest you lose the substance by grasping at the shadow."

Aesop

THE DEVIL

1

QUILLAN

Quillan Sullivan had, over the course of many years, developed the skills necessary to endure his father's legendary lectures. He could successfully mask his complete lack of interest with an outward appearance of contrition. Twenty-six years of experience in this made him damn near an expert.

"Right, sure," he answered, nodding furiously, as Patrick Sullivan paced Quillan's humble living room. His father's protracted, heavy steps nearly shook the cheap lamp from Quillan's equally cheap desk, both accouterments his father hotly disapproved of. The Sullivans didn't work hard for nearly two centuries to live in such affront to good taste, after all. Quillan smirked.

"This is funny to you?" his father demanded, halting his relentless pacing.

Oops. "Not exactly. You see—"

"What I *see* is a child I raised, who's ungrateful, immature, spoiled, and completely out of control! Do you know how difficult it was to convince Colin to let you stay? Do you understand how absolutely outlandish it is that we even had to sit down to discuss whether or not a *Sullivan* would be allowed to continue practicing law at our *family* firm?" Patrick's jowls trembled as the word *Sullivan* spat from his lips.

Quillan was quite aware. Sullivan and Associates was practically a birthright for any Sullivan choosing to go into law. Getting removed would be about as likely as the Prince of Wales being stripped of his title.

Quillan wondered at his strange sense of pride about the current state of affairs surrounding his actions.

His father's tomato-red face matched his hair, and the veins in his thick neck protruded, as they often did when dealing with his only son. A veil of control settled over his face, a telltale sign of his preparedness to reign in a conversation going nowhere. "I'm weary of these discussions, Quillan. I have better things to do than lecture my grown son on how it's unacceptable to consistently drop the ball at work. I've decided to pass this babysitting job on to someone else."

Quillan looked up. This piqued his attention. "Sorry?"

"Lauren Weatherly." Patrick studied Quillan's blank face. "Your cousin Cameron's sister-in-law? Been with the firm about five years now? Seriously, Quillan? You work in the same office."

Well, it's not like I spend a lot of time there, is what Quillan wanted to say, but instead replied, "I'd probably know her if I saw her."

His father groaned in exasperation. "One would hope, Quillan. Well, you'll know her soon enough. I've asked her to keep an eye on you and give you direction. Maybe remedial lessons on how to actually *do* the things you were *supposedly* trained to do in law school."

Quillan shifted in his seat. "Sure, okay."

Patrick Sullivan rolled his eyes to the ceiling and sighed

again. "Of course, tell me what I want to hear like you always do. It doesn't matter. You're *going* to succeed, whether you want to or not. You're *going* to because you're my son and I want to see you be successful. More importantly, you're *going* to pull your head out of your ass because it's not only your reputation on the line, it's mine. I'm proud of where I come from. You could learn some personal pride yourself." His father laughed at the last part, a grating, derisive sound, as if pigs would fly around the world before this happened.

"I said I would," Quillan insisted, ushering his dad toward the door, fatigued of listening to everyone in his life offering passionate diatribes about what he *should* be doing. What he *should* have done was not listen to them in the first place, and pursue something that actually interested him. *First and foremost, I should have moved far away from these crazy, superstitious Irish kooks.*

But you don't like anything. What would you have done if not this? Riley's words resonated in his head. *I would do anything to have your worries.*

No one else had the power to reach Quillan and appeal to his better nature the way Riley could, yet his words changed nothing.

"When you come in Monday, go straight to Lauren's office." His father positioned his body between the door and frame as if he thought Quillan might close it in his face. "Woe betide you if she has to come looking for you!"

His father finally gone, Quillan went to the kitchen, opened the cupboard serving as their wet bar, and started to pour a drink. He stopped halfway, glancing at the clock to see it was only noon, shrugged, and continued pouring.

"You weren't very nice," Riley interrupted his misery.

"And?"

"He just wants you to be okay. He loves you."

"Ah, things are so simple to a seven-year-old," Quillan declared and brushed past Riley, shuffling out onto the small deck overlooking a shared garden area. Sweet scents of jasmine and oleander filled his troubled head, calming him.

"I'm not like other seven-year-olds," Riley insisted, following.

"Be that as it may, you have absolutely no idea what you're talking about."

Riley wrinkled his nose, as he often did when trying to give Quillan advice on a topic foreign to him. "I wish I did," he said finally.

Quillan softened. "I know, buddy. Anyway, it's no big deal, right? I just have to meet with this chick, and then Dad will cool off for a bit, and it will all be good. For a while anyway."

"Do you think so?"

Quillan nodded. "You really think they'd kick a Sullivan out of their own law firm? I mean, c'mon, there's, like, fifty of us there. It's not an office, it's a collection."

Riley giggled. "As long as you don't lose your job. That would make Mom sad."

Quillan thought his mother's sadness was often over-exaggerated, but Riley couldn't understand that, so he offered, "It's all good, buddy. Don't you worry. I've got this under control."

A large smile spread across Riley's face. "Can I watch you play video games?"

Quillan finished his drink and left the glass next to all the other empty ones that someone, probably Leander, would have to take care of later. "Sure."

Leander arrived home that evening in an especially foul mood. It was sometimes hard to discern the direction of Leander's disposition as the scowl on his face was an ever-present feature, but Quillan picked up on the thud of Leander's old backpack hitting the floor, and the fact he was still wearing his shoes when he stomped into the living room.

"Thy panties appear to be in a twist," Quillan remarked without looking up, embroiled in finishing the last lap of his racing game. Riley disappeared the moment Leander's key turned in the lock.

"Clearly," Leander snipped. He marched toward the balcony, observed Quillan's glasses spread out on the table and chairs, snorted, then flopped down in the old recliner instead. His hand moved instinctively to brush the bangs from his eyes, but stopped in mid-gesture. He'd shaved his head the day before in a moment of particular frustration.

Quillan finished his game and tossed the controller carelessly into a cardboard box. "Want me to tell you about my shitty day? I had an awesome conversation with my father."

"Not especially."

"Want to talk about yours then? Wishing you had enough *cojones* to ask that shark chick out?"

Leander shot him a look.

"Well, she studies sharks, does she not?"

"She's a marine biology major," Leander clarified evenly.

"Exactly, the shark chick. She shoot you down?"

"No."

"Then what?"

"Not everyone's problems can be summed up into booty call complications," Leander volleyed, and slumped into his room without another word.

"Alas, there are other shark chicks in the sea," Quillan called out after him.

Leander's moods were nothing new, nor were the glaring differences between the two men. Riley had explained their individual natures best: *Leander is the kid in class who keeps his head down when the teacher says good morning to everyone. You're the kid who screams good morning back, as loud as he possibly can.*

Quillan and Leander had been best friends since the third grade when Leander had shown up to class after having been skipped ahead a grade. Years later, Quillan would reflect on what a horrible decision that was. Leander was smart, there was no doubt, but he would always struggle socially.

Where Leander resisted making friends, Quillan had problems turning them away. He didn't understand what made him latch on to the quiet, odd boy who came into their class that day, but he never regretted it. Not then, and not now, years later, when they lived as roommates in their dusty French Quarter flat.

Their differences didn't stop there, though. Where Quillan had grown up in a relatively normal family, everything about Leander's home life was steeped in bizarre. His parents, Pandora and Jasper Broussard, were local celebrities, known for their pandering of occult artifacts, tours, books, and bogus magical services. Their profession was horrifying to Leander, a medical student pursuing a life of research science.

His youngest sister, Harriett, went over a decade without speaking, and then only began again when she fled home. Quillan always interpreted her silence as a disgust equal to Leander's.

Leander had another sister, though. Estella... ahh, Estella. Estella with the blonde silken hair that glimmered in the sun. Estella of the tiny nose and full, voluptuous apple-red mouth. Estella of the moonlight-pale skin and crystal blue eyes like a clear spring day.

Estella was the great love of Quillan's life, though the sentiment remained unrequited. She had been away at college in France studying the occult for the past four years. In the time apart, Quillan's fascination for her had dulled only somewhat.

The attraction had always been a bone of contention between Quillan and Leander. Leander didn't like his sister. Quillan wasn't sure Leander even *loved* her. *She's an angel*, Quillan would say. *She's a foul bitch*, Leander would respond.

For Leander, Quillan was an escape from the prison of his own mind and the world he grew up in. For Quillan, Leander offered a breath of fresh air, and a reminder that perhaps his problems were not nearly as dramatic as they seemed.

For all their closeness, Quillan had never talked to Leander about Riley. Never discussed him directly, not even in the context of their childhood, before everything had gone to hell. If there was anyone Quillan could have told, it would have been Leander, the man who'd grown up in a household of complete crazies and was more than a little nutty himself.

But Quillan couldn't bring himself to tell anyone. Not Leander, not his parents, and not anyone else he'd ever known.

How exactly *does* one tell someone they have regular conversations with their dead twin brother?

2
FINNEGAN

Finn's pleas to Thorvald, no matter the angle attempted, fell on deaf ears.

"Your place is here," the ancient said, never searching for more creative or softer ways to deliver the message. "At *Ophèlie*."

"My place is with my family," Finn countered, thinking of his son upstairs and his wife, somewhere across the world, mired in unknown dangers.

He wouldn't choose one over the other. If he'd taken any lesson from Aidrik's sacrifice, it was the equality of love.

"Your mate is safe with the Brotherhood. Your son requires the protection the two of you created. No, halfling, you'll not be joining us in Farjhem."

If we can create the shield here, we can create it anywhere, Finn thought, but Thorvald may as well have been constructed of titanium.

In the end, Finn conceded Thorvald's particular journey was not his, anyway. Thorvald would be leading a team to investigate all that transpired in Farjhem after Finn was forced to flee, without Ana or Aidrik. Whatever they found there, Ana would not be among the lists of dead. Nerys made that clear with her reassurances Ana was with the Brotherhood, far from the warfare that left the primeval land in ruins.

Finn's faith in Ana's safety was tenuous, despite trusting Nerys. No deception existed in the warrior princess—none he could see, anyway. He sensed her agenda belonged with no particular group, but with her belief in the eventual peace of her people.

Aleksandr was his responsibility, and it was one he took to his soul. But Aleksei's physical well-being was only half the matter. The longer his mother's fate remained unknown, the more he despaired and retreated into a place Finn had difficulty reaching him.

Finn could neither sit back and hope for the best, nor ask his son to. In the end, if joining Thorvald on his quest wasn't meant to be, he would find his own way to Ana.

MATTERS AT *OPHÈLIE* HAD EVOLVED IN A NEAR-IMMEDIATE MANNER, from perilous excitement to a calmness bordering on suspended animation. With the property and family once again safe, and the Senetat purportedly destroyed—*Thanks to Ana... my god, how I need to see her, to relieve the weight of this burden from her*—the dire urgency permeating everything had dissipated.

Anders, along with Tristan and Harriett, left the day prior, leading a search party for the missing refugee children. Lucia remained behind, for reasons she reserved to herself, keeping Hakon and Livia with her. Markus had left for D.C. to see his parents, after his visits with his broken sister, Katja, resulted in more heartbreak.

Nerys stayed, with a kind but stalwart reminder that her

primary concern was Aleksei's safety. She tailed him around the property, in unfailing vigilance.

Which left Nicolas and Mercy, who were thick in the midst of dealing with something they didn't share with anyone else in the household.

"Finn, I need to take her to Colleen. If anyone asks, make something up. I don't care what, as long as it doesn't turn everyone into busybodies. I can count on you, yeah? Okay?" Nicolas leaned over the kitchen sink, pouring out bottle after bottle of Hennessy.

"You know you can," Finn assured him. "But I won't be here when you get back."

Nicolas dropped the bottle he was holding into the basin with a sharp clatter. His shoulders sagged in a heavy sigh. "That isn't a good idea. But you know that, and you don't care. If I were you, I wouldn't care either. Hell, if Mercy didn't need me so fucking bad, I'd be at your side."

Finn said nothing.

"I know what it is to love Ana." Nicolas bowed his head lower, shaking it with a short series of huffs, the sound equally pain and laughter. "How consuming it can be, destroying everything else, including whatever is left of your better sense. To know that, and love her all the more."

"I've never felt I was giving anything up, to love her."

"Yeah. It's different with you two. I know that. Of course it is," Nicolas rambled.

In a flash of rage, he flung one of the empty bottles against the side of the fridge. The glass shattered, and both men jumped.

"Don't listen to anything coming out of my mouth, brother," Nicolas muttered, stumbling from the room. "Love has always been an affliction I misunderstood at the outset, and ruined in the final stretch.

"Take care of yourself, and Aleksandr. God, how I love that boy. Okay? Don't let anything happen to him, Finn. Not a hair."

Finn didn't respond, feeling it unnecessary.

But he did offer a smile to Nicolas, saying a silent prayer to Aidrik to look after the man once he and Aleksei were on their way.

THERE EXISTED ONE OTHER IN THE HOUSEHOLD, OF COURSE. A CERTAIN brother Finn had left to his own devices. Finn's revulsion for him had only grown since disaster struck his family. Not waned. Not even slightly.

You put her on this path, Jon. If not for you, we'd have settled into a quiet, happy life in Maine.

Yeah, another voice in his mind countered, *but then you wouldn't have Aleksei. Your bond with Ana would not have been strengthened by your shared experiences. You'd be ordinary.*

None of that excuses or changes anything.

Finn pushed this additional bit of narrative far from his thoughts.

ONCE NICOLAS AND MERCY WERE ON THEIR WAY TO NEW ORLEANS, Finn sat down in the study and fingered through Nicolas' address book. He easily found the two contacts he was looking for.

On a handy yellow Post-it note, he scribbled down the numbers for Colin Sullivan and Augustus Deschanel, then put everything back where he'd found it. Once the others realized they'd fled, it would be better if the trail were not so easy to reconstruct.

A tall, youthful redhead appeared in the doorway, Forbia at

his ankles. Aleksei's drowsy smile and heavy lids gave his insomnia away. "What are you doing, Far?"

After folding the square carefully in half, Finn rose to join his son, resting a hand on his back as he guided him from the office. "Making plans."

3
LAUREN

Lauren Weatherly switched on both coffee pots, and the break room filled with a deep, floral aroma.

The steady dripping patter was the first sound to be heard at Sullivan and Associates that morning, and there would be no additional noise for another thirty minutes or so. Although Lauren had been chided several times for making the coffee—this was the assistants' job—she didn't mind. No work was beneath her. Besides, she was an early riser and first to arrive every morning.

Lauren turned her gaze out the window facing Julia Street. The world lay blanketed in dark, rows of galleries and shops still dead to the world. Some of the stores remained shuttered, years after Katrina. She wondered if they would ever re-open.

Great oaks resisted the booming gusts of wind that bowed the bare lavender and empress trees, while the rest of the world remained oblivious to nature's morning call. The late October air seemed dry but electric, as if an off-season storm perched on the horizon.

When the pot chimed its finish, Lauren filled a mug half

with coffee, the balance milk, and went to her small office. Calling it a cramped space would be polite. Unlike the break room and many of the other offices, there was no window. Lacking room for a bookshelf, her books and binders were stacked tidily against a wall.

Lauren set the mug down on the old oak desk and glanced at her calendar. With a sigh, she slumped in her seat. Today was the day she'd begin "mentoring" Quillan Sullivan.

Her flattery at being chosen by one of the partners to help was quickly supplanted by apprehension at what she'd gotten herself into. Quillan hardly ever showed up for work. Most of his clients had requested a change in representation. On the rare occasion he did actually wander in, he spent his time playing practical jokes on his uncles, aunts, and cousins. From everything Lauren had seen so far, there weren't any indications he even *wanted* his job. She suspected only his Sullivan name kept him employed... at least until now. His father had evidently reached a breaking point.

It would be a tall order, saving that one.

Other than his ridiculous behavior, Lauren didn't know much about Quillan. He was Patrick's son, Patrick being one of the Sullivan partners, his oldest brother, Colin, presiding as senior partner. There were so many damn Sullivans at the firm she had a hard time keeping track. They had another brother, Rory, and a sister, Chelsea. The siblings were all partners, as was Colin's uncle, Jamie. From all she'd heard, and seen, working well past retirement wasn't uncommon amongst this family.

The number of Sullivan associates changed with the wind... or, every time a new flow of graduates entered from Tulane, Loyola, or, occasionally, some far-flung East Coast Ivy League school.

There were, of course, non-Sullivans at the firm, but not

many. In fact, when Lauren joined, she was the seventh, although, in a way, she was an honorary Sullivan, she supposed. Her older sister, Cassidy, had married Cameron, Rory's son, a nepotistic connection that got Lauren the interview in the first place.

Her father hadn't balked at all when she went to law school instead of pursuing a degree in business like Cassidy. Cass was the oldest, after all, and would be the next in line at Weatherly Department Stores. Still, Lauren wished it had bothered her father more. Knowing that Cassidy—beautiful Cassidy Weatherly, the chief financial officer at WDS, model, and public face of the company—was all that mattered to him made it even more difficult.

Of course, Cassidy wasn't perfect. Lauren knew quite a bit about her older sister. Knew she had, for example, made her way through many of the young lawyers at S&A. That these dalliances didn't stop after she married Cameron. But Lauren said nothing, because, while she disliked being second choice, she appreciated the freedom it offered her. Comparable to being the second child of the king, the "spare," Lauren could do as she pleased. And if Cassidy had, unintentionally, taught her anything, it was how to keep her business discreet.

Lauren squinted at her calendar, wondering if she checked it from another angle, might Quillan's name might fall off altogether.

Her assistant had left two stacks of files on Lauren's desk. On the right were files for her clients that she needed to meet with. On the left, a disproportionately larger stack, were Quillan's. She wondered again if she'd made a mistake. If she should simply *talk* to Patrick and suggest he find someone else.

Listen to yourself. You're already giving up and you haven't said so much as two words to him yet.

"I told him to be here at nine. So you'll probably see him around noon," Patrick grumbled the day before.

"I'll arrange my day accordingly, sir."

"And he will no doubt be quite resistant to almost anything you say," he continued, "but the thing about Quillan is, he pretends not to listen, ego and all that, but he usually takes things to heart."

Lauren thought perhaps Patrick Sullivan was fooling himself, but she'd nodded, smiled, and agreed.

In light of her musing, Quillan surprised her entirely when the secretary called to tell her he'd arrived.

She glanced at the clock. 8:50.

"Send him in," Lauren said, straightening her blouse and jacket. She hadn't even had a chance to look over any of his clients yet. She took a deep breath and stood as the door opened.

Quillan Sullivan was laughing with Cora, Lauren's assistant, as he walked in, making ridiculous faces at her while she doubled over. Lauren wanted to retch.

Sullivan men commonly had jet-black hair and green eyes, while some sported strong jawlines and deep-seated dimples. Quillan had been gifted with the entire package. He was still grinning when he turned to face her and, for a moment, she was taken with his bright smile as Cora must have been.

"I'm early, I know, but I always like to go above and beyond," he said and winked at her, his smile expanding.

Lauren cleared her throat. "I suppose your inherent inclination to consistently go *above and beyond* is why we're here?" She gestured at his stack of files. "Or when you said always, did you mean to say never?"

The smile died on his face. His lips separated as if to impart another witty reply, but then promptly snapped closed. She motioned toward the old chair in front of her desk and he waved to indicate he'd stand.

"Fine," she said. "Let's clear the air here, Quillan. I'm not doing this because I don't have enough work on my plate. Believe me, I do. I'm doing this purely because your father asked me, and I'm not entirely sure I'd keep my job if I'd said no."

"Laurie—"

"Lauren," she replied firmly.

"Lauren," he continued without missing a beat, "neither one of us has time for this—"

She interrupted him with a laugh. "I'd love to know what you're doing with your time, because we both know it isn't *work*."

"I don't want to be here any more than you do, so let's spend a few minutes and figure things out." His hand signaled the files on the desk as if they were merely dirt to be swept up. "And then we can both go back to doing our own thing."

Lauren's pale face radiated cherry red, and though her hands were in her pockets, she didn't doubt he could see the distinct shape of fists protruding from her slacks. Her short, blonde bob kept falling defiantly into her face but she left her hands in her pockets, instead grunting in frustration. "This," she said, nodding at the desk, "is going to take more than a few minutes. *This,* might take weeks. You're right, I don't want to be here, but you're going to sit down and let me help you."

Quillan cocked his head to the side and ran his tongue over his lips. "Features are harder... hair shorter... eyes bluer... and —" He tilted his head further to the side. "—sufficient. You definitely don't have her legs. But you pass for Assidy Cassidy's sister."

Lauren bit her tongue, recognizing the bait. "Why have you been missing meetings with your clients?"

He grinned. "I wouldn't exactly say I've been *missing* them."

"Why haven't you asked your paralegal to file the paperwork for any of these?" she pressed on. "One of your clients threatened to pursue legal action against you for negligence. Did you know that?"

"Do you know how underpaid paralegals are? Jordan was telling me the other day their starting salary is down by almost *twenty percent* of what it was ten years ago, well, when you adjust for inflation, and I just don't feel—"

"Like doing your job?" she finished. "Yes, that's clear. What's not clear is why you're even here, because it's obvious you don't want to be."

"Well, I'd like to think I'm doing my part in not contributing to our ghastly unemployment rate," he quipped. "Putting New Orleans back to work post-Katrina, and whatnot."

"Quillan," she said evenly. "I'm going to keep this simple since abstract concepts seem to be a challenge for you. If we don't fix whatever your problems are, you're going to lose your job. Your father said as much to me, so I can assume he said the same to you." She paused then, a new thought settling over her. "Is that it? Are you *trying* to get fired?"

Quillan shrugged. He wasn't smiling anymore; his dimples had all but disappeared. His green eyes, brilliantly sparkling only moments prior, were muddy, shadowed. "Tell me what you need me to do and I'll do it."

She watched him in surprise, expecting more of his snarky comebacks. "I'll make nine to eleven available every morning, to help you go through and get this all cleaned up. If you show up late, I'm not going to give you more time, and if we don't get everything done, I'll tell your father why." She gauged his face for a reaction, but he remained impassive. "If you let me, I can help you. I will."

Quillan nodded slowly. His green eyes twinkled once again, his smile rejoining. For a moment, she could see how he'd been able to charm so many all his life.

"Is it cool if we start tomorrow? I have somewhere to be."

"Of course you do," Lauren said with a sigh, speaking to her sparse wall instead of her recent visitor, as he'd left without waiting for her response.

4
FINNEGAN

The three men who held his family's future in their hands sat before him in the mahogany-laden office, processing his implausible story.

Finn couldn't have known that Nicolas had sat in this exact room with these same men, not so very long ago, and relayed all the dark, salient secrets plaguing the Deschanels. That these men had played a part in propelling the events forward, resulting in Finn's marriage to Ana, allies without him ever knowing.

Aleksei waited in a café across the street. Finn didn't underestimate Colin and Oz's understanding of the matter, but Augustus would be a stretch. Finn's few interactions with the man had left him with a strong impression of the armor guarding the man's unyielding resolve.

"Documentation should not be a problem," Colin said thoughtfully. He offered Finn another glass of water, but he shook his head. "We've assisted the Deschanels in matters of this nature for years, and I expect we can have something for you within a week."

"Sooner," Finn cut in. "If you can. Please."

Colin raised an eyebrow. Oz scribbled some notes to his left.

Augustus stared ahead, saying nothing, betraying no thoughts. Judging from his expression, he could have been considering his afternoon schedule.

"We can get the necessary paperwork by tomorrow, Dad," Oz said. "I'll call Gatz."

"Of course. He owes us some favors." Colin folded his hands on top the table. "We'll need pictures of both you and your son before we can proceed. Do you have them?"

Finn swallowed. Nodded. With a tentative glance at his father-in-law, he passed an envelope across the table.

Prying up the metal prong with his thumb nail, Colin opened the manila packet. Both brows went up this time as he came upon Aleksandr's photo. "This is your son? Aleksandr?"

"Long story, Dad. For another time," Oz offered.

Colin's slow nod seemed to indicate this was nowhere near the first *long story* he'd been privy to over the years of working with Deschanels. "Very well. Ah, yes, and you included all your dates and vitals as asked, too. Thank you. Seems everything we need is here. Oz will drop the completed documents at *Ophélie* tomorrow night, once we've secured them."

"Ana's as well?" While Finn trusted their professionalism and attention to detail, he couldn't risk the oversight. Everything had to fall into place, or nothing would. "Even though I couldn't get a picture?"

"We keep copies of all Deschanel passports on file here at the firm, as they come to us first for handling," Oz said. "As it happens, Ana renewed hers only two years ago, so the picture we have will be current enough."

Finn half-expected Augustus to break his silence once his

daughter's name was raised, but his deportment remained wholly unreadable.

The ease of the conversation left Finn as wary as he was grateful. Could it be this easy? Truly?

"We should discuss the means of your travel, Finnegan," Colin interrupted his reverie. "Planes are out of the question, thanks to the detailed tracking at the TSA. Some train lines don't require official records of travelers, so we can arrange at least partial transport there. Renting a car may also put you at risk, but is less a gamble than flying."

Finn tightened his jaw. This, then, is where the ball would drop. "I assumed the false documentation solved all that."

"You need to consider ways to limit your exposure. It would be best if no one could concoct a travel trail for John Smith, or whatever your name will be when the passports come back. You understand?"

Finn nodded, trying not to over-analyze the complications ahead until absolutely necessary.

Colin returned all the contents to the envelope, sliding it over to his son. "I'll have Oz deliver a list of approved communication and travel channels for you when he brings the passports. We'll send other resources as needed. This isn't our first time. Rest easy, Finnegan. We'll have options for you."

The attorneys stood, and Finn took the cue to rise with them. Everyone exchanged handshakes, all except Augustus, who remained seated.

"Finnegan, stay a moment," he directed. A command, though a weary one.

Colin nodded at Oz, then smiled at Finn. "We'll give you two some privacy."

. . .

Finn watched the heavy door as it clicked closed. Augustus waited at the table. With held breath, Finn turned and sat down across from him.

"I have properties in Charleston, and on Long Island. The carriage line will deliver you to Charleston direct, in less than a day. Rest there, and then take the same line to New York. Once ready, I will have a steamship available in Brooklyn to take you to Ireland. Galway. It departs every Tuesday and Saturday. Your choice. I'll give word to the director and your passage will be secured, no questions asked.

"From there, you will travel to Northern Ireland, where you'll take a Belfast freighter to Bergen, Norway. Depending on your pace up to this point, you may have a few days' wait. I've detailed everything here for you."

Augustus passed a folder, not unlike the one from earlier, across the table, offering no explanation on how he knew to construct these details prior to the meeting. His eyes followed the movement, but didn't rise to meet Finn's. "I would like to meet my grandson."

"He's not far. I can bring him in," Finn recollected, his mind catching up to the quick direction the conversation took. "He isn't... well, he isn't what you'll be expecting. I think you need to prepare yourself."

"My sister Colleen already advised me on the situation," Augustus replied with a tight frown. "I may never see my daughter again, but I won't send my grandson across the sea without seeing him with my own eyes."

"I'll get him now. He's been asking about you," Finn said. His pulse had settled upon realizing he wouldn't be tasked with difficult explanations. "But Mr. Deschanel, sir, you *will* see your daughter again."

Finn reached for the door, but Augustus was upon him, one hand on his shoulder. "I've been unfair to you, Finnegan. A man true to himself can admit his faults. Had I not turned away when Ana was floundering, perhaps her journey would have ended in more favorable circumstances."

Finn sucked in a deep breath and turned to face his father-in-law. "Maybe. But in another journey, we wouldn't have Aleksei."

"She's fortunate to have you," Augustus managed. "It may not matter at this juncture, but I can acknowledge it now."

"It matters," Finn answered. His eyes stung.

"Bring her home, Finn."

"On my life, sir."

Finn made small talk with Oz while Aleksei spent some time with his grandfather. He'd offered to join them, but Aleksei said he would be fine. Finn understood his son needed to do this alone.

When Aleksei emerged twenty minutes later with a smile, Finn's heart relaxed.

Jon cornered them upon their return. He'd attempted conversation several times, but Finn managed to dodge each overture.

Not this time.

"I'm going with you," Jon insisted, trailing Finn, Aleksei, and Forbia up the central stairs.

"To bed? Not interested," Finn muttered. Forbia growled at her master's distress.

"I know you, Finn. And I know you're going after her."

Finn whispered, instructing Aleksei to head on upstairs without him. Forbia paused, but Finn clicked his tongue at her, telling her it was okay to go.

"You don't know what you're talking about." Finn exhaled. "You never did."

"I don't blame you. I would do the same, in your shoes," Jon pressed, ascending another stair. Finn tensed.

"Don't compare our motives. They've never been in line," Finn said through gritted teeth.

Jon's heavy steps trekked back down the stairs, but when he reached the bottom, he said, "You can hate me until the day we die, Finn, but I'm coming. I came here to help you, and you've never needed more help in your life."

Finn pushed forward, toward his room, away from the heaviness of his brother's presence and words.

5
LEANDER

Leander Broussard begrudgingly signed for the latest delivery at The Soothsayer's Coffer. That he'd agreed to help his parents was unusual, but they were busy preparing for the return of the Great One, better known as his sister Estella, and he'd never hear the end of it if he wasn't helping in some way. Truth be told, he'd rather be here than subjected to their endless fussing over the planned perfection to welcome the bitch home.

Leander sliced the top of the box open in one quick move. Spell books and candles. He flipped the lid back over and checked the return sender: Magician's Wholesale Warehouse. "Yeah, I'm sure all legitimate witches purchase their sacred relics at the Costco of witchcraft," he muttered.

Tourism was slower this time of year, so he'd only had to suffer through a handful of customers. But every one inevitably had their share of ridiculous questions. Will this cure my lifelong asthma? Will there be any side effects, other than securing the man of my dreams, if I drink too much of this lust potion? Leander, knowing very well everything his parents sold in their store was a load of crap, simply nodded or shook his head. Most didn't want the truth anyway, only seeking some form of validation for their poor purchases.

People often asked about their palm reading services—"We have a certified palmist onsite three days a week"—or their magic contracting business where one of Leander's parents could be hired to solve any number of supernatural quandaries for a rather substantial fee. Leander would hand them the brochure, nodding, rolling his eyes behind their turned backs, wondering at the mind's proclivity to suspend disbelief at all the wrong times.

By far their most popular service was cemetery tours. Even in the sweltering summer months, they rarely cancelled for lack of interest.

The Soothsayer's Coffer had not always been such a mockery. Jasper and Pandora Broussard were cultural anthropologists, with a special interest in the occult. After college, they'd traveled the world together in search of rare and interesting magical artifacts, collecting enough for a meager display.

Back in New Orleans, they'd opened a modest museum to share these with the public. But with astronomical Quarter rent and a general lack of interest in anything which did not immediately dazzle, they did what any self-respecting scholars with a passion for their subject would do: they sold out. The museum swiftly turned into The Soothsayer's Coffer, and the Broussards brought in ten fake artifacts for every real one. Neon signs advertising astrology and palm readings went up, and Jasper began writing books on voodoo that he marketed and sold straight from the store. Add in Pandora selling her services as a sorceress and public speaker, and precipitously the money began rolling in. What had once been a labor of love became a farce.

Leander suspected that, as with most deluded individuals,

his parents still believed in what they did. Jasper found ways to insert topics from his books into almost every discussion—"I read Katrina reconstruction is picking up in the Lower Ninth. Did you know voodoo was critical to the success of reconstruction after the war?"—and Pandora was known to engage in very lively debates with any skeptic who walked through the door. In spite of having more than enough money to hire others to run the store for them, Pandora and Jasper Broussard were onsite every day.

Leander couldn't understand why his father never engaged his *real* abilities. The ones he'd inherited from the Deschanel line.

Except, he did know. Peddling fake occult services made them a dime a dozen. If people knew they could *really* turn lights off from across the room, or read minds, the conversation would shift in a far more uncomfortable direction.

"Ruby, scan this stuff in," Leander said brusquely to Quillan's younger cousin, who worked at the shop part time. She scurried over and pulled the box into her arms, prancing lightly away. Leander scowled.

Jasper's latest book, *One Man's Conversations with Marie Laveau,* sat on gauche display all along the front half of the store. The cover featured a picture of the great Ms. Laveau, alongside a badly Photoshopped picture of Leander's father, hands under his chin, posing in what he must have assumed conveyed pensive thoughtfulness. Leander reminded himself he was fortunate his father had chosen to embarrass the family *after* Leander had left home.

He checked the clock. Only noon. Five more hours until Estella would arrive and another two on top of that before he would have to put up with a public dinner and reunion.

Estella was a delicious mystery to most people. Lovely on the eyes, even sweeter on the ears, and outwardly charming and agreeable. Famous for keeping much to herself, and betraying little of what she was thinking. To Leander, there was nothing at all mysterious about Estella's behavior. Anytime she kept her mouth closed, trouble of some sort would follow. He knew her coldness, how mean she could be.

While Leander could handle her cutting malice, what bothered him most was her treatment of Harriett, their younger sister. Constantly calling her awful things like "half-wit," and "imbecile," words that often brought poor, unstable Harriett to racking sobs. Estella laughed and laughed. Tears didn't give her pause, they sustained her. Her weapons were invisible, but no less potent.

She did the same things to Leander, but he never needed friends the way his sisters did, and never really had any, until Quillan had come around. Quillan was shallow but never looked for ways of hurting or abandoning Leander.

Unfortunately, Harriett *had* cared, all too much. She had cared enough that she eventually withdrew to her room for longer periods of time, only speaking when spoken to. This gradually grew to where Harriett stopped speaking entirely, and eventually had to be homeschooled. Therapist after therapist gave different diagnoses—psychotic, borderline personality disorder, schizophrenic—and each one prescribed some procedure or drug to fix it. Not one of them touched on what was really wrong with Harriett: Estella.

Finally, the failure of other fixes led to Harriett being institutionalized, a move Leander fought tooth and nail but his parents insisted was "the only way."

But then a miracle visited Harriett, in the form of their distant cousin, Tristan Sullivan. She found words again, along with pieces of her confidence. Leander hoped this also meant freedom from Estella's cruelty.

Of course, no one else saw Estella through Leander's eyes.

Not his parents, and certainly not Quillan, who'd never been exactly lauded for his judgment.

Leander's lips twitched. If only she'd stayed in France. If only there was any excuse acceptable enough to get him out of going to dinner. He couldn't stomach Estella's high laughter and saccharine smiles.

"Lee, did we get any other boxes?" Ruby chirped from behind him, springing lightly to his side. He groaned inwardly.

"No."

"Should I rearrange the west shelves again?" she suggested brightly.

"Yes."

She bounced off again, with an energy Leander had never possessed in all his life.

A thought occurred to him, one that brought an infrequent smile to his stoic face. He picked up the phone and called Quillan.

"Yo."

"Busy tonight?" Leander asked.

"I'm not into that sort of thing," Quillan said, laughing at his own joke. "Even if you are kind of pretty."

Leander didn't laugh. "Are you or not?"

"Depends. I could be convinced to hit the clubs tonight."

"Don't you work tomorrow?"

"Yeah, so?"

Leander paused. To ask this of Quillan would mean having some relief this evening, but would come at the cost of having to hear his friend's misplaced excitement on a topic where their opinions were now, and always would be, diametrically opposite. But Quillan would find out sooner or later. "Dinner with my family. Estella is home."

Quillan made several half-worded proclamations on the other end. His pure joy dulled Leander's mood further.

"Estella! Home? For fuck's sake Leander, why haven't you told me? Estella—home—God, I'm not prepared, I haven't even... wow!"

Leander groaned. "You want to come or not?"

"Yes, of course I want to come! Man, Estella. It's been so long. Has she said anything about me at all? You know, like, does she know I'm coming tonight? What did she say?"

"You realize you sound like a thirteen year-old girl," Leander said.

Quillan scoffed in indignation. "No need to resort to insults. This is a glorious day, my friend. Holy shit, Estella is home!"

"Well, be at Commander's at seven. Nah, make it seven thirty. My parents are always late for everything."

"Yes sir!" Quillan exclaimed and hung up, leaving Leander to wonder if inviting Quillan had been a bad idea after all.

6

FINNEGAN

So much for sneaking away.

He'd managed to avoid discovery by any of the Deschanels, even dodging their "mind reading" by employing the blocking Ana had taught him when they were living abroad.

In the end, nothing divine gave Finn away. Only his brother's unrelenting insistence.

"I care not whether your brother goes," Nerys had said, overhearing Jon's rising pitch. "But you'll not leave my sight. Aleksei's well-being is my charge as much as yours, Finnegan. I'll hear no argument on the matter, and you'll raise no objection." Frustration edged her words, but beyond that, she seemed unsurprised at Finn's determination.

She may have been more surprised that Finn was relieved, rather than put out, by her assertion on coming along. His secret fears of what lay ahead dwarfed any bravado on the matter.

Oz, good as his word, delivered their travel documentation the next evening, adding, with a touch of abashedness, Jon's paperwork. “He called and asked to be included. You didn’t answer your phone when I attempted to confirm, and I didn’t want to run the risk of causing delays.”

“It’s fine,” Finn replied, offering a gracious smile despite the fact it was *not* fine. Also not Oz’s fault. “Thank you, Oz. Please thank your father again, too.”

“She’s coming as well?” Oz tilted his head toward Nerys. Panic visibly covered the man, in fear he’d missed a detail.

“I have my own paperwork,” Nerys assured him.

Oz relaxed with relief. “All the travel routes, keys to the estates, a few burner phones, and money are in here,” he said, handing Finn a thick envelope.

“The money isn’t necessary,” Finn said quickly. “Thank you, but—”

“From Augustus,” Oz interjected. “He insisted. See it as his way of helping Ana and Aleksei, and you might find the support easier to accept.”

Finn nodded. “Everything helps, I suppose.”

“Oh, also,” Oz went on, nodding at the envelope, “I’ve left a travel kennel on the porch for Forbia. It’s dark and covered for a reason... we can’t risk anyone seeing she’s a *wolf* or they’ll call animal control, and you can imagine how that unneeded distraction might make things far more complicated for you.”

Forbia dropped her head toward Finn’s feet and let out a light whimper.

“Sorry girl,” Finn cooed, leaning down to give her an encouraging pat. “He’s right. And it won’t be for too long.”

“Right. Well, I think that’s it,” Oz declared, glancing around at the empty house, heavy with the lack of its master. Finn felt Nicolas’ absence as well. The house responded to no one the way it did the heir and his vivaciousness. “We’re only a call away. Anything you need, we will see to it, Finn.” Oz stepped forward and embraced him in a quick hug. "Be careful."

Finn nodded and saw him out with one final thanks.

In the end, there was little Finn could do to stop Jon's tagging along, short of physically restraining him, and Finn had far more productive and important things to spend his energies on.

"You'll stay out of my way," Finn commanded, turning away before Jon could attempt further discourse.

The next morning, Jon mercifully found his own compartment on the train. Nerys settled in with Finn and Aleksei, refusing to be parted from them for even a moment. Thanks to a generous bribe, Forbia's crate was secured in a nearby corner where she could watch, her head pillowed on her front paws.

"It may seem overzealous to you, but the further we get from *Ophélie*, the weaker your protection is," Nerys explained.

"Can't we just make another ward?" Aleksei asked.

"There are limits. The protections cast are an extension of your power, which has a beginning and an end. The more protections you cast, the weaker each individual ward will become. You'll risk exposing your family if you go around casting wards all over the globe."

Finn listened to her words eagerly. Every moment since accepting the Sveising from Aidrik had been one of discovery for him, as he slowly absorbed the boundaries of his new life. How much could Nerys teach him? She was an arborkinetic, where he was a bestiakinetic, but she'd lived many, many years and had encountered abilities of all kinds.

"Emergencies only," Aleksei surmised with a yawn. "Got it!"

The conversation died off as morning stretched into afternoon. Forbia whined and twitched, nails scratching the hard plastic, chasing rabbits in her dreams no doubt. Aleksei slept against Finn's shoulder, snoring softly. Nerys gazed out the window, brows furrowed in thought.

"I need you to be upfront with me," Finn said, venturing forth into the conversation he'd wanted to have with her since she secreted him out of Farjhem. "I can't keep wondering what you're not telling us."

Nerys glanced across the train car at him. "You mean what I said about Aleksei," she answered.

Finn was relieved not to have to play games or dance around the topic. "Yeah. You said he must be protected at all costs. And while I'm grateful for you being here, I want to understand why he's so important to you."

"You're right. You need to know," Nerys agreed. She glanced again out the window. Closed her eyes. "There's so much to tell you. But the words are better said away from his ears. He's not ready to hear them, and he could wake at any moment."

Finn looked down at his son, then back at her. "I won't be separated from him again. Whatever's on your mind, you should know that."

"It's not separation ahead for Aleksei, but a joining."

Her answer produced more questions, but he agreed this wasn't the place. "In Charleston, then."

"Aye."

"No secrets."

"No. No secrets."

7
QUILLAN

Quillan drove past the familiar blue and white awning of Commander's Palace, parking his car down the street. He spotted both Leander's bike and the Broussard's Bentley. For once, the Broussards had arrived on time and he was late.

Inside, the atmosphere was hazy, the voices loud. He informed the host he was with the Broussard party, and the man promptly asked if he'd read Jasper's latest release. Changed his entire life, he said. No, Quillan informed him, he had not. Disappointed, and a touch frostier, the host led him to the table.

He spotted Leander first, sulked over his salad while the rest of the table engaged in discussion. Pandora flapped her heavily braceleted arms, Jasper nodding in hearty admiration of his beautiful wife. At the head of the table, *her.*

Quillan had been kicked in the chest. Estella. *His* Estella. She wore a bright yellow sundress that made her long, blonde hair appear a waterfall of gold, flowing from a halo. She twisted the straw of her hurricane around in her mouth, her tongue flitting out here and there as she laughed at her mother's story. Her eyes betrayed her bored detachment.

He didn't have time to wonder what was on her mind, as Leander jumped up in a display of uncharacteristic enthusiasm and beckoned him over before the host could seat him.

"Where have you been?" Leander mouthed under his breath.

"You told me to be thirty minutes late," Quillan countered, but his eyes had not left Estella. She reached for a roll, the lean cut of her delicate arm outstretched, bringing the bread back in one fluid, beautiful motion. When Quillan felt a small, stinging punch to his arm, he realized he'd been fixed on the spot, staring.

"Quillan!" Pandora exclaimed, standing and kissing him on both cheeks. "You've put on some weight, I dare say."

"My mother would be happy to hear you say that," he replied, still watching Estella, who rolled her wrists around in front of her face, admiring her watch.

"Catching any bad guys?" Jasper chimed in, reaching out to shake Quillan's hand. "Did you know Marie Laveau helped the police on more than one occasion?"

"I'm a lawyer, sir."

"Well lawyers catch bad guys too, do they not? Right into the prison system." Jasper slapped the table and laughed, looking around to gauge the reactions of everyone else. Estella fixed her gaze across the room at the band, playing *When the Saints Come Marching In*.

"You got me there, sir," Quillan said and rolled his eyes out of Jasper's sight.

His heart thumped so hard in his chest, each beat resonated like the march taking him to his death. Estella still looked the other way, and he didn't know how to get her attention without making it awkward for them both.

Quillan cleared his throat, but she continued to watch the band play. "Estella," he croaked out.

She turned around, slowly and deliberately, as if his voice were an unforgivable interruption. When their eyes met, Quillan's voracious heartbeats stopped altogether. "Oh, it's *you*," she muttered, and with nary another look, she snapped back to watch the band.

"Estella!" her mother exclaimed. "You haven't seen Quillan in over four years!"

Estella flicked her wrists in the air in a dismissive motion and continued her apathetic people watching.

"Poor dear is so jet lagged. You know she was up before the sun rose in Paris, and oh my *goddess* those flights are so long," Pandora apologized, but Quillan's heart had already crashed clear to the floor. His heartbeat returned to the hard, jagged beats as the flush in his cheeks grew painfully visible. *Oh, it's* you. Of all the things she could have said.

"Still a ray of sunshine," Leander whispered, making no effort to hide his infuriatingly gratified smirk. Quillan thought Leander had probably enjoyed that little exchange, maybe felt it validated how he viewed his sister. But Quillan was not so easily deterred.

"So, Estella, how was France?" Quillan yelled across the music. She didn't turn around, clapping her tiny hands in tempo with the beat.

"Estella, Quillan is talking to you," Pandora chided, tapping her bony fingers on her daughter's shoulder. Estella recoiled as if her mother had thrown holy water on her.

"Quillan never did care much for courtesies," Estella declared. "Obviously, I'm in the middle of something."

"But you're home now, and we're all so eager to hear about school," Pandora insisted, shooting a look at Jasper. He didn't catch his wife's signal, and continued the laser-focused buttering of his bread.

"Are you now?" Estella sounded amused, in the way of a child about to destroy an expensive toy. "Well, let me tell you about France then. I drank cappuccinos on the boulevard and swam in Nice. But mostly I fucked a lot of octogenarians." With that, she abruptly returned her attention to the musicians.

Pandora flew into a flutter while Jasper tried to calm her. Quillan, far from being discouraged, kept on.

"How many is a lot? Because I know whatever number women give you, you usually need to multiply that by five."

Estella slowly turned back around and narrowed her eyes. "Quillan, I'm afraid you wouldn't be capable of calculating a number this large."

"Allow me to dazzle you with my math skills."

Her lips twisted together, her eyes neat slits. "My mother tells me you're some kind of... lawyer now," she spat out with distaste.

"Some kind, yes," he replied.

"Sorry to hear that." She examined the down on her arm as if it were infinitesimally more interesting than the conversation at hand.

"Sorry you're home," Leander mumbled so only Quillan could hear.

"Most women already have their panties off when I tell them what I do," Quillan edged on.

She snickered. "The type of women who would take their panties off for you *would* be into something so pedestrian."

Pandora fanned herself with increasingly rapid determination. Jasper looked around as if he might find a reasonable escape with enough hope.

"You're right, I forgot your degree was in something so much more respectable. Occult artifacts, is it?"

"Exactly the type of response I'd expect from someone with your base interests," she chirped.

"Says the girl who bragged about the plethora of foreign old men she's fucked."

"That's a five dollar word, there, Quillan. Plethora. Saved it for this occasion, did you?"

Pandora gave off a muted yelp, and Jasper said awkwardly, "Estella, when do you think you'll be able to start down at the shop?"

She turned to her father, seeming to notice him for the first time. "I'll need a few days to sort myself out," she replied. "And we still need to discuss the precise nature of my role. I've already told you I want nothing to do with any of your tours and such."

"No, of course not, darling, of course not. We only want you to be involved in the things you feel will be the most enriching for you," he assured her.

She smirked. "What I'm saying is, I think most of what goes on down at your *shop* is a bunch of bullshit. Do you know what people here think of you two?"

"Well, I—" Jasper started.

"They're rich, aren't they? Paid for your expensive fuck-fest in France, right?" Leander piped up. Quillan was surprised to hear Leander defend his parents' business, but that just showed where Estella ranked on the scale of things Leander disapproved of.

"Rich? For being ridiculous. What's next, a reality show?" she spat.

"We stalled in negotiations," Jasper fussed.

"For heaven's sake, dear, we thought you *wanted* to come

home," Pandora jumped in, reaching across the table for her daughter's hand. Estella quickly snatched it away.

"Wanted to? You stopped sending money... *remember*?"

Pandora snapped her head toward Jasper in astonishment.

"So much for being independent," Leander said.

"When the opinion of a social reject matters to me, I'll be sure to come find you," she snapped. "This is between Jasper and me. I imagined the discussion would be more private, but I was wrong."

"Is this true?" Pandora asked, leaning forward onto her elbows. Her bracelets clanked against her wine glass, which was perpetually empty and in the process of a refill. "Is this why she's home, Jasper?"

Jasper squared his shoulders and grunted. "We paid for four years of college and plenty of her amusements. If she wants graduate school, she can get a job—"

"You are such a hypocrite. Your parents paid for all eight years of college, and never complained about it," Estella lashed. All her carefully planned mannerisms were gone now, replaced by anger and a clear difficulty controlling how she came across. "You want me to work in the store so you can have a pretty face, now that Mom is getting old. You need me, you're bribing me, and it's *despicable*!"

Pandora's neck whipped back and forth between her daughter and husband. She kept opening and closing her mouth, unable to form questions.

"That's not entirely true." Jasper paused, realizing he must choose his words carefully. "If I've learned anything, it's that nothing replaces genuine work experience, and if you're going to get respectable work in your field, you need to have practical experience. I am not only offering to give that to you—and pay you no less, young lady!—but after a year I will pay for your graduate studies, as long as you stay in New Orleans. I would say that's more than fair."

"I... Jasper... I cannot believe... our own daughter." Pandora excused herself and hurried off, presumably to the bar for something more potent.

"Then consider it fair that *I... hate... you*," Estella seethed, and pushed violently from the table, marching toward the entrance.

When Jasper stood up to go after her, Quillan quickly put his hand out. "No, I'll go," he said and didn't stop to catch a look at Leander's disgusted face before rushing after her.

He found her outside, hailing a cab, her petite wrists blurring in the chilled air.

"Let me drive you home," he offered. He slipped his blazer over her shoulders, but she shrugged it off and made no move to grab the jacket before it fell to the muddy ground.

"I'd rather walk."

"Estella—"

She spun to face him. Her cheeks were bright red. The tears in her eyes sparkled. "Go fuck yourself, Quillan."

He reached for her shoulder. She slapped him on the face, the cracking sound reverberating in the quiet air around them.

Quillan clutched his wounded face. "What is *wrong* with you?"

She laughed, a dark, ugly sound. "When are you going to get it through your thick, ridiculous head that I do not now, and never did, want anything to do with you? You're an idiot. You disgust me. If you were the last man on Earth, I would jump off a bridge and call it a day. *Leave me alone*."

Quillan blinked, studying her. "So, can I pick you up tomorrow at eight?"

Estella set her mouth, finally at a loss for words. She turned back toward the street, waving wildly as a cab finally slowed and approached.

"Leave me alone, Quillan," she said as she slid into the backseat.

Not a chance, he thought.

8
JONATHAN

Augustus Deschanel's property rested upon a private outcropping on Sullivan's Island, near Charleston, South Carolina. A coastal cottage, Jon imagined the brochure would call it, a quaint escape, but the estate resembled the sprawling homes of Cape Cod, with expansive wraparound porches, circular drives, and a span of private beach. Palmettos blanketed the property in complete privacy, though the house was set a quarter-mile off the main road.

The home boasted seven bedrooms, so Jon had his pick. There was no question he'd seek out the one furthest from Finn, who was too distracted to even pretend his brother's presence wasn't an intrusion of the worst kind.

As he opened the French doors leading into his room for the next night or two, he found himself standing before a young woman, her face pale from fear.

They both jumped backward at the mutual intrusion. The girl spoke first. "Leave now, or I'll kill you! I swear it, I will!"

Jon threw his hands up. "Hey!" he declared, despite the

many other questions and objections on the tip of his tongue. “Hey now!”

“You think I’m unarmed, but I’m not,” she went on. Her face peeled back, resembling a snarl. “You don’t want this!”

“I’m not here to hurt you. I don’t even know who you are,” Jon countered, backing slowly toward the hall. *This is what I get for picking the furthest room.* “Or what you’re doing in a house that doesn’t belong to you.”

“It definitely doesn’t belong to *you*. You’re no Deschanel!” she screamed. This last outburst finally drew the attention of Jon’s traveling companions.

Finn was first on the scene. From his peripheral, Jon observed his brother’s expression evolve from one of alarm to total confusion.

“Anne?” Finn called, in a half-whisper. He approached the feral girl with one tentative hand out.

“Finn!” she cried and rushed forward, barreling into his sturdy frame. “How on Earth are you here? Where’s Ana? I don’t understand what’s going on.”

“That makes two of us,” Jon’s brother replied, gently peeling her from his arms. “Nicolas said you’d run away, after the Empyrean children. How did you find yourself here?”

“Chasing them. When I lost their trail, I needed to go somewhere while I sorted things out. Aunt Colleen had a list of all Deschanel owned properties and their access codes, and I... well, borrowed it.”

Jon snapped his bewildered gaze between Finn and the girl.

“I take it you didn’t find them,” Nerys said, appearing with Aleksei in tow. Her long red hair had been taken down from its braids, a crimson cape.

Anne twitched her head. “Who are you? And who’s he?”

“This is the Duchess Nerys. She’s here to help,” Finn

explained. He nodded at Jon without shifting his gaze. "This is Jon." Not *my brother.*

Anne narrowed her eyes at Jon. Finn's vague acknowledgment evidently wasn't enough for her. "No," she said after a long pause, returning to look at Nerys. "I didn't find them. Tracking was my brother Jesse's specialty. Apparently it doesn't run in the family."

"You have another specialty, though, don't you?" Nerys said with a curious, impish grin.

Anne dropped her eyes. "What would you know about it?"

"An arborkinetic always knows a fellow master of flora."

It occurred to Jon that if he were keeping score, this would be number five hundred seventy-seven on the list of things that made zero sense to him since joining the world his brother married into.

Such as the fact that Finn kept insisting, despite it being entirely impossible, that the grown boy named Aleksei was his son.

Not that Jon was expecting, nor did he even feel he deserved, explanations. He'd have to earn that level of respect, something he was now finally ready to do.

Anne watched the duchess with hard wariness, but didn't reply. She turned back to Finn. "Where's Ana? And Aidrik?"

Aleksei's face fell at the mention of his dead father. Finn's matched. "Aidrik is gone," he said. "And Ana needs our help. We're on our way to her. We'll be out of your hair in a day. Two tops."

The girl named Anne stepped forward. Her spine straightened, as she shrugged off some of her initial wildness. "I don't think so, Finnegan St. Andrews. I came with you the first time you rescued my cousin. What makes you think I'd stay behind this time?"

. . .

Anne made turkey sandwiches for dinner. Then she huddled around the table with Finn, Aleksei, and Nerys, demanding to know everything they'd been through, in exchange for news of her own adventures.

Jon gravitated toward the fireplace with a cup of coffee, understanding he wouldn't be a welcome member of this reunion.

The decision to come after Finn had taken months, first hitting his subconscious with hints. The inexplicable desire to pick up *Walden Pond,* Finn's favorite book. Rising with the sun as Finn always had, breaking his own beloved habits in the process. Later, as anniversaries of difficult events they used to acknowledge together, like their parents' deaths, came around, Jon's anger became something he could separate from himself entirely, and analyze.

Until this slow unraveling of his motives, Jon could find slivers of justification in all his actions. His love for Ana had not been his fault. His subsequent abuse of her trust, and of Finn's, was an inadvertent result of his attempts to drive her intrusive presence from their lives. His continued lack of remorse held these motives together into something cohesive, allowing him to project most of his anger toward Ana, long after she'd left. And to Finn, for following her. For not seeing Jon's pain. For choosing her.

None of these reasons held together with the gift of distance. Jon's feelings were his own, but his actions... his *actions* painted a picture of the darkest period of his life. Even darker than the months after Carla died.

Ana hadn't committed any crimes against him, no matter how his heart ached at her defection. And Finn loved her. No passing love either, because he'd *married* her, and followed her across the world.

Jon missed his brother. He missed their opposite yet

complementary natures, best expressed by late nights before the fireplace, comparing notes of their days.

Could he ever make amends for the wrong he'd done Finn? That he'd done Ana?

Jon didn't know the answer to this, but his relentless nature propelled him toward a powerful resilience Finn might be impressed by, if he didn't hate him.

Jon awoke to the sound of Anne moving coals around in the fireplace. The fire had died to embers, and would burn out soon.

"So, who are you, Jon?" Anne blurted, spinning around. "I know why Finn and Aleksei are here. Even Nerys. But what's your story?"

"I'm Finn's brother." No matter his crimes, this fact hadn't changed.

Anne twisted her lips. "Brother. Finn's never mentioned you. Why is that?"

"I can't say."

Anne's jaw started in with another dig, but then it slowly fell. A light passed over her face. Her mouth parted. "Oh. Ohhhhh. I know who you are now. I heard Aunt Colleen talking to Uncle Noah about it, after Ana came back to New Orleans. You attacked her! You drove her away from Finn."

Jon turned toward the dying fire and nodded.

"Wow. You have nerve showing up here, when your brother is grieving and his wife is God-only-knows-where in God-only-knows-what condition." She knelt by the grate, to meet Jon's eyes. "Whatever your reasons are, he can't deal with you on top of everything else. He's already shouldering too much."

Jon glanced up, stifling a smirk. "Does he know you have a thing for him?"

Red rose to Anne's face in an instant blush. "You don't know anything about me. But I'll tell you this. I've never assaulted someone. Never wronged any of my siblings the way you wronged yours." She paused briefly, eyes shifting downward. "So think what you want, I don't care. But if you love Finn, you'll go home and let him deal with things his own way."

Jon stood, towering before her. "As it happens, I do love Finn, and that's why I'm here. And *you* don't know anything about *me,* either, Miss Anne. Are you defined by the bad decisions you've made in your life?"

Anne opened her mouth, then snapped it shut. Without another word, she pivoted, marching down the long hall toward her room.

Once he was sure she wouldn't re-emerge, Jon made his way to his own room.

9
QUILLAN

All of Quillan's attempts to contact Estella had gone painfully awry. Undeterred by her behavior at Commander's Palace, he persisted in calling and stopping by the store, the former perpetually unanswered, the latter resulting in her disappearing into the back without a word.

Pandora tried to explain her daughter's moodiness as readjusting to the culture, but Quillan sensed there was something altogether different about Estella Broussard.

"You're realizing what an arrogant cow she is," Leander had said without looking up from his textbook.

"No, something is definitely different," Quillan decided.

"Maybe now you can move on."

Try as Quillan might to get Estella out of his head, his thoughts were consumed with her after their ill-fated encounter at Commander's. And, despite Leander's sarcastic jabs at a sister he couldn't stand under the best circumstances, Quillan sensed something *was* off. Sure, she had always been standoffish and bitchy. It was part of her charm. You never had to wonder where you stood with Estella.

The tears, though, were not like her. Her cool aloofness, the behavior he had always known her for, always liked her for, was clearly an act now, and he'd witnessed her complete meltdown over the course of that unpleasant evening. Those cruel words she spat at him as she waited for the cab were a fear of being seen out of her element. For, the moment their eyes locked, an understanding had passed between them, and it was one Estella hated him for.

Quillan couldn't move past that. At first, he called her out of old habit, but at some point he realized he needed to understand what had happened to her. Why she had changed. Connecting with her became a single-minded goal that consumed him and made it even more difficult to focus on other things, such as the growing problem at work.

Lauren was a genuinely nice person, if vanilla, and Quillan made things far more difficult for her than he needed to. It would take such little effort to listen, and absorb her advice, but he'd never been capable of managing several important things at once, and his concerns for Estella soared far above all else.

He'd been relieved when he came into the office and Lauren had an entirely different exercise for them. One that had nothing to do with his perpetual failures as a lawyer.

"I," she said, carrying in two large file boxes that wobbled dangerously, so old they looked past rotting and on to disintegration, "have been tasked with a really exciting project that you're going to help me with."

"What in the hell is that crap?"

"There's more where this came from, and you'll be fetching it shortly." Lauren opened one of the box lids and, as she did, a puff of musky grime furled out, eliciting coughs from them both. "We picked these up from *Ophélie* today. Nicolas Deschanel is engaged in a special project, unrelated to this I'm told, but it resulted in unearthing boxes upon boxes under some old floorboards in the *garçonierre*."

Quillan sneered in disgust. He disliked old things, which he believed offered no value to the present. "What are they?"

"No clue. That's what we're here for."

"What are we supposed to do with this stuff?" He plugged his nose, though the scent had dissipated. "Put it in the document shredder?"

She raised an eyebrow, settling the lid back. "Inventory, Quillan. We need to inventory every item so they can be sent to an antiques assessor for appraisal."

"Why don't we write 'really old shit' and call it a day," he said, wiping his finger across the lid to remove several layers of dirt and grime. He sneered and quickly wiped his hand on the oak boardroom table.

"Because the Deschanels pay us to be useful, although I suppose your fantastic suggestion *would* explain quite a bit about your current predicament here at the firm." She eyed him with a raised brow.

"I've got jokes too, Lauren. Like how much it's going to cost you to dry clean that shit off your suit." He pointed at her blazer, covered in box muck.

"Another reason you should pay attention at work, Quillan. We have a company account for that." She winked at him and gestured to follow her.

He helped her bring the rest in from the hired van, and when they sat down to start their task they had twelve boxes to sort through.

Lauren pulled out a box of latex gloves, removed a pair for herself, and tossed the carton to Quillan. "You're not leaving until we're done, so suck it up."

Quillan took one last look of despair at the boxes and then opened the first one. It was full of old books and clothing, but the original colors were lost to the fading and dinginess of being stored for so long. "These are really, really old," he remarked obviously.

"Hopefully the appraiser can tell us how old," Lauren said as she carefully removed an oil lamp from the box she was sorting. "Our job is only to document what the items are, so we can account for all of them. It may feel like grunt work to you, but they've trusted us for many, many years. If that means going through old, smelly boxes to account for things, to make sure nothing gets nicked by a frisky appraiser, so be it."

Quillan lifted an old petticoat, which fell into pieces, melting before his eyes. "Be careful!" she snapped.

"Yeah, yeah," he rejoined, gently putting the fabric remnants aside.

The sorting continued through the morning, into the afternoon. Whenever Quillan would complain, Lauren snapped him back to reality with some chiding comment, ignoring Quillan's insistent complaints and under-the-breath insults. Around four, he got a reprieve as Lauren's phone rang, and she excused herself.

Taking a break was his initial inclination, but seeing they had only one box left, he decided finishing and lighting out early would be a better idea. Opening the final box, he found another box, wrapped in old cheesecloth several times over. The rectangular chest was made of what looked like dark mahogany, and etched in gold on the lid was a large, cursive D. Although it was clearly timeworn, the box itself was still in good shape, the hinges looking almost brand new.

Quillan opened the lid, finding inside a bundle of letters tied together with a strand of light green satin. Beneath the letters were several pewter charms, none of which Quillan recognized. Symbols of some sort. One was a cross but the top was finished into a loop. Another, a small round painting with two eagles looking opposite directions. The third resembled an infinity sign with a double cross on top.

"How do I label this crap?" Quillan mused. He wrote down "lots of letters" and started to label the other artifacts when a thought struck him.

"Estella," he whispered. Estella would know what these symbols were. They were obviously occult of some sort, though Quillan didn't know or care what in the slightest. But Estella might care... and if she did, she might be willing to have dinner with him.

This could be exactly the "in" he needed.

"Quillan, no." Riley jumped in, nearly knocking Quillan over with surprise. Riley hardly ever appeared away from home, because he said it was too risky. "That's stealing."

"Oh, bugger off," Quillan said with a dismissive gesture. "No one will even miss these."

"She's not nice," Riley replied with a frown.

"Aw, she's not so bad, she's just doing her job."

"No... the *other* one."

Quillan looked back up. "Estella?"

Riley nodded.

"She's always been cranky."

"You shouldn't be trying to talk to her," Riley insisted, sounding every bit the seven years old he always would remain. "She's not good."

"*So* sorry about that," Lauren exclaimed as she rushed back into the room. Quillan whipped his head around toward Riley but his brother had vanished. He quickly piled everything back in the box and shoved it under the table behind him, out of sight. "One of my clients was supposed to receive a settlement today and it didn't go through, so I had to call the other attorney to get it sorted out. Jeez!"

"And how did it turn out?" he asked absentmindedly, thinking of how he was going to get the box out without her noticing or wondering what had been in the now empty box in front of him.

She eyed him with growing suspicion. "Well... turns out there was a misunderstanding. *How* there was a misunderstanding is beyond me because we clarified this date and amount at least a hundred times, but they assured me it was a sincere mistake. At this point it was easier to resolve the apparent confusion than to drag the settlement out further." She laughed. "I swear, if being a lawyer has taught me anything, it's that people almost never act rationally."

"Totally," he said, thoughts tethered on the box hiding behind him. He eyed the one in front of him, guiltily, hoping she wouldn't notice, and ask questions.

Lauren ran her hands through her short blonde hair, and, looking around the room, let out a relieved sigh. "Wow. That was a lot more work than it looked, eh?" Her eyes stopped on him. "You know, Quillan, I really appreciate your help today. You didn't have to... well, yes you did, but you could've half-assed it and you were honestly helpful. So, thanks."

Quillan realized she was giving him the first compliment anyone had offered him in his career, but his mind was too distracted to do anything except nod. She gave him a quizzical look, but moved on to label the boxes, affixing their inventory sheets to the sides.

"Some of this could be worth a fortune, not that the Deschanels really need it," Lauren said. With her back turned, Quillan quickly snatched the box and moved it to the other side of the room, to a shelf behind some books. He wouldn't be able to remove the chest with her looking, and would have to come back for it later, but he was thrilled at his discovery. It was fate. He knew it.

Finally, she came to the last box, the one Quillan had been dreading. She frowned. "What was in here? I know it wasn't empty."

He shrugged, afraid if he said anything he'd give himself away. She watched him carefully for a few moments, Quillan's heart racing as each second ticked. *This is it. She can see right through me.*

But she surprised him when she said finally, "No matter. Things probably got mixed up in different boxes." Quillan released a slow, guarded breath, but didn't miss the curious look she gave him as she left the room.

10
FINNEGAN

The sharp pierce of Aleksei's cries awoke Finn from the light rest he'd only recently fallen into.

With a quick shake, he roused his son, who shot straight forward in the bed, gasping. Sweat pasted his copper hair to his forehead. Tears stained his cheeks.

"What is it?" Finn asked.

Aleksei's chest heaved in heavy, rasping bursts. Finn stroked his back, waiting for him to catch his breath. Forbia crept up onto the bed, lying over his son's legs in silent support.

"Mora," the boy panted. "I dreamed of her, over and over. She's in a lot of pain, Far. I wanna help her but she's so far away."

Finn pulled his son tight to his chest, searching for words to reassure him, but coming up short. Though young in years, Aleksei was a wise boy, sometimes even more so than Finn himself, he felt, and wouldn't respond well to empty platitudes.

Finn's painful truth was that he had no idea how to find

Ana. He didn't know where she was, nor what to do when and if they found her. Whether anything they did would even make a difference.

He only knew they had to. And because they had to, they would.

FINN ALLOWED THEM A SECOND NIGHT ON SULLIVAN'S ISLAND. THEIR journey ahead promised to be long, and trying, sleep difficult to come by.

Jon trekked off in search of camping supplies, preparation Finn was ashamed he'd overlooked in his urgency. They wouldn't need them in America, or even Ireland, but they couldn't possibly know what awaited them in the Norwegian wilderness and beyond.

He was even more chagrined to find himself incapable of thanking his brother for this valuable gesture. However, if Jon had stayed behind as asked, Finn wouldn't be wasting precious thoughts on someone who'd caused his wife inexcusable pain. A fact only amplified by the void left in her absence.

Anne made sandwiches again. No one had the energy for anything more robust, and most of the food went uneaten anyway.

After dinner, Anne retired to her room, and Jon to his. Aleksei passed after them, with a drowsy shuffle, Forbia on his heels.

Once he heard everyone's doors click closed, Finn turned to Nerys. "Now seems as good a time as any to share what you know about Aleksei."

"Aye," she agreed, as she slipped into the kitchen, checking on the kettle she'd put to boil. "I apologize for not sharing these words with you sooner, Finnegan. In truth, much intrigue exists within the bounds of the Brotherhood. Who is allowed knowledge and privilege."

"Sounds like our government."

"Take my brother, Agripin, as an example. He's been brought up to believe he's the chosen leader. The golden prince, set to unite the drekar toward a common cause. I assure you, he doesn't know the half of what I'm about to share with you."

"But you're going to tell me anyway."

Nerys handed him a cup of tea, and settled into the seat across from him with hers. "I was never one for politics." She winked, and drew a light sip. "He's your son, Finnegan. You have a right to know these things. Most of all, you have a responsibility that you can't rise to without this knowledge."

"Responsibility?"

"To assist him toward meeting his destiny. Without him, all is lost. On *that,* at least, the Brotherhood is united. This promise has been our single uniform beacon."

"You're saying the Brotherhood knows about Aleksei?" Once the question left his mouth, he realized this didn't surprise him. Agripin had known, before he'd even met them. Eldre Maxima went out of her way to taunt them about their son.

"They've known about him since long before his birth. It was foretold," Nerys explained. "For thousands of years."

Finn stood. He turned slowly, each word settling in like a blanket of fog. A dizziness swept through him, from head to toe.

"Overwhelming to hear that, I'm sure," Nerys replied lightly. "None of your questions will have satisfying answers until I've told you everything, I'm afraid. Ready to settle in for a story?"

. . .

Nerys told a tale of two races, Empyreans and the forerunners of the Quinlans, the Tuatha de Danann. Once great allies with complementing strengths, one born of fire and the other nature, equal benefit to offer one another. Their alliance was built on the promise of their mutual survival, sealed with a blood oath.

When war came to the Tuatha, the Empyreans broke this oath, choosing their survival over aiding their friends. The Tuatha were nearly wiped out, with those who survived seeking shelter in small, hidden tribes, regrouping as the Quinlans.

Along with the breaking of this sacred oath came the promise of strife for both races, one which seemingly had no end. Famine, war, and a myriad of other misfortunes sat upon their weary shoulders for eons.

The goddess Morrigan, of the original Tuatha de Danann, descendant of their goddess Danu, brought forth a prophecy said to be from Danu herself, one that brought the first sliver of hope.

> *Two millennia of wars and strife, which cannot be avoided, but can be stopped. One descendant from each of the four to emerge. Four become two, their offspring the peace that unites the two races again.*
>
> *From Falias, a male, draoi, pure of heart and an affinity for creatures.*
>
> *From Murias, a female, born of fire and darkness.*
> *From Findias, a female, reincarnated over the many moons.*
> *From Gorias, a male, draoi. The lover of the Findias heir.*
>
> *A son shall spring from Falias and Murias. Findias and Gorias join after many reincarnations, bringing forth a daughter. This*

son and this daughter will join together, in peace, uniting the Quinlans and Empyreans once more, thus ending the long days of war.

"Most think the core purpose of the Brotherhood is to unite the rebels against the Senetat," Nerys explained. "And for those scattered across the world, this may be truth. But those at the core, the leaders of the drekar, know better. For some of them were there when the blood oath was made, and later broken. It was Birger's blood which sealed it from our side. He stood with the Tuatha when the time came, but the meager help we brought to their aid was not enough." She paused, watching.

"I'm still listening," Finn said, having retaken his seat. "I don't understand, but I'm listening."

"The Brotherhood exists to find, and then protect, the daughter and son of the prophecy. Only when they unite will the Empyreans and the Quinlans find lasting peace. You might think these problems fall far from your threshold, but they are closer than you believe. Your wife's family's supposed curse?"

"I've seen enough to believe it isn't *supposed*."

"Of course, it's all as potent as it seems. But it doesn't have to be. The Deschanels suffer, as descendants of both races. This suffering will cease, Finn. It can and *will* stop, once Aleksei and the daughter of Findias and Gorias join together."

"Nerys, I hear everything you've said, but I don't understand. Or maybe I do... I don't know." Finn shook his head. He pushed the tea forward on the table, then dropped his head on his closed fists.

Nerys reached over and lay a hand on the crown of his head. "You and Ana each descend from one of the four original Quinlan tribes. Your coming together was long foretold, as was Aleksei's birth. Aleksei is one-half of the prophecy we've waited thousands of years for."

Finn pushed out a sound resembling a laugh. "And the other half? How are we supposed to find them?"

"You already know them," Nerys declared, her face spreading into a welcoming smile. "Amelia and Jacob will give birth to the daughter who makes up the other half."

"Amelia and Jacob?" Finn repeated, hoping parroting her words might bring further understanding. "They don't want children."

"They will," Nerys replied, though her words, for the first time that evening, sounded less than convinced. "They must."

"And what if... what if Aleksei doesn't want this chick? No one has a right to expect he's going into some pre-arranged marriage because some goddess says he should." *And I'm not letting him date for at least another eighteen years!*

"He will," Nerys insisted. "As you wanted Ana, and Jacob wanted Amelia. He'll lay eyes upon her and there will be no question of whom he loves, and who his heart demands."

"I don't know," Finn muttered, drawing in breath. "I don't know about any of this."

"I cannot make it easier for you to accept, Finnegan, but I can answer any questions you have and hope it arms you toward helping Aleksei when the time comes."

Finn met her eyes, looking for signs of deception. He found none. Lie or no, though, the words were all too much. A prophecy. Everything in their damned lives being foretold. He'd been angry when his grandfather insisted Ana and his meeting was a result of fate's hand. Here the story came again, from someone else. Maybe it was all true. Perhaps they'd been on this trajectory since before they all were twinkles in their mothers' eyes.

But tonight, Finn's mind could only settle on one important task ahead. "Thanks for telling me," he said, and rose, stretching. "We can talk about this again, once Ana is safe."

"Finnegan, I know you may not want to hear this, but finding Amelia and Jacob is the most important thing—"

Finn put his hand forward. "Stop, Nerys. Please. While I still really like you."

Nerys nodded, looking down.

"First, we find Ana. Help me do this. Please. And then, I promise, we'll figure this out, too. I'll believe whatever you need me to believe, as long as none of it puts my family in danger." Nerys nodded again. "And please don't mention this to Aleksei. He already can't sleep at nights, he misses his mom so damn much. He doesn't need further distraction."

"I leave that task to you," Nerys said graciously, with a nod. "For now."

"Thank you," Finn replied. He glanced toward the fire, where the logs had burned down to embers. "Train is at nine."

"Aye. Rest well, Finnegan."

"As well as any night since my wife went missing," he replied, and offered her a tight smile before moving down the hall, toward his room and Aleksei.

Finn had promised himself, some time before taking his leave of Nerys, that he wouldn't let her words sink in too deep until he had Ana, but one thought in particular would not leave him.

Though he suspected no deception in the words she'd shared, he sensed, on an even stronger level, there were others she left out.

Nerys was hiding something. He'd no doubt of it. His only hope was that, whatever it was, it wouldn't get in the way of finding Ana.

11
ESTELLA

Estella slammed the door to her childhood bedroom, shutting out the searching voice of her mother in the hallway. This sequence of events flooded Estella with many memories, memories she'd never wanted to remember or relive.

I hate all of you, she thought. Her disgusting and indulgent mother... her father's lack of backbone... her brother Leander's self-satisfied glances... and Harriett's slobbery silence, which by some strange miracle, was now over. Even more so, she hated this lumbering mansion, gradually falling into disrepair because her parents only had enough sense to purchase it, but not to maintain it.

The ironwork banisters on the spiral staircase were so rusted they turned to dust in spots when you touched them. Harriett had fallen through one last year. The carpets smelled of hundred-year-old mold, the ornate patterns long faded, now looking like several unfortunate shades of dying gray swirled together. Cobwebs remained ensconced for years in the chandeliers and ceiling corners, with no one willing to climb up and clear them.

What she hated most, though, were the horrific murals gracing the walls of the dining and sitting rooms, depicting the Haitian slave revolution in vivid, gory detail. And if their existence were not bad enough, her father had hired artists to touch up the paintings so they looked fresh and somehow even more vivid and real. She'd chided him for spending money to fix the murals while letting the rest of the house rot, but he assured her she'd understand, when she was older.

Well, she was older now, and understanding never came.

Estella was relatively certain the house listed slightly to the east, but her father insisted with a grin that it was she who was crooked. She, the most graceful and perfect creature for miles, was crooked. Right.

Her mother relentlessly complained about the vines climbing in through cracked windows, but would do so from the comfort of her chaise, wine glass in hand, heavily medicated. She'd point and say, "Why, look, the crown molding over there has clearly rotted off," as if she expected her words would magically repair the damage.

Her father, the man who'd written in earnest a book entitled *The Upside of Slavery*, would miss the hints entirely and they'd both lounge in their lazy, languid bliss.

Thankfully, Harriett was no longer part of the scenery at the decrepit Broussard manor. Her silent slobbering in the corner, despite being fully capable of speech, was no doubt an attempt to prove some idiotic point. Oh how her father had gushed with joy at her apparent miraculous recovery. Stupid attention whore.

Leander, of course, continued to blame Estella for the blubbering mess their younger sister had been for years. But how could attempting to better someone be a fault? Harriett was so much like their father, spineless and lacking entirely in gumption. She *let* herself be bullied. Sat there, twirling her long, muddy blonde hair as people ridiculed and cajoled her, doing nothing.

Estella knew coddling the little twit would not solve a damn thing. So she bullied Harriett herself—yes, she would admit it, and why not?—because she hoped she would push Harriett to the point of finally standing up and defending herself. She'd tripped her in front of boys she had crushes on, teased her about her awkwardness, spread horrible rumors about her, and hadn't done a damn thing to hide it. She wanted Harriett to grow a pair. To stand up and be brave, because how else would she ever survive in the real world?

Estella could not be blamed for this. Would not. It wasn't her fault Harriett was weak. For all anyone knew, Estella had saved her from jumping off the Crescent City Connection, like other kids pushed to the brink.

Whereas Harriett and Leander took after their father, Estella fancied herself more like her great-grandmother Blanche, a Deschanel and a fine lady in the early twentieth century New Orleans' social circles. Estella was only six when she died, but Blanche had lived with Estella's family since before she was born, Jasper having taken her in when she lost her home after *Grandpère* Claudius died.

The story they told was that Blanche had sold the family home in Lafayette, but the truth was for almost two years, no one had been paying the taxes on the large property, nor was any attention paid to the stacks of liens piling up. The police were afraid to kick out the venerable Blanche Broussard and so they, eventually, called her family to come do it for them.

Jasper was the only one to answer this call to arms, which was such a damn shame, Estella thought. Blanche was a Deschanel, for the love of god. The last of the great ones, and the founder of the Broussard dynasty. A goddamned fixture, and they had all let her stay out there to rot. And Luther, who'd stood to inherit her larger lakeside property, suggested she just live there instead. All alone. Disgusting.

But just because Blanche didn't bother with paying bills didn't mean she'd lost her senses. Right to the last, she sat on her front porch with her daddy Charles' old sawed-off shotgun, shooting at the feet of the foreclosure agents, wearing her Sunday lace.

Estella remembered very little from her early childhood, but her recollections of her great-grandmother were startlingly vivid. Sitting on her lap, tracing the pattern of her Sunday lace, the smell of jasmine, the stories Blanche would tell her about growing up with her brother, August, the heir. About how the Deschanel family was cursed and she'd moved far away to protect her family, praying the dark omen would not reach. How she worried she'd not run far enough when her two youngest boys, Wyatt and Noble, died in childhood. Her contrasting joy in seeing her other two children, Eugenia and Cassius, thrive. Eugenia had married a Fontenot, one of the few families in Louisiana who rivaled the Deschanels in wealth and renown. Cassius had helped grow the Broussard name through his descendants, Estella being the finest of them all.

Estella's great-grandfather, Claudius, had been Blanche's third husband. Her first two husbands, Johnson Guidry and Ellis Kenner, both died under unusual circumstances.

Estella believed, with all her heart, that her great-grandmother had killed both of them. The thought thrilled her. Most of the relatives tried to brush these rumors aside, but Estella wished nothing more than to go back in time and witness the power Blanche exerted over men. The moments when they knew, when they finally figured out, that Blanche Deschanel was not a woman to be messed with. The fear. The dominance.

Blanche counseled her to never, ever trust a man. Not a lover, not a father, not a brother, not a friend. Blanche had learned this from her Aunt Ophelia, another woman Estella would have liked to share a cup of coffee with. It gave her such strength to know she came from a family of exceptionally strong women. How unfortunate that she was the only one left. No other thoughts troubled Estella quite like this. Her family, once great, and now she stood alone.

What she would give to speak to her great-grandmother again. To ask her, now that she was older and could understand, what had happened. Blanche would tell her. Blanche would see the reflection of herself in the young and vivacious Estella, and confide any number of secrets. Estella was as sure of this as she was she did not belong in this old, rotting house.

Her presence at home had little to do with belonging. She had been kind enough not to say it at dinner, instead making up the reason that her father had needed her young and pretty face to sell books, but in truth he wanted her home for an even more selfish reason: her mother was slipping further and further into drinks and delusions and he didn't know how to handle her.

Life had been good in France. For the first time, Estella had been surrounded by others worthy of being in her presence... people who challenged her and had impeccable taste in wine, dining, and fashion. Her studies had been going exceptionally well, and she'd even formed her own club of adventurers who met and planned field trips across Europe, to study the occult and bring back artifacts and discoveries. Most importantly, she'd almost cracked the secret to necromancy, that vague and complicated form of devilry that would allow her to finally reach out to Blanche, her soul mate, the one person she needed. The one person she could not have.

After all, Estella was a mind reader, a Deschanel trait she'd inherited, to her great pleasure. Those who already possessed such skills of the mind were often ripe for learning new ones, and being able to grow and expand the abilities they already had. Was necromancy not a form of mind reading, in its own way? Couldn't then she, Estella, learn this? Through her circle of friends they'd tried, many times, and failed, but they were getting closer. Surrounding herself with like-skilled individuals had produced an otherworldly strength she could literally *feel* all around her. Success was only a matter of time.

Charlie claimed to be a necromancer but then he'd died. Heart attack, the coroner's report read, but she knew, and so did the others in their group, it was not a heart attack at all. And then Alice had wanted to try, despite what happened to Charlie, despite the warnings from others. All but Estella that is... who was Alice to her, against the possibility of success? She went through with the ceremony, tried to make contact. Alice, too, had died. Brain hemorrhage, hers had said. That was when their little group disbanded and Estella started her search for a new, stronger circle.

Then her father recalled her.

If she'd told him she only went into occult studies to communicate with her dead great-grandmother, he'd likely have pulled the money sooner.

She was surrounded now by a glut of fake artifacts for a very real interest she needed to master. Her hometown should have been the best place for this exploration, but her parents had long since gone off the deep end. Any legitimate scholastic endeavors had been replaced by woeful inadequacies and new ways to completely sell out.

If only she had fostered better relationships with her Deschanel cousins. There were rumors there'd been a handful of real necromancers throughout their history. She knew many of them had other abilities: telekinesis, telepathy, healing.

Conjuring of elements. A wealth of people who would be entirely useful for her, but none of whom she knew well enough to approach and ask, "Hey, wanna help me try to talk to our dead relatives?"

She looked up at the old photo of Blanche, taken when she was in her early twenties, a picture Estella had long ago positioned above her bed, the way some kids had Jesus above theirs. She resembled her physically, as well as in temperament. Same wide, blue eyes. The tiny features and blonde hair that flowed around their faces and shoulders like waves of silk. Most of all, though, Estella loved to study Blanche's gaze. It was a knowing expression, as if she knew what you looked like without your clothes on. As if she knew what was in your very soul.

Estella's ringing phone startled her. Quillan. Again. She hit the ignore button. Her face spread into a slow, ugly smile.

Power. He made it so easy.

12
NERYS

They boarded the train for New York with no issues, though this time Forbia and her crate were forced to ride in a separate area, for animals. Her mournful howls could be heard throughout the first class car. Finn slumped against his window, looking progressively more heartsick as her cries increased.

"All Emyr's creatures possess the capacity for forgiveness. And perhaps even the will to forget the unfortunate," Nerys reassured him, but he didn't even attempt a polite smile. Nor did Aleksei's affections cheer him up.

Jon, the estranged brother, sat in his own car. There was a story here, one involving a great deception, but Nerys didn't wish to impose her wisdom where it wasn't wanted. She could not claim to have great kinship with her own siblings.

But her natural empathy toward other creatures caused her to nudge the high-strung Anne to go stay with him. Anne, who always seemed one push away from full-on wrath, started to object when Nerys placed a tender hand on her arm and reminded her that the greatest way they could serve their own souls was to soothe those of others.

Nerys enjoyed the passing views of the Appalachians as they traveled north. Her journeys seldom found her in North America. She marveled at the raw beauty. At how the towering mountains seemed to be the only land still sacred from technology and development.

Once in New York, they'd stay only one night, for their ship to Ireland would depart the next morning. From there, they'd journey to Norway. And from there... with an inward sigh, Nerys accepted she had no direction.

Several, select Brotherhood leaders had always maintained their own private telepathic channel, one they created by combining their power; one incapable of a breach by mystics. No matter where she was, or where they were, she could reach her most trusted friends—Birger, Astrid, Thorvald, and Trygve—and they her.

This sacred communication channel came to an abrupt silence somewhere on the path between New Orleans and Charleston.

More unsettling than the loss of contact, was not knowing why. Had something befallen her old friends? Had they, for reasons she couldn't guess, no matter how much thought she placed on the matter, cut her off?

Nerys couldn't take Finn and the others to the safe house without understanding this critical shift. And she couldn't grasp the shift without speaking to her friends.

The cyclical dilemma weighed against her heart, a secret she could share with none of her fellow travelers, whose troubles were far heavier than hers.

"I know I'm not very old, but my mora says I'm a good listener," her sweet charge, Aleksei, cut in with an earnest look, breaking her from her reverie.

"I don't suppose empathic qualities are part of your mystic's spread?" Nerys replied with a smile.

"I'm still learning what I am. Anders said it might take years."

"Aye," she agreed. "Few or many. It is different for all. Worry not about me, though, Aleksei. I often wear this face when my thoughts wander."

Aleksei observed her with unveiled skepticism, but didn't press the matter.

So she would have to be careful around him, as she was with Finn, who also exhibited his own share of empathic abilities.

Nerys loathed deception of any kind. A large part of her longed to share the burden of her worries. This sentiment was not only selfish, but dangerous.

The other half of her apprehensions centered with a revelation Thorvald had left with her, before the communication was severed.

He'd intimated to her he'd seen visions of what lay behind this "curse" of the Deschanels. Something not even the family yet knew, despite spending centuries trying to understand the evil tormenting them.

"Plague is coming, more determined than ever," Thorvald had said, in their secret channel. "*Seduction to sinners. A legacy in splinters. Beware, the myths of midwinter.* Do those words mean anything to you?"

Nerys told him they did not.

Thorvald paused. "We have bigger issues at hand than deciphering riddles."

"They are our blood. We must protect them. Aidrik gave his life to keep them safe, and we owe him."

"Aye, Nerys. But you well know even if we intervened, it would do no good. Another evil would rise, because we have not yet stopped our problems where they took root. The prophecy is our only chance at posterity."

"Has anyone determined where Amelia and Jacob escaped to?"

Thorvald was silent for several moments, and she had her answer. "Your responsibility is with Aleksei, and finding his mate. They are the key to their salvation. To *all* our salvations."

"Only if we *find* the other heirs and they beget a female."

"Aye. There were no signs of conception when they disappeared. For now, we protect Aleksei. Focus on what we can control."

"With Cianán and Cerridwen seemingly disappeared off the Earth, how many will fall before we find them? If we don't protect them from this latest nuisance?"

Thorvald had no response. There was no measurement for the pain ahead if the prophecy remained unfulfilled.

Nerys tried not to think on the evils awaiting the family in New Orleans. Thorvald's wisdom, this time, was on the mark. They must focus their energies on attacking the source, not patching wounds.

As the lush mountain flora and fauna sped past her window, Nerys beseeched Emyr to not abandon them in their most critical hour.

13
QUILLAN

Poof. Crack. Poof. Crack. Riley disappeared from one side of the room and reappeared on the other, ignoring Quillan's increasingly impatient requests for him to knock it off. *Poof. Crack. Poof. Crack.*

"Riley, *stop*!" Quillan searched for his shoes, swatting the air where his brother was one moment, and gone the next. "Knock it off."

Quillan felt a gust of air rush past his face and then Riley came to a stop, sitting in the folding chair at the end of the bed. "Don't go."

Crawling around on his knees, Quillan searched for his other shoe. He didn't look up. "You're getting a tad obnoxious, little brother." In frustration, he sighed loudly. "Goddamn shoe, I was just wearing it earlier."

"You're not going to find it," Riley said. If he could stomp his feet, he would.

Quillan stopped crawling and looked up. "Where's the shoe, Riley?"

Riley shifted his face toward the ceiling, ignoring him.

"Fine. I have other shoes," Quillan said and moved to leave the room. But then Riley was in front of him, again. Quillan walked right through him.

"Pleasssseeee Quillan, you don't understand!" Riley pleaded.

"What I don't understand..." Quillan started, locating another pair of shoes and quickly putting them on. He was in a hurry to get down to the Coffer before Estella closed up. He didn't want to wait another day to show her the box. "Is why you're acting like a shithead?"

Riley's eyes teared up, or appeared to. Riley's days of crying were long over. "I've already said, I can't tell you."

"Won't is more like it," Quillan replied. He reached for his jacket and checked to see if he had everything, looking around for his keys.

"Can't," Riley insisted. His lower lip turned up in an overstated pout.

"Whatever," Quillan said distractedly. *Jacket. Keys. Box. Wallet.* "I'll be sure to let you know how it goes," he added with a wink, secretly enjoying the pained look on his brother's face as he walked out and left him standing there.

Well, what did Riley expect? He was a seven-year-old boy. Would always be a seven-year-old boy, and there was nothing either of them could do about it. And as far as the doctors could all ascertain, there was nothing they could have done to prevent his death, either.

"I don't understand. How does a healthy seven-year-old boy have a *heart attack*?" Quillan remembered his mother crying desperately at the team of doctors who had come together in their curiosity over the mysterious case of Riley Sullivan.

"It's very uncommon, but it does happen," one doctor, the old one, had insisted. "Usually there's some sort of event, some trauma that is a catalyst. And you're sure nothing happened to—"

"I'm *sure*!" his mother had screamed, bringing the entire attention of the hospital to her distraught family. "He was *sleeping* for Christ's sake!"

"Isabella," his father, Patrick, had whispered, holding her tenderly, his large hand grasping Quillan's tiny one.

"The trauma can be latent," a younger doctor piped in sheepishly. "It could have been from days earlier."

"He's—was—a child," Patrick had said. "He played like all children do. What were we supposed to do, lock him in his room?" Quillan remembered his father's large hand trembling, shaking his own.

"I'm sorry, sometimes things like this cannot be easily explained," the older doctor concluded, and despite a number of inquiries, the mystery of Riley's death had never been solved beyond those words. *Things like this cannot be easily explained.*

At seven, Quillan hadn't completely understood death, and this situation didn't serve to thrust him into that understanding. The day after Quillan's parents drove home from the hospital without Riley, patiently telling Quillan that his brother would never be coming home again, Quillan found Riley sitting on the end of his bed as if nothing had happened.

"Mom said you weren't coming home."

Riley shrugged. "I guess I'm staying."

But Quillan learned quickly that while he could still talk and play with his brother, no one else could. When Quillan would talk to Riley at the dinner table—Riley, sitting in his old seat, no food before him—his parents were unsettled. They exchanged looks, pulled him aside for talks, and tried to engage him in sharing how he was feeling about Riley's death.

"He's not dead," Quillan had insisted. They'd taken him to see a therapist.

"They can't see me like you can," Riley had told him. "Don't say anything more to Mom. It makes her sad."

Quillan never mentioned it again, and was careful never to talk too loud in his room, or to laugh too much when they would play. But sometimes his mother still looked at him strangely. He knew she worried, and suspected that Quillan maintained his delusions about his dead brother.

While Quillan grew, first into his teenage years and then into an adult, Riley stayed the same. His appearance never shifted from the tiny black-haired child he was the day he died, and his mannerisms and speech never evolved much, either. Although he'd existed as long as Quillan, and tried very hard to speak and act like they were of the same age, he simply couldn't, because he'd missed out on the experiences Quillan got to participate in. This caused great frustration for Riley, who had trouble accepting his twin might have grown into a different person.

But Riley followed Quillan, nonetheless, through college, and into his first apartment. Quillan was so used to the sound of his voice and his presence that he couldn't imagine a life without his brother, and wondered how he'd ever managed to keep it a secret for so long, especially from Leander.

He didn't know how to deal with some of Riley's newer insecurities, though, and so Quillan handled them as he did anything else that caused him frustration: he simply didn't. He dismissed them as idle jealousies of a child in a unique and awful position, and pushed them to the back of his mind.

Quillan pulled up to the store several minutes after dusk. The neon light switched off, and he rushed to the door, hoping it wasn't too late. As he reached for the handle, he looked up to find himself staring directly into Estella's eyes. Her gaze hardened, and without a second thought, she turned the key in the lock, spun on her heels, and headed to the back of the store.

His phone buzzed. He looked down at it. *Lauren*. Ignore.

"Well, shit," Quillan spat, and raced around the side of the brick building, running down the narrow alley. He saw her getting into her Lexus, and reached out to put his hand on her shoulder.

"Quillan, what the fuck is wrong with you?" she snapped, and slammed the door on his arm. He recoiled in pained shock.

"I could ask the same of you!" he cried, clutching his arm. As he rubbed the growing red lump on his forearm, the mahogany box slid out from under his left and fell to the ground, spilling the contents.

Estella moved to close the door again, then spotted what he'd dropped. She slowly climbed back out and knelt down in the gravel, picking up one of the symbols. Oblivious to Quillan's pain, she inspected the object, turning the metal disk in the dim streetlamp.

"Where did you get this?" she demanded.

Quillan panted, the pain almost unbearable. "I... came... to show it to you," he breathed.

She narrowed her eyes at his show of pain, and went back to admiring the emblem. "Do you even know what this is, you ridiculous boy?"

He shook his head, biting his lip so hard the taste of copper spilled on to his tongue.

"Necromancy," she whispered with a smile, and for a moment Quillan forgot about his pain.

"There's more," he managed to say, gritting his teeth.

Estella rifled through the other symbols. "Brimstone," she said, holding up the infinity sign with the double cross. "An alchemy symbol. Also enjoyed by Satanists." She looked up. "Or so I'm told."

She picked up the third one and squinted at it, turning it over in her hand. Quillan watched her, fixed. "I don't know what this one is," she mused, clearly a painful admission. "But I can look it up. Now, tell me, where did you find these?"

"They were brought to us from *Ophélie*. From the Deschanels," he added.

"Yes," she said evenly. "I, too, am a Deschanel."

Oof. He'd completely forgotten, but this fact could work in his favor. "Yeah, I know that."

She smirked. "What are these papers?"

He shook his head. "Letters, I think. I haven't had a chance to read through any yet, but thought you might want to."

She laughed, and when she did, her blonde hair shook in rippling waves that gave Quillan chills throughout his whole body. "Oh, you thought so, did you?"

Quillan didn't know how to respond. He'd never known with her.

Estella glanced at the papers, handling them roughly as her eyes scanned. *My dearest Blanche.* "My dearest... Quillan, what... where did you get these?"

"I told you—"

"These could not have been at *Ophélie*!"

He threw his hands up and backed away. "Calm down. I don't know anything more than what I told you. I don't know anything about them, and only wanted to spend some time with you, for once, Estella."

She glared, and he worried she might throw the entire box at him and drive off. But then she said, "Well, let's see what they are, and then I can figure out what to do with you."

She closed the door to her car, picked up the remaining contents, and Quillan followed her into The Soothsayer's Coffer, with absolutely no idea of what to expect next.

14
JONATHAN

Jon liked the Deschanel house on Long Island.

It recalled memories of home, of the old Victorian his parents had bought with cash when they emigrated from the Highlands of Scotland to Summer Island, Maine. History and character in every piece of trim, unique by room, telling stories he might like to hear under better circumstances.

They wouldn't be here long enough to uncover the secrets of this old house. The ship would leave tomorrow at ten in the morning, a fact he'd learned from Nerys, not Finn, who vacillated between flashing him hard stares and ignoring his presence altogether.

He has a right to his anger. He has a right to it forever, if he chooses, Jon continued to remind himself, but he couldn't help wanting to tell his brother, *This will be so much easier if we work together. We always were a great team.*

After dinner, Jon wandered down the long dock, the setting sun warming him from behind. His head fell back, toward the orange and purple sky, as his shoulders rose in a deep breath.

When had things gone so wrong? It was easy to blame Ana's arrival in Maine, but months of reflection helped Jon see the fuse had been lit back in his youth, when Carla died. A grief he'd been forced to process alone... if he'd even processed it at all. Every moment thereafter was a latent reaction to his pain at envisioning himself in the life he wanted, rather than the life he'd chosen.

Ana's presence, in hindsight, was not the source, but a greater push into the darkness. A place Jon thrived in, because it was safe.

His entire life now hung in the balance because of his comfort there. It wasn't too late; he had to believe that. If anyone taught him that inexplicable endless capacity for human compassion, it was Finn.

Slow steps plodded down the dock, and Jon turned to see that strange girl, Anne, hands shoved deep in her pockets. Her dirty blonde hair was pulled back, in a tie that reminded Jon of something Laura from *Little House* would have worn. As odd and out of place as it was—not to mention her floral gingham dress, straight out of the 19th century plains country store—she molded into the style in the most natural way.

"We're leaving at nine. Thought someone should tell you," Anne offered. Her eyes shifted toward the water. She squinted, focusing.

"Nerys told me," Jon replied. "Do you need glasses?"

Her ponytail whipped around with her head. "That's awfully presumptuous!"

Jon shrugged. "I've noticed you've been squinting a lot the last couple of days. When was the last time you got your eyes checked?"

"None of your beeswax," she snapped, her brief cordiality gone. "When was the last time *you* got *yours* checked?"

"Three months ago," he answered without missing a beat. "My appointments are always scheduled a year in advance, and I never miss them. I've never needed glasses, though."

Anne gaped at him. She started to squint again, then, catching herself, grunted in frustration. "You're nothing like your brother."

"No, I'm not."

"He doesn't seem to want you here."

"Congratulations on your astute observation."

Anne made a face. "Why are you here, then?"

Speaking of none of someone's beeswax. "I don't have to explain myself to you."

"Maybe you should explain it to Finn, then. He had no idea you were coming. You're just agitating him further."

"He told you that, did he?"

Anne shifted, shielding her eyes from the setting sun. "He didn't have to. Deschanels have a way of sensing things."

So they keep saying. "And why are *you* here, Anne?"

"You know why. Our paths crossed in Charleston."

"Sure, but why are you coming along overseas?"

"To help Finn."

"And Ana?"

"Her, too."

"Uh huh."

"Uh huh?"

"I may not be a Deschanel, but I'm not blind. You're not a fan of your cousin Ana, but you're very fond of my brother."

Anne's frame sagged, as if trying to sink through the cracks of the dock. A fierce and immediate blush rose up. "Would you stop with that? He's my friend and I want to help."

"I notice you didn't deny the other part of what I said. About Ana."

Anne balled her fists at her side. A light whisper passed through the tall blades of grass on the shore. "You're one to talk about Ana! No wonder Finn doesn't want you here. You have no idea how to talk to people. I'm going to ask again, why on *Earth* are you here?"

"I already told you—"

"You think you can make up for what you did to him? To Ana? You can't take it back."

Jon tensed. He wanted to escape in the worst way, less because of her accusations and more that her bringing them forth meant discussing them.

He also saw no point in rising to her bait, though. "I'm not proud of my past actions. I would take it back, if I could."

Anne snorted. "Says every criminal on the planet who got caught, I suppose."

"You've never done anything you regret?"

"Nothing like that," she retorted smartly, but Jon saw the darkness pass over her face. One he recognized.

"Then you're fortunate, Anne. Because there's no feeling that eats you alive more than regret."

"What do you expect will happen by your being here? That Finn will forget?"

"No," Jon replied. "I don't expect he ever will, nor should he. Ana is his wife, and I hurt her. But I'm not here looking for him to forget what I've done. I can tell him I'm sorry, but what good is that? Words are words. Change has to come through action."

Anne's expression lost some of its fire, plainly surprised by his earnest confession. "Do you really think people can change?"

Jon took one last glance at the sun, now disappearing to the west, and started back toward the house. He considered her question with the seriousness it deserved. "I hope I can. I think I have. At the least, I have to believe it's possible. If not, I may as well shut up shop now."

"What about paying for your crimes?" Anne asked, though her question seemed directed at a situation other than the one at hand.

"Some crimes have no worse punishment than realizing what you've lost for your troubles," he replied. "Goodnight, Anne."

Her voice was small and faraway as she replied, "Yeah. Goodnight, Jon."

JON RAN INTO ALEKSEI AS HE ENTERED THE BACKDOOR, INTO THE kitchen. Under Forbia's expectant supervision, the boy sacked the cupboards for something to eat.

"I saw some crackers in the pantry," Jon suggested.

Aleksei smiled. "Awesome!"

"Goodnight, Aleksei."

"Goodnight, Uncle."

Jon's heart skipped at the words, but he didn't let the feeling permeate much deeper. His scientific mind could not grasp that this "child" could really be Finn's son, despite that he resembled him—and Ana. Beyond his disbelief, though, was the understanding he could not have a relationship with Aleksei until the wound with Finn mended.

Jon passed by his brother's room on the way to his own. A sound halted him.

Through the cracked door, Jon saw Finn leaning over the foot of the bed, face buried in his hands. His body quaked with sobs.

"We'll find her, Finn. I promise," Jon whispered, in a voice too low for anyone but him to hear. Saying the words out loud made them real. They made him believe there was an end to his brother's agony.

The promise gave him the power to be a part of Finn's relief.

15
QUILLAN

Estella sat in the corner of her pink and white striped bedroom, curled in her velvet armchair, perusing the stack of letters. Quillan had been tasked with researching all Deschanels alive in the early twentieth century, and notating their ages at the time, where they were living, what they were doing, and any other pertinent information.

Quillan could not be less interested in the mysteries contained in the letters, a fine contrast to Estella's dogged determination to spend every waking hour solving them. He began to realize his fine idea to snag time with Estella was perhaps not as well-planned as he'd thought.

He legitimately attempted to perform his tasks as assigned, but would find himself gazing up at her—the way she twisted those silken locks around her long, slender finger, how she'd part her lips ever so slightly when she was particularly deep in thought—and lost all focus entirely. Focus had never been Quillan's strength, but fortunately, determination was.

In the two days they'd spent reading through the letters,

they discovered only a couple of things, and neither actually explained anything.

The first was that over half the letters were written by a woman named Anne to a man named Amos, and appeared to never have been sent. The two had been locked in some sort of forbidden relationship, the letters written in so vague a fashion it bordered on code. In fact, as there was no Anne or Amos Deschanel alive when the letters were dated, they assumed the names were code as well.

The second discovery was the other half of the letters were written from "Anne" to another woman, but these letters were signed in an offhand way: *Love, Your Favorite.* The only telltale sign that "Your Favorite" and "Anne" were the same person was the handwriting, particularly the remarkable way she constructed her "y," with sweeping tails that swooshed across the whole page.

This second set of letters were all addressed to a woman named Blanche and *that,* at least, *did* mean something to Estella.

"We need to find out who Anne was, who she was fucking, and why she was writing to my great-grandmother," Estella had said after the first read-through, providing a nice summary of the task ahead.

But with letters written in code names, and no other identifying facts, that task seemed far too daunting for someone as unfocused and easily distracted as Quillan. Even Riley laughed at him, teasing it served him right she put him to work doing the one thing Quillan had always hated: research.

Stop being such a jealous twit, Quillan had said under his breath.

She's a bad person, Riley repeated, a broken record. *But it* is *kinda funny she has you doing paperwork!*

Quillan had to believe once they figured out what these

ridiculous old letters said, and the silly symbols meant, she'd find some way of thanking him. He knew just the thing.

As for her interest in the letters, the only thing he could glean from her was that Blanche was her great-grandmother and they'd been close.

"Progress report," she demanded from across the room, with the stern timbre of a schoolmaster.

"Uh... er..." *Shit.* "I still only have a few names."

"Well, spit them out!"

Quillan shifted awkwardly. He'd rattled these off earlier and made no progress since. He hoped she wouldn't notice. "There's an Amelia Deschanel. She died in 1910, when the letters are dated, so maybe—"

"Negative," she interrupted. "There are several letters past 1910. Continue."

"Um... there's an Elizabeth Deschanel, born in 1903, but died in 1905, and then—"

"For fuck's sake, Quillan, these letters were not written by children, nor were they written by *ghost* children, so what else?"

His discomfort grew to anxiety. "Er, Eliza Deschanel born in 1908 and married to August Deschanel... er... scratch that, she would have been two... fuck... um. You know, most of these people were dead or kids in 1910. What the hell..."

"Yes, yes, the Deschanel family Curse," she said with an impatient wave. "We all know about *that.* Was there no one else?"

Quillan perked. "A family curse?"

"Focus!"

"I'm still looking," he mumbled.

"Yes, do that," she said, and went back to her reading. "Start by not being such a failure."

This had been the nature of things since they started, but

the experience wasn't entirely without its perks. The image of Estella's fingers twined through her hair, pen slipping in and out of her full lips, the occasional glimpse of her tongue running over her pink lip gloss... all far better than his wildest fantasies. Her sex appeal was even more potent when she gave him orders, demanding this or that from him. His legs remained perpetually crossed.

He suspected, though, that her pert demands would become more volatile if his research continued to turn up nothing. She might remove him from the project entirely.

Quillan's phone had been buzzing all day, and after a while he'd turned it off. He couldn't deal with Lauren when he was focused on pleasing Estella.

"Estella," he said, embarrassed when his voice cracked at the edges. Even more horrified when the small smile on her face said it hadn't gone unnoticed. "May I see some of the letters between Anne and Amos?"

Estella rifled through the papers and thrust several out in front of her, clearly expecting Quillan to come fetch them. *Like a dog.* His hand brushed her slender fingers as the paper exchanged hands, and a chill coursed through him. She didn't even look up.

He sunk back into the chaise and squinted at the tight, flowery cursive.

My Dearest Amos,

As I have attempted to tell you on far too many occasions now to put number to, there is little benefit to the continuation of this discourse; with certainty, far worse a misfortune should greet us both. It is not without some sorrow that these words doth part, but it is with great wisdom and knowledge of such things that we have discussed, far more than was ever necessary, that I say these words now and for a final time. Thusly, the product of such liaisons, as it were, may lead us both into a ruin that can only be filled with a finalization akin to death itself. Of all this, you know and must, thusly, move forward without further thought of such discourse and liaisons continuing. Strike it forth from head and heart, you must, and with such expediency as to be remarked upon.

With Love but Mostly Regret,
Anne

What in the hell did I just read? Quillan's head ached. The other letters were even longer. *What have I gotten myself into?*

A small sigh escaped the petite girl, whose long legs were dangling scintillatingly over the arms of her tall chair.

Quillan refocused on the letters, trying harder. Estella had said they were written in code, but Quillan didn't think it was code, so much as *vague.* Anne seemed to write in circles about a topic that she and Amos knew intimately but didn't want conveyed in letter.

Probably having an affair, he thought. *Maybe he's her servant or something.* But he'd found no Deschanels of marriageable age, or, hell, even any that were alive at all. Perhaps the dates were also a diversion?

The product of such liaisons...

That last sentence jumped out at him, but refused to offer him meaning. What would the product of an affair be? Divorce? Banishment? Disinheritance?

Maybe Anne wasn't a Deschanel after all? Maybe it was Amos?

He returned to the website he'd found, with the Deschanel records, and tried searching for Deschanel men. He scanned through the names and years, and found this opened up a couple of options. There was a Jean Deschanel, who would have been sixty-six in 1910. His son, Charles Deschanel, thirty-five. Other than that, only a few scattered male Deschanel children. Although Jean and Charles were both married at the time, given the scandalous nature of the letters, he knew neither could be ruled out.

So, that left him with zero females and exactly two males to work with, if these records could be trusted. It occurred to him the firm would have the best chronicles on the Deschanels around, but he thought of Lauren's nonstop attempts to call him. Not an option.

He pulled out another letter and read:

My Dearest Amos,

What is done is done, and it is my utmost wish you cease the inquiries. We have discoursed at length regarding the absolutely real and relevant reasons why this decision was come to, and there was no other possible outcome. Even you must know this. And yet, I continue to receive correspondence that you have sent further inquiries and are now threatening to come by and investigate matters for yourself?

You claimed to have full faith in the assertions of my family and the terrible burdens placed upon it by greedy and monstrous ancestors, yet your actions would speak clearly in an entirely untoward direction. Were your reassurances merely the products of comfort in a moment? Were they outright deceptions? I ask this not because I seek a direct response or answer—for you know, I do not, no—but for I would have you ask these questions of yourself instead.

What do you seek to gain? A torment that is unfixable, unquenchable? Satisfaction to a morbid curiosity? No, there is no gain in either, Amos, and you must come to that realization with

expediency, either through my pleading and tearful words, or your own deeply abiding intelligence and good sense.
This blight, this plague, this enmity of the devil that my family has earned, has no cure. You cannot seek to fool it or charm it, or bargain with it. This choice I have made was a choice I never ere wanted wrought upon me and yet it was, and I made it with sound mind and the purest of judgment and cause. You must respect my decision. To do otherwise would be to condemn yourself, and to condemn him. I know you do not want this!

With Love but Mostly Regret,
Anne

To do otherwise would be to condemn yourself, and to condemn him. Him... him. Now there was another person involved? He wondered if Estella had caught that last word of the letter. He opened his mouth to ask, then thought better of it. If she'd caught it, she would've said something. Bringing it to her attention now would only seem to be calling out her oversight. *Yeah, that'll go over like a pregnant pole vaulter.*

But the mention of this additional person could prove useful if the pieces started coming together. *Him* could refer to her husband or lover, of course. That definitely seemed the most obvious answer... but the line following... *I know you do not want this!* made no sense in that context. Why would Amos care about Anne's husband's feelings or reputation?

This is the most work I have ever done for a piece of ass.

Quillan rubbed his hands across his tired face, grunting and stretching, causing the box to fall off the table and spill on to the floor.

"Careful!" Estella barked as he knelt to pick everything up before she could snap at him again.

As he did, he noticed that, on the inside of the lid, on the red velvet liner, were two barely visible, faded letters:

OD

16

OLIVIA

Olivia considered the twin babies in awestruck affection.

She'd never supported Alain and Katja's twisted liaison, no matter how noble they declared their reasons. Cousins reproducing was unnatural. An abomination! Trading one predicament for another far worse.

Her disapproval had quickly shifted, veering down a road toward necessary acceptance. Olivia's brother, Alain, was gone, a victim of his own hand. Katja had nearly lost her life in the ordeal as well. Their beautiful twins, Stella and Sebastian, now rested in the nursery Olivia had originally set up for her own baby, stillborn only two weeks before, filling both gaps, in a way.

Stella and Sebastian slept, side-by-side, with a small space between them as if waiting for Nora, their lost sister. Their birth into this world had been traumatic: a single gunshot to their mother's stomach had ripped Nora from this world before she could even enter it, and left their mother paralyzed and broken. Their father had then turned the gun on himself, ending not only his life, but any hopes the Deschanel family had resting on their salvation.

Despite the completely ridiculous notion, to varying degrees, many in the family chose to believe in the remote possibility of their solution, mainly because no one had a better idea.

Olivia slid silently into the rocker and watched the babies sleep. Her toddler son, Rory, slept in his own room, already lost to his dreams. Greg worked late, a steady condition recently, and one Olivia suspected was caused by the turmoil she'd brought into their happy home.

In her mind, no other choice existed. As she'd watched Katja slip away, blood rushing from her plump belly, Olivia changed. Not eventually, or gradually, but in that exact moment.

She knew she'd give anything—yes, anything—to save Katja and her babies. It was too late for Alain, but not for his children.

Greg said little on the subject, understanding that even if his opinion differed from hers, the twins were all she had left of her beloved brother.

To love them meant to love Katja, and she would, no matter the road ahead.

Stella and Sebastian's tiny breaths traded off, creating a small, muffled song as they slept. Olivia's heart leapt at the amount of love she already had for these two tiny people. Babies who were her cousins, but who would be raised believing they were her children. *I know Katja must love them too. If only I could reach her. If she would only listen. I know I could get through to her.*

But Katja was unreachable. The death of Alain and Nora was an unthinkable tragedy, but was not what had ultimately broken her. Nor was it the paralysis that would leave the twenty-year-old confined to a wheelchair for the rest of her life, as she'd refused healing from any of the family's shaman.

Katja Gehring was lost to the knowledge of what she perceived to be the biggest failure of her life.

"I was so damned sure, Olivia," she'd said, the night she demanded Olivia take her children from her.

"I know," Olivia replied, soothingly, though she didn't know and never would. Her hands pressed to Katja's brow. "But so did others, dear." She didn't add salt to the wound by reminding Katja that she, Olivia, had been one of the few who knew it would never work. There *was* no cure, because there *was* no curse, other than their staunch unwillingness to be a normal family.

"Because of me! Because I was a stubborn bitch!" Katja flipped her head to the side, knocking Olivia's hand away. "He's dead because of me. My daughter is dead, because of me. Others will continue to die, *because of me!*"

"The family's beliefs have nothing to do with you," Olivia told her, evenly. "You were the first person to come up with a reasonable way to end this madness." Olivia paused, swallowing her innate need to remind others when they've been wrong. This new, kinder Olivia would have to say what Katja needed to hear, rather than what her mind desired to convey. "It isn't your fault."

"Reasonable? I suppose you think fucking your first cousin and producing mutant offspring, all in order to please some vengeful, incestuous French cunt, is reasonable? Maybe Brigitte would have been happier if I fucked my brother, Markus," Katja sneered, tears of anger rolling down her face.

Well, no, none of it was reasonable, dear. But it is done, and we can't go back. We can never, ever go back. And I wish to God I knew the words you needed to hear to help push you forward.

Katja was a brilliant girl, a child of two scientists, and her theory had been based on a logic she wholly believed. But that logic had resulted in a chain of events culminating in unspeakable tragedy. Katja would never accept she was not at fault for Alain and Nora's deaths, because, logically, she was partly right. If she had not persuaded Alain, and others, to believe in her theory, then Alain would still be alive. *But then, these children never would have been born, either. In all this senseless tragedy, two lives were created and we can't let that be overlooked.*

Then Katja made what she believed to be the most logical decision of all: that it should be Olivia and Greg who raise the twins.

"I know you're going through something unthinkable right now, Katja, but they're your *children.* They need you," Olivia insisted. She could understand Katja's pain, but she could not relate to her dismissal of her own children, no matter how young she was. No matter what she had been through.

But Katja had laughed. Then laughed, and laughed some more. "You really don't get it, do you? I'm never going to get better. I will never get over what I've done. And worst of all, I will *never be able to look at those mutants with anything but contempt.*"

Katja had the paperwork signed before she even discussed the arrangement with Olivia. Not simply guardianship, but a complete signing away of her parental rights. *The mutants are yours now.*

"I'm not signing this," Olivia insisted. "It's staying in a drawer for the day you come to your senses, and I can tear it up."

Katja threw her head back and laughed again. There was little left of the beautiful, kind, brilliant girl she once was. "Don't hold your fucking breath, cuz."

A month had passed since that discussion. Katja slipped further into the recesses of her tortured mind, retreating to an old basement bedroom Greg had once used for storage, speaking to no one. She refused any company. Even her parents and brother were forbidden from visiting.

"Thank you for letting me know she's okay," Aunt Evangeline said with a choked sigh, the day Olivia had called her to advise of Katja's wishes. "You've done so much for her. I wish she would let us help."

"One day," Olivia said graciously. "When she's ready."

"Darling," Evangeline replied, her voice cracking. "If you decide, at any point, the children are too much, Johannes and I will take them. I know my little girl, and I don't expect her to ever come around to this."

"I refuse to believe that," Olivia said, stubbornly.

"Then you don't know Katja," her aunt had said, with a sad, resigned exhale.

OLIVIA AWOKE WITH A START. SHE HADN'T MEANT TO FALL ASLEEP IN the rocker. A glance outside told her it was late. As she sat up, a blanket slipped to the floor. *Greg,* she thought, and smiled.

Cooing sounds emerged from the crib, and she realized what had awakened her. The babies were up, making baby sounds only they understood. Smiling and refolding the blanket, she reached for the bottles she'd prepared and left in the warmer. After a quick meal, and dry diapers, she'd join Greg in bed.

Leaning over the crib, Olivia saw the two were facing out of their crib, toward the closet. Stella's eyes were wide, the light dancing in them, and Sebastian was smiling.

Are they... playing? It seemed unusual for two so young, but Olivia had never had two babies of the same age.

At once, Olivia had a strong sense of a fourth presence in

the room. She turned to the door, expecting Greg or Rory, but they weren't there. No one was.

Turning back toward the twins, she saw again they were both staring toward the closet, to her left, and fixated on, seemingly, nothing at all.

Olivia picked up a strong sense from Stella. *She's talking to someone.* But no... that was impossible. Stella was hardly four months old, her brain not yet developed enough to experience the kind of connection Olivia was detecting. What was it Greg had said the other day? *They're bigger than Rory was at six months, and he was no small baby.* At first she thought he was waxing esoteric on how fast children grow up, but then she realized he was right. They *did* appear to be growing rapidly, and at a faster rate than made sense, especially given their premature birth and weeks in the NICU. She chalked it up to the stress of their new life, but it made her nervous about scheduling their next checkup.

Olivia had the wind knocked out of her as she picked up another sensation, this time from Sebastian. *He's intrigued by this other entity. Protective of Stella. He wants to play.*

She couldn't begin to know what to make of this. Sure, growing up as a Deschanel, she'd seen plenty of inexplicable things. Still...

Olivia reached for her cell and selected the contact record for Aunt Colleen.

She stopped short of hitting send.

17
ESTELLA

Estella had been mostly pretending to read the letters. It was not that they didn't interest her—because oh, Lord did they ever—but Quillan's thoughts were equally perplexing.

Of course, most was quite unsurprising: all the myriad things he would do to her once he solved her silly mystery and got his reward. *He sure has another thing coming if he thinks I would ever hook up with him, but if that dangling thought keeps him going...*

It wasn't that she needed him for his intelligence, as he possessed little, or his problem-solving skills, which seemed to be another not-so-strong point for Quillan. The rub was, he'd been the source of the boxes and remained insistent he could not let them out of his sight, as they were "on loan."

"On loan, my ass," Estella had said. "You stole them to hang out with me."

He hadn't exactly denied it, but he insisted on being present. And, as the items didn't belong to her, she had no solid ground to stand on.

Besides, he had access to resources at his silly law firm that she, despite her resourcefulness, could not match. She couldn't imagine what secrets lay at the end of the search, but they involved her great-grandmother and that was more than enough. She couldn't care less about a ridiculous love affair, but whoever wrote the letters to her lover had also written letters to her great-grandmother. And those letters contained warnings... warnings to stop, to turn back, to change course. Warnings Estella didn't understand.

She'd kept those letters to herself and let Quillan focus on whatever the others were about.

On the peripheral of his convoluted mind were concerns about work, which he perpetually convinced himself to ignore rather than address. *Lauren is going to be so mad... ugh, and I promised her... but what can you do, she can't always expect me to drop everything...*

Typical Quillan, thought Estella. Lazy to the last.

His thoughts about someone named Riley were more interesting. Quillan had never mentioned a Riley. Most likely a male, but could be female, which might explain Quillan's fear of Riley's reaction. Whatever Riley was likely thinking right now, as a result of Quillan's associations with Estella, seemed to be the only thing on Quillan's mind that mattered.

It was really no surprise he was making so little progress on *any* of the tasks she had assigned him.

Of course, he was worried about that, too. She had to stop herself from giggling. *What in the hell am I doing here... oh God, she's so hot, what I would give... keep reading Quillan, keep reading!*

Though she didn't know Riley, Riley apparently knew her. Had, in fact, been warning Quillan to stay away from her. *She's bad. She will hurt you.*

Already, Estella despised this Riley. Who did he or she think they were? Quillan's mind had settled on jealousy as the reason for Riley's warnings, which piqued her curiosity even further. Why had Quillan never mentioned this person?

Because you aren't friends. You think he's beneath you. You treat him like crap. Remember?

Oh, yes. Well, either way, something about this Riley situation wasn't sitting well with her, and she added it to the list of things to figure out. She could ask him, but, like any decent mind reader, she enjoyed the challenge.

Estella returned to the letters, fixating on the words as if answers would jump from the page.

My Dearest Blanche,

I find myself in a deeply emotional turmoil since our discourse of Christmas last. I believe your good and kindly heart may be leading you astray—nay, I am quite sure of it. We are all the victims of our good intentions, and as we well know, the road to hell is paved with them.

I, of anyone, understand and empathize greatly with the immensity of what lays before you as you begin the journey, once again, recently married for a third time and with designs to start a family. But I say to you thus: what you propose is preposterous. More, even if it did produce the results you are expecting (and I truly, do not, in my heart of hearts believe that it will), the cost of said results would be far more burden than I would ever want laden on your kind and goodly heart. I plead with you, Blanche: do not do it. Your great-grandfather's greed and arrogance is what brought this upon us, not some vengeful single-minded spirit. Do not overcomplicate this with flowery explanations... accept it for what it is and pray for the safety of those you love.

Remember the warnings, with the fervor of faith: Seduction to sinners. A legacy in splinters. Beware, the myths of midwinter.

With Love,
Your Favorite
January 1940

Estella had heard there were Deschanels who could touch something—a letter, for example—and pick up the thoughts of the writer. She wished she had such a handy skill right now. They were arguing about the Deschanel family Curse, but what was new? The Deschanels *still* argued about the damned curse and it was the twenty-first century.

Remember the warnings, with the fervor of faith:

Seduction to sinners. A legacy in splinters. Beware, the myths of midwinter.

Why did people have to speak in riddles? Estella always said exactly what she was thinking.

There were altogether ten letters to Blanche, spanning over the course of six years, from 1940 to 1946. The last letter had a note of finality to it, and was the only correspondence not addressing Blanche as "My Dearest."

Blanche,

It is for the last time you have left me thus, at such a loss for words. My own heart, you are the child I was never allowed to have, for the consequences of such an action were always apparent, always present to me. That you could not understand the simplicity of the terrible decisions of your ancestors has always pained me, but never in the way it does now.

Two of them... two of them, and for what? You believe that this will satisfy a requirement but that would indicate a compassion and logic that does not exist in such a horrible situation as the one our family has been thrust into. To the last, I believed you would change your mind... that you, my dearest heart, could never be capable of

such acts of horror and disregard for beloved kindred. Alas, you have surprised me, but in no way I ever wanted to be surprised.
It is with the heaviest heart that I turn this letter toward goodbye. Had you allowed things to take their natural course, as is our cross to bear, I would have borne the grief with you, side-by-side, holding your hand. As you have chosen a course that is so unthinkable, so unnatural, you must bear this grief instead alone.

With Great and Profound Sadness,
Your Favorite
1946

More talk about the curse, perhaps, but whatever Blanche had done was so reprehensible in the eyes of the writer, she was cutting her out of her life. And with no further letters, that might be exactly what happened.

Could the writer be referring to Blanche's murder of her husbands? Estella thought it was possible on the scale of "horrific acts." The only trouble was the years didn't match up. Blanche's first husband, Johnson Guidry, had "disappeared" in 1930, and Ellis Kenner died in 1940. Whatever had happened, whatever Blanche had done that had been so displeasing, happened six years later. Blanche married Estella's great-grandfather, Claudius Broussard, two months after Ellis' death. By 1946, all of Blanche's remaining four children were born, and she was well into her new life. Happy, from what Blanche had always told Estella, when she rambled stories of her youth, great-granddaughter in her lap. *With Claudius, I finally got it right.*

Estella set the papers down and closed her eyes. She tried to visualize her great-grandmother then, as she had been in her youth. Long, loose blonde curls, bouncing with her swift step. Engaging blue eyes that never shied away from locking with others in conversation. The firm, full mouth that opened as wide as her face when she laughed. *What did you do, great-grandmother? Who did you anger and disappoint so much? You never mentioned it. Or did you? I wish I could remember everything you told me. Lord knows I've tried, but I was so young...*

The memories did sometimes come back to her. That morning she'd been in the shower when she recalled one of the last conversations she had with her great-grandmother, words forgotten until just then.

...And then there were necromancers too, but they were quite rare, of course.

How rare, great-grandmother? Rare like snow?

More rare than that, child. I am the only one of my generation, though that hasn't stopped others from trying to make a necromancer where one does not exist.

I don't understand.

No. But you will someday.

Estella wondered if someday was nearing closer than she thought.

AN HOUR LATER, SHE STOOD OVER THE SHOULDER OF QUILLAN, WHO'D carelessly dropped the antique letter box and spilled everything on to the floor.

"OD? Really? You don't know?" Her hands gripped her hips, nodding at the faded embossed letters.

"Should I?"

Disgusted, she taunted, "I'll give you one guess. There's an entire fucking plantation named after her?"

Quillan gawked at her the way her father's dog did when she issued an order he couldn't comprehend. She sighed again. "Ophélie, you twit."

Then he was shaking his head, with that same befuddled

look, and she thought she might slap him if he continued to act so dense. "That's not possible, though. She died in 1863."

Estella's mouth was already open to abuse him when she stopped. She privately fumed at being bested by someone she held in such low regard. "It doesn't mean it's not her box," he suggested meekly, compromising. *Yet another reason I hate you, Quillan. You have no backbone.*

"No, it can't be," she conceded, thinking. Ophélie's mother, Brigitte, had burned all her things after she died at the hands of soldiers. She'd been so young. "You know, I'm still amazed Ophelia Deschanel hasn't come up in any of your searches. I could have sworn she would have been at the right age for these letters..."

"Ophelia?" he asked. "With an a?"

"No, with a z, you twit."

He ignored her. "So there're two Ophélies? One with an e and one with an a?"

"Are you serious right now? Of course there is! Ophélie died during the Civil War, as you pointed out. Ophelia was her niece and lived to be some ridiculously old age. She was my great-grandmother Blanche's aunt. She's the one who gave us everything we know about the Curse. Isn't your firm supposed to be experts on the Deschanels?" And as she said those words, something at last clicked. *Blanche's aunt... Blanche was born in 1908... which would mean Ophelia would have been an adult when the love letters were written, and even older when the letters to Blanche were crafted.*

How did we miss this?

Quillan fumbled with his laptop again, furiously smashing keys. "Quillan, are you daft?"

He looked up, eyes wide. Fearful, apologetic, but also, vindicated. "Ophelia Deschanel would have been thirty-two in 1910."

"Well, then. I think we finally have our letter writer."

"There's something else," Quillan said. "I think... well, I think maybe Ophelia Deschanel had a child with whoever this Amos fella is."

Estella didn't care about a baby, or Amos, but since Ophelia was a part of this mystery, she realized she must *find* her interest. "Why, pray tell?"

"It would be easier to figure out if we knew who Amos was, and why they were running around in secret, but..." He pulled out a letter and pointed to a sentence: *Thusly, the product of such liaisons, as it were, may only lead us both into ruin.* "I get the distinct feeling the product is a child."

"But that still doesn't explain why she's upset," Estella said impatiently.

"I think maybe she gave it up."

"And?"

He took a deep breath. "And, I think maybe he figured it out and tried to do something. Maybe he even got his hands on the baby somehow."

She laughed at him. "That's a pretty broad assumption from all those vague words, would you not say?"

Quillan didn't seem to have an answer. Estella had no idea if his theory had any merit. He could have said the sky was blue and she would have declared him unfit for polite society.

His face lit up. "You said she's the one who knew the most about your... er... Curse, correct?" Estella affected a dismissive nod. "And if she never married because of it, because she was afraid of something happening to her children?" Estella nodded again, pursing her lips. "Then maybe she gave up this child for that same reason."

She rolled her eyes to the ceiling. "Then why would she let herself get pregnant in the first place?"

"Not everyone had access to the birth control you have

available now," he reminded her. "And from everything I'm getting from this letter, it was the last thing she wanted to have happen."

"I think this is presumptive at best," Estella snarked, but was slowly coming around to the idea. She didn't tell Quillan this, but there had been rumors Ophelia had her share of casual lovers. In fact, Blanche compared her to Queen Elizabeth I, who had famously refused to marry, but nonetheless enjoyed her carnal pleasures. Not impossible one of them might have knocked her up.

Still... Estella felt like this would have been somehow known. There were no secrets inside the Deschanel family, only ones kept from the rest of the world. Like the Curse.

Blanche had chosen to leave New Orleans and disown the main Deschanel branch, in hopes of saving her family from the fate that befell many her kin, over the years. She'd done so on the urging of Ophelia, who saw herself as the family's voice on the Curse.

If Ophelia's own words had backfired on her, Quillan was right. She would not have had the option of a safe abortion, so would not adoption be her only hope? It would still be a gamble, for that child to be born with Deschanel blood, but perhaps a better chance than keeping it.

Estella didn't tell Quillan any of this.

Better for him to think his idea was ridiculous.

18

NERYS

Oh, what Nerys would do for a terrakinetic right now!

A couple days travel was nothing for her, under the ordinarily easy, lazy journeys of her freedom to wander. But eternity could not be longer under the tension of her fellow travelers, who gave no effort toward even pretending to relax or let go.

The interchange between her companions, the underlying stench of deep deception running between the brothers, and the way Anne reacted to Jon, was a curious thing. Nerys hoped none of it would prove troublesome in the days ahead, where trust in one another would be more important than any past wrongs.

More than a terrakinetic and a portail, she desired to rediscover the comfort of access to the minds of the Brotherhood, which remained silent and inaccessible.

The night Farjhem burned would remain etched forever to memory.

"Events have taken a terrible turn," Birger had told her.

"Agripin has made a sacrifice of Aidrik. He'll be executed at Farsengel, and Anasofiya with him."

"No!" Nerys cried. Beside her, Astrid wept silent tears. "How could my brother do this? This wasn't the plan. We're no better than the Senetat if we would give up our own to save ourselves."

"I have to believe he had no other choice," Birger said in a reasonable tone. His eyes, dark and troubled, showed her he was questioning ever trusting Agripin. Nerys had no guidance for him. She hardly knew her brother, but doubted the veracity of a plan that placed the swaggering duke in a position of power. A place where he was a partial architect for all their fates.

"We must at least try to save them."

"We cannot breach Farsengel without an army. News has already spread about this throughout the drekar and many have scattered, believing this to be another Runean War." Her old friend gave a weary sigh. "Finnegan has escaped. He awaits Ana at the waypoint they agreed on, though he doesn't yet know she won't be joining him. You and Thorvald, with Stian's help, must go to him and see him safely back to New Orleans, and Aleksei."

Nerys had gasped. "Aidrik's ward! They'll all be exposed. Without a Quinlan to adhere it..."

Birger offered a small smile. "You're tired, old friend. Finnegan is a Quinlan. A draoi. Aleksei, as a mystic, can create the ward, and his father can adhere it."

"Of course. I knew that." She'd found her forgetfulness worrisome.

But this was before, when the prophecy existed solely as pretty words spoken by an old race they'd once called friends. Aleksei's birth had changed everything.

When Aidrik was executed, Ana had manifested powers

others had only guessed at, annihilating the Senetat and sending Farjhem up in smoke and ash. She emerged no longer the same, a danger to herself and others, and so they'd bound her magic and secreted her out of Farjhem, taking her to the Brotherhood's apartments in Bergen. Agripin stayed by her side, refusing to leave despite her vows to destroy him the second he let his guard down.

All this Nerys learned from the thoughts of her friends. Her last intelligence informed her they would be moving on. The Senetat was not entirely destroyed, as they'd initially believed. The danger not past.

Then everyone went dark for Nerys.

Her final thoughts from Thorvald. *Nerys, I've seen the newest evil plaguing the Deschanels. A necromancer.*

How? Their numbers have dwindled down to nothing over the years.

Don't underestimate the science behind this halfling family. Many of them have manifested powers as great as ours. Some greater. I won't speculate. Why bother? I am quite sure a necromancer plagues this family. My dreams are infected with the warning: Seduction to sinners. A legacy in splinters. Beware, the myths of midwinter. Remember?

Aye, though the words make no more sense. What could they possibly want? To talk to ghosts? Nerys nearly laughed.

What necromancer has ever been satisfied to simply speak to one?

But that would require no mere necromancer... She'd left the actual words unsaid. Even Empyreans were not immune to a touch of superstition.

Yes.

If this is true, and you've discouraged me from intervening, why tell me at all?

To light a fire? Because I refuse to deceive? Because no army wins a war without the knowledge needed to defeat their opponent? Duchess, how many years have you known me?

Since Canaan.

Aye. You may disapprove of my propensity for bloodlust, and I may rail against your frustrating neutrality, but I would not deceive you. A lie by omission is still a lie.

And so Thorvald had armed Nerys with knowledge that kept her up nights, carrying the burden of a worry her companions did not need.

The time would come, though. If they could not find Ana quick enough—and at this point, with no link to the Brotherhood, Nerys doubted their success more and more—she would be forced to present Finnegan with a choice: save his wife, or save her family. Their son's family.

Nerys closed her eyes, and tried once more to find her friends.

19
QUILLAN

Quillan braced himself for what was sure to be an epic reaming from his father. He wasn't disappointed.

"I am without words, Quillan Patrick Sullivan!" Patrick's voice quavered as hard as his hands, balled into large fists that resembled swinging boulders. His face matched the red stripes on his candy cane tie.

Quillan's eyes darted across the room at Lauren, who sat quietly observing. He looked to her for help, but she avoided eye contact.

"One hundred thousand dollars! You may think that isn't a lot of money, but it's more money than you've brought into this firm altogether. And you *lost* it!"

"Well," Quillan said, looking again to Lauren for support, with no luck. "I wouldn't say that it's lost, exactly..."

"You watch your smart mouth with me, Quillan. In here, I'm your boss, not your father," Patrick warned. He braced himself on the bookshelf, a big man out of breath.

"Technically..." Quillan started to say it was actually his

uncle Colin who was his boss, but his father's face was already turning purple. "Can't we have the secretaries resend the bills?"

Lauren's lips twisted around in a hidden smile, and Patrick spun so hard the bookshelf rattled. A snow globe crashed to the floor. "Are you really as thick as you let on? Surely I haven't raised a child this dense."

Lauren cleared her throat. "We've already invoiced them for final charges, so sending a new invoice now would cast a bad light on the firm."

Quillan laughed in relief. "Well, we sent them the invoices, so we just need to get them to pay, right?"

"No," she replied. "Because time sheets were not submitted, the invoices were grossly understated." She looked at Patrick, who gawped out the window in furious contemplation. "By about a hundred thousand dollars," she added.

Quillan felt the floor swept from under his feet. His father got worked up about everything. He was used to this. When the lawn wasn't edged properly, he'd throw the gas can across the garage. When he ordered a pizza and the order wasn't quite right, he'd call and berate the manager for hours. Always barking, rarely biting; a challenge to figure out how serious he was when he treated small and big problems the same.

But Lauren's face sealed the deal for Quillan. The confidence was gone from her voice and demeanor, and Quillan imagined she had taken the brunt of the screaming before he'd come in. She was, after all, the one tasked with helping make sure they avoided exactly this situation.

"So, now what?" Quillan immediately regretted how nonchalant the question sounded.

"NOW WHAT?" Patrick's neck veins popped out in a grotesque purple maze.

"*Now*," he continued, his heavy steps thumping as he paced

the room, eyes trained on Quillan. "*Now* we pray to every saint we know that Colin doesn't initiate a vote to have you removed! And you *will* answer when Lauren calls you, and you *will* do everything she says!" Patrick left and slammed the door, his thundering steps echoing as he stormed down the hall outside.

Until that moment, Quillan hadn't really believed it could ever come to that. But the anger and disappointment radiating from his father, coupled with Lauren's defeated head bow, put things in a new light.

You've really fucked up this time.

"I tried to warn you," Lauren said, throwing her hands out, "I tried—"

"I know," Quillan assured her. "I was busy. It wasn't your fault."

"For two days?" She laughed. "Quillan, most people do their extracurricular activities on their days off. You were supposed to be here, in the office, the last two days. What could be more important than coming to work and saving your job?"

There was no way he was going to tell her. Even he could see how ridiculous it would sound if he explained that he was hanging out with a girl in hopes he might eventually get laid, even if it was a plan years in the making.

"It's complicated," he offered finally.

Lauren crossed her arms and leaned forward. "Complicated? No, Quillan, I'd argue this is actually extremely simple. You are in real danger of losing your job and you just *don't care*!"

Her steel-gray eyes flashed, wide, and the blonde of her short bob tickled her jawline, swaying back and forth with her heavy breaths. In her own way, she was nearly as worked up as his father had been.

"Of course I care," Quillan said and smirked. He thought maybe he was telling the truth, too.

"You have given neither me nor your father any indication this is true," she spat, leaning over the desk on her hands, glaring at him. "You are making a fool of yourself. And me."

"I'm sure it's so easy for you, Lauren," he said, leaning against the tall windowsill. In the street below, people waited for the streetcar to take them back into the Garden District. "Top of your class, parents always expected great things from you. You earned this job, which says something at Sullivan and Associates, because we have a real hard-on for keeping business in the family."

She eyed him warily, gauging his sincerity. "I don't see how that makes it easy for me at all."

"You're good at this. I'm not here because I was smart, or because people expected me to do well. I'm here because my father is here, as his father was, and my uncles, and cousins, and every other goddamned Sullivan who's alive in New Orleans. Everyone knows I'm a giant fuckup. And yet, for God only knows what reason, they hired me and let me deal with clients."

Her face was slowly moving from anger to annoyance. "Am I supposed to feel sorry for you, Quillan?"

This was not going as he had intended. "I'm just saying I'm not good at this."

She closed her eyes for a moment, searching for a response. "I know that. And you're right, so does everyone else. But you're supremely lucky in that people are still trying to help you anyway. What makes you a fuck-up, Quillan, is not that you aren't good at your job. It's that you keep turning down every opportunity to possibly *become* good at it."

Quillan didn't know how to respond to this.

Lauren's voice softened, and she relaxed her posture. "We're really not that different, you and I."

He laughed. He couldn't help himself. "Trust me, we are."

"I know what you think of me, but I don't get all my enjoyment from work. I like to have fun, too." She walked toward him and leaned back against the desk. "And I know you were with a girl."

This startled him. "How?"

She smiled. "Because of the look on your face when I asked where you'd been. You're not the first person to throw away their responsibilities for some tail."

"Maybe," Quillan conceded, studying her. "But you and I... we're on different wavelengths. Trust me on that."

"Okay," she agreed. "But I can drink you under the table, Irish or no."

He laughed and slapped his hand against the bookshelf. "What kind of a woman challenges a man, an Irishman no less, to a drinking contest? Are you mad?"

"If I win, you have to do everything I say, from now on. No avoiding my calls, no complaining. If you win, then... well, you should probably still listen to me, but I'll let you pick a prize."

He'd been thinking for some time now that he should be putting effort into helping Leander meet someone. "Okay, if I win, you go out with my friend."

The smile faded from Lauren's face. "You want me to date your friend?" Was that disappointment?

"He's a nice guy, I promise. Just not great at meeting people."

Lauren frowned for a moment, then stuck her hand out. "All right, then. When shall we do this?"

His phone rang and it was Leander. He held his hand up to Lauren, to hold on a moment. "Man, your ears must have been burning," he joked, and winked at Lauren. She smiled half-heartedly. "What's up?"

"Dad needs a plant for tonight." Leander sighed. "I got conned into it."

"Sucks to be you." Quillan laughed. The Broussards often brought along people on their cemetery tours disguised as tourists, who were there to make the tour look good by asking interesting questions and getting the crowd going. Quillan couldn't imagine a world where antisocial Leander would make a good "plant."

"Yes. You're coming with me, okay?"

"Negative."

"You have plans with Estella? No, I didn't think so. She has a date tonight. Not with you."

An invisible hand punched Quillan in the gut. She hadn't mentioned a date. But were they even the kind of friends who told each other what they were doing? Were they friends at all?

"I have to work," he said, eyeing Lauren.

"Bring the whip-cracker with you," Leander suggested.

He covered the phone with his hand and looked up at Lauren with a twinkle of mischief. "Got plans tonight?"

"Depends."

He gave her the rundown, hoping she'd insist they stay in and try to fix his invoicing mess. It was a fine situation, when he'd rather work than go out.

"Sounds *fabulous!*" she exclaimed, and returned the same exaggerated wink, then walked out of the room.

"We'll be there at seven," Quillan grumbled.

20
KATJA

Katja ignored Olivia's knocks, focusing harder on the paper in front of her. She'd been up nearly forty-eight hours straight, but wasn't tired. *No rest for the wicked,* she would have said, but Katja Gehring was long past the point of ironic jokes. She was focused, not giving up when she was *so close* to stringing the threads of her research together.

"Greg is threatening to cut the power to your room if you don't get some sleep," Olivia warned. Though her words were direct, and her threats not likely empty, Katja didn't care. If they turned her lights off, she'd open the window and read by moonlight if she had to, like her ancestors must have done.

Katja ignored her, not lifting her focus from the sheet in front of her. It didn't look especially different from the thousands of other sheets strewn across her desk, and room, but something about it *felt* different. Her gut told her that all the blurred words and thoughts were finally going to come together and reveal the answer to her soul's greatest question.

"Kat, please," Olivia pleaded. Katja's mind acknowledged

the desperate kindness in her cousin's voice, but she didn't react as she might have two months ago, before the entire world flipped upside down. The feelings of others reigned so small and unimportant in the face of all that had happened. Sometimes she wanted to slap Olivia for such trivial concerns; to say, *Are you really such an ignorant bitch, that you think this* matters *compared to everything else?*

In the midst of her scattered delusions, Katja simply needed her, and everyone else, to stay out of her hair, and out of her space. She needed time to figure things out, and she was *so close.*

She'd called Markus, a couple weeks ago, to come to her, feeling him out for suitability to assist in her research. He'd already consumed too much of the Deschanel family crusader Kool-Aid though, and so she sent him away.

Katja heard the soft sounds of her cousin's steps as they faded and let out a small breath, but her heart continued to race at the prospect of what she might uncover next, if she could simply finish her reading.

Research had always been a strong point for Katja, having been born from two award-winning scientists. She and her brother, Markus, both were drawn to the same world—one of logic, and sense, and a reason for everything. So when Katja moved into her teenage years, and started absorbing the details of the Deschanel Curse, she did the only thing she knew to do, the thing she had been raised to do: she researched it. Her initial interest morphed into a full-on fixation, and by the time she graduated high school, her findings had taken her on a path that veered far from theories the family held so dear.

The presumption, held by nearly all Deschanels who believed in Brigitte's Curse, was that its origins centered on one single, horrible sin committed by their ancestor Charles Deschanel.

But that did not make an iota of sense to Katja. Sure, it wasn't implausible that Brigitte, in her grief, may have made some horrible pronouncements on Charles and his kin. However, it seemed unlikely that a woman who could love her daughter that much, would want her grandchildren, and their grandchildren, to suffer for something not their fault. Even emotions followed a logical pattern. A logical thing for Brigitte to do, under duress, would be to strike down vengeance upon Charles himself, not innocent children in generations to come.

Logical or not, it didn't change the fact the family was, in fact, definitely cursed. Entire generations were thinned out, leaving the family's future hanging in the balance more than once. Katja's research wasn't designed around debunking the Curse, but determining its true origin.

Katja had to think beyond the information she'd been surrounded by her whole life, and instead forge a broader path. What else could she learn about Brigitte? Charles? Ophélie? What about the town in France where they had emigrated from? And what of their parents?

Her research uncovered odd patterns. Though it was well-known that Charles and Brigitte were first cousins, Katja had been astonished to learn their parents were brother and sister. Going back another generation, *their* parents were also brother and sister. This continued on and on, as far as Katja could find records. All brothers and sisters, with a couple instances of first cousins, but nothing further in relation.

Katja knew this had to mean something; that it was not merely coincidence. Though close-relation marriages were somewhat common in rural European towns in the 19th century, brother marrying sister had never been accepted. Katja could find no other families in their region who followed that behavior. This rampant incest was unique to Deschanels.

Katja was struck by the obvious break in the pattern:

Ophélie. Ophélie, being Charles and Brigitte's only daughter, severed that link with her untimely death. She would not be able to marry one of her brothers.

But what, if anything, did this mean?

Katja's research further uncovered the few other families in Europe who were engaging in the brother-sister unions, were all doing it to sustain something of genetic importance. The Deschanels were known for their unusual abilities. It was believed these other families had forced inbreeding to protect these abilities and keep their bloodline strong. With this, Katja wondered, what if her ancestors, in France, had been more powerful than the Deschanels of today? What if they sought to protect and sustain that?

If this were true, and nothing else in her research had produced a conclusion half as logical, then the only solution would be to reconnect those ties. A brother and sister, or two first cousins, would need to continue the task of strengthening the bloodline.

Certainly not ideal from a number of angles, but it was the only hypothesis that had both a solid explanation, and a course of action to follow.

But what if you're wrong? Alain had said, that night at Lake Pontchartrain after she poured forth her years of research. Though nearly a decade older than Katja, his face possessed a lightness and innocence that she had never known in her own short life. Alain had the soft, kind look of someone who held on to the belief that everything would always be okay, if you simply believed it would.

I'm not, she'd responded simply, confidently. Katja had a pride bordering on hubris, and she would never have whispered a word of this to anyone had she not vetted it thoroughly. She'd been as sure as any scientist could be after they put forth their grand hypothesis.

But how will we live? How will our children live?

She'd been prepared for his questions, but had not predicted his innocence; his eagerness to please. Despite his reasonable reservations, he was very nearly convinced before she finished speaking. And though her short-shorts and braless tank top had not technically been part of the experiment, it was a smart manipulation of the variables.

She'd been *so sure*. Sure enough to convince Alain. Sure enough to convince most of the family, despite their fears and concerns about her and Alain's future. She'd maintained her confidence through Alain's slow descent into madness. Kept it right up until the moment she opened her eyes and saw his distraught, lost face, and the gun pointed at her belly.

No one understood why she couldn't raise her babies. They assumed she saw them as a sad reminder of all that had gone wrong. There existed some truth to this, but such a sentiment didn't even begin to scratch the surface. The memory of her failure, of Alain's final, desperate act, was almost an afterthought now.

No, there was something *off* about the babies. Not their unfortunate entry into the world, or even jitters Katja had over being the mother of twins when she was hardly an adult herself. It went much deeper than that... beyond even the oddness that Deschanels gave off to non-Deschanels.

Stella and Sebastian were evil. She was sure of it. And she was positive this evil, whatever it was, and whatever reason it had entered the world through her and Alain, was the answer to why the Curse didn't break with their birth.

Mutant babies, she'd called them to Olivia. Because *devil spawns from the seventh circle of hell* did not seem like an appropriate thing to say to her cousin, who had done Katja a solid by taking them off her hands long enough for her to figure things out.

Upon further study, Katja was convinced that the birth of these two children may have fulfilled a prophecy far deeper, and more sinister, than anything she'd uncovered in her initial research. Whatever it was, it spelled terrible things for the family. She would figure out what it was, and she would stop it. She would stop *them,* whoever *they* really were.

This was why, no matter how much Olivia, or her parents, begged, Katja would not be swayed from her research.

21
ESTELLA

"Have a lovely time on your date tonight, dear," Pandora slurred. Jasper braced her swaying body as he guided her toward the door to take her home.

Estella smirked, not bothering to hide her disdain for her mother's growing problem with the bottle. "I'm sure I will."

Jasper cast a quick glance back. "I'll return in ten minutes to close up. Thanks for watching the store." They disappeared out the door.

"As if I had a choice," she mumbled, but was still relieved she'd found a way out of filling in on the tour of Lafayette Cemetery No. 1. When Leander's lies about not feeling well fell through, she had to think of something her parents would respect. She decided to play on her father's half-hearted guilt for bringing her home, and claimed to have a date. "I'm trying to readjust to being home again," she simpered. "Like you suggested."

With every day, her hatred of her parents grew. She'd always held them in low esteem, but now, witnessing their behavior through adult eyes, she despised them. Her mother, once a great beauty of New Orleans, reduced to a drunken, slovenly mess, unable to perform the duties of this farce she called a career. As a child she interpreted her father's doting as kindness; she now saw it for what it truly was: cowardice.

That morning when he'd cornered her in the store, to con her into filling in, she finally confronted him. "Why would I help you out? Isn't it enough you brought me here to be your shield, because you can't handle your own wife? Isn't that your job, through sickness and in health, till death do you part?"

Jasper looked down, away, anywhere but at her. "That's ridiculous, Estella, I didn't bring you home to take care of your—"

"Bullshit! You know damn well my education is far superior than spending my days holed up in some shitty store. Is that why she's a drunk, Jasper? Because she's finally realized what a mockery her career has turned into?"

"Your mother is not a drunk. She simply likes her spirits from time-to-time," he said pleasantly. Estella snorted with laughter. "And I do wish you would call me Father..."

"A *father* would not use his daughter to do his dirty work."

He sighed, defeated. Jasper's tactic for dealing with difficult conversations was to end them. "I still need your help tonight."

She rolled her eyes and turned from him. "I can't. I have a date."

"Oh!" His voice tilted up, excited, and she hated it. "How lovely!"

Like I would actually date anyone in this shitty town. "Yes, I'm sure it will be." Her eyes caught the letters sticking out of her purse. They filled her with an unusual sense of calm. Knowing she would return to them tonight soothed her.

As her father hovered awkwardly, she realized he might be of some use to her. In spite of the ridiculousness of the Coffer, he'd once been a great scholar of the occult. Respected, even. *You would be remiss not to use all your resources, especially those right in front of you.*

"What do you know about necromancy?" she blurted.

He threw his hands up and laughed, clearly relieved at the subject change. "Whoa there! That's quite the topic, Estella. Any reason for the interest?"

Like I would ever tell you. "No, just had a customer come in the other day asking about some symbols they found."

He crossed his arms and leaned back against the counter. He smiled so big, so happy at the thought of being useful, Estella *almost* smiled back. "Well, tell me about the symbols and perhaps I can help."

"The first was the symbol for necromancy. The second, the Leviathan cross..."

"Sulfur, yes. Popular with Satanists."

She ignored him, already regretting her decision to ask. "The third was a double-headed eagle."

He nodded, stroking his chin. "Yes, a symbol of power, authority. These are all very potent symbols your customer showed you. They would have been owned by someone of great aspirations, I believe."

"Do they mean anything when used together?"

The question on his face told her he didn't know the answer, but that wouldn't stop him from guessing. "There are many symbols with enough power on their own that it is difficult to know what someone meant when using them in tandem," he mumbled, deep in thought. "But the presence of the necromancy symbol stands out as primary. I would say the wielder of these symbols believed... hmmm... possibly they were aspiring toward necromancy in order to achieve some great power or dominion over others. They may be in dealings with Satan himself."

She wanted to slap him, then herself, for starting this discussion. "That's a pretty bold assumption, don't you think?"

"My dear, without the opportunity to speak with the owner of the symbols, assumptions are all we have," he insisted, waving his hands. "I suggest calling them back in."

"Well, that's not possible," she said quickly. "The customer... found the symbols and didn't know who they belonged to. They're very old. Maybe a hundred years or more."

He chuckled. "Then it's safe to say whoever owned them didn't achieve their aims, eh?"

"Excuse me?"

"If they were trying to gain power through necromancy, they'd still be around, no?"

Estella wasn't in the mood for his self-indulgent riddling. She'd made a mistake thinking he would be useful to her. "I think I have what I need, thanks."

Jasper beamed. "I'm so happy I could be of service to you."

There had to be another meaning for the symbols. It was not possible that Ophelia Deschanel, a woman whom Blanche had respected above all others, was using necromancy for evil gain. Nor that Blanche was somehow mixed up in this nonsense. She'd hoped her father might be able to shed some insight beyond the most obvious interpretation, but whatever brain cells he'd once possessed had apparently fled.

Or was the answer right in front of her? Estella had spent the last four years trying to recruit masters of divination to aid her in speaking to her great-grandmother once again. What if Ophelia, through Blanche, had been trying to do the same thing?

It didn't sit well with Estella. If Blanche only wanted to communicate with the dead, then why the other symbols? What did Ophelia's warnings have to do with any of it?

She pulled out the letters, searching for the section that had been on her mind the most.

I do not believe in your theories as I have lived too long and seen too much not to know the actual truth of the matter. But no matter the belief, you must realize that what you seek to do is so preposterous, so against the natural order of things, that you will never succeed in a way that is satisfying and redeeming to you. There are some things that must and always should be left alone, always and forever. This ability is no skill, but a product of the same Curse that afflicts us all. Your skill, above all others, should be ignored, pushed back down inside of you, and never spoken of again. Cast it from your thoughts! Banish these endeavors forthwith! I must repeat again: You will not gain what you seek, but will instead gain something much darker and more horrible than you ever imagined.

Was Ophelia referring to using powers to commune with the dead, or something more sinister?

Whatever the case, the world did not come to an end. Whether Blanche succeeded in her efforts or not, she lived a long life. The letters from Ophelia stopped cold in 1946, even though Ophelia lived almost another thirty years.

Estella scattered the letters on the counter with a grunt of frustration. Until they could learn to talk with the dead, all she had was supposition and vagueness.

The tour would start soon. She grinned, thinking of Leander having to be the plant. Served him right for always being a self-righteous asshole.

Briefly, she wondered if he'd talked Quillan into joining him. He hadn't called her once all day. She frowned, wondering what he could be up to that was more important.

Why do you care? You should be happy he's leaving you alone.

Was it that "Riley" again, putting thoughts into his head? If Quillan was at the cemetery tonight, would Riley be there too?

Estella glanced at the clock. It had been more than ten minutes, and she wasn't waiting around for her father any longer. She left the store without locking up, not caring if anyone walked in.

It wouldn't hurt to take a longer route, and drive past the cemetery on the way home.

She turned down Washington, easing her car ahead of Commander's Palace. A growing crowd congregated near the large metal archway marking the entrance to Lafayette Cemetery No. 1. Esmerelda, the flamboyant gypsy her parents hired to lead the Garden District tours, lifted her hands in the air to signal the start of the tour.

Estella scanned the group. Leander stood near the gate, hands shoved deep in his pockets. She spotted Quillan nearby, mimicking Esmerelda's exaggerated gestures. A tall blonde next to him snickered. Quillan turned to the girl and whispered something in her ear. She nodded, laughing. Quillan's gestures were too familiar for a stranger. He knew her.

Estella's jaw tensed. Her hands squeezed tight to the leather steering wheel. Was this the mysterious Riley?

"Riley" was tall, with short, chin-length blonde hair and a very angular jaw. Little or no makeup, and her clothes were nearly as plain as her face. *Why, she's not Quillan's type at all!*

But then, why was she there?

And more importantly, why is this bothering me?

22

NERYS

The hustle and bustle of Galway put Nerys on immediate and acute alert. Senses torn in all directions, she struggled to keep up with every movement, every thought, every errant look, all which had the potential to be a threat.

We are so exposed, she considered, over and over, the feeling worsening with every step through the old city.

Finnegan brightened the moment his feet transferred from ship to stones. His increasing optimism abruptly contradicted with her accelerated fears, but Nerys preferred the halfling like this. The other travelers looked to him for emotional direction. Budding hysteria would not do.

He went to see about train tickets with single-minded determination, leaving the others huddled around their luggage near the port. Forbia had found a perch on top of the gear, her nose pointed into the wind, twitching at all the unusual scents. Nerys excused herself, determined to follow the nagging instinctual fear that would not leave her, and needing space from her companions to avoid further muddling of thoughts. The sensation was there for a reason, as her senses always and often were.

She cast eyes over the crowd, her glance quickly moving from sailor to traveler, from merchant to vagrant. No immediate explanation for her alarm, nor did the feeling subside.

Nerys turned to see Anne and Jon having a row, then Jon storming off. Aleksei and Forbia were nowhere to be seen.

A knot formed in her belly at the realization her group was no longer safely huddled in one spot. This loss of control spread through to her chest.

Her attention diverted toward a rising cacophony in the market. Vendors and patrons rushed toward the commotion, abandoning posts and wares without a second thought.

Nerys approached the source, the panic within coming to a sharp peak with every step.

She forced her way through the thick crowd, where she knew, without seeing, one of her own was in danger.

When she stumbled into the center of the ruckus, she found several men pinning Aleksei facedown into a stall, one calling for additional help. Another held a snarling Forbia at bay with an empty wooden fruit crate. On the other side, Jon broke through nearly the same time she did, and forced himself to where the men held his kin.

"Come on now," Jon said amenably, as if the situation at hand were far less serious than whatever had caused these men to apprehend the young man down like a violent criminal. "Whatever it is, we can sort this out."

"This child is from the devil! I saw it with my own eyes!" one of the men declared through tightly clenched teeth.

"Aye, we've not tolerated this wickedry in Galway for many years. We've no place for it," another of the captors added.

"Let's start by telling me what happened," Jon said in the same, even tone. But Nerys knew. She knew, and her mind spiraled and twisted, searching for a solution that would not somehow make things drastically worse.

Finn burst through, face colored with anger. Nerys shot him a sharp look of warning. When he continued to charge forward, oblivious in his rage, she employed persuasion. *You'll accept my apologies for it later.*

He paused in confusion, shifting a curious glance toward where his brother's misplaced diplomacy cast an anxious lull over all gathered. Next he noticed Forbia. With a sharp hand signal, he ordered the beast to a sit beside him. A low growl rumbled from her chest. She was physically still, but nowhere near calm.

"I was only trying to help," Aleksei moaned, muffled against the wood as one of the men pressed a firmer hold on his neck.

"We don't need this kind of help," the man answered, then turned toward Jon. "Are you responsible for this whelp? Did ye teach him to do this?"

"I still don't understand the nature of his crime," Jon replied reasonably.

"Sometimes a pot gets overturned, and that's the way of it. This boy got it in his head he had more say than fate and stopped it. With his mind. His *devilry*."

Jon chuckled. "We all would wish to have that skill. I assure you, though, he has no such gift."

"I saw it!" "We watched him!" Several voices replied in frenzied unison.

"His eyes rolled back and he swayed on his feet," the first man, the one with his hand at Aleksei's neck, said with wide eyes. "And then the broth hung in midair, suspended."

Jon gestured toward the mess of beef and liquid covering the cobblestones, near an overturned cast iron pot. "Seems to me, if he's being accused of having the skill to stop time, he isn't very good at it."

This was followed by several chuckles. *None of them truly want to lynch a young boy.* But Nerys dared not relax.

"Aye, 'cos we grabbed him and broke the devil's trance before he could bring a curse upon us."

Jon made a visible effort to bite back a certain humor at the superstitions being conveyed, but Nerys, sensing his trembling, unsteady fear, knew better. He played a dangerous game, choosing to take a tender bite rather than barking. "This child? He can hardly be counted on to tie his shoes properly. Really, you'd find more magic in the rats eating your meat pies."

One of the men whipped his neck toward his booth, to discover Jon wasn't lying about the vermin. Two of them perched on the cutting board where he'd been preparing meat before the ruckus.

He dropped his hold on the boy, apparently deciding his livelihood held greater sway than proving a point. Aleksei breathed out in relief, but the two men remaining affected a firmer hold.

Nerys, fixated, lost her focus on quelling Finn, and he shot forward, Forbia in eager agreement at his side, yanking the assailant with his hand at Aleksei's neck back into the stall of the man busied with chasing off the very large, persistent rats. With a shrill curse, both men and one angry wolf, toppled over one another, topsy turvy, along with a good amount of pie fillings.

The crowd gaped and gasped, slowly backing away, not necessarily from Finn but the uncertainty of the situation and what a strange turn things had taken since the first accusation struck. Perhaps even sensing the very *real* magic in the vicinity, from all involved. Including Jon, though he wasn't aware of it.

Nerys resumed her binding of Finn, who stopped short of

strangling the last fisherman obstinately holding firm to his son. *We have to keep our wits. A fight will only incite them, and worsen the problem.* Forbia barely achieved a half-sit this time, her attention torn between Aleksei and the meat strewn over the uneven stone.

The remaining man looked around at those gathered, first in silent appeal, and then voicing it. “None of ya? No? Most of you remember the last time we allowed darkness into our town. How long it took us to be rid of it!” Wide eyes and quiet stares met his words. “The losses!”

Jon, sensing the tide turning, stepped closer. “Whatever happened here, to you, I’m sorry. But this is not the same. My ward is only a child. We’re here to visit a distant relative, nothing more. We wish you no trouble. On my honor.”

The man gave Jon a long, stubborn look. He’d already made up his mind to relent, Nerys read from his thoughts, but he didn’t wish this stranger to see him so easily bent. “If we see ye again...”

“You won’t,” Jon assured him, barely masking his relief. “We’re only passing through.”

“Then pass through,” the man spat, garnering the last word.

Jon knelt long enough to make sure his nephew was okay before making a swift exit off the quay, leading the boy toward a cluster of transportation buildings.

Nerys slipped a hand through Finn’s elbow and jerked him along, away from the noise and questions, before someone else decided to take up the mantle of the prior thugs.

They caught up with Jon and Aleksei, the latter of whom was shaking so badly the former had two steadying hands under his elbows. Anne rushed forward, from Nerys couldn’t guess where, demanding to know what had happened.

“Hush,” Jon barked at her, leveling a kinder eye at his trembling nephew. "Aleksandr, what happened back there? What on Earth were they talking about?"

Aleksei mumbled something at the ground while Forbia leaned against him in silent support. Nerys pushed forward, releasing Finn from his binding as she did so, and the man launched himself at his son. "Come," she said, taking firm command. They were not yet far enough from the scene of the trouble to be clear of it. "Forget the train. We'll need to rent a vehicle."

Jon released Aleksei into his father's embrace and flashed her an incredulous look, as if she were speaking some foreign language no longer in practice. "Why, because of a few bullies?"

"No, because word of what Aleksei did back there will spread, and reach ears of those whom we do not want aware. We must change our trail."

"You're no better than they are with that talk. He did nothing wrong!" Jon exclaimed. "And who would want to come after him, I can't even imagine. He's a child, nothing more."

"He's everything," Nerys countered without elaboration. "As to the rest... it isn't my place to tell you this story. Either Finn will, or he will not, but we are not staying in this city another minute."

Anne gave Jon a prolonged, exasperated stare, then shook her head, declaring him some sort of lost cause in her mind. She turned to Finn, who held his son, his eyes red with vengeance. "Let's go rent a car, something big enough for the six of us, and get moving."

Finn waved her away, his attentions divided between the comfort of his shaken son, and thoughts of marching back to the quay and tearing the heads of the rough men from their shoulders.

"I'll take care of it," Jon huffed, looking past Anne. She followed him anyway. Nerys caught the tail end of her thoughts. *Can't be trusted. Probably mess it up and we'll end up with a sidecar.*

Aleksei wiped his eyes and ran off after them, his thoughts unreadable.

"Finn—" Nerys started.

"I know. I know what he did. A time shaper. He's done it once before, and Anders told him to never do it again. He didn't mean to, either time. I won't scold him for something no one has even bothered to teach him to control."

"That isn't what I was going to suggest."

"What, then?"

"Anders is a capable scout, and a decent trainer. But time shapers are so very rare, and his hesitance was a form of fear—of causing more damage. I knew a time shaper once, and he confided in me much about his ability. How to harness it. How to use it, when the need arises."

Finn's expression went blank. "I think... I think he means to try and use it to save his mother."

Nerys nodded. "Aye. But we cannot abide such a risk. No matter the cost. He isn't anywhere near ready to use the ability responsibly and to do otherwise will cause irreversible disaster."

Finn ran both hands over his face, his eyes fixed on the door the others had disappeared through. "Then I suggest we don't put off training him."

JON DROVE. ANNE GRUDGINGLY TOOK THE FRONT PASSENGER SEAT, allowing Finn to stay with Aleksei in the back. As an added benefit, this provided her the opportunity to point out his inadequacy at driving on the left side, and his unforgivable proximity to the curb.

Aleksei slept, leaned against the window, exhausted by his earlier efforts and the near-violence done upon him. Forbia had also made herself comfortable amid the luggage, her head pointedly placed in close enough proximity for Nerys to rest a hand on the soft fur between her ears.

Finn turned in his seat, whispering to Nerys in the third row, hoping to tickle more information from her. How he knew she was holding back, Nerys could not deign, but she held her ground with a firm hand, leaving him comfortably in the role he needed: Father. Rescuer.

No place for his fear, when hers was developing nicely on its own.

23
QUILLAN

There were at least thirty people in the tour party. Leander explained they used to limit it to ten, "back when they cared about the quality of the whole thing." This particular excursion was known as The Glamorous Dead, designed to highlight the glory of dying wealthy. White-washed history at its finest.

Quillan had been in Lafayette Cemetery No. 1 many times, but never on a formal tour. Many Sullivans were laid to rest there over the years, and every funeral he'd attended had been in this old sea of crumbling, above-ground tombs. Visiting out-of-town cousins sometimes remarked how all the marbled, rotting crypts were morbid. He loved telling them they were re-used once the bodies had decomposed enough to be dumped into the bottom. It was weird for foreigners to see everyone in New Orleans put in a vault, but to him it was strange to think of putting people in the ground.

"Lafayette Cemetery No. 1 was originally part of the city of Lafayette, and this particular piece of land has been used for burials since 1824. When the city was annexed by New Orleans in 1852, it became the first official city cemetery." Esmeralda's large voice boomed over the crowd of people gawking at the half-open tombs, whispering about whether or not they could see bones inside.

"So how does this work?" Lauren asked Leander. She'd been overly kind to him since their introduction, attempting to get him to warm up to her. *The woman loves a lost cause.* "Do you have questions already planned?"

Leander smirked. They lingered behind, although they were supposed to be mixing in with the crowd. "I was given a list of questions but they never made it off the store counter," he said slyly. "I thought I would make up my own."

"Well, I, for one, am excited!" Lauren exclaimed, and Quillan thought she genuinely looked it.

"You're going to be sorely disappointed," Leander assured her.

"In 1847, tragedy struck New Orleans with an epidemic of yellow fever. Over three *thousand* people died that year, and some six hundred of those are buried right here in Lafayette No. 1!"

"Isn't it true that another eight thousand died here a few years after, but they were left piled up at the gates because certain people didn't want the proletarians in their cemetery?" Leander shouted. Lauren's eyes widened. Quillan grinned.

Esmeralda's smile died on her lips. Her eyes narrowed at Leander, who was supposed to be supporting her. "Well! Fantastic question, sir. Their exclusion was not because the rich didn't want them," she countered with a chuckle, looking around at everyone to make sure they weren't too put, "but because there simply was not room. There are, after all, only about a thousand vaults here."

"So how did they bury six hundred from the yellow fever outbreak?" a man asked.

"Good question—"

"You don't think there's only one person in each of these, right?" Leander shouted. He had the attention of the entire tour now. "Some of these family crypts have dozens or more, in each. And before you wonder how small tombs could have so many people, once a body is all bones, they get dumped down into the bottom—they call it an oven, but let's call it a toilet—to make room for new dead. Don't worry though... state law says they have to wait at *least* a year and a day before they re-open a tomb and stir up the contents."

The tourists exchanged looks of shock and disgust, and Leander's smile grew.

"You're terrible," Lauren whispered but was grinning too. Quillan had never heard his friend speak with such confidence before, and was too amazed for an appropriate reaction.

"This is true," Esmeralda boomed, apparently accepting it would be easier to go with it at this point. "This has long been a practice in New Orleans, and it allows families to remain together for all of eternity!"

"Except," Leander butted in, "most of these tombs have been sold many times over and are reused. So there's a whole hodgepodge of different families in each of them. That doesn't sound very intimate to me."

"Is this true?" people were asking all around. "How many families are in each?"

"There are over seven thousand people buried here, so you do the math," Leander responded.

Esmeralda positively glowered. "Let's move on."

"Well, you learn something new every day, now don't you," Lauren whispered, eyes twinkling. "Really, I don't know why you don't do this more often, Leander."

Leander grunted but Quillan saw he enjoyed Lauren's interest.

"So, who is Estella out with tonight?" Quillan asked, attempting casualness, and failing.

Leander snorted again, louder this time. "We can't go one day without talking about her?"

"Who's Estella?" Lauren piped up from behind them.

"My bitch of a sister," he replied, turning back to Quillan. "Stop with the obsession. Really. She's evil. She'll spread it all over you."

You sound like Riley, he almost said. "She's really enjoying this mystery we've been working on," he said, intentionally vague so Lauren wouldn't know he was talking about the stolen letters and artifacts.

"She doesn't enjoy anything that doesn't give her personal gain," Leander replied. Lauren kept up behind them, listening closely. "Trust me."

Quillan shrugged. "I think she's interested in her family history."

Leander laughed and several people turned back to see if he was about to ask another crazy question. "Estella hates the Deschanels, like any self-respecting Broussard. She's up to something."

"Estella Broussard?" Lauren asked, jogging to keep up. "Leander, you're her brother? A Deschanel?"

Quillan tensed, worried this might lead to a line of questioning ending with the stolen box. "Unfortunately," Leander replied.

"So," she said, putting things together, "Estella Broussard is who you've been skipping work to hang out with?"

"Sort of," Quillan admitted. His cheeks burned. He wished he hadn't brought it up.

"You really need to stay away from that girl. She's crazy!" she exclaimed. "No offense, Leander."

"None taken. See, Quillan, her reputation precedes her."

Was he really the only one who didn't think she was a psycho?

"I'm serious," she said, dropping her voice. "That girl is no good."

"Well, I didn't ask for either of your opinions on the matter," Quillan snipped. "Anyway, we've hit a wall because we can't figure out who the recipient of some of the... correspondence is."

"Why?" Leander asked, one ear to Esmeralda's words, waiting for a chance to jump in.

"Because it's in some sort of code. But we think—well, *I* think, Estella isn't real keen on the idea yet—maybe they had a baby together that was given up for adoption. Which could mean there's a whole branch of Deschanels in New Orleans that no one knows about."

"Yawn," Leander said.

"You didn't find anything in the convent records?" Lauren asked.

"Sorry?"

She shook her head. "Really? You haven't checked them?" She sighed at his blank look. "Mothers in New Orleans often had unwanted children in convents, and the nuns were responsible for finding adoptive parents. Chances are, the mother used an assumed name, but if you had the year and timeframe, you might be able to narrow it down and start from there."

Quillan gaped at her. "You're a genius."

"It's why I get paid the big bucks," she said, and flexed her arms.

One of the tourists called out, "I heard voodoo was practiced here?"

Esmeralda's eyes lit up. "Why yes! Marie Laveau herself

held many séances on these grounds, and is rumored to be buried here, according to old legends!"

"Bullshit!" Lauren called out, and the eyes of Esmeralda, Quillan, and Leander all turned to her in shock. "Everyone knows she's buried in St. Louis Cemetery No. 1."

Esmeralda looked as if she might murder all three of them. "That's what historians would like you to believe. But those of us who are in the know—"

"Well, I'd love to hear what a famous priestess of the Quarter would be doing buried with all the rich Americans in Uptown?" Lauren countered.

"That information isn't anywhere in this guide," a woman was saying to her partner, and others were checking their brochures as well. Murmurs rippled through the crowd.

"How is it that some of us seem to know more than you, lady?" another woman called out.

"This is really going sideways." Leander beamed at Lauren.

While Leander and Lauren managed Esmeralda and the crowd, Quillan snuck away. All throughout the walk, he'd sensed Riley's presence, but as soon as Estella was mentioned, he started boldly interrupting. It was always weird to Quillan that Riley could be so loud to him and no one else could hear him at all.

"What are you doing here?" he demanded, when they were well-hidden behind a large tomb.

"I'm always here," Riley said sadly.

"I mean *here*. Tonight."

"I follow you all the time, Quillan, you just can't always see me."

Quillan frowned in disbelief. "That's not true. I'd sense it if you were."

"I know how to be invisible, even to you," his little brother asserted.

"You shouldn't be here," Quillan said, looking around. Two rows down was the Sullivan family tomb, where the physical form of Riley Sullivan would remain for the rest of days. He didn't know what Riley was, and wasn't, aware of, outside of their conversations. Up until now, he'd assumed Riley went off and did his own thing when Quillan was busy.

"I have nowhere else to go."

"You're a goddamned ghost, you can go anywhere you want!"

"No, I can't," he said with a sad, slow shake of the head. "I'm attached to you. I go where you go. It's my job."

"Job... you've been saying that for years. I don't think you know what a job means," Quillan said testily. "I'm not your job. You don't have a job. You *can't have a job, Riley.*"

Riley looked at him like *he* was the one incapable of understanding. "I can only go where you go."

"Well, what if I go to France? Would you go there?"

Riley shrugged. "Yes... no... I don't know. It's hard to explain."

Quillan let out a deep breath and tried to think of a way to say what was on his mind without hurting Riley's delicate feelings. "I need you to stop with the Estella hate. You don't like her. Okay, I get that, but we're going to have to agree to disagree on this. And most importantly, *you can't keep showing up in public and doing this.* It's distracting, and one day I'm going to slip up and start talking to you!"

Riley's lower lip trembled. "It's my job," he repeated.

"Quillan, who are you talking to?" Lauren's voice called from nearby. Quillan froze.

"No one, just checking my messages," he said quickly, and flashed Riley a meaningful glance before joining her.

"We were wondering where you went," she said, but her

voice told him that by *we* she meant *I. I sure hope she's not getting any wrong ideas here.*

The worry was wiped from his mind when she said, "Your friend Leander... he's not so bad." She had a peculiar look on her face. "What I mean is, if I lost the bet—not that I will, but if I did—I think that would be okay."

Between Riley's bizarre revelation and Lauren's unexpected behavior, Quillan was ready for the night to end. Too many thoughts swam through his head. *How did I not know Riley was always with me? Who is this girl that came with us tonight, because she isn't the uptight, by-the-book girl I thought she was. What is Estella doing?*

"Did you hear me?"

"Yeah," he said, absentmindedly. "Loud and clear."

"Tour is wrapping up soon. Leander thinks we should jet before Esmeralda can corner him."

"Yeah, yeah, good idea," he said, still looking toward the spot where Riley sat moments ago, issuing his usual warnings. He couldn't see him, but now he knew that didn't mean much.

All Quillan wanted to do was lay down and shut the day out.

He told Lauren he'd take a rain check on the drinking contest. When she countered and said that a reschedule was the same as a forfeit, he let her win. He was out of sorts and not in the mood for company. Even if Estella had shown up at his door, Quillan wouldn't have been excited to see her.

He didn't know why it bothered him, what Riley had said in the cemetery. It made sense, in a way. Riley either did not, or could not, reveal himself to anyone else, so what other purpose did he have for sticking around, if not to follow Quillan wherever he went?

For years, there were many unspoken feelings between them. Anytime Quillan had asked why Riley was here, with him, and not off in heaven or whatever the afterlife held, Riley insisted he couldn't tell him. He'd never elaborate beyond that, no matter how much Quillan prodded. Quillan didn't know if Riley was bound by some kind of code of the dead, or if he truly didn't know.

Somehow this had all been bearable when he'd thought of Riley as having some sort of other life, away from Quillan. Tonight's confirmation, that Riley existed in his state of limbo only for Quillan, left him standing in an overwhelming shadow of guilt. He could do nothing to save Riley when he was living, could do nothing to send him to a place where he could be at peace, and was now responsible for his eternal happiness and entertainment.

Quillan closed his eyes and sunk into his bed, shutting out the world. He was home alone. Leander had stayed with Lauren. He didn't know how to feel about that, either, but his mind couldn't handle that on top of everything else.

"Are you mad at me?" Riley's small voice said from across the room.

Quillan's eyes flew open. Of course Riley was here. "No, buddy," he said with a sigh. "I'm not mad."

"But you were supposed to go out," he insisted. His voice took on the desperate whine of a child. "You came home because of me."

"I didn't really want to go out anyway," he assured him. He wished Riley would go away so he could rest, but the thought made the guilt worsen.

"I like Lauren," Riley said brightly. "She's very nice."

Quillan nodded. She was nice. She would be good for Leander, too. Lee had only had one or two girlfriends in his whole life. He deserved a break.

Riley lowered his head. "I like her a lot better than Estella," he said cautiously.

Quillan closed his eyes and sighed. He didn't want to have this conversation with Riley again, especially not tonight. "Let's not go there, Riley."

"She was spying on you tonight," Riley said, clear he thought that would drive his point home. Quillan's ears perked.

"Come again?"

"I saw her! She drove by the cemetery when you were at the gate, waiting. She made ugly faces at you guys, then peeled out and drove off."

Well, this was an interesting turn of events. Why would she be following him? Unless she was following Leander? No, that made no sense. She hated Leander.

She hates you too. Or, maybe that's what she wants you to think.

Quillan's heart swelled in his chest. He'd been so occupied with the fiasco at work, he hadn't called her all day.

Was it possible she missed him?

The day that had felt so heavy was slowly lightening. "You're sure it was Estella?"

Riley's head nodded furiously. "Oh yes! It was her!"

"Thanks for letting me know," he said, but Riley frowned when he saw Quillan smiling.

"Why aren't you mad at her?" he demanded.

"It's complicated."

"You always say that." Riley's hands balled into fists. He stomped his feet, though no sound was made. "It's not complicated if you'd just explain it to me!"

"Riley, you're seven years old. I don't know how to explain it to you," he said softly.

"No, I'm not seven, I'm twenty-six, like you, I just don't *look* like you anymore." Translucent tears rolled down Riley's tiny face. "I understand a lot more than you think."

Quillan sat up. "Really? You thought telling me about Estella spying was going to put me off her, but now I want her more than ever. Do you know why?"

Riley shook his head, crying silently.

"Because I've *always* wanted her, Riley. I love her! She's the only girl I've ever loved. I'm not an idiot, I know she doesn't love me back, but what you told me tonight makes me think maybe she could."

"Quillllaaaaaan," Riley sobbed. "Please don't see her anymore. You don't understand. She's bad, she will hurt youuuuu."

"Goddammit Riley! Stop fucking saying that. If you have something substantial to tell me, then out with it, but otherwise, shut your mouth!"

Tears rolled down Riley's cheeks. "I want to tell you, Quillan, but I can't. You don't know how that feels." A crack filled the air and he was gone.

Quillan took a deep breath and held it in as he fell back on to the bed. He exhaled slowly, and all the thoughts and worries of the day left him. He was asleep within minutes.

24
OLIVIA

"Liv, wake up. Do you hear that?"

Olivia slowly came to as Greg shook her. Her eyes blurred and strained as they fell on the clock: four in the morning. She'd only been asleep for a couple of hours, and needed to be up in another hour to feed the twins.

"I hear nothing except my will to live slipping away," she moaned, yanking the pillow over her head. Greg snatched it back, pulling her gently to a sitting position.

"Shh," he said, with a finger to his lips. "Listen."

Olivia was too tired to be anything other than annoyed. "I don't hear anything," she whispered, but then she did.

Laughter. Voices. Olivia looked at her husband, eyes wide, and he nodded, no further words necessary. Someone was in the house.

She started to slip quietly off the edge of the bed, but his hand shot out and gripped her arm. He shook his head, and then turned to his bedside drawer, pulling out the 9mm. He installed the clip and slid out of bed, Olivia tailing behind.

Halfway down the hall, Greg abruptly stopped, and turned.

He pointed at the twins' room. *He wants me to listen with something other than my ears. He'd just as soon never speak about the oddities of my family, but that doesn't mean he'll turn his cheek at them in an emergency.*

Olivia closed her eyes and did as bidden. She heard the giggles and the low adult voice still, but it was muted, distant. Thin vibrations began their trembling through her body and then, she sensed the thoughts and feelings of the twins, in addition to a third, foreign entity.

Stella is happy. The third presence is giving her extreme joy. She defers to the presence in the way she would her own mother. Sebastian is also happy, but is feeling protective of Stella. The third presence...

Olivia realized, with a start, that she couldn't sense details of the third presence. She could detect it through the reactions of Stella and Sebastian, but not using her own abilities. She looked at Greg in confusion, who stared back with eager bewilderment.

Olivia was positive there was someone in the room with the babies. Whoever it was, both Stella and Sebastian seemed to know him or her, and, more, seemed very comfortable with them.

Had someone been sneaking into their house nightly? Had they only just heard it tonight?

She beckoned Greg forward. He gave her a fleeting glance, then moved.

As Greg slowly reached for the doorknob, the giggles stopped. There were no sounds at all coming from the room anymore. Impatient, Olivia reached for the knob and flung the door open herself, rushing into the room to catch whoever was hiding.

Greg came behind her, flipping the gun back and forth in

front of him as he inspected the room. "Who's in here?" Olivia called. "Come out and we won't shoot you!"

No one did. She glanced at Greg and gestured toward the crib. *Cover me.* He nodded. She rushed to the twins, both silent and sleeping.

I'll buy that one of us imagined it. Not both.

They checked the room several times. The window remained locked from the inside. Whoever it was had disappeared into thin air.

"I don't understand," Greg ruminated. "I was so sure I heard someone."

"I heard it too," Olivia agreed, but her eyes were drawn to the twins. *Is it possible? No, it cannot be.* She wanted to ask Greg if he saw it too, but was afraid. Afraid he would say yes.

"Liv, tell me," he urged, the familiarity of years together prompting his sensitivity to her smallest changes.

Olivia didn't know what to say. She sighed and pointed at the twins. He peered into the crib.

"How is that... how is that possible?"

"I don't know," she admitted, breathless.

"They've doubled in size since this morning," Greg said, putting voice to their mutual thoughts. "They're way too big for four months."

She nodded. Yes, that was her assessment too. If she took them to a pediatrician, they'd be mistaken for over twelve.

"Liv... how?" Greg asked again. He sounded like a child himself; unsure, nervous.

"No idea," she replied. "I've seen a lot of weird things, but this takes the cake." *Oh, if only my mother were here.* An empty platitude Olivia had called upon many times in her life, only to realize her mother had no interest in anything she couldn't easily label or explain. Now they weren't even on speaking terms, as Maureen couldn't get past her illogical hatred for Katja.

"But, we're really seeing this, right? These little monkeys are growing up way too fast?"

"We're seeing it all right." Olivia sat down in the rocker, lightheaded. Black dots swam before her eyes and a gasp escaped her as one of her panic attacks started. Greg rushed over and knelt before her, taking her face in his hands. She allowed the comfort, even welcomed it. Not so long ago, their marriage had been steps from ending. It had taken these two unusual babies to bring them back toward one another.

"We need to talk to your Aunt Colleen," he said.

"Katja would kill me."

Greg didn't miss a beat. "Katja never has to know."

Olivia enjoyed this new, fearless side of her husband. "Can you call her?" she asked. The tears in her eyes were not of sadness, but frustration. A startling lack of control. "Careful not to wake Rory."

Greg kissed her and disappeared, not pointing out the fact that it was four in the morning, and Colleen Deschanel might not appreciate a wake-up call.

When he was gone, Olivia took a deep breath and attempted to tune in with the twins again. No use. Whatever heightened, and unnatural, emotions she had sensed earlier, they were gone now.

Her aunt arrived thirty minutes later. Though she must have been sleeping when she received the call, her tan suit was pressed and her dark hair perfectly groomed. Her makeup was fresh, clean, and flawless. Colleen Deschanel was already ready, even at 4:30 in the morning.

"Olivia, my dear." Her voice rang kind, and supportive, as if no cruel words had ever been exchanged between them. "Tell me what's wrong. I'll help any way I can."

"It's the twins," Olivia said. When Colleen's eyes widened, she added, "They're fine. Actually, I don't know anymore. I don't know if they're fine. I don't even know what to think."

Greg's hand wound through hers and squeezed. "Maybe you'd better see for yourself, Colleen," he added, helpfully.

Colleen marched up the stairs and straight into the twins' room. When Olivia and Greg entered, they found her staring thoughtfully at Stella and Sebastian.

"I've heard of this happening before," she started, calmly. She lifted Stella into her arms and inspected her, then cradled the child in a practiced motion. "But never seen it."

"Heard of what?" the couple asked in unison.

"If you're expecting a scientific explanation, you're going to be disappointed," Colleen said, as she handed Stella to Olivia, and then lifted Sebastian to examine him next. "There were old wives' tales our Aunt Ophelia used to tell us, about Deschanel children who grew to adulthood in less than a year—"

"Stop right there," Greg interrupted. "I know y'all are different, but at least there's some kind of *precedent* for mind readers and empaths and whatnot. But, c'mon, Colleen. What you're suggesting is impossible."

Colleen placed Sebastian back in the crib. "If I've learned anything in my life, it's that nothing is impossible. Even if it *is* beyond explanation. You both have met Aleksei. He's more Empyrean than human, which explains his growth, but we're all at least *partly* Empyrean. Just because it hasn't happened before, doesn't mean it was impossible, either." She cooed at the smiling baby. "Are these two going to grow to adults in a year? I have no idea. But I do know these little ones are measuring in at about fifteen months, not four."

Fifteen months. That's more than I estimated.

Yet, now there were three witnesses.

"Did Aunt Ophelia ever say if there was a way to stop their growth? Or why it happened?"

Colleen shrugged, and took a seat in the rocker. "She never said much on the topic. I do know she'd never seen it with her own eyes. They were stories from the old world, from before her grandparents left France. It was supposed to be a good sign. Children with this affliction were blessed."

"Blessed," Greg repeated, with a hollow laugh.

"So, what do we do?" Olivia asked. Deep down, she had hoped Colleen might swoop in with some grand, reasonable explanation that put their minds at ease; that she might allay their fears. Instead, she'd confirmed them.

"You do exactly what you would have done if they were growing like normal babies," Colleen said, reasonably. "You raise them, love them, and care for them, as Katja wanted you to."

"I wish Katja were here to hear this, and be a part of it," Olivia said.

"She would have no more insight into this situation than you," her aunt reminded her. "In her current state, she might even be less-equipped to handle this development. I hardly think she would take them back."

"We don't want to give them back," Greg said quickly.

Olivia tilted her head, watching Greg's eyes dart to the twins, protectively. *He loves them like they're his own. He loves them even more than I do. Maybe this is related to our recent loss. Maybe not.*

"Of course you don't," Colleen soothed, and put a hand on Greg's shoulder.

25
ESTELLA

Estella opened the email Quillan had sent containing all convent records in Orleans Parish for the year 1910. He mentioned someone at the firm had helped him retrieve them, and she'd bet it was that Riley girl from the other night.

Utter hogwash, that she was giving this girl a minute's worth of her thoughts. She was rather plain, though not ugly, so Quillan might have thought she was more in his league than Estella. Estella didn't want Quillan, but he'd wanted *her* for so long that the idea of him wanting anyone else bothered her in a way she couldn't explain.

"We're looking for a child born around May or June, 1910, to a mother under an assumed name. The father will have been someone local and from a less fortunate family, or at least, that's what I think. It sounds almost like she is talking down to him in the letters... you know, like he's from a part of society, or whatever, that her family wouldn't be too cool with. I'll be over after work to help ya out," Quillan's email read. She'd forgotten he had a job, probably because he'd gone to work so rarely since she'd returned home.

His comment about the less fortunate father surprised Estella. She'd read the letters and hadn't picked up on that herself. That observation showed a keen sense for subtle details. Until he was proved right, though, she would not give him too much credit. He was, after all, a Sullivan.

Estella scanned through the records. There were over a hundred babies born that year given up for adoption, but only twenty were born in May or June.

"He said local," she muttered and started removing all the parents from outside of New Orleans. This exercise narrowed the list further, as most of the parents were from other parts of the state or region. Only three babies were adopted within the city of New Orleans. She reviewed the now much shorter list:

1. Mother: Jane Doe
Child: Cassandra
Born: May 25, 1910
Adopted By: Andrew and Joan Cutwright

2. Mother: Elizabeth Benoit
Child: Mathilda
Born: May 29, 1910
Adopted By: Craig and Mary Banner

3. Mother: Anne Smith
Child: Patrick
Born: June 3, 1910
Adopted by: Seamus and Claire Sullivan

Estella's heart dropped when she read the last record. *Anne.* Adopted by Seamus and Claire Sullivan.

What were the odds Ophelia Deschanel had an affair with Seamus Sullivan, who was surely related to Quillan? She didn't want this to be true and yet, she knew the Cutwrights. They were a very wealthy family, and had been around since before the Civil War. The Banners she was unfamiliar with, but when she read the additional notes it said they had moved to New Orleans only a couple of months before the adoption. Craig Banner could not have been the father of this child.

Estella stepped away from the computer, and walked to the window. On the streets below, tourists snapped pictures of the house, a phenomenon she was used to since childhood. Part of the life of a Garden District resident.

Her ears buzzed alongside a growing tightness in her chest. Estella was horrified at the idea of being related to the Sullivans. No, it was horror at *them* being related to *her*. Oh, how this Seamus had aimed high with Ophelia! What a presumption, to think he could have her, and then go behind her back and steal the child, raising it as his own. And what did this say about the man's wife, to go along with it? Estella had no respect for a woman who let her man run around and do whatever he pleased. She would never allow such a disgusting betrayal from her own husband. She'd inherited that from Blanche.

Her first instinct was to keep this revelation from Quillan. She couldn't bear to see the satisfaction in his face at learning he didn't descend purely from heathens. But she knew he would have been looking at the files too, and surely he'd seen the Sullivans.

It seemed all too cozy to be coincidence.

Of all the things that could come out of this! It would be too much to hope for that Quillan had planted the information as a joke. This didn't strike her as the type of thing he could come up with on his own. Besides, these files bore the markings of a formal stenographer, likely whomever Quillan had tasked with doing the research.

Well, she would find out when he arrived, whether he was willing to tell her or not.

LATER THAT EVENING, WHEN QUILLAN ARRIVED TO THE HOUSE, HE looked as if he might burst out his skin, on the verge of a breakdown. Was he waiting to hear if Estella had found the match? She wouldn't give him the satisfaction.

As hard as she tried to pry the thoughts from his mind, he had other things on the brain pressing him harder. The trouble with mind reading was you couldn't pick and choose what you gleaned. It was all a jumble, and often only the most clear and vivid thoughts would become apparent. Whatever he made of this family revelation, it wasn't as important to him as whatever had happened with Riley.

Estella strained to pick up a clear stream. She must have had a foolish look on her face because, at one point, Quillan asked if she was all right. She tried to be subtler from then on.

Quillan had upset Riley, and Riley being upset hurt Quillan. Quillan had tried to talk to Riley afterward but Riley was missing in action. Sounded like a pretty standard fight to Estella, except Quillan was in torment about it. He was so distracted she didn't pick up a single thought about *her*.

There was a momentary break in his thoughts of Riley for her to glean something more relevant to the day. *She thinks I made it up. She doesn't believe it. How am I going to prove this to her? God, she's pissed about this. What am I supposed to do? It's not my fault! Why are women always so damned moody?*

Estella had quite enough for one day. "Quillan, I need you to leave!" she exclaimed, startling him into dropping the letters.

"It's still early..."

"*Now*!"

He looked dumfounded for a moment, then decided she was serious. He lifted his jacket off the couch and headed for the door. "We didn't get a chance to talk about the records I sent over..." he said meekly.

"I know what you want to talk about! Well, *I* don't! Deschanel blood does not make you a Deschanel, and certainly you were not raised with the same decency—"

"If this is true, then I have as much Deschanel blood as you," he insisted, surprising her by standing up for himself.

She opened her mouth to yell at him but all that escaped was a frustrated gasp. She wagged her finger at the door. "I don't care what the records say. Get out!"

"Goddammit, Estella, what in the hell is *wron*g with you?" he cried as he rushed toward the foyer. She reached around him to open the door, pulling it right into his face. "Ouch!"

Rubbing his nose, he ventured, "When are we going to continue this then?"

"I don't know! Whenever I feel like it. Go! Go pander to Riley, or whatever her stupid name is!"

"Wait, *what*? How do you know about Riley?" he asked in a panic, but she had already slammed the door in his face.

26
NERYS

F*arjhem is being rebuilt. War is imminent.*

Nerys didn't question how Trygve found them on the road to Belfast. How, north of Dublin, outside the village of Balbriggan, he'd been waiting in the dusty parking lot of a lonely roadside pub, hands crossed over his torso, patience of the ancients plastered across his alabaster face.

"Eat," he commanded, "then we can discuss matters."

The travel-weary group accepted the order with gratitude, having been on the road nonstop since the incident in Galway. They watched Trygve in open curiosity through their small feast, as he perched upon one of the wooden stools like a giant, observing something uninteresting in the field outside while he waited.

Finn paid the bill in cash, making arrangements for the waitress to put the leftovers in a to-go container for Forbia. Trygve turned to Nerys. "Can we speak in private?"

"No. Sorry, no, you can't," Finn cut in. "Trygve, whatever you have to say, you can say to me as well."

Trygve blinked, nonplussed. Apparently sensing his

request could go either way, Finn quickly offered, "We can send the others away. But Nerys and I have a mutual understanding about keeping secrets."

"Very well," Trygve agreed, but shot Nerys a look bordering on annoyance.

Aleksei excused himself without complaint, taking Forbia's dinner to her. Jon followed, having fallen easily into the role of the boy's secondary caretaker, a position Nerys wondered if Finn was aware of yet.

Anne lingered behind, flashing Finn a look, but his focus fixed solely on Trygve. After a pause, she went off after the others.

"Farjhem is being rebuilt," Trygve had said, once they were alone in the small meadow behind the empty pub. "War is imminent."

Both Finn's eyebrows shot up. "Maybe you should start at the beginning," Nerys suggested.

"Are you certain you want the halfling draoi to hear this?"

"He's one of us now. His investment is as great as our own."

Trygve kept his own counsel regarding any residual feelings on the matter, his strong, ageless face betraying nothing further. "The emperor. Your brother. He's been afforded far too much power."

Nerys regarded him, without the expected questions. She needed to understand what Agripin had done to draw this ancient's ire, but she wouldn't inquire on it until after she understood the reason he'd tracked them down. "Any power given him can be as easily taken away. A gift of your Brotherhood."

"Our Brotherhood."

"Trygve, I have always maintained a position of neutrality. I assisted your cause when it seemed to be leading toward the potential for peace. I have never been a true drekar."

"That is not how the others see it. How I see it."

"I've given you no false ideations on this. Beyond that, if I were truly one of you, the communications would not have been terminated." Nerys stopped, remembering Finn's attentive presence.

Trygve's blue eyes flickered. "I closed mine to all when I left. As to the others... I cannot say."

"You left? When? Why?"

"Agripin," Finn decided, finding his first words. "He betrayed you, too?" Nerys sensed his painful struggle to resist asking about Ana until the right time presented itself.

"He cannot betray what he does not understand," Trygve replied. He turned to Nerys. "He is ruled by emotion. Day and night, he sits at the bedside of the Empress Anasofiya, posturing, rambling, evangelizing. He'll listen to no one if their words involve a reprisal for bringing her along."

"He should have left her there to die, then?" Finn retorted, biting back much more.

Trygve leveled his eyes on Finn. Watching him, in what would have been an awkward silence for anyone other than the ancient, who measured time on a different scale. "Your mate destroyed the Senetat. Farjhem. In vengeance for Aidrik. Most of us would have done the same. I'll not stand as judge for her actions. In fact, I may thank her for them one day. But the empress entered her cell in one condition. She left in entirely another."

"I don't know what that means," Finn countered. He shook his head, as if tossing away any words which might cause them further challenge on the journey to his wife. "She saw her evigbond murdered before her eyes. Yeah, she's changed. We're all changed. *I'm* changed, and I wasn't there."

Nerys alone understood where Trygve was going. The sinking feeling that began on their journey, growing to new heights in Galway, had never disappeared. It swelled now.

"The rumors were true, then? What Eldre Maxima conjectured about her? An etheric summoner?"

Finn opened his mouth to voice the obvious question. Closed it.

"Aye. She calls her familiar Wraith. For lack of a better understanding of its nature, perhaps. For creativity. Who knows? When it burst from her and brought forth the bedlam in Farsengel, she was not prepared. It left her... changed. A witch gone mad."

"A witch gone mad." Nerys tried the words out, rolled them around in her head. Her heart ached for Anasofiya, though she hardly knew her. Mostly, it burned at the realization Aleksei would never seek to fulfill destiny's kiss with his mother's fate so tenuous. Etheric summoners being scarce, who could she seek out to heal Ana's soul? Or, what was left of it.

"I still don't understand," Finn said. "And why shouldn't Agripin have rescued her? Doesn't she deserve your aid after all she's done for you?"

"We've given her our succor, as much as she will allow," Trygve assured him. "But we are not dealing with the empress. With your mate. She may yet be inside, but the creature bound in Agripin's chambers is a far more dangerous adversary than the Senetat ever envisioned. An organism of vengeance."

Finn didn't hesitate. "Then we have no time to waste."

"Finnegan, still your restless soul," Nerys said in as gentle tones as she could manage under the weight of such heavy and unexpected news. "She's safe with the Brotherhood." But Nerys was no longer so sure.

"Is she? Then why is this guy tracking us down to lodge a complaint about the leadership?"

"That is not why I sought you out," Trygve replied. "Farjhem is already rising from the ashes. Longtime rumors of a secondary Senetat, one waiting in the wings, have become more than whispers. War is coming. Whether it be a fortnight from now or twenty years, time is immaterial for us. A whisper. I believe it will come sooner than later, though."

"Agripin asked you to warn us," Nerys concluded.

"Your brother did no such thing. He does *nothing* unless it involves platitudes toward his changed empress. I am not the first to disappear under the cover of night, disenchanted."

"Thank you, then," Nerys said quietly. Processing. A dark and growing rift in the Brotherhood. The ancients, scattering to the winds once more.

"Where can I find her?" Finn pressed.

"She may not know you," Trygve warned. "Or her son. She has room in her heart for nothing but vengeance. She subsists from it. You may not know *her.*"

"It won't keep me from her, either. I made a promise to my son." *And to myself,* Nerys heard him add.

Trygve affected a shrug. He then gave the last known location of the Brotherhood conclave to Nerys, with the caveat he could not be certain they were still there.

"You could stay with us, Trygve," Nerys offered, immediately regretting her hopefulness. He would have better things to do, surely, than join them on what may be a futile rescue mission.

"Brynja and Einar will be expecting me," he rejoined. "And I will benefit greatly from their guidance in this dark hour."

"Will I hear from you again?"

"I'll know you in your hour of need."

. . .

After Trygve departed, Finn turned to her. His dazed expression struggled for clarity, then, seemingly deciding none would be found, shook his head to clear it. "We're going straight there. To the safe house."

"I'm not certain this is the best course."

Finn reached for her arm, no malice in the gesture. "You knew when you came with us, what our goal was. The *only* goal, Nerys. When we started out, we had nothing to go on, except that they'd fled. Now we know where they are. We *know* where they are! Why do you look so sour about it?"

"You heard what Trygve said."

"I heard him tell me where my wife was."

"You're a smart man, Finnegan. Don't be so thick."

Finn ignored the slight. "Determined. Where do you think Forbia gets her name? If Ana were in my shoes, she wouldn't hesitate."

Nerys sighed. "Let's finish the drive to Belfast and find an inn that takes currency. We all need rest."

27
LAUREN

Lauren was doing everything she could to calm Quillan's secretary, Carla, but the woman was consumed by hysterics. "I call him. I schedule everything! I reassure people when he misses appointments. But I am done, just done! This man yelled at me for over an hour, Lauren! For something I had bent over backwards to fix because Quillan is so irresponsible!"

"I know, you've done a great job," Lauren said, trying to placate her, but Carla wouldn't stop.

"I did this as a favor to Patrick, a favor! You know, I was perfectly happy working for Rory? I worked for him for ten years. Ten *years*, Lauren. He never missed an appointment, was never late, and he never had any mix-ups on my watch. Not one. And you know, when Patrick came to me, saying I was the best and that he needed the best to help his son, I thought maybe it was another chance to prove my loyalty to this company. But this... child... is unprofessional and going to get us both fired!"

Lauren held her tongue, letting Carla vent. Quillan had

gone too far this time, even for him. He'd not only blown off an earlier appointment with this client, but then also missed the reschedule.

Lauren didn't know how to help someone who didn't want to be helped.

"I'm going to Patrick." Carla sniffed, blotting her eyes with a tissue. "I'm going to tell him how I feel, and be honest with him, even though I know it will hurt him. I can't protect his son at the cost of my own job. I won't work under these conditions."

"No, don't do that," Lauren said, too quickly. Carla narrowed her eyes. "Let me talk to him. Let me be the bad guy. You don't want to be the one delivering this news."

Carla brightened at the suggestion and put her hand over the top of Lauren's. "You're one of the good ones, sweetie. I always said that."

Did you now? I could have sworn you were the one who started the rumor I was having an affair with Oz Sullivan before his wife died. "Thanks, Carla. I'll take care of this."

When Carla left her office, Lauren flopped into her high-backed leather chair. She wanted to sink down into it until she disappeared completely. Like Carla, she feared Patrick would want a scapegoat for his son's failures. It would be easier than admitting Quillan was a fuck-up. That Patrick might somehow share in that responsibility.

That ate at her the most. Patrick had enlisted the help of everyone else in the firm, except himself. He was keeping an arm's length distance between him and his son. People were whispering that he was doing so not to protect Quillan, but himself. The Sullivans liked to outwardly hold themselves to sky-high standards, but weren't above self-preservation.

Lauren suspected Quillan had never had a solid role model in his father. Patrick was a large, booming figure who loved to be the center of attention when it was for something good, but would throw anyone in his path when something went bad. His reputation at the firm was of a good lawyer, but he had the loyalty of a mother cat who abandoned their kittens at the first sign of illness. Had he inadvertently taught Quillan how to shirk responsibility? Lauren wondered what Quillan's mother was like.

She looked at her phone. It would have been too much to hope he would return any of her calls. She should have known winning a silly bet wouldn't change his behavior.

Lauren tried calling once more. This time, the phone went straight to voicemail. She tried again, with the same result. *That bastard turned his phone off.*

Picking up her desk phone, she began dialing Patrick's secretary, then paused. *If you do this, he's going to lose his job. Maybe he deserves it. Probably deserves it. But you're the only one who has sincerely tried to help him. If you want to help him, help.*

"He doesn't deserve my help," she muttered and cradled the phone. She was angry at herself for wanting to give up, but even angrier for realizing she was resigned to continue trying to help him. *He's going to drag you down with him. And what's worse, he won't feel the slightest bit of regret.*

She suspected that was true, but, unlike Patrick, Lauren Weatherly was more concerned with being able to look herself in the mirror and believe she'd done all she could.

She scrolled through her phone, and found Leander's number. He'd given it to her the other night, over the weirdest round of drinks she'd ever had.

Leander had spent the entire evening talking about Quillan. What a good guy Quillan was, how he was smarter than people thought, and such a nice guy at heart. She realized, about halfway through the evening, Leander was trying to do exactly what Quillan had been attempting: set up his friend.

"For two guys who live together, you sure don't talk much." She laughed and explained the situation. Leander was genuinely touched Quillan had thought of him.

"Isn't that what friends do?" she asked.

"That's not how it is with us," he had said, and left it at that.

This sort of awkward confusion was exactly why she didn't like the dating scene. Leander wasn't interested in her, she wasn't interested in Quillan, and the whole situation should never have come up.

Leander might know where Quillan was, and that was the more pressing issue than ridiculous adventures in dating.

"Yes," Leander answered on the second ring.

"Leander, hi. It's... Lauren." Pause. "From the other night."

"Yes," he said. "I know."

"Oh. I'm looking for Quillan. He's in some trouble."

Snicker. "When is he not?"

"I'm serious," she insisted. "His phone is off, and if I don't reach him soon and get things sorted out, he's probably going to lose his job. For real this time."

"Haven't seen him," Leander said, "but that's because he spends all his time with Estella."

Lauren was privy to many, many stories about Estella Broussard, and all of them pointed to her being a terrible influence on Quillan. Worse was what Leander had told her over drinks. *He's wanted my sister since they were kids. She's never wanted him back, but she doesn't let him move on, either.* It was no wonder Lauren couldn't get him to focus, with such a temptation dangling in front of him.

"Do you have her number?" Lauren asked.

He laughed. "If she has a number, I don't care to have it." There was silence on the other end for a moment before he added, "She's working today, at The Soothsayer's Coffer. You might stop by there. At your own risk."

Lauren didn't wish to deal with Estella face-to-face, but if it was the only way to find Quillan, she saw no other choice.

She said her goodbye to Leander and drove to the store. She'd never been there before, but the establishment wasn't difficult to spot. It was something of an eyesore, obnoxious even by Quarter standards.

The exterior of The Soothsayer's Coffer was lined in bright green and purple stripes, and a large, badly crafted statue of Marie Laveau stood guard outside the door. The effigy was so obstructive, people walking by had to slip into the street to go around.

Several neon signs in the window advertised their services: palm reading, fortune telling, spell casting, and remedies. Most of their business came from tourists, but Lauren knew there were plenty of locals who ate into the stuff as well.

Lauren parked down the block and jogged toward the store, spotting Quillan's car parked across the street. The knot in her belly started to dissolve. He was here. There was hope.

She shoved the door open, and several large, loud bells of different sounds and volume rang all around her. "Come in!" a deep, Caribbean-accented voice boomed over the loudspeaker.

Lauren pushed her way toward the counter, dodging haphazard shelving, plaster statues, and various objects hanging from the ceiling. Estella sulked behind the counter, flashing her a look so unpleasant it made her skin crawl.

"I think you may have come to the wrong place," Estella said, the iciness in her words chilling the air between them.

Lauren straightened herself. She wasn't going to let this girl ruffle her. "I'm looking for Quillan. I know he's here."

Estella twisted her lips around, laughing under her breath. The petite girl was sizing her up; Lauren felt naked and self-conscious. Her tiny wrists flicked to the right and left. "Do you see him?"

"His car is across the street."

"There are many piece-of-shit cars in New Orleans. Quillan's is hardly unique." Estella chuckled coldly.

"I work with Quillan," Lauren said. The urge to slap the smirk off Estella's face was strong. "I need to talk to him about a client and his phone is off."

"Oh, I *know* who you *are,* Riley." Estella enunciated every word as if Lauren could not understand her otherwise.

"Riley?" Lauren made a face. "Who is Riley?"

"Right. Well, Riley, if Quillan wanted to talk to you then I'd guess he wouldn't have turned his phone off."

"I don't know who this Riley is, or what you're talking about, but I need to speak with Quillan urgently. His job depends on it."

Estella's look suggested she wasn't the least bit concerned about Quillan's peril at work. She appeared to be mulling something over.

"What *is* your name?" she demanded.

Lauren gritted her teeth, sorely tempted to give Estella the answer she deserved. But time was running out. "Lauren. Lauren Weatherly. I'm a lawyer at Sullivan and Associates."

For a moment, Estella's cool demeanor seemed to crack, replaced by ruffled confusion. She quickly righted herself. "Quillan!" she snapped, without looking back to where she called. "Get out here!"

She studied Lauren with a cold smile on her face while they waited for Quillan, who took forever. He emerged, smiling, but his smile faded when he saw Lauren.

"What are you doing here?"

"Can we talk privately?"

He looked to Estella for permission. *Are you kidding me?* She nodded at him and he gestured toward the back.

Lauren followed him through the back office and out the back door, into a gravelly lot. No sooner had she emerged through the door, when he spun on her and snapped, "I turned off my phone for a reason."

"We have a problem or I wouldn't be here."

"Did you ever stop to think that maybe I don't care, Lauren?" He was looking at her with a gaze she hadn't seen before. He sized her up and down with a disgust that made her feel dirty.

She righted herself. "Yes, Quillan, that's crossed my mind quite a few times. But then, I thought, maybe you do care. Maybe you need someone to believe in you, someone who doesn't just, I don't know, pass you off on someone else."

His eyes narrowed. "Is that a dig at my father? The same man who hired you, and gave you a chance, even though you had no experience? Oh, that's right, your sister is married to a Sullivan so I guess I'm not the only one who got a charity job."

She'd struck below the belt and so he'd returned it. She would always be sensitive about being hired right out of law school, the odd man out compared to the other non-Sullivans, who were recruited from top firms and the DA's office. "Thanks, Quillan, for reminding me what a selfish jerk you actually are."

He rolled his arms in front of him, falling into an exaggerated bow. "At your service, Miss Weatherly. I aim to please."

"Then you aim too high. You might want to lower the bar," she snapped back.

"Maybe you could teach me a thing or two about securing success I don't deserve and didn't work for," he seethed, kicking up gravel. A man nearby stopped to watch.

"Such an astute observation from someone who is about to

get kicked out of his birthright! I mean, how fucking bad do you have to be to get fired from a job that was a sure thing?" She laughed, throwing her hands up. "God, what was I thinking trying to help you? Why did I agree to this?"

"You're only *just now* asking yourself that question? Wow."

"And you really are the most selfish, stupid person I have ever met, Quillan. You have everything you could ever want or need handed to you, and you'd rather sit here trying to bang a chick who'd rather screw the dust under her feet than give you even a moment of the attention you've earned!"

"I have had enough with people and their bullshit about Estella! She has done nothing to you, nothing to Riley, nothing to Leander, so all I can figure is that you're all jealous of her!"

Riley. There was that name again. She didn't care at the moment. "Jealous? If by jealous you mean that I feel pity for her? And you. You're both assholes, and you deserve each other." The tears stung her eyes as they pooled under her lids. She wouldn't let him see them.

She turned to leave and he called out, "Hey Lauren?"

She bit her lip and turned. For a heartbeat, she thought he was going to apologize.

"Go fuck yourself."

28
KATJA

Katja regretted her sojourn into the kitchen.

For one, the trek felt like agony on her arms. Greg had built a ramp from the basement, including a crude pulley system, when she outright refused to live upstairs with the rest of the household; with the mutants. She knew she should be practicing getting around in her wheelchair more, but she didn't have the desire or temperament to deal with the task. It wasn't lost on her that a visit from any one of the family healers could make it all go away. Even had she wanted to forget such potential, Olivia made mention of it at least once a week.

But worst of all was that she had underestimated her cousin. She should have known Olivia would find a way to take advantage of Katja's rare presence on the main floor.

"Stella has grown so big! She has your enormous blue eyes, and Sebastian—he has Alain's mouth..."

"Yes, babies grow. Yes, they look like their parents. Are we done?" She eyed the hallway for a chance at a clean break. Greg hovered in the doorway. *Ass.*

"I can hardly believe how fast they're growing. Come, let's go see them."

"I already told you, I don't want to see them."

"I don't understand you, Katja," Olivia said sadly.

Oh, here we go. She's going to harp about how I was raised better than this.

"I may not understand your mother's ideas about childrearing, especially as it relates to the curse, but I trust she couldn't have ever encouraged you to abandon your children?"

"That would be an excellent question to ask someone if our *family was normal.* You can sit there and judge me all you want, but we both know I would never have *abandoned* my children under normal circumstances."

"So, they were born under a less than desirable set of variables," Greg chimed in from where he stood sentry in the hallway, evidently deciding throwing out a few scientific terms might appeal to her. "That does not make them less yours."

Katja laughed, smirking. *Oh, the things I could tell you. How I could dance circles around your simple minds.* "I don't expect you to understand."

"There are plenty of parents in wheelchairs," her cousin asserted.

"Right, *that's* the problem," Katja cackled, her voice dripping with only half the sarcasm she felt. "I'd rather have a pity party than be a mother. Don't want to put in the extra effort. Hell, maybe I don't think I'm good enough. Yes, perhaps that's the problem."

Katja spun her chair around and wheeled toward the hallway. She was going back to her room, and Greg could either move or be plowed over.

"Katja," Olivia's calm, but sad, voice called from behind her. "What happened to Alain and Nora was not your fault."

Katja froze. There was an unspoken agreement in the house

that Alain and Nora would never be talked about. She had overlooked the earlier mention of Sebastian resembling his father, but she would not ignore something so glaring, and so obviously meant to garner a reaction.

"You're right, Liv," Katja responded, speaking slowly, letting her words burn. "It's *your* fault. You... Aunt Maureen... Aunt Colleen. All of you selfish cows who insisted on bringing children into this world without a solution. Without a cure. Thanks for leaving the burden of solving this problem on the rest of our shoulders."

Greg moved swiftly aside as Katja wheeled her chair past him and back to her basement bedroom.

Dear Alain, Katja began, writing in the leather-bound journal that had been a gift from him before he died. Katja found it ironic the gift had been intended as a way for her to express some of her fears and concerns, when Alain's bottling of his had been what killed him.

I am supremely glad you are dead.

If I had known what I know now, I would obviously not have sought you out. But if I had known you were a giant, weak-minded pussy, I would have ignored you altogether.

Your children are, apparently, growing well. The two that lived anyway. The third—you know, the one you killed?—is not so good, although it could be argued she's better off. We both know giving them to Olivia was like handing her a ticking time bomb. The only question that remains is what will happen when the bomb goes off? Not that you need concern yourself. You took the easy way out. The shitty way out.

The coward's way.

My research is getting me closer to answers. I would say that you wouldn't be happy with some of my early hypotheses, since they involve less-than-positive thoughts about our offspring, but clearly your fears about them were already moving in that direction since you tried to kill all four of us. So, as much as I loathe you, you're also the only person I can share these revelations with because you're the only one who is going to understand when I say, I think our children are evil. And I think they need to die.

Katja closed the notebook, and slipped it into the top drawer of her wooden desk. She then locked it, and slipped the strap holding the key back over her neck. She couldn't risk Olivia or Greg reading any of her letters and thoughts. They weren't ready to understand. Well, they might never be ready, actually. She was in this alone.

Katja could admit now, for the first time since she dove into this research, she'd limited herself. She had seen, and latched on to, the obvious pattern of incest. There were numerous families across Europe with powers, many of whom practiced inbreeding to preserve those abilities. Genetically, that made sense. And as Brigitte was known to be a powerful witch, her ability to curse her descendants also made sense. The two things were logical, if anything about the supernatural world of Deschanels could be considered logical.

But, there was more to the story. Had she not been so excited about her discovery...had she not been ecstatic to be the Deschanel who *finally* figured it out, who saved the family, then she might have seen the other pattern. Alain would be alive. And perhaps she could have discovered the real way to end the madness, finally.

Well, her eyes were open now. She decided that, rather than the twins being a simple miscalculation, they might, in fact, be tied to the real answer. Katja suspected they were a critical component.

Her recent research veered more into the nature of various abilities. Back before the Curse began, it was not uncommon for Deschanels to be incredibly powerful, with abilities measuring at the highest levels. Now, with the blood more diluted, the abilities had followed suit. Elementals and astral projectors used to be a dime a dozen, but now, less than a handful.

As she pushed further into the world of the paranormal in the eighteenth and nineteenth centuries, she noted there were several abilities revered far above others. These were the gifts families tried to reproduce, or mimic, through their breeding. The ones they most wanted to preserve:

Etheric Summoners: *Individuals who could conjure a familiar, spawned from their own spirit and magic. The combined force of the witch and her familiar was near limitless.*

Resurrection Shamans: *A subset of shamans able to bring a corpse back to life within a limited period of time.*

Necromancers: *Individuals capable of communicating with the dead to varying degrees. Some could accommodate a possession for temporary periods. Stronger necromancers maintain longer possessions.* ***The ultimate necromancer, called a starlight awakene****r, was said to be capable of sustaining a permanent possession, and said possession also resulted in immortality.*

As far as Katja could find, there were no Deschanels with any of these abilities currently in existence. Her cousin Anasofiya was reportedly a resurrection shaman, but by all accounts, Ana was more Empyrean than human at this juncture, so she hardly counted.

Katja decided the absence of these abilities in current generations was as telling as the presence of them in generations past.

She pulled the notebook back out of the drawer, and continued writing. Perhaps she wasn't so tired, after all.

Logically, then, we can assume the lack of inbreeding allowed those powerful abilities to slowly weaken or die out. If we know they were desirable, we can logically then also deduce these were the abilities they sought to sustain via incest. But other than the fact they're ridiculously awesome, why else would these abilities be important?

She paused when she heard noises outside the basement door. Her cousins had finally given up and gone to bed. Katja continued.

Resurrection shamans seem obvious. Bringing people back to life could be useful in a number of situations. Problem is, the ability only works for a limited time. Once the body starts to decompose, it's already game over. The shaman can only bring the individual back to the state they are in, so unless they want to create a zombie, they have limited time to perform the ritual.

Etheric summoners... now, this, Alain, I could get behind. To have your own familiar? Can you imagine? But, unless I'm missing something critical, this feels like an amplified version of other powerful abilities.

Necromancers seem equally cool, but without any real, practical use. Communicating with the dead might be fun if you missed your mom, or to scare some folks, but what, really, is it needed for? Katja paused again, thinking.

Of course, the starlight awakener could be an interesting development, but there's no proof they ever existed. What would it mean if a starlight awakener were to be made immortal? Would they gain additional powers? Would they be functionally immortal, never aging, or would they also be immune to mortal injury? More and more this seems to be an important ability, but in the absence of any useful information, or examples, it's impossible to know.

What did any of this have to do with the curse Brigitte

placed on their family? And what did it have to do with the twins?

I don't know, she concluded. *I really don't know, but I understand, in the same way others in my family inherently understands things, this is relevant. One of these abilities is key to understanding how all of these circumstances came to be. Why we are here. Why simply attempting to "fix" the issue did nothing but make it worse.*

Most of all, it has to do with the twins. It must.

29
ESTELLA

Estella's telepathy was not as acute as she would have liked. She'd heard of Deschanels who could hear thoughts from several buildings over, and one who was able to read the thoughts of someone in the next town. Even with practice, the furthest she could reach was across the room. On a good day, through one wall.

Estella had to employ more than mind reading, then, to listen to the heated exchange going on between Quillan and Lauren. She slipped into the back room and put her ear to the door, then opened her mind to both of them.

I just want to help him, why won't he let me help him? Oh my God, he is so stubborn. How can he not see he's throwing his future away with this undeserving wench? Estella tensed up at this. *What am I going to do if he doesn't follow me? Why, why, is it my fault? If he would only listen to me, I could help him.*

Who was this desperate bitch?

Quillan's thoughts amused her further.

Why won't she go away? Go away, Lauren, just go away, I'm right where I want to be. I don't need you. Why are you so damn stubborn? Is this why my father chose you? Fuck off, fuck off, fuck off, leave me alone. I can't do this job, I can't do this life. Let me be.

Both continued in this same spirit as they hurled insults back and forth. Estella knew now that this girl was not Riley, but this only confused her. If *she* was not Riley... who was?

The fight ended. Quillan told her to fuck off and his feet crunched hard in the gravel as he headed back in. Estella sprinted toward the front of the store and pretended she hadn't moved.

"What was that all about?" she asked, affecting bland disinterest.

"Nothing," he replied, but she observed his shaking hands and rapid breathing. "I'm going to step in back and make a quick phone call," he added, and disappeared.

She couldn't follow him this time, it would be too obvious. But only one room away, she could hear everything he said.

"Riley, for the last time, stop leaving the house!" Estella couldn't hear Riley's response.

"You can't change my mind on this. Not you, not Lauren, not Lee. I'm done talking."

Silence.

"Go away, Riley. Go home."

The conversation continued, with Quillan insisting Riley stop, go home, leave him be. Estella grew bored, then she spotted Quillan's cell phone sitting on the counter.

Her eyes widened. If his phone was there, who was he talking to?

Estella slipped her shoes off and tiptoed around the corner, holding her breath. Quillan faced the wall, talking to...

No one. He was alone.

"Riley, you think I don't understand? I would do anything to bring you back so we could hang out and do stuff together, but I can't. I can't change what happened to you."

Estella was dumbfounded. Quillan was clearly insane, and Riley his imaginary friend.

"You can't save me, Riley, just as I couldn't save you."

She started to slip back to the front of the store when a thought popped into her head. *I have as much Deschanel blood as you do.*

Estella froze. She remembered something else now, something awful her parents had told her. *Leander made a new friend, and he's going to come over. Please be nice to him, Estella. Something very bad happened to him recently. His little brother is in heaven with the angels, and he's still hurting very much.*

Riley.

And now she remembered where she'd heard that name before. Quillan's twin, who'd died of some bizarre and unexplainable problem. Quillan was talking to Riley... Quillan was a Deschanel...

Quillan wasn't insane.

Quillan was a necromancer.

ESTELLA COULDN'T MUSTER FOCUS THE REMAINDER OF THE EVENING. Her thoughts were all over the place. Quillan was, for once, quiet and wrapped up in his research. It was all she could do not to scream, *WHY DIDN'T YOU TELL ME!*

Digging in his mind became more focused with this new information, and she listened for things she hadn't considered before. Knowing Riley was his dead brother changed how she perceived his thoughts about him, and they made more sense. The more she listened, realization dawned: Quillan wasn't keeping anything from her. The idiot genuinely didn't know.

He seemed to think talking to Riley was a fluke. He didn't realize he could, if he wanted, make contact with others like

Riley. That he'd inherited this from his Deschanel ancestors, just as she'd inherited her telepathy.

How would he have known? Until a couple of days ago, Quillan had no idea he was related to the Deschanels.

Oh, the power he unknowingly wielded! All this time, the answer had been sitting right in front of her, staring her in the face, annoying her to no end. Quillan, a necromancer. To think of it!

A more delicious present could not have been dropped into Estella's lap. Here was a Deschanel, a necromancer, and in the body of the one person in the world who would do absolutely anything she asked, without question.

The situation was almost enough to make her reconsider her staunch atheism.

Estella could hardly sit upright in her chair, she was so giddy. It was going to happen, finally! She would have her opportunity to talk to Blanche once again, ask her all the questions she'd amassed over the years alone, without guidance. And they could solve the mystery of the letters... the mysterious warnings... all of it. Within her grasp, finally.

Remember what happened to Charlie. To Alice. They'd been necromancers too.

Yes, but they were not Deschanels. And for all she knew, they hadn't even been *real* necromancers. They'd been all too eager to try, and she hadn't questioned them properly. No, she was certain of Quillan's abilities.

Tapping his abilities was a risk she was willing to take, in order to finally achieve this goal. If it worked, she would have a lifetime of access to Blanche, and Ophelia, and anyone else who struck her fancy. And if it didn't... well, Quillan was throwing his future away anyway, was he not? He didn't seem to care about anything except her. To die doing something meaningful...

Oh, stop waxing poetic. The truth is, you don't care if he dies or not.

No, and had Leander been the necromancer in this generation, she'd have used him. Or Harriett. Or anyone. There was not a single person she cared about more than her single-minded pursuit of her great-grandmother's companionship. No one she would not sacrifice.

The only question now was *how* to approach him.

Estella couldn't blurt the question out, much as it burned in her chest. The news needed to be fed to Quillan slowly, in a way he could digest and process. He would need to be in a state of complete acceptance before attempting any contact. Not for his own sake, but for the success of the encounter. She wouldn't risk ruining his mind, when it was so valuable to her.

She didn't know for sure, but guessed Riley had first sought out Quillan, not the other way around. Neither Blanche nor Ophelia would be looking for Quillan, and so he'd require a bit of training.

What if he says no? Maybe he'll be afraid, or won't believe you.

True, those were both reasonable outcomes. His fear she didn't worry about. He'd do anything to appear brave to Estella. His disbelief she would counter by demonstrating her own powers. If he saw he was not alone, he might warm to the idea quicker.

Still, even if he believed her, she was asking a lot. Estella, even in her most selfish moments, could understand that. He would want something in return... something more than her sniping at him every five minutes for being inadequate.

Estella glanced over at Quillan. *I didn't realize he had green eyes. His black hair is soft, clean.* If one could get past the personality defects, he was not hard on the eyes.

You know what will work for certain. But if you go there, you can't undo it. He will never leave you alone after, and you'll never be rid of him. This is not a decision to be made in haste.

No, it wasn't. But it was also not a decision for which Estella saw any other option. She wanted to talk to her great-grandmother. She needed to. There was so much to ask her, now that she was older and understood more.

30
JONATHAN

Jon's brother had changed.

He'd had plenty of time, whether it be in cars, trains, or ships, to ruminate over the differences. A year since he'd seen him, give or take, but the young idealistic man who'd fled Maine in pursuit of his heart had evolved into something with harder edges and even deeper passions.

This was not to say the changes Jon observed in Finn were bad. He'd feared for Finn when he fell in love so easily, half-believing it was another one of his little brother's whims. Like college. Like every other woman he'd dated.

The Finn leading the mission to rescue his wife left little doubt as to where his mind and heart lay. The intentions of both were equally determined toward their goal. The Finn who'd left his home and his past a year ago might not have been capable of the trial ahead. This one would find Ana or die trying.

Jon's disbelief on the matter of Aleksei also waned. The boy's laugh, his subtle but borderline rough sense of humor. His tendency toward introspection, and internalization.

That Aleksei looked like Finn, and Ana, was unmistakable. Had he only resembled Ana, Jon might have been able to dismiss him as a Deschanel cousin, posing for reasons Jon couldn't begin to comprehend. But when he looked into the ocean of Aleksei's eyes, he saw Finn gazing back.

Jon was a man of medicine. Of science. The mystery of Aleksei's parentage couldn't be solved with anything he'd learned, and yet he could see no reason why it would be untrue. A conundrum his brain, and his deeper emotions, could not now, and might never, resolve.

Perhaps, by and through his bond with Aleksandr, Jon might also find his way back to Finn.

THE INN OUTSIDE BELFAST WAS SMALL, AND ISOLATED. THE LOCATION wasn't amenable to travelers, and it was a wonder they kept the lights on. This, of course, was exactly why they'd chosen it.

The suite consisted of two bedrooms linked by a small hall, and a shared bathroom. Aleksei and Finn claimed a bed, and the two women—was Nerys a woman, exactly? Yet another mystery that would remain unsolved—claimed the other, leaving Jon to pull out the trundle. He lamented the short length, picturing his long legs dangling over the time-shorn rug as he tossed and turned. The cantankerous innkeeper refused to allow Forbia inside, but the young wolf had proven she could fend for herself well enough.

Dinnertime arrived, but no one felt like venturing out to eat. Finn remarked they had several days before their next ship, and may as well pick up some groceries, so he left with the rental and took Aleksei with him.

Nerys wandered off shortly after, with Forbia for company, claiming to need time alone with her thoughts. Jon understood. He had trouble thinking in the presence of others. With these cramped quarters, he supposed he might follow her lead, sooner or later.

No one told him anything. If they had a plan—and Jon wasn't clear if they did, or if they were simply moving forward with hope and prayer—they hadn't bothered to share it with him. This, more than being left out of casual conversation, and more than the hard looks from Finn, made him feel ever the interloper.

Not enough to deter him, though.

Jon wandered down the hall and into the second bedroom, where Anne and Nerys settled, in search of blankets for his trundle. He stopped in the doorway. Anne knelt by the bed in the traditional posture of prayer, whispering north.

Sensing him, she stopped, turning slowly. "Did you need something?"

"Blankets, but I can come back."

"No need. Get your blankets. I'm done."

Jon stayed put. "Do you really believe someone is listening when you pray?"

Anne blinked. "Someone? I believe *God* is listening."

"Does he answer your prayers?"

Her face scrunched, then went blank. "I take it you don't accept God in your own life?" she replied, without answering his question.

"I was raised to believe in God," Jon answered, acutely aware that she hadn't yet risen from her knees. In some strange way, though she was beneath him, the power dynamic had shifted in her favor. "Never taught to understand Him, though."

"Maybe you aren't meant to."

"Faith without understanding isn't in the cards for me. No one I knew could meet any of my questions with an answer more precise than 'because God wills it,' and so I never learned anything stronger than begrudging acceptance. I need my world to make sense. So I turned to science." As the words left him, Jon wondered where they'd come from. How long they'd been true.

Anne looked ready to tear his heathen face to shreds, but she surprised him when her face crumbled into something resembling sympathy. "A shame your parents never took the time to answer your questions properly. I guess it's no wonder you turned away and found something that made sense."

"Finn had God once," Jon mused. "I don't think he believes anymore. Or maybe he does. He doesn't confide in me anymore."

"You've helped him a lot with Aleksei," Anne offered graciously. An improvement.

Jon had a response loaded, about how his affection toward his nephew didn't erase the crime against his brother, but that wasn't a conversation which would ever come naturally or easily. "Your prayers sound dutiful. What do you expect to gain from them?"

Anne's face turned to fire, and Jon immediately realized his words had, like so many other times in his life, been taken wrong. "Gain? What do you, an atheist veterinarian, know about a relationship with a higher power?"

"I'm sorry. That isn't—"

Anne rose, one foot at a time. "If you truly felt remorse for what you did to Finn, you'd be on your knees every moment of every day begging God for absolution! You wouldn't simply hope the crime washed away with time and good deeds. You wouldn't just *hope* you could somehow be forgiven for never learning to tame the power that spiraled out of control and killed your own mother because you couldn't stop yourself!"

"Huh?" She wasn't talking about Jon, not anymore.

Tears coursed down her splotchy cheeks. The bushes

outside heaved against the dingy panes of glass. "Stop it right now!" she screamed. "Just stop it!"

Anne's body rippled with sighs and deep-formed sobs. He feared she might explode with the grief living within her, erupting into a geyser of destruction.

Outside, the flora rustled, whistling a low song Jon understood was for Anne, and Anne alone. Taunting her, inviting further ruin, or simply offering consolation, he did not know.

Before Jon could find a single thing to say, Anne fled, her tiny feet tapping down the hall. He heard her pause and then a door slam.

Jon sunk down on to the hard bed, in a daze with this knowledge. *We've both done terrible things. Anne understands what it is to betray the person you love most in the world. She comprehends the guilt. Lives with it. Festers in it, like darkness, waiting for it to take her away from the pain forever, even if it means her own demise.*

Perhaps... perhaps, Jon thought, they might learn something from each other about the nature of atonement.

31
QUILLAN

Quillan jumped off the streetcar at Canal Street, and made a slow approach toward the offices of Sullivan and Associates. He expected to be fired and so his very next visit would be Bourbon Street, where he'd drink until he passed out in a corner somewhere. Maybe a cab ride home if he was coherent enough to give someone his address.

He'd fucked up. Badly. Nearly the moment Lauren left the Coffer, remorse had taken root. He'd sat in the shop and read the same sentence over and over again for hours, getting nowhere in the letters, the lump in his stomach growing larger every second that passed. Finally, he left without saying goodbye to Estella. He doubted she noticed.

Quillan experienced a rare moment of clarity where he could see his entire life for what it was: a giant ball of failure. From his career, to his relentless pursuit of a girl who had never wanted him and never would, all the way to his treatment of the myriad of people who'd tried to help him. His father, Leander, Lauren, many others. And why? Because they loved him? Why did they, when he'd given them nothing in return, and no reason to care?

Yet this wave of rare self-awareness would accomplish nothing for Quillan. He wouldn't call Lauren and apologize, and wouldn't admit to Leander he'd been right, nor would he open up to his father and thank him for all the opportunities given him. He wouldn't do these things even if they saved his job and friendships. Quillan's cowardice kept his mouth sealed. And so, head hung in shame, he approached the office doors and prepared for the worst.

The boom of his father's voice carried all the way into the corridor. Quillan took a deep breath as he swung the door open and walked into the office.

He expected his father to turn his thundering words on him, but it was a group of secretaries he yelled at. "I don't care how you do it. Be creative. Find it!"

They scattered, frazzled. Patrick's eyes locked on Quillan's and the younger man's stomach turned into knots. "Son!" he said jovially and strode in Quillan's direction. *He's... smiling.*

"Hi," he said cautiously. "What's going on?"

Patrick's thick neck strained with frustration. "One of those nitwits lost a box that came from the Deschanel estate. I swear, I could wring their necks."

Quillan found yet another reason to feel bad. "I'm sure it will turn up."

"They better hope so." Patrick laughed and spittle flew from his lips. "Lauren's in her office if you want to go celebrate with her," he added and clapped his son on the back, then walked away, leaving behind a very confused Quillan.

Celebrate? Was this some sort of joke? Were they going to make him the butt of a prank for all he'd done? Quillan glanced in the direction of Lauren's office. Her door was closed, and blinds drawn.

He swung his gaze around the office, but everyone was wrapped up in their own work.

Might as well get it over with. Quillan maneuvered through the admin desks and approached her door. He heard the rapid ticks of typing, and knocked.

"Come in," she said. As he entered, she continued at her laptop without looking up. He hovered awkwardly and waited for her to address him.

"Close the door," she said coolly, and gestured for him to have a seat across from her. She seemed like an entirely different person from the angry, frazzled girl who'd stood fighting with him in the alley yesterday. Composed. *Probably ecstatic about what comes next, after how I treated her.*

"So he's letting you fire me, huh?"

Lauren blinked a few times, leaving him to sit and further stew in his thoughts. "No, you're the new office hero," she said evenly. Her face betrayed nothing more than her vague words.

Quillan laughed, choking on his spit. "Hero? Look, let's make this easier. Why don't I quit and save everyone the trouble of whatever you assholes have planned."

She watched him. Quillan grew further agitated when she didn't react to any of his words.

"Quillan, no one wants to fire you. You did, after all, bring in the largest account that the firm has seen in... well, since they signed the Deschanels."

This joke was going way over his head. His mind spun in various directions, searching, but he wasn't finding the punch line. "Stop toying with me, Lauren, and say whatever it is you want to say."

Lauren stood up and walked around her desk. She towered over him in her heels. "You lost the account you messed up. I couldn't save it for you, because the damage was already done and you refused to save it yourself. But I'd been working on something else, secretly, that I hoped to present to Colin and show him." She paused and looked out the door's window with a whimsical expression. "I was hoping to prove I had earned my spot in the firm."

"I didn't mean what I said yesterday," Quillan amended quickly. "I know you didn't get this job on charity."

She laughed. "I know I'm worthy of it, and I wanted to show others that, too. So I'd been working on the O'Keefes for a while. John O'Keefe is a friend of my dad's, and I knew he was unhappy with his current business arrangements."

"John O'Keefe of O'Keefe Oil and Gas? You mean the dude who owns half the state of Louisiana?" Quillan asked.

"And part of Florida," she said. "He'd been using a firm in New York. One of those fancy outfits that fly you up on a private plane for all your meetings. But John didn't want that. He's a local boy, from Lafayette, born and raised. Wanted to be treated like a Southerner. So I took a chance."

"Wait... you signed John O'Keefe? Lauren, are you serious right now?"

She nodded, but there was no excitement in her face. In fact, the color had drained away and she looked ill.

"Actually, Quillan, you did."

The realization of what had occurred slowly came over him. Lauren had saved his job by giving him credit for her work. And not just any work, but the absolute biggest thing to happen to the firm in over a hundred years.

"No," he said, standing up. "Lauren, this is not... I appreciate what you've done, but no, not like this. This is your baby, you earned this!"

Lauren's face pointed at her feet, nodding slowly. "Life isn't about doing what's fair, Quillan, it's about doing what you must. Losing your client was more than lost revenue, it's negative publicity for us. Worse that, it was the son of a senior partner responsible. The only thing that would remedy the situation is to counter with news so amazing the loss would be forgotten. To do that, I had to save your reputation."

Quillan was overwhelmed with the enormity of her sacrifice. "I don't understand why you keep helping me."

When she looked up, her eyes were glassy. It was the first moment of weakness he'd witnessed in Lauren Weatherly, and the sight of it dropped his heart. "Because it was the right thing to do."

He took one of her hands in his. "Lauren—"

She pulled away. "Quillan, don't. Your pity will only make me feel worse."

"I need to make this up to you."

"Need? No, you don't need to do anything. This was my decision."

"I *want* to make it up to you." He saw a goodness in her he'd never seen in himself. As the silent tears rolled down her pale cheeks, he wished more than anything he could find it in himself to love someone like Lauren. Someone who was warm and caring, thoughtful, and held themselves to a higher calling. He wished he wasn't drawn to women like Estella, who would step over him as many times as she needed if it gave her even the slightest reward.

Most of all, Quillan wished knowing this had the power to change his feelings.

"Stop fucking up, then," Lauren said in a teary voice. "Make an effort. Don't make this," she gestured toward the door, and the rest of the office, "for nothing."

"Let me take you to dinner," he said. "Anywhere you want."

At first it appeared she would refuse, but then she said, "Arnaud's."

"You would pick the most expensive restaurant in town!"

"You would complain about money when I just landed you the best deal of your career."

He narrowed his eyes teasingly and smiled. "Fine. But wear something pretty. You scare me in a business suit."

"Don't worry, Quillan," she said, as a slow grin spread across her tear-stained face. "I clean up real nicely."

32
OLIVIA

Olivia inhaled the soft, delicate scent of the white roses as she closed the cooler. Over twelve dozen she'd prepared today, and they were exquisite. Perhaps her loveliest arrangement yet, a rewarding result, because she also intended it to be her last. She couldn't run a flower boutique *and* deal with the cascading events at home.

That morning, Greg had woken her to calmly let her know the twins had grown another few inches. She brought the twins in to see Colleen, who took the official measurements and made her pronouncement.

"Well then," Colleen said, slowly, "I'd say they are measuring in at about eighteen months, give or take."

"Hell's bells!" They were past the point of pretend. "They're going to be bigger than Rory by breakfast tomorrow."

Her aunt nodded, as if the subject at hand was rising gas prices. "It seems our theory is correct," she said.

"Will they stop growing at some point?" Olivia wrung her hands.

"From what I've heard, they will slow down around sexual maturity and begin to age at a normal rate."

"So, what you're saying is, in a few weeks I'm going to have teenagers on my hands?"

"It's entirely possible."

Tears burned the back of her eyes, but Olivia Claiborne would not show weakness in front of a relative she'd considered a nemesis not so very long ago. "This should be interesting."

After Olivia finished the last of the rose arrangement, she had locked the door, drawing the blinds. She would have to go home soon, but needed a few moments to herself.

When their growth started to become obvious—*Was that really only a few days ago?*—Olivia had politely dismissed the nanny. She'd been with them since Rory was several months old, but they couldn't afford inevitable questions lacking reasonable answers. Greg had taken a week off from work until they could sort things out.

Well. I'd say things are officially sorted.

On a whim, Olivia reached for the phone. She dialed her Aunt Evangeline in DC.

"Ahh, Liv!" A deep, welcoming voice boomed from the other end, after only one ring. "We got your pictures. I cannot believe how the children have grown! They are so lovely."

Olivia smiled. *They really are lovely babies, all other concerns aside.* "That's the thing..." She stopped. "Are you alone? Do you have a moment?"

She heard her aunt shuffling in the background, and a door close. "I am now. What's going on, dear?"

There was neither the need, nor the time, to skate around the point. "The pictures I sent aren't recent. The children are growing at an exceptionally fast rate. Too fast to overlook. I think it's going to continue."

Evangeline paused only for the briefest moment. "What does Colleen say?" she inquired. It chaffed Olivia that she'd had to seek her aunt's counsel, but there were bigger problems than her bruised pride.

"She's got it in her head they've inherited some rare Deschanel trait where they will keep growing like weeds until they hit sexual maturity. Which should be, oh, in a few months."

"Hmm," her aunt said, thoughtfully. Olivia tried to imagine all the things she was *not* saying. Scientists could be unbearably maddening.

"You don't sound especially concerned about your grandchildren." Olivia tried to pull the accusation from her tone.

"You're in good hands with Colleen. I daresay there are no better. But as for Katja... I assume you called for advice on how to appeal to her? To perhaps involve her now, before her children become adults?"

Olivia confessed she had.

"I wish I could tell you the words you want to hear," Evangeline replied, in a soothing voice. "Katja may yet come around, but it won't be because of this. In fact, I would keep this from her as long as you can, for fear of making things worse."

"I'm sorry," Olivia said quietly. "I wish there was more I could do."

"You're already doing so much," Aunt Evangeline said, sniffling. "You're raising those babies. Johannes and I would have gladly done so, but she has her reasons for not allowing it, or allowing us near them, and I raised her to be independent. You're doing what Katja either cannot, or will not. We owe you everything."

Olivia had been on the verge of telling her aunt the rest of the story; about how the twins had seemingly discovered a "friend" of sorts. But until she had answers, she couldn't bear to explain something that would sound patently ridiculous.

"Greg, Rory, and I love Stella and Sebastian," Olivia assured her, though she failed to mention Rory had been kept from the twins recently for fear of terrifying his young mind when he saw babies turn to playmates, and more. She'd debated sending him to Greg's sister temporarily. "They're welcome in our home for as long as is necessary."

They said their goodbyes, and Olivia cradled the phone. Along with everything else, it was time to start considering that the children might become a permanent arrangement.

When Olivia arrived home that evening, she found Greg standing in the foyer, frozen to the spot. He didn't seem to notice her, until she wound her arms through his waist.

"Look," he whispered, breathlessly, and she followed his gaze. The twins were standing—*standing*—upright in the dining room, eyes fixed on the chandelier, which swayed back and forth at a frenzied pace. Stella giggled, but Sebastian was *talking*. Pointing and crying, "More! More!"

"Mother of God," she whispered, loosening her grip. She moved to Greg's side and he laced his trembling hand through hers.

"I put them down to sleep twenty minutes ago," Greg whispered. She sensed he was less worried about distracting the twins and more about drawing the attention of whatever had the power to swing their chandelier. "I read a book to Rory and then started to fix dinner when I heard the crystal clinking together. I came in and..."

Olivia squeezed his hand, sharing his fear that their invisible, uninvited guest was here to stay.

33
QUILLAN

Quillan spent the entire day in the office. For most people this would be entirely unremarkable, but it marked the first time he'd done so willingly, without being forced, in his entire career. He sat and tried to patiently listen as Lauren walked him through things he should already know: client details, upcoming meetings, case particulars. The more she talked, the more aware he became of how close he'd been to losing everything.

His cousin Oz stopped by unexpectedly. "I didn't always know I wanted this job," he said, and Quillan suspected he was in for a fine lecture. "I almost threw it away, too."

Quillan had only ever heard great things about Oz, whose father, Colin, was the most senior partner. Oz was the heir apparent; the next in line, as it always had been for the Sullivans.

"There was this girl..." Oz trailed off and smiled. Deep dimples betrayed his youthfulness, even behind the polished look. "Anyway, I thought life held other things for me. I didn't want a job that fell in my lap, I wanted something that challenged me."

"So why did you stay?"

Oz looked at him, watching him in the way an older brother might. "I grew up. And I realized a job didn't need to be glamorous to be challenging, and interesting."

"Except you're good at it," Quillan argued. "You inherited the damned lawyer gene."

Oz laughed. "No, trust me, I did not. I had to work for it, like everyone else. There are very few natural lawyers in this firm, *especially* among the Sullivans. Did you know your father took three tries at the bar exam before he passed?"

Quillan's eyes lit up. "He never mentioned that."

Oz nodded, laughing. "Half the other Sullivans in the firm didn't fare much better." He leaned forward on Quillan's desk. "I'm going to let you in on a secret no one out there wants you to know."

"I'm listening."

"The Sullivans are not excellent at being lawyers, Q. We're excellent at being a family. We look out for each other, and our clients, and we project that to everyone in the community. That doesn't make us good at what we do, only good at how we do it."

"Have you ever wondered why almost *all* of us are lawyers?" Oz continued. "I mean, seriously, there's no such thing as a lawyer gene! I'm pretty sure half of us would have been better suited to sitting in a cube processing code, or building houses. Particularly your ox of a father," he said with a flex of the arms. Quillan chuckled. "We're not here because we're excellent. We're here because we stuck together and all work toward the same goal, every day. That's what makes us great. You know our motto, I'm sure."

"Family before all else."

"Exactly... *family before all else*. Before talent, before pride, before failure. It took me a long time to realize this, Quillan, so I don't expect you to nod your head and fall in with the pack when you walk out of here. But I advise you to at least try to pull your weight in the meantime, so you don't throw it all away before you realize what you want."

Everything Oz said seemed so obvious to Quillan, yet the thoughts had never occurred to him before. Quillan had always been so focused on the "greatness" surrounding him, and his own fear of inadequacy, that he'd never questioned why, or whether it was great to begin with.

Looking at Oz—his black hair combed neatly, suit pressed, no signs he had ever struggled as Quillan did—Quillan realized he could be successful too, if he wanted it. Had Oz sat in a similar office having a similar conversation with a similar cousin once?

"I don't know what I want," Quillan confessed, surprising himself with the admission. His voice sounded foreign to him.

"You will," Oz assured him. He stood up. "Just don't mess things up while you're figuring it out." As Oz turned to leave, he added, "Lauren's a great person. Stop treating her like garbage."

"I agree with Oz." Riley popped up the instant the door closed.

"I thought I told you to stay home," Quillan grumbled, but didn't have the heart to really argue with Riley. He was still processing everything: Lauren's unreasonable sacrifice, Oz's unexpected wisdom.

"I forgot," Riley said petulantly, and flitted from one side of the room to the other. "Are you taking Lauren on a date?"

"It's not a date," Quillan said. "I'm taking her out to thank her for doing some stuff for me around the office."

"Sounds like a date," Riley said, and his face erupted in a large, innocent smile. "You going tonight?"

"Tomorrow," Quillan said impatiently. "And it's *not* a date."

The door to his office opened and Riley disappeared with a crack. Lauren entered.

Instead of her usual pantsuit, she wore a black dress, cut open in the back. Her long legs were bare, stretching high in her ridiculous heels. He had no idea how women walked anywhere in those.

Lauren noticed him noticing and blushed. "Came to see if you needed anything for your appointment this afternoon."

He was, astonishingly, prepared, having spent the prior hour reading over a file he should have already been familiar with. "No, I'm good, thanks."

She smiled, lingering. *If Riley is watching this, it's no wonder he thinks we're going on a date. Now she's wearing sexy dresses and smiling at me like a schoolgirl.*

"All right then," she said, still beaming. "Wanted to check before I left."

"Left?"

"Yes, for the day."

Quillan looked at the clock; only five. Lauren usually stayed in the office until seven or eight. "It's a little early."

Lauren's face flushed pink again. "I'm meeting someone."

The lump that had finally disappeared in his stomach returned.

"Oh," he said, for lack of anything better. "Well, have fun."

"Thanks." She giggled to herself, increasing the awkwardness. "I think everything going on at work made me realize I need to live a little. In a way, I guess I can thank you."

Quillan stared at her. "Uh, you're welcome?"

"Looking forward to our dinner tomorrow," she said as she opened the door. Lauren was beautiful. Not beautiful like

Estella, his exotic China doll. Beautiful in the way of someone who cares about others enough to give selflessly.

"Me too," he said, and watched her leave, questioning why he felt so glum.

QUILLAN WONDERED WHY HE'D AGREED TO COME. THE WOMEN WERE a mess of long, flowing skirts, colorful scarves, so much jewelry most of them had a slight droop in their walk. The men fared not much better. Bright blue hair covered in turbans, pants something a genie from the Far East might wear, jewelry even more elaborate than their women. They all knew each other, all falling over themselves to talk to Pandora and Jasper, whose flamboyance trumped everyone combined.

Quillan's eyes fell on Estella, and he remembered why he was here. Her smile glowed radiant, a beautiful but seldom occurrence. He would have joined ten of these seminars to see her face light again. He wanted so much to squeeze her hand, but envisioned the smile dropping from her face and the disgust that would follow.

Pandora and Jasper pushed through the crowd to reach the stage, as the assembly was about to begin. The sign above the podium read: NECROMASTERY: OWN IT. Quillan smirked. If nothing else, he'd be entertained.

"Why are we here again?" he whispered to Estella, who beamed at her handbill.

"This topic might help us with our research," she said, and turned back to look at the stage, where her father attempted to secure the attention of the lively, raucous crowd.

"I don't see how," he mumbled.

"Shh! It's starting," she admonished with a flick to his shoulder.

"Ladies and gentlefolk! Witches and warlocks! Priests and

priestesses! We welcome you all! Merry meet!" Pandora threw her arms open wide in a show of welcome. Quillan found it hard to believe this was the same woman who could hardly be bothered to hold her own drink.

Jasper stood off to the side, admiring her in awestruck devotion. "Those of you who are already masters of necromancy might be thinking, why am I here today? What could I possibly have to learn about a topic I'm already versed in?" Pandora scanned the room, eyeing each of them in a most supercilious manner. "Well, I say to you this: are we truly a master of something that leaves us less of who we were before we started? Are we an expert if we leave a part of ourselves behind with every contact? No," she answered her own question. "We are not. To master the art of necromancy, we must learn how to make ourselves not weaker with each encounter but *stronger*! We must become *necromasters*!"

The applause was deafening, but it was nothing compared to the clank and clanging of beads and banging of instruments. Even Estella clapped.

"She's not serious," he said to Estella. "Right?"

She looked at him, blinking incredulously. "Of course she's serious."

"So your mom talks to dead people?"

"Listen!"

Quillan sighed and flopped back. Clearly he was among crazies. The only nonbeliever in the room, the odd man out.

"We must learn to give back to the dead without giving ourselves to them. Because," she laughed, looking around the room as if surrounded by her closest friends, "let's face it. Dead people are greedy!" The room cheered. "They've had their lives and they want *more*!" Louder cheering. "They cannot accept that their time is done and past, and that by simply talking to them we are giving them the greatest gift one could give those of the no-longer-living!" The room positively erupted now. Estella stood and whistled.

I have entered the Twilight Zone.

"But to that we say, no, spirit! No more! You will haunt our dreams, our families, our lives *no more*!" The room boomed with applause, and to his left, Quillan saw a woman sink to her knees in tears, reminding him of a man he once saw "healed" at a revival his mother had dragged him to. "It is a gift, I say. But not a gift to us. No, it is a gift to them. One they must be grateful to accept and become our minions in exchange for this large mercy we give them."

Quillan had to do a double take when he saw Estella taking diligent notes.

"Show us!" a woman jumped up and screamed, hands thrown out in submission.

"Are you mad?" a man chimed in from across the room. He had one hand on his hips, the other pointing accusingly at the woman. "That is a flagrant disregard for the laws that bind us! 'Never attempt to summon the dead in groups larger than eight.' There are over two hundred of us here!"

"Ian is right," Pandora supported, silencing the rubble. "We mustn't ever summon the dead in groups as large as this. To do so would be to invoke the wrath of Satan himself. So no," she said with a sad shake of her head, "we cannot show you. We can merely teach you the skills to do it on your own."

Quillan snickered. "Rules. Sure. They have no idea!"

Estella smacked him again and shot him a warning look.

Something obscured his vision. The wavering form of Riley materialized in front of him, stern and disapproving.

"You need to leave right now, Quillan!"

Quillan panicked. How could no one else, in a room full of supposed necromancers, not see this screaming ghost in front of him?

"This is a trick! She's tricking you!"

He couldn't respond. If he did, he'd surely look insane. He tried to look around Riley, to ignore him, but there was no getting around a slippery ghost.

Another smack from Estella. Her lips pursed together and she wore the look of a mother tending to her petulant child.

"QUILLAN LEAVE NOW, C'MON, WE HAVE TO GO!"

Quillan stood so fast he tripped over the chair in front of him, taking a chunk of weave from the woman seated there. "Ouch!" she hissed. Estella was tugging at his arm, whispering in a terse voice, asking where did he think he was going and what on Earth was wrong with him.

"I'll be back in a minute," he grumbled, ignoring her protestations. He could see only one thing: Riley's back as he followed him out the door and into the humid night.

Quillan ran around the side of the building and into the alley, behind the large dumpster. Riley appeared the instant he stopped.

"What in the hell is wrong with you?" Quillan demanded. He gripped the dirty dumpster, doubled over in anger. "Riley, this is *not* funny!"

But Riley wasn't smiling, nor did he look pleased. "I wish you would listen to me. I don't know how else to tell you, I just wish you would listen."

Quillan laughed, panting and clutching his sides. "You are a real fucking piece of work, Riley. You are always in my ear, going on and on about Estella and how terrible she is, but you won't tell me why. You won't tell me what is actually the matter, or why you care so damn much! Jealousy is the only explanation that makes sense."

Riley shook his head. "I want you to be happy. You're my brother. I want you to have a happy life and have good things. That's the only reason—"

"Bullshit! Bullshit, bullshit, bullshit! If you can't be specific with me about your problem, then it's not a real problem." He stood up, dusting himself off, wiping the sweat from his brow. "I want you to go home, Riley."

"You have to leave, Quillan, you can't go back—"

"Go *home*, Riley."

"Quillan, no, please, come with me. You can't listen to them, you can't listen to Estella. Please just come with—"

"Riley," Quillan managed to say in as calm of a voice as he could manage in his anger, "I don't want you here."

"I know you don't like what I say, I know—"

"Riley," he continued, "I don't want you here anymore. At all." He looked at his brother, a child who resembled the little boy Quillan once was. Quillan's best friend and one of the only constants that had ever brought anything positive to his life.

"I want you to go away and never come back."

Riley's lip trembled and the invisible tears began to pour. "You don't mean that."

Quillan nodded, years of frustration at the helplessness of his brother's situation boiling over, mixed with exhaustion of the constant arguing. Had he been keeping Riley here all these years?

"I mean it, Riley. Go."

Riley opened his mouth to protest once more, but then his tiny hand lifted in a short, slow wave of goodbye. He looked down and then he was gone.

Quillan stood alone in the alley. The breath and life had been sucked from him.

34
KATJA

Katja began to grow suspicious of the silence of those around her.

Until the past week, Olivia and Greg had been relentless in their efforts to force Katja to acknowledge her children. Like clockwork, rotating efforts from the moment she woke up until she willed herself to sleep. She'd learned to tune their voices out, and they became an ambient background noise, akin to the cicadas humming, or cars passing by.

But then both her cousins went unexpectedly silent on the topic. Their only requests were that Katja eat regularly, and emerge from her room from time to time for exercise. While she had little desire to do either of those things, she acquiesced to buy their goodwill. What remained of the old Katja drove her to do this, that same part didn't want to see her cousins run themselves ragged with worry.

While no part of her was willing to compromise on the twins, Olivia and Greg had stopped talking about them in her presence. Instead, she found them, more than once, whispering quietly in the kitchen, or in their bedroom, stopping when they sensed Katja's presence nearby.

Katja knew better than to ask what they were hiding. If they thought she was suspicious, they 'd take their conversations to a more private place. This would not do as Katja was determined to figure out what the heck was going on.

One evening, Katja found her chance, when their landline rang. Olivia, who usually let calls go to voice mail, answered on the first ring.

Olivia started in whispers, then her voice drifted beyond Katja's ears. She wheeled herself from the room and up the ramp, but her cousin had gone into the pantry. The cord trailed out from under the closed door.

Seriously? I'm in a wheelchair, I'm not deaf! Katja maneuvered herself into the study, and carefully picked up the second phone. Holding her breath, she lifted it from the receiver and tapped the mute button.

"I have to take new ones every day, because they keep changing. Truly, I'm afraid to take them, lest they fall into the wrong hands," Olivia said. *Why can't they have this conversation in front of me?* "Have you had any luck in your research?"

"No," Katja's mother answered, heavy with resignation. "Johannes has been making calls, too, but with no success. We're not giving up, though."

"Greg has been spending day and night on the internet," Olivia said with a sigh. "I think he regrets working so much when Rory was a baby, and he'd hoped to get more time with the twins at that stage. Especially after..."

"Yes, dear," Evangeline said with a soft touch. "You're going to have to enroll them in school soon," she added.

"How can I?" Olivia demanded. Panicked, upset. "If I enroll them in kindergarten tomorrow, they'll be in first grade by the end of the week, and fourth by the end of the month. How can I explain that?"

What in the hell was Olivia talking about?

"Do you know any private tutors? Are there any on the Sullivan payroll, maybe? They've maintained a list of trusted business partners for years. Discreet. People *we* can trust."

"I didn't know that," Olivia said. She sounded old and weary. "I'll call Colin tomorrow, see if he can help. If not, I think one of our Guidry cousins might be a teacher, but I'd prefer not to involve them if I can help it."

"I'm still thinking about coming out and helping," Evangeline went on. "I know Katja doesn't want us there, but perhaps if we were in town, close by..."

"Thanks, but we'll be fine. Colleen has been very helpful. And, I have to respect Katja's wishes."

Evangeline sighed. "Keep me posted, okay?"

"I will."

"And most importantly, please don't mention this to my daughter."

Katja quickly cradled the phone and wheeled down to the basement before Olivia could piece things together.

With her door shut and locked behind her, she let out several choking, gasping breaths. She couldn't wrap her mind fully around all she had heard.

The twins... they're growing. Somehow, they're growing at an accelerated rate, and they're big enough the family is worried about suspicious eyes. No wonder Olivia stopped trying to shove pictures under my nose. She doesn't want me to know what mutated bastard spawn I've created.

Unbelievable. First, they harassed her over her decision. Then, they kept valuable information from her. Well, she was done. Past her tolerance of being treated like an invalid child, she wasn't going to stand for it anymore.

Katja unlocked her desk drawer, and pulled out her journal.

Children growing like mutants. Size of four-year-olds? Some kind of gene retardation. No mention of special abilities, but without doubt those will manifest as they grow. Need to compare to my notes on special abilities, to see if there are any known correlations between growth and paranormal power.

There is no longer any doubt in my mind that the children are unstable. My research will prove that, and once it has, I will decide the proper course of action to eliminate any danger they pose to my family.

Katja closed the journal, and slipped it back into the desk, re-locking the drawer. Another thought occurred to her, one that didn't sit well at all.

My mother must somehow know what I've discovered. Maybe one of the seers tipped her off, I don't know. Her warning to Olivia at the end was not concern for my well-being.

She's not protecting me. She's protecting them.

35
FINNEGAN

Time crept slowly in Northern Ireland, sneaking by at a pace that reminded Finn of dreaded naptime as a kid. He'd stare at the clock, unable to read it, but knowing where the long hand needed to hit before his mother would let him go play.

His mind occasionally wandered back to New Orleans, where the rest of the family waited in limbo. Their Curse lay dormant, a sleeper cell waiting to come alive. They were protected from the Senetat, at least, a problem Finn now, thanks to Trygve, understood remained very real and potent.

Hopefully Nicolas was garnering more sleep than he was. Perhaps he'd already seen to Mercy's needs, however deep they ran.

Aleksei alternately played with Jon and Forbia, or conversed with Anne about the family's history. Finn watched them, a heaviness keeping him rooted firmly to wherever he happened to be seated, unable to enjoy the same reprieve.

A draoi, Aidrik had branded him, casually, and only hours before his death. He'd offered Finn no explanations, only a demand he return to *Ophélie* to help Aleksei adhere a new ward. How he could do this... *why* he could do this... what else he could do, aside from asking questions no one wanted to answer, remained cloaked in mystery.

Ulfberht lay across Finn's lap. He'd never, not once, unsheathed it since it was bequeathed to him. She was Aidrik's sword. Always would be. One day, he'd return the steel to her rightful owner. Finn couldn't see any other outcome, despite what he knew to be true. He hadn't seen the Senetat pull the life-force from his brother, but he no longer felt the soul-deep connection to him. Aidrik *was* gone. But the sword would always be his.

And what if Finn did decide to take the old, crucible steel in his own hands? What would metal do against magic? Was this a fool's errand, leading them all to their doom?

"Far." Aleksei's soft voice pierced his distress.

Finn forced a smile. "Is it lunchtime already?"

"Aidrik isn't gone completely," Aleksei said, dropping down to sit with his father. "He's dead, yeah. But he's been with us all along. I can still feel him. It's different, of course, not like before, but he's here."

"Are you reading my mind again?" Finn teased, pulling his son away from the same cesspool of dark thoughts. He carried enough darkness for the both of them. *Now I sound like Ana.*

"I don't need to. You're my father," Aleksei explained, his earlier wisdom fading to wide-eyed innocence.

Finn pulled him in for a hug, planting a kiss on the top of his head. "Of course he's with us. He sent me back to you. And, you know, I don't like to brag, but it *did* lead to us saving your family from imminent danger."

Aleksei grinned. "Tristan would say, 'that was a pretty boss move.'"

"Tristan would be right, too, dammit."

"Probably a good thing we don't have any desires for world domination, huh?"

"Speak for yourself, kid."

Aleksei's gaze traveled back to the small porch, and Finn's followed. Jon sat reading a book Finn recognized as from his own collection, back home.

"Uncle Jon is sad."

"Aleksei..." Finn started, then questioned the conversation's direction. While candid parenting had been his style thus far, there were some truths children should never be subjected to. "Your uncle has some things in his past that are his to deal with. We need to focus on finding your mom."

"Make peace with him, Far." Aleksei turned his eyes on Finn. Ana looked back at him. "For you, but also for Mora. She won't until you do."

Finn's skin turned to ice. Surely, Aleksei couldn't know the crimes Jon had committed against his mother, but he spoke with unusually wise confidence. "There are some matters too complex to explain in words, son."

"Let it go, Far. Uncle Jon didn't put Mora on this path, fate did. Fate's a wheel, always moving, whether we move with it or not. Fate put him on our path, too, you know?"

Fate is a sick bastard, then. Where had this ageless wisdom come from? What was Aleksei thinking... doing... while Finn ruminated on an old sword and his own helplessness?

A deep ache, one which hadn't gone away since Jon did his terrible deed, grew keener as Ana's battered face, juxtaposed with Jon's unrepentant one, filled his mind.

He looked away from his brother. Fate or not, Finn had not yet developed the wherewithal to bury Jon's horrific, selfish act.

"Let's go find Anne and see about lunch."

36
QUILLAN

Lauren insisted on meeting him at Arnaud's, stressing that this was *not* a date. This was perfectly all right with Quillan. He preferred walking. Made things a lot less awkward when he ended the night drunk.

His thoughts hadn't been his own for the past week. Lauren's decision at work left him with a feeling he couldn't describe. She had no vested interest in his success, unlike his father or the other Sullivans. What she'd done for Quillan had been unreservedly selfless, with no tangible gain for herself. A nice dinner would hardly come close to balancing the score.

As for Estella, he hadn't talked to her since he abandoned her the night before. She hadn't called to ask where he'd gone in such a hurry, if he was okay—not that he expected her to. Riley also remained silent, respecting his brother's wishes, but his absence made the pain in Quillan's gut sharpen.

Arnaud's was packed, but he'd wisely made a reservation. For the first time in years, Quillan arrived early. His debt to Lauren ran deep enough without affronting her further by making her wait.

The waiter escorted him to their table.

He sat and waited, watching the other couples around him. Women in black dresses and pearls, men in expensive suits. He looked at his khakis and plaid shirt with a frown, estimating if he had time to duck around the corner and buy a change of clothing. At least a nicer shirt.

Quillan fidgeted with his silverware, rearranging the order, stacking them, anything to pass the time. At exactly seven, he started folding his napkin in the shape of an airplane, officially worried.

He sunk further into his chair, aware of how much he stuck out both in appearance and lack of a date. Did everyone think he got stood up? Were they thinking he deserved to be stood up for the ridiculous way he was dressed? Were they thinking about him at all?

Quillan wondered if this was how everyone felt when they had to wait for someone who was perpetually late. He made a mental note to never arrive early anywhere again.

He didn't recognize Lauren at first glance. Her short blonde hair was curled in waves that reminded him of a flapper; endless legs peeked out from the tassels of her silver dress, running lovely lines to her glittery stilettos. In that glowing moment, Lauren outshined her sister Cassidy, the girl so photogenic their entire department store business had been revived.

The host guided her toward their table. Quillan knew he should stand and hug her, or shake her hand, or *something*, but was stuck mesmerized by the way her wavy hair caressed the flushed pink of her pale cheeks; how her whole body sparkled with gold and silver.

I don't deserve all you've done for me, and I don't deserve how beautiful you look tonight. When she spotted him, her eyes lit up and she rushed forward, leaving the host behind. Quillan found his wits again and stood to embrace her.

His hands found the softness of Lauren's warm, toned back, wondering if Estella would feel this good. *You're an asshole for thinking of Estella when Lauren looks so beautiful.*

"You look... amazing," he breathed.

"You look... nice too," she returned as she eyed his clothing choice, hiding a smile.

"I already know I look like an imbecile."

"Thanks for getting that out in the open," she teased, eyes twinkling with amusement. "Would hate to have that lingering over our evening."

Quillan couldn't believe how different someone could seem in a new setting, under changed circumstances. Gone was the uptight, determined frustration. Lauren proved relaxed, in her element. Glowing. Yes, she seemed to be radiating with a warmth and happiness he desired to absorb and experience along with her. *Why, she probably has a whole life outside of the firm.*

It occurred to him he knew absolutely nothing about Lauren.

"So," he said.

"So," she agreed. "Thanks for taking me to such a swanky joint. I'm guessing you might not have realized what you were getting yourself into," she joked, with a nod at his shirt.

"Hey." He laughed. "I've got no shame in my game."

"I'm not sure you have any 'game' at all. But on the upside, you're making me look good."

That was an understatement. If people weren't questioning his fashion choices before she arrived, they certainly were now. He was a mound of dirt in the shadow of her sunbeam.

"I wanted to say thank you, again—" he started, but she put her hand up.

"I don't want to talk shop tonight," Lauren said. "Do you know how many hours of my life I spend there?"

"Still, thank you."

"Accepted," she said, and lifted her menu. "I would ask you for a recommendation, but clearly this is your first time."

"Clearly," he mumbled. It was easy to forget where Lauren came from when she worked within the Sullivan's domain, but tonight her Weatherly grace shone through every gesture, from the way she unfolded her napkin to the placement of her glass.

"Why do you do this?" Quillan asked. "You could have been a socialite and never lifted a finger your whole life. Sorry, I guess that's shop talk."

"It's all right." Lauren set the menu aside. "Yes, I suppose I could have been a socialite. My father would have allowed it. He definitely wanted Cassidy to remain... unspoiled." She frowned, and Quillan gauged the comparisons to her sister were a sore subject. "But I didn't want to be known as one of the 'Weatherly girls,' I wanted my own accomplishments. I wanted to contribute."

When Quillan said nothing, Lauren added, "That must sound like a ridiculous cliché to you... the rich girl wanting to be known for something other than her money." She sipped her water, long fingers gripping the flute with a delicate touch. "You see so many people famous now for being the sons and daughters of someone with money. It's a disgusting testament to the society we live in that we encourage this, and I don't want any part of it."

Quillan thought of Estella, who had, in contrast, done everything possible to use the Deschanel name, fortune, and position to her advantage. "I think I understand."

"Maybe you do." She cocked her head, watching him. "You're sort of the anti-Sullivan, aren't you?"

He chuckled. "I guess that's one way to look at it."

"Everything looks different when you're on the outside looking in." A whimsical shine lit her eyes. "I can guess what people think of Cassidy and me. And before I joined the firm, I thought all Sullivans were gods in the legal field."

"That must have been quite the wake-up call."

She laughed. "Indeed."

"Did you know I'm also part Deschanel?"

She looked up, surprised. "Wait... sorry?"

"I'm probably as much Deschanel as I am Sullivan," he went on, "or as much Deschanel as any of the other Deschanels around."

She shook her head, leaning forward. "What are you talking about? I'm very familiar with the Deschanel file, and I've seen no mention at all of any cross-overs with the Sullivans."

Crap. In his attempt to be conversational he'd backed himself into a corner, and the correct answer to her question would land him in hot water. "It's, well, not on record, exactly."

Her eyes widened, followed by a knowing smile. "Of course. That's why you wanted those birth records."

"It's a long story—"

She put her hand up to stop him. "Quillan, I know you took that box from the Deschanel inventory, and I know why."

The lump in Quillan's throat loomed larger than ever. He could think of nothing to say.

"I suspected it right off the bat, but couldn't figure out *why* you would take something like that. I mean, you're not exactly fanatical about your work and there was no logical reason for you to go out of your way to hide such an interest. But that night at Lafayette, when Leander mentioned his sister... that's when I knew. You took it to her, trying to get yourself laid."

The temperature rose to his face so violently that his head started to swim. "That's not exactly—"

Lauren laughed, putting her hand up again. "It's okay. Please, don't hurt yourself explaining. I get it. She's hot, you've wanted her forever, she's a frigid bitch, and you saw a way in. You are not the first guy to invent creative methods for a booty call."

Quillan choked down his water, emptying the glass. He needed air... was anyone else hot? "It wasn't for a booty call."

"Call it whatever you want," she teased, "but know your secret is safe with me. I'm not going to tell anyone, but I will ask you to return the items once you've gotten what you wanted." She winked.

He *wanted* to thrust his head into an ice-cold bowl of water, the awkwardness of the scolding made worse by the fact that she was not angry but *amused* by the whole thing.

"I thought she might be interested because there were some occult thingies in the box," he said, feeling properly set in his place. "She's into that."

"Yes, I'm familiar with the Broussards," Lauren said, bemused.

"Estella isn't like her parents," he said quickly. "She has a genuine interest in the subject."

"As I'm sure her parents once did, before they took a genuine interest in a solid revenue stream."

"They're a tad on the extreme side, I realize, but Estella has a pure love for the occult."

"There is nothing even slightly pure about Estella Broussard."

Quillan's pulse quickened and heat flooded back into his face; beads of sweat danced on his forehead. His hands balled into fists at his side. He had all he could take of this tired argument. "What is *with* everyone and their irrational hatred of

Estella? You, Leander, my brother, Riley. I can't take it anymore! You all rant about her like she's some sort of serial killer or child predator, but she's only a girl!"

"Riley? Your brother, Riley?"

Quillan froze. In his anger he'd grown careless.

Her lips parted slightly as she studied him, a slow smile spreading across her face. "Quillan, can you talk to Riley?"

He started to shake his head and protest, but she slipped her hand over his, squeezing. "I've been around the Sullivans long enough to have seen some things. Colin can slide objects across his desk. Rory can make the water hot for his tea in seconds. Robin can persuade people to do anything she asks. And you..." She lifted his hand in the air, turning it over in both her hands. "You're special, too, aren't you?"

Quillan stared at her, mouth agape. Sullivans with special abilities? Colin moving things across desks, Rory making water boil?

He snatched his hand back. "You're out of your mind."

"No," she said slowly, "I'm not. I've lived in New Orleans my whole life, like you. I've seen a lot of weird shit, and your family's parlor tricks don't even budge the scale. But you..." She backed away from him. "Quillan, does anyone else know?"

He would know if his relatives had special abilities, or parlor tricks, or whatever she called them. And what a waste, if it were true. The Sullivans were far too dull for such gifts.

One look at Lauren's face made it clear she wasn't joking. "No, no one knows."

"Wow," she whispered. The color drained from her face. "A necromancer. A real life necromancer."

"No, no, no." He laughed, picturing all the absurd quacks from the night before. "That shit isn't real, Lauren. I just..." Was he really going to have this discussion with someone? Now? To confess this secret he'd kept for nineteen years?

Her face plainly said she wouldn't let him out of this so easily. "I don't know why I can talk to Riley, but there's nothing supernatural about it. I assumed it had to do with our twin connection. He's there, and it's better than him not being there."

Quillan couldn't get a read on her expression.

"I won't tell anyone, if that's what you're worried about," she said finally.

The knot in his stomach began to slowly dissolve. "Thank you. No one else can see him but me."

"I don't doubt that," she said. "It's a gift, being able to hold on to your brother. I wish I could still talk to my mother. I miss her every day. Have you ever tried talking to anyone else?"

"Why would I?" he answered, taken aback. "Riley came to me, not the other way around. I didn't hold a séance or something. I was seven."

"That's not what I mean," she said, shaking her head. "Have you ever heard the voices of anyone else you've lost?"

"I haven't lost anyone else."

"No one?"

"No one I've been close with."

"Hmm."

Lauren's line of questioning perplexed him. Here he'd revealed he could talk to his dead brother and instead of asking what that was like, she wanted to know if there were others?

"Is he here right now?"

Good question. According to Riley, he was always with Quillan, but Riley hadn't returned since his dismissal. "I don't know. Maybe."

"You said Riley warned you about Estella?" she pressed.

"Yes," he retorted, "he says the same stupid, vague shit all of you say. That she's bad, that she's going to hurt me, that I need to stay away. He's jealous, like Leander is jealous. What I can't figure out is why you care."

Lauren lifted her napkin, refolding it nervously. "If I knew the answer to that, I'd be out celebrating the new client I signed with the partners tonight. As it is, I'm sitting here with you, having a far more interesting conversation."

"What about your date last night? How did that go?"

Lauren smirked at the jarring conversation shift. "He's a good guy. Calls when he says he's going to call. Shows up on time. Laughs at my jokes. Has a high regard for my feelings and respects me." Her eyes bored holes clear into his soul with those words.

"You deserve that."

"I do," she agreed. "I absolutely do. I don't deserve to be treated like garbage. But we can't choose who we care about."

Quillan had forgotten his annoyance with her questions and could now only see how beautiful she looked, and how understanding she was. How kind she was. "I'm sorry," he said in a low voice, with words that came from a deeper place than Quillan had been in many years. "I don't know who I am sometimes."

She smiled sadly. "I know who you are."

He reached across the table and took her hands in his, touching his lips to them, feeling their softness, their warmth, their delicacy. He let his mouth linger as all the turmoil, sadness, and regret boiled up from within him, threatening to spill.

Quillan's eyes were heavy with things unsaid and more, the same look reflected in Lauren's expression.

As he opened his mouth, to voice these feelings, his phone rang, startling them both from the trance.

Estella.

No... ignore it. You cannot let her string you along forever. Open your eyes, and see what you have right in front of you. If you answer this, you'll never get this moment back.

He hit the ignore button, but his phone rang once more. On the third ring, he excused himself to answer, hating himself, wondering if Lauren hated him, too.

37
OLIVIA

Olivia hiked up the narrow green-carpeted staircase of the old office on Julia Street. Sullivan and Associates had been a staple law firm in New Orleans for over a century, but the august group of lawyers held a more significant meaning to the Deschanels, having been the trusted family attorneys for nearly as long. They also held the distinction of being the only non-Deschanels who had any inkling of the family's darker secrets.

Olivia, admittedly, knew very few Sullivans intimately enough to call upon them. Oz would have been her first choice, but her last interaction with him had been horrifying.

Instead, she contacted his father, Colin.

Olivia assumed they hadn't updated the decor since the office opened, judging from the dark wood paneling, and leather on sensory overload, but the space had a welcoming, and comforting, old-world charm.

She ran headfirst into one of the attorneys in the lobby, who quickly apologized and straightened her out. "Can I help you?"

"I'm looking for Colin Sullivan's office."

Olivia recognized her, from their school days: Lauren Weatherly, heiress to the Weatherly Department Stores. They hadn't known each other well enough to consider themselves friends.

"At the end of the hall, on the left," Lauren said pleasantly. Upon closer inspection, Olivia observed deep lines etching her old classmate's face, darkness under her eyes.

Lauren's face twitched marginally at the inspection, and she gazed at Olivia with a curious expression. She shook her head, and walked away.

Olivia made her way down the paneled hallway and knocked on Colin's door. He answered immediately, and a deep, long-held breath escaped her as she stared into his kind and familiar face.

She smiled and embraced him. "It's been years," she said as she pulled away, remembering his presence at family events, when she was a girl.

"It's good to see you now, though," Colin said amiably, and held the chair out for her. She sat, and then he took his seat behind his desk. "On the phone, you said something had happened and you needed the help of someone you can trust."

Olivia nodded. "I'm not sure where to start."

Colin relaxed into his chair. "I've been around Deschanels all my life. Represented them for years now. My son and cousin married into the family." They both laughed, uneasily, but his next words had a serious tone. "There's little you could say about your family that would surprise me."

"I might prove you wrong," Olivia challenged. "In all my life, I've never come across anything like this. Defining it is the least of my worries."

"Tell me about it," he said, comfortingly.

Olivia told him in plain, clear words about the twins' rapid growth. Evangeline's suggestion that the firm could help them find a way to educate the children without questions asked. The only part of the story she left out was the invisible friend the children had continued to converse with.

After a long period of consideration, Colin said, "You're right. I'm shocked. Then again, I've seen Aleksei, so I suppose you could say that's softened the blow."

"Can you help?"

He paused, in thought. "Have you met my niece, Grace?"

"I don't believe so."

Colin sat forward. "She's a teacher. Fifth grade down at one of the inner city schools. Troubled kids, from troubled families. She's miserable, but too kind to walk away.

"More importantly, she's also like *you,*" Colin continued. When Olivia narrowed her eyes, he quickly added, "She has special abilities. Like the Deschanels."

"Oh?"

"She can move objects across the room, or manipulate items, make them bend, stuff like that," Colin explained. "Sometimes she can't help it, things happen by accident. That's why she's not in a better school, teaching children whose parents actually ensure attendance."

"You're suggesting she can help?"

Colin nodded. "Grace is a loyal Sullivan, through and through. Also she may prove to be more open-minded than others."

"I don't mean to sound ungrateful, but do you think she'll be capable of keeping up with them? Stella and Sebastian are growing *fast*. I suspect they might be ready for high school curriculum in the next month or two."

"It won't be a problem. And if we need to get her certified, we will," Colin said confidently.

Olivia slipped back in her seat, and let out a long,

exhausted sigh. "I don't know what I would have done without the firm here to help us figure things out. I mean, how is it your family came to not only represent us, but accept us? Embrace us, even?"

Colin smiled. "Loyalty is our mainstay. The Deschanels are as much family as they are clients."

She wanted to smack herself for the tears that welled. *Goddammit, stop, Olivia, stop before you start crying like a damned schoolgirl and can't stop.* "Thank you," she whispered, through her cracked voice.

Colin came around the desk and knelt before her. Taking both of her hands in his, he smiled, a gesture as warm as the outside sun. "I can't imagine what you're going through right now. But you're never alone, Olivia."

GRACE SULLIVAN WAS A TINY WISP OF A GIRL. OLIVIA REMEMBERED Colin's words. *She doesn't look like much, but she's tough. She's your girl.*

"So, what did your uncle tell you about this assignment?" Olivia asked, as she led Grace into the kitchen. She eyed the suitcase, wondering if this was all of Grace's belongings. *I did tell him she should bring all she will need, as this assignment could be indefinite.*

"That you have twins growing faster than they have any business doing. You need someone who won't be bothered by it, or ask too many questions." The girl's voice was unexpectedly deep. Olivia realized she had been expecting a squeak.

"That about sums it up," she said with a humorless chuckle. "I've been trying to copy some of the kindergarten and first grade curriculums I found on the internet. I think they should be in about the second grade now, although it's difficult to tell..."

Olivia turned to gauge Grace's reaction to the flippant way she talked about what was, in fact, a real crisis. Grace peered around the room with her saucer eyes, and said nothing.

"Thing is, both Stella and Sebastian are ridiculously smart. They've blown everything I taught them out of the water. I'm not a teacher, of course, but it seems to me these kids are reading at a fifth grade level."

"It's possible," Grace said casually. Olivia found her calm manner and chocolate voice unexpectedly soothing. "Many children test above their age level, and in the case of yours, with their growth and brain development, it could be they will need a very different schooling from what a normal child would receive."

Grace said the word normal without a flinch or a pause. *She really has seen things.*

"Colin indicated you're qualified to teach at any grade level?" Olivia queried.

Grace smiled; a shy gesture, tinged with kindness. "Not exactly. I'm qualified to teach middle school, but technically, in the state of Louisiana, as long as you have a teaching degree they will happily slap you into any classroom. The wonders of our great education system. But yes, I'm comfortable teaching them all through high school content if necessary. I'm a quick study with curriculum. I have an eidetic memory."

Olivia smiled politely. She didn't know what to make of this tiny, confident girl. "Really? That's fairly uncommon."

Grace shot her a sidelong glance. "So is being a seer, but I understand there might be one nearby."

Is she toying with me? Bonding? Playing?

"I suppose it's no secret to your family what the Deschanels can do," Olivia conceded.

"The Deschanels aren't the only family with secrets," Grace replied, breaking the palpable tension with another one of her kind, furtive smiles. "Olivia, your children, and your secrets, are safe with me."

It wasn't the words that comforted Olivia, but something in the way she'd said them. She wasn't sure she believed in the concept of reincarnation. Like most Deschanels, she'd been raised Catholic, but also like most Deschanels, she rarely practiced. There was something about Grace that stuck with her. *She's an old soul. I've heard people use that expression so many times, but this is the first I've actually understood what it meant. I could believe this girl came from another time and place entirely.*

"Thank you," Olivia replied. There were still a lot of unknowns, and unanswered questions, but Grace was here, and she was going to help. They were no longer alone. "Would you like to meet the twins?"

"Boy would I!" the small girl exclaimed.

Olivia led her up the long, narrow staircase. As they entered the upper hallway, Olivia froze, throwing her arm out to stop Grace from going further. *Voices. Three.*

Grace tilted her head; Olivia caught her knowing look in her peripheral. She heard it too.

Grace gestured to Olivia to stay put, and moved forward into the hallway. With her tiny build, her steps made no sound. Olivia's heart raced as Grace slowly approached the door to the twins' room. Her arms rose in front of her, eyes snapped closed.

Olivia had seen plenty of telekinetics, but she had never *sensed* one as strong as Grace. A deep and trembling power radiated from her small frame. As her arms moved up and forward, the air around them changed; it appeared to grow, expand, and swirl. *Why, she's no mere telekinetic. She's also a conjurer. An elemental conjurer, perhaps. Hell's bells!*

With a loud crack, the door to the twins' room blew open, and with it came an enormous burst of air that knocked Olivia straight into the wall. Grace stood planted firmly in her spot, arms spread wide, hair blowing up and outward, wildly.

Stella screamed, and then Sebastian. Another change in the atmosphere as a shape took form, a phenomenon that reminded Olivia of Lake Pontchartrain's surface when a wind passed over.

Grace's arms twisted around this invisible form, subduing it. Then, with a powerful burst of energy, she threw this shape down the long hallway, collapsing to her knees as she released. Olivia saw nothing fly from the girl's arms, but the octagonal stained glass window at the end of the hall shattered.

Olivia rushed to Grace's side, pulling her into her arms. All the power radiating from her moments ago had dissipated, and now she was only a young girl again, bowed over and gasping for air. "Are you okay? What just happened?"

The twins bolted down the hall, toward the broken window. Stella screaming and crying, Sebastian holding his sister, protectively.

"Olivia," the girl in her arms said, drained of energy. "Is there something else you want to tell me?"

Olivia said nothing.

"Were you going to mention the twins are necromancers? That they can speak with the dead?"

Olivia released her and fell back against the wood floor.

38
QUILLAN

"I need you," Estella purred, delivering to Quillan the exact words he'd desired to hear from her for all of time, delivered in the same tone of his vivid and hopeful imagination.

He thought only briefly of the beautiful girl waiting inside the restaurant. "I'll be right there," was all he could get out before his legs were moving, running, carrying him not quickly enough to the intersection of St. Charles and Canal. He saw it in slow motion: the streetcar slowly pulling away, ambling back into the Garden District. He jogged in place, the decision bubbling in his head. No, he wouldn't wait. He would keep running until he reached her house.

He raced down upturned sidewalks, knocking people to the side as he pushed clumsily through the crowds, oblivious to anything but what waited at the end of his journey. His legs were a blur, loafers smacking hard on the pavement. The sweat poured from his brow, down his face, blurring his vision, so he ran blindly. He could run this path in his sleep, or with his eyes closed. He knew the way to Estella without thinking; a homing device burned into his heart.

Finally, businesses faded into homes and when he passed the Pontchartrain Hotel, his heart swelled at the prospect of getting closer. The streetcar bumbled past him, beating him to his destination. With a second wind, he turned down Prytania and pushed through the last of the distance to his precious Estella's house.

She awaited him on the porch. The vision of her standing there sent his heart to the pavement. Her long legs peeked from beneath a thin white t-shirt that barely covered her panties. They tilted in, provocatively. Her long, bouncy blonde hair curled around her arms, and breasts, inviting him.

"Where have you been?" she pouted.

"I... came... ran," he panted. The exertion had caught up to him, adrenaline nearly worn off. "As soon as..."

She pulled his hands into hers, lifting herself, and as she rose, he realized she *wasn't* wearing underwear. He swayed, dizzy with intoxication.

"I need you," she said again, the gift that would never stop giving. She shifted to the side, tilting one hip, and the large shirt slipped off her shoulder, revealing a bare breast. His mouth parted, blood rushing to his groin, lost in a dream as her hand pushed the back of his head to her pert nipple. He took the hard bud in his mouth, suckling hungrily. She moaned, and led him into the house.

He couldn't be sure any of this was happening. She kicked the door closed, and the sound was deafening, final, shutting out the rest of the world. Estella stood before him, white shirt still askance, her perfect white breast staring at him, legs spread invitingly apart. Before he could make a single move, she wrapped her tiny hand around his and set it between her legs.

When he moved to kiss her, she pushed him away. With the hand holding his against her wetness, she slid his fingers up into her core, her fingers alongside, moaning as they pleasured her, together.

"Oh, God," he groaned, "my God, Estella, I want you so bad."

She swayed her hips up and down, side-to-side, as their joined hands worked inside her, slipping in and out, fingers twined together. Her nectar slid over his hand, down his wrists, tickling his arm. He had never experienced anything so erotic in his life.

"Taste me," she gasped, using her free hand to shove his head, forcing him to his knees. "Now."

Estella pulled their soaked hands out, and he snaked his tongue in, overcome by her sweetness, so hard now he worried he would spill before he could have her. She smiled in satisfaction as he licked his fingers, then nudged him down for more. As he buried his face in her warmth, and his tongue slid inside her, his hunger elicited animalistic moans, unable to get enough, wanting all of her. She straddled his face and bucked in rhythm, riding him. He cried out, begging for more, wanting to shove his tongue so far inside of her it disappeared entirely.

"I want you to drown in it," she hissed before pushing him to the carpet, rising over him. Wetness glimmered from beneath the hem of her shirt.

I want to violate you until there's nothing left of either of us.

"I expect nothing less," Estella demurred.

QUILLAN LAY NEXT TO HER ON THE CLOYING SOFTNESS OF THE bearskin rug, playing every moment over again in his head, from her neediness on the porch to the demanding, and even cruel, sexual being of the past few hours. She was selfish, requiring all of him, but he enjoyed giving, more than he'd ever enjoyed anything in his life. He hoped her selfishness only grew from here, if this was how it now manifested.

She sighed and rolled languidly over, exposing her bare, soft skin. He wanted to take her again, but she was already sitting up and pulling clothes on, so he put the thought from his head, for now.

"That was—"

She stopped him. "Better not to ruin it with words."

"Yeah, sure," he agreed, but for the first time in his life he *wanted* to talk about sex. There were so many things he wished to ask her, to clarify, to tie everything up. Had she been playing hard to get all these years? Why give in now? And with such passion and surrender. She'd ruined him for other women forever. *I love you,* he wanted to cry out. *I am yours. I am yours for eternity, Estella.*

He watched her dress, still swimming through his daze of thoughts. Lauren, who at first must have been confused, later angry, and by now at home furious, never crossed his mind. He was Estella's, mind, body, and soul. No one else existed. Nothing else existed, not even his guilt.

She rolled her socks over her ivory skin. "So, what did you think of the necromancy seminar we went to? Or what you heard of it before you so *rudely* left."

Quillan looked up, dizzy from the abrupt shift in tone. "What was I supposed to think of it?"

She frowned and pulled herself up into a chair clear across the room from him, sliding her legs under in one quick move. "I'm asking what you think, not for you to tell me what you think I want to hear."

Quillan wasn't ready to start into one of their usual conversations. He didn't want to move past this moment just yet, this magic they'd created. But this was Estella, and she could never be swayed by any force other than her own will. "It was a little silly," he confessed, flinching at the response he expected. "Hard to take serious."

"Maybe if you'd have stayed you could have learned something," she admonished.

He feared saying anything that might cause her to revert too far from the mood which had brought him there. "Something urgent came up, I'm sorry."

"It's fine."

Quillan gaped at her. Was Estella being... understanding?

"But I was hoping you might learn something. It's a topic that should be important to you."

"If it's important to you, of course it's important to me," he said quickly.

"Goddammit, Quillan, stop agreeing with me. You sound like a simpering idiot." She rolled her tongue around in her mouth, clearly annoyed. "Do you really not know?"

He shook his head in place of a verbal response, afraid of angering her further.

Estella emitted one of her signature sighs and leaned forward, meeting his eyes. "*You* are a necromancer, Quillan."

He nearly laughed. Was it not earlier this evening that someone had misjudged his abilities for more than what they were? It seemed a lifetime ago. "No, Estella. I'm not, that's absolutely ridiculous."

She closed her eyes. "I wish she would stop talking about this stuff. All I want is to take her again on this rug. I still can't believe this happened, what does it mean? Can we talk about that?"

Quillan felt all of the color drain from his face as he listened to words that flowed directly from his mind out of her mouth. "What did you do?"

"I read your mind," she snapped. "I can do that. Like you can talk to dead people."

Had she always been able to get into his head? He felt naked and on display. How did she do it?

She waved her hands in front of him, snapping her fingers. "Quillan! Did you hear what I said?"

He blinked away his disbelief and met her gaze. "How did you do it?"

"I'm a Deschanel, remember? We can do things. Some of us can read minds, some of us can move things from one end of a room to another. Some of us are healers. But necromancers..." She paused for effect. "Now, those are rare indeed. They say only one per generation."

"Why do you think I'm a necromancer?" He recalled Lauren telling him about his uncles sliding objects across desks and influencing people.

"Because I'm a mind reader, obviously. I know all about Riley."

In one night, he'd gone from having a secret of twenty years to being discovered by not one, but *two* different people.

He wanted to protest, to disagree, to keep Riley safe from the world, but Estella was probably in his head again, listening to him bicker with himself. "I can talk to Riley but that's it."

"I can see why you think that," she replied, "but trust me when I say you're a necromancer. You wouldn't be able to talk to Riley if you weren't. Now that we know you're a Deschanel, it all makes sense."

"I can talk to him because he's my *brother* and I love him." He knew as the words left his mouth how ridiculous they sounded.

"Oh, so you think everyone can talk to their beloved dead relatives then, do you?"

"If I were a necromancer, I would be able to talk to others. I would see dead people all the time, all around me," he argued weakly.

"It doesn't quite work like that." Estella curled her lip in condescension. "You either have to force contact on your own, or the spirit has to seek you out. I'm guessing Riley came to you after he died, not the other way around?" Quillan nodded. "And I'm guessing you've had no other relatives die whom you loved the way you loved Riley?" He nodded again. "Right. So you would need to seek them out to test my theory. You'd have to make contact."

"Why in the hell would I want to do *that?* Managing Riley is a full time job all on its own, trust me."

"Do you really not know where I'm going with this?"

He didn't, and felt like even more of an idiot than he had when she initiated the discussion. "Maybe you should just come out and tell me."

"Blanche. Ophelia. Seamus. Quillan, we hit a wall with our research because there's nothing left to be found unless we ask them ourselves. We could actually *have a conversation* with them!"

The letters seemed like a lifetime ago. "You're kidding, right? You're fucking with me?"

"No, Quillan, I am not *fucking* with you, though you can thank me later for the great time I showed you earlier. Are you honestly conflicted? This is a no-brainer. We can *talk* to the dead. We can have a real conversation with them!"

"I don't know..."

"You don't *know?*" The anger returned. "As in, you don't know if you're too big of a pussy to go through with this? Or you don't know if you're capable of having a conversation with them because you clearly struggle with the English language?"

Emotional walls closed in on all sides and, for the first time in his life, he did not want to be in Estella Broussard's presence. "I don't know if I can talk to them. If I'm actually what you say I am."

She laughed, a deep, cruel sound. "I'm certain of what you are. Absolutely positive. Do you even know what kind of a gift this is? How blessed you are? God must have quite the sense of humor, giving this incredible talent to such an undeserving half-wit."

"Stop insulting me," he pled in a near whisper. "I'd do anything in the world for you, so it's not necessary to cut me down in order to get what you want."

Estella sat back, contrite. "The first sign of a backbone. Is there more where that came from?"

"Look," he said. She'd put him into a corner, and she knew it. Now, he knew it. For once, he wasn't enamored with her manipulations, but sickened by them. "You might have all the confidence in the world about this, but I don't. I need to think." He raised himself up and began looking for his clothes. "I'm gonna leave now."

She laughed again, the same cruel taunt. "Leave? After all we shared?" Her tone cut sharper than a knife.

He spun on her. "Why do you act like this, Estella? Why do you find it necessary to treat people so horribly?"

She reached out and touched his face. "The better question is, why do you keep coming back for more?"

In spite of the context, the warmth of her hand against his face filled him with the same conflicted love he'd always had for her. His voice trembled. "Because I love you."

He half-expected her to laugh again, and break his heart forever. Instead she inspected him thoughtfully.

"If you really love me, you'll do this for me."

And there it was. The point of the whole evening; the seduction, the persuasion. She'd given him a gift he'd wanted almost his whole life, and now the scales were tipped.

She was owed.

Behind her words lay a promise of more rewards for Quillan if he played along.

"I need to think about it," he said, turning before her words or touch could sway him further. He needed sleep and a clear head. He needed to talk to Riley.

"Do that," she called after him, as he dressed quickly and headed for the front door. "You could have everything you've ever wanted, Quillan, and it would cost you very little."

The hollow feeling deep inside told him otherwise. The voice of Riley spoke inside his head, telling him what he feared all along: *It will cost you everything.*

QUILLAN ARRIVED AT THE FLAT TO FIND HIMSELF HOME ALONE. Leander wasn't there but Quillan didn't care where he was. He needed to talk to Riley, to confront him, ask him more about his warning. Most of all, apologize.

He tossed his keys without looking where they landed, and threw his arms up in submission.

"I'm sorry, Riley!" he cried. "I'm *sorry*. Please... come back, buddy. I need to talk to you!"

He waited for the whoosh and crack announcing Riley's appearance, but it didn't come. "Riley!" he called out, his voice cracking. "*Please*! I need you!"

Where the sound of Riley's small, laughing voice would have been, only the deafening call of Quillan's loneliness remained.

"Come back," he whispered, as he sunk into the couch. Tears erupted and flowed freely down his cheeks, dousing him in his own inadequacy, regret, and shame. He had done this. He had driven his brother away.

Quillan's best friend of twenty-six years was gone.

39
JONATHAN

"Not gonna eat?" Finn called after Anne. He'd grilled fish caught from the nearby freshwater pond. Not the great Atlantic cod or marlin he'd bake up back home, but Jon guessed it gave him a sense of purpose to engage in something he was skilled at, in the midst of all the unknowns.

"Not hungry," Anne said, pausing at the door. Her shoulders sagged. She seemed to know Finn wouldn't leave it at that. "I need to clear my head. I'll be back in a bit."

"Did something happen?" Aleksei asked. "Is she okay?"

"We all need a retreat from time-to-time," Nerys explained and guided him toward the dining room table.

Jon watched the door. A visceral pull tugged somewhere within him, one that understood the unsaid words following the erratic girl as she fled for solace.

He rushed toward the same door, quickly, so as not to draw inquiries for explanations he didn't have.

• • •

Instinct carried him. The purple hues of dusk cast violent shadows over the still pond. A second silhouette caught his attention.

"Anne," Jon whispered, wondering whose voice he was hearing. Surely this tenderness was not his. Only once, a lifetime ago, could he have ever prescribed such a thing to himself.

Anne's shoulders shook with the weight of her grief. Her hands protected her face from the cascade of tears in accompaniment.

Jon sank to the soft grass beside her, awaiting her inevitable demands asking why he was here. But she said nothing. The only audible contributions were the soft songs of the crickets and the hum from dragonflies skip-dancing the surface.

"You can tell me. I'll listen."

"And do what?" she muttered, but he felt her soften, and she didn't pull from him when he draped a tentative arm over her shoulders.

"Maybe saying the words will be enough," Jon replied. Her hair smelled of strawberries and an honest perfume of evening sweat. "Have you ever had someone you could talk to?"

"I don't know how to talk," she choked out between the sobs she struggled to restrain. "My mother taught me feelings were best served buried deep, where they couldn't make me more undesirable than I already was."

"Is that why..."

"Why I killed her? No. Not exactly, anyway. It was an accident, I didn't mean to. But I must have, right? Plants obey my commands. My whims and desires. They wouldn't have done what they did if it wasn't at my bidding." Anne drew in a shuddering breath. "I'm an abomination."

Jon had witnessed how plants reacted to Anne's presence,

but without an explanation that made sense, he'd dismissed it outright. Now she was saying she'd killed her mother with this same anomaly.

This was her darkness, but he had his own.

"Anne... if you'd truly meant her malice, you wouldn't be torturing yourself about it, years later."

"I'm not torturing myself for killing her. I'm doing it because I'm *not* sorry she's gone! I hated her, Jon. I loathed the woman, and all her horrible words, and judgmental looks. The way she could never bring herself to love me, only tolerate me. She raised me to believe I was nothing! And the worst part? She was right."

Jon tried to speak, to rebut. Anne's words couldn't be slowed.

"It doesn't end there, it only begins," she rushed on. "I wished my cousin Ana harm, and she nearly died. And now she very well still might. I lusted after a man who was not mine, and never will be. And now, I've lost the Empyrean children who were under my charge. I bring nothing but pain and suffering to anyone who dares love or trust me."

"Good intentions gone astray," Jon mused, thinking of his own penchant for causing pain to loved ones. "And then, at some point, the intentions cease to be good, and you've lost the desire for anything else but a determination toward something pointless and irrelevant."

"Good intentions," Anne repeated, softly. She lifted her head to look at him for the first time since he sat down. "Is a good intention still good if it's entirely self-serving?"

"Aren't we self-serving by nature? It takes considerable effort to serve others first."

Anne's laugh was bitter. "For us, maybe. For most of the world, the gesture comes quite naturally."

For us, he considered. *Could it be true, to be weighed down by such tremendous darkness that you are removed from the human condition?*

"I've tried to atone for it." Anne sniffed. "But I know now, I'm cruel and wicked at heart. There's no fixing me."

Jon's lips grazed hers before he could consider the action. Her mouth parted with a gasp. She backed away.

"No," she whispered, turning away again, burying her face into her tear-soaked palms. "I was wrong about you, Jon, and I'm sorry. Whatever injuries you did Finn and Ana, I see you're trying to right that wrong. This contrition separates us, though; it puts you on the other side of the line, on the list of those I'm capable of crushing."

"You have no idea what I'm capable of." Jon's voice cracked.

"You made a mistake. That doesn't make you evil. It doesn't make you an abomination."

"Anne, you're so quick to judge yourself, but you can't see the darkness in others? I didn't just *make a mistake.* I knowingly and willingly pursued Ana, to hurt her. Maybe to hurt Finn, but whether he was hurt or not was of no matter to me, because *I wanted her.* It was me, Jonathan Andrew St. Andrews, who did these things, and I don't think I'd do anything differently if time were reset."

Anne dropped her hands. Her head tilted back toward the sky, and her eyes closed. "I don't understand what you're saying. Why are you here then?"

"I could throw myself from a cliff to rid the world of my darkness, or I could attempt my own version of atonement. It may not look like the redemption of others, but intention matters. It has to."

"Are you sorry for what you did? To Ana and Finn?"

"I'm sorry I pulled them into my downward spiral," Jon replied. "I'm sorry they were hurt in the process."

"That's a very nihilistic outlook," Anne countered, but she was listening.

"I don't know why I'm this way. But I'm tired of fighting myself. I believe... maybe... I can find a way to channel my emotional distance to something good. That instead of trying to squash it, if I cultivate this perspective, and learn to control it, I can affect better outcomes. It's why I came back. I sensed Finn needed me. Maybe I can't offer him what Nerys, or what others, can, but perhaps my uniquely tortured soul will come through for him in a way no one else could contemplate."

"You're being hard on yourself," she said with a hint of sarcasm. "You went after the wrong girl and things went too far. This does not a lifetime of errors make."

Should he tell her? There was nothing to stop him, other than his own buried regret. No one else had ever heard the words, but when had he been in the presence of such a kindred spirit? *You thought you'd found it in Ana. But Ana's darkness was her greatest strength. Yours eats you alive.*

"I watched the love of my life fall to her death," Jon said after a pause. Well, the words were out now. She could do with them as she pleased.

Anne's sniffling stopped. Her silence seemed permission to go on.

"Carla was too good for me. I saw it that way, at least, and that would have been how the entire island saw it, had they known about us. She was the most beautiful girl in school and I was... well, I was me. It would take many hands to count the times I'd been at the end of her bullying or teasing, but I couldn't stop from falling in love with her when circumstances brought her to me."

"Someone who hurts you is *not* too good for you, Jon," Anne said, but she nodded for him to go on.

"She had a boyfriend. Her social equivalent, but Lionel was

a sociopath in the making. Had he lived, the guy would have gone on to terrorize many women, I suspect. When Carla found her way to me, she'd been fed up with him, and wanted better for herself. In helping her, I loved her.

"Carla ended up pregnant. We were both so foolishly caught up in our secret affair, we didn't think about precautions. I convinced her to leave Summer Island with me, and start a life together. She was terrified, but I insisted I could protect her, having not even the first clue what those words meant. When she went to break things off with Lionel, really break them off, they both ended up dead. Murder-suicide. All three of them. Carla, Lionel, and my unborn child."

"Jon!"

"I never told anyone. My family knew Carla and I were close, but they never suspected the depth of what had grown between us. And they never learned about the baby. Not even Carla's parents knew, because they waived the right to an autopsy."

The first of Jon's own tears fell, cutting a solid line down his cheeks. "I'll never know if the moment I saw Carla fall to her death is the same moment I became who I am now... or if it was a catalyst, bringing me over the edge of my potential, which had always lain dormant. The only thing I do know, Anne, is that atonement doesn't come from prayer, or regret. Regret without change, without evolving and adapting, is the most self-serving thing we could ever do for ourselves."

Anne laced a hand through his. She set the other over his tears on one cheek, and turned his face toward hers. "Thank you for telling me."

"We have a chance here," Jon answered, his voice choked with emotion that had built up over nearly two decades. "To do the right thing, Anne. To help those we love. We can find our recompense, through becoming the people we were meant to be."

Anne pressed her whole body forward, kissing him, running her hands over his cheeks, through his hair.

Jon fell back against the grass and she came over him, raining kisses wherever her lips could graze. "Monsters, we are," he murmured, pulling, tugging, desiring her.

"Then let us be monsters together," Anne moaned, unbuckling his trousers, suckling at his neck. "Let us save our family, together."

Jon lifted her skirt and entered her, every flash of hatred, sorrow, and love from his life... yes, even love... coursing through his motions.

Anne cried out, a soft, crisp cry of pain, and he understood, with beautiful, delicious clarity, that she'd saved herself... for him, though she'd likely not known it until that very moment. He would receive this gift with open arms, an open soul, maybe, an open heart.

The merging of souls created a cocoon, sheltering them from the broader world, but also bringing them closer together, to a place free of judgment and overflowing with the joyous gift of mutual understanding.

40
KATJA

Katja dropped her pen.

Throughout her research, she'd been firmly prepared for the truth, anticipating the revealed facts would lead to a significant shift in the family dynamic. That they might, in fact, lead to an all-out war between the Deschanels.

But now that the truth was before her, and she was absolutely certain of the implications, her stomach twisted in knots. Knowing meant she could not sit back and do nothing; inaction would be criminal.

She picked up her abandoned pen, and, with a shaky hand, began to write.

I did not think it possible for this family to have a starlight awakener. There is not a single instance of one in any record kept on the Deschanels, nor are there any strong accounts outside of the family. The SAs are mythical, along the same lines as vampires, werewolves, and fairies. In other words, they were never truly believed to exist.

Yet, there is no other explanation. The growth. The conversa-

tions with deceased relatives. The only question remaining is whether or not one, or both, holds this power. Without seeing them, I cannot make the assessment. My theory is they draw strength from each other. They are somehow linked. Perhaps the power would disappear entirely, or at least lessen, if they were removed from each other's presence.

Or perhaps I'm wrong. What if one were to perish? Would the living cannibalize the powers of the dead and form a much stronger being than what we currently have?

The biggest question remaining: Who is trying to come through?

41
QUILLAN

Quillan slept all through Sunday. On Monday, he called out sick. His father chuckled and told him he'd earned it. On Tuesday, he said he was working from home, though all his files, and computer, were still at the office.

Quillan's stomach threatened to turn over at the memory of every awful thing he'd said or done to Lauren, a list that only continued to grow. His cowardice, his selfishness, were overwhelming, and yet he couldn't resist the lure of Estella.

After dropping such a heavy request in his lap, Estella should have been falling all over herself to check on him, to see how he was handling the news. But this was Estella, and *only* Estella could drop such a bomb and sit back, watching it play to her advantage. Quillan suspected he was doing exactly what she wanted him to do.

The idea his gift of talking to his brother might be part of a dark, sinister ability tied to his family's history was an unthinkable concept to process. Estella insisted he would have to hone his skill in order to talk to other dead people. Quillan couldn't put aside the belief that if he really was "blessed," he would have talked to someone other than Riley by now.

A part of him wondered if Estella wasn't intentionally making a fool of him for her own twisted amusement.

She went to a lot of trouble getting you there, delivering herself on a platter. She does nothing without some personal gain, and you know this. You've always known this.

Riley reached out to you, not the other way around, both Estella and Lauren had said. So what if he could reach out to Riley? If he could learn to harness this so-called ability they both seemed to think he had, could he appeal to his little brother and get him back? Riley might even be impressed by Quillan's resourcefulness.

Under this motivation, Quillan found himself back at Estella's house. She greeted him with a dazzling smile. "I'm glad to see you've come to your senses."

He took her on the stairs, even though Pandora was home, only a few rooms away.

"So, what are you doing this weekend?" he asked as she pulled out the old box, carefully removing the letters and symbols.

"We fucked, Quillan, we're not in a relationship," she asserted. When his face fell, she added, as if afraid he might change his mind, "Nothing interesting. Working for my father."

Quillan wanted to ask her more, but feared sacrificing her good mood, even if it was artificial. He couldn't handle his sadness and her displeasure in tandem.

"Where do we start?" he asked instead, forcing an enthusiasm he didn't feel.

"Well," she perked up, "I've done significant research on the subject. There are many unnatural ways to force communion with the dead, and that's traditional necromancy. Like the people you saw the other night," she explained with a wave of the hand, as if they hadn't been complete frauds, her parents included. "But there's not much information out there about *natural* necromancers, such as yourself. And unfortunately, there are a lot of phonies who *pretend* to be natural necromancers, but they're employing the dark arts like all the others. But..." she handed him a piece of paper printed off the internet, "I'm encouraged by what I did find once I weeded out some of the crap. It would seem if one is predisposed, as you are, it simply requires a certain degree of concentration, belief, and focus."

He wrinkled his nose. Estella continued, "Yes, I realize none of those are your strong points, Quillan, but I'm hoping your natural strength in this ability will outweigh your lack of intellect."

Quillan ignored the slight. "So what, exactly, do you suggest I do? Do we need to hold hands and close our eyes and chant some shit?"

"You watch too much TV. We need to block out all external distractions. Any noises, interruptions. Turn your cell off. Now," she commanded, when he made no move to do it. "I've already closed all the blinds in the house and unplugged the land lines. Pandora is locked in her room. We won't hear from her." Quillan raised an eyebrow, but she went on. "My father isn't expected home until late tonight. Some psychics' dinner.

"Once we start, you'll need to clear your mind entirely. Focus on something bland. The color black should work. You need to expel any thought that competes with this. Once your mind is completely clear of distractions, then introduce one thought and one thought only: Blanche."

"What will you be doing?"

"I can't do anything except guide you," Estella sighed, as if that alone were a huge burden. "I cannot speak while you're clearing your mind because it might distract you. Once you start focusing on communicating with Blanche, though, you need to speak your commands out loud."

"My commands?"

"Yes, yes, like 'Blanche Broussard, I request your presence. Blanche, I would like to palaver.' Or improvise. You need her to know you're seeking her, so she can hear her name from the nether and come forth into our plane to communicate."

Quillan had no idea what she just said. Palaver. Nether. Plane. Communicate. She might have listened to her parents too much. "What if she doesn't come?"

"She will, because a spirit is incapable of refusing the call of a true necromancer."

"What if—" He started to question, again, whether she was sure about his ability, but her eyes narrowed and he was quite certain he'd be incapable of clearing his thoughts with the wrath of Estella Broussard hanging over him.

"What happens if—when, sorry, when—she answers?"

"Well, then we ask her all the things we want to know." She sounded like a little girl on Christmas morning. "They say the strongest necromancers can channel a connection so robust, others without that skill can participate in the communication. I have high hopes."

I have high hopes toward your disappointment. "So, what should I ask her?"

She smacked her palm into her forehead. "Let *me* do the talking when we get there, Quillan. God help us if you're forced to."

"So..." Other questions formed in his head, but they were vague. He didn't know what he didn't know.

Quillan realized he was stalling for time.

"So... *what*? Is there a problem?"

"Is there something else we need to do before we start?"

Estella waved her hands in his face. "Only waiting on you to get your panties out of a twist and start clearing your damn head."

Like I can when you're staring me down like that. But he did as Estella asked, closing his eyes, trying to think of nothing. Nothing turned out to be something. At first it was an empty room, and then he tried to focus on black, like she'd suggested, but shapes started forming and emerging from the black and then he saw a room again. He commanded himself to clear everything at once, but instead he envisioned nearly everything at once, leaving his head swimming with images. Meanwhile, he could *feel* Estella's impatience from several feet away. Her body radiated with annoyance and apprehension.

I'm trying he wanted to say, but speaking would start the process over and incite more anger. Yet, here he was, thinking about it, which, inevitably, also started the process over. He frowned in frustration at the whole exercise and heard a small grunt she couldn't hide. *You're not helping,* he wished he could say, but he had spent his whole life tiptoeing around Estella and this was not the time to stop.

Seconds turned to minutes; the minutes dragged into more. The harder Quillan focused on removing the myriad things crowding his thoughts, the more he thought about them. The longer time dragged on, the more aware he was of Estella's presence and growing annoyance. Finally, she seemed to realize her influence, because she stood and left the room.

In her absence, the room went completely still. The house made no sounds. Quillan inhaled a deep breath and held it. When he slowly exhaled, he pushed out the people, places, and ideas crowding his busy brain. With each breath in and out, he expelled more of the invaders. The more progress he made, the faster his brain allowed him to release. Quicker and quicker the thoughts left, and his pulse and breathing slowed.

And then, all at once, he was empty. His concept of nothing was not black, as Estella had suggested. It was off-white—gray. An explosion of absolutely nothing.

"Blanche," Quillan whispered. The rest of the words were heavy on his tongue. He forced his reservations aside, another unwelcome intruder.

"Blanche Broussard," he said, louder this time. "Blanche Deschanel Broussard, I would like to palaver." The word sounded good on his tongue; it felt natural, though he'd never heard the term before Estella spoke it.

The air around him grew cold and a small draft blew past his face. He opened his eyes to see the space in front of him wavering and distorting, like a television with a bad picture. More colors and shapes came into focus as a young, beautiful girl materialized before his eyes. *Estella.* Yes, Estella. The woman in front of him was Estella.

Yet, he could immediately see it was not. She had the same blonde ringlet hair and tiny features, same petite frame, and certainly the same mordant darkness in her eyes. But this girl was bewitched with a softness Estella had never had.

"Quillan Sullivan," the deep, milky voice of Blanche said. "I wondered when one of you kids was going to figure out how to talk to us."

"Great-grandmother?" Estella whispered in awe as she moved back into the room. She gaped at the figure before him.

"Estella, my darling," the woman said, her smile kind. "Do come join us."

Quillan's heart threatened to beat right out of his chest. He had done it. He had made contact with the dead, and was exactly what Estella said he was: a necromancer.

Quillan deferred to Estella to gauge her reaction. She was staring in astonishment at her great-grandmother, on her knees, reaching out with tears in her eyes. He'd given Estella a gift no one else could, rendering himself invaluable. She would choose to be close to him solely for what he could do for her.

He could live with that, more than he could live without her.

"There are so many things we want to ask you," Estella breathed. Blanche smiled indulgently. Until now, Quillan had not seen Estella humbled.

"Shh, my child. We have all the time in the world, thanks to our darling friend, Quillan!" She reached her hand out to him. He knew he could not physically touch her, but he reached by instinct.

"I don't understand why I have this ability," was all he could think to say. Estella glared at him.

"Why, many of the Deschanels have abilities," Blanche declared. She flipped her wrists emphatically in the air, reminding him of Estella. "They go back hundreds of years." Quillan and Estella watched her, both loaded with questions. "Of course, you know I'm a necromancer, too. I've had many wonderful talks with our ancestors, though not all of them were as willing as I am to appear."

"Why was your Aunt Ophelia threatening you?" Estella blurted out.

Blanche chuckled. "Slow down, my darling. That's a very long tale and we haven't seen each other in years."

"Estella says, if I can make you appear to others that means I'm powerful. Is that true?" Quillan jumped in.

"Oh, I'd say so," she replied with a knowing wink. "Even I could not project spirits for others. In fact, I've never heard of a Deschanel who could."

He beamed, proud of something he did not yet understand. "So I can talk to anyone? Any dead folks, I mean."

She shook her head. "You may only seek out those who want to be sought. My, there is so much to tell the two of you, but I am not at liberty to say! I can reveal this. Some of us choose to wait, and watch, and look over those we loved. Others do not. If they've chosen the other path, you'll be unable to make contact with them, no matter how powerful you are."

"Can..." He didn't know how to form the question without angering Estella further. "Can someone choose to 'move on' after they initially chose to stay?"

"Do you mean, could I move on and out of your reach, my child?"

"Well, yes."

"I do not know. There are some spirits I used to connect with who are no longer available, but where they went? I am not privy to that."

"I've missed you so much," Estella whispered. Quillan found himself touched by the depth and purity of her emotion. It gave him hope she might yet have love in her heart.

"I cannot say I have missed you, my darling, because I am always with you," Blanche said to her in a maternal fashion. "Though I am grateful that we've been able to reconnect face-to-face. You were always my favorite, you know."

Estella nodded. "I know."

Blanche eyed her for a moment and then chuckled again. "You are one in a million, child. I always imagined you would be the 'chosen one' but life does not always work out the way we expect, now does it?"

Quillan and Estella both opened their mouths to ask what the 'chosen one' meant, but at that moment the door opened and blinding light filled the hallway. Jasper had come home early.

Quillan looked toward the door and when he looked back, Blanche was gone. "Fuck," he muttered.

Estella rocked back on her heels, shell-shocked. She'd

probably not expected Quillan would succeed, despite her belief. Or perhaps it was that one cannot adequately prepare to see someone they love again after so many years.

"Thank you," she whispered.

Once certain Leander was asleep, Quillan closed his eyes and attempted to clear his mind. The task proved harder the second time around, because his desire to reach his brother was not so much inspiring as distracting. His failure would mean not talking to Riley for the foreseeable future, and he couldn't take that risk.

He squeezed his eyes shut and flinched. No, this wouldn't work. He couldn't simply force the thoughts out with more thoughts. He remembered Estella's words:

Focus on the black. Push out all the light.

Quillan filled his lungs with fresh breath and released it slowly, lettings his thoughts flow alongside. In. Out. In. Out. Black.

When finally his mind was clear, he whispered Riley's name.

He called out louder, despite being fearful of waking Leander.

Nothing.

Again and again. Over and over. Desperate, he resorted to begging. "Riley, *please*!"

But Riley either would not, or could not, come.

42
NERYS

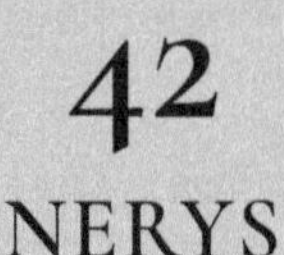

"Nerys."

"Thorvald?"

"Don't awaken. It isn't safe to send you thoughts when you're conscious. Watch. Quietly."

The blackness of Nerys' dreamless sleep shifted to waves of green grass and bowing live oaks. A stately plantation sat sentry in the middle. Ophélie. *No, not* Ophélie, *but the sense of being owned by Deschanels rang strong.*

Shrouded figures moved toward a small family cemetery. They gathered around a central individual, masked by their circle. A circle of the dead.

"He is a very powerful necromancer. Perhaps the most powerful any of us have ever seen," one whispered, though the voice was separate of the joining, narrating from the sky.

"I brought him to you," another voice said. Hope and evil rolling from this one's tongue.

"He is not who you think he is, child. You misunderstood me."

The narration continued as the figures drew closer to the being in the center.

"What do you mean? I did all this for nothing?"

"Not for nothing. Only through him was communication possible. Planning. Now, we finally have our starlight awakener. Behold!"

The vision ripped Nerys away. She stood somewhere she'd been before: the hills of the Costa del Sol, *near the ruined* alcazar *Thorvald called home.*

"Thor, they can't mean what I heard. They haven't found..."

"Not yet. But they will. Soon." His deep red hair, the hair of the ancients, rippled in the balmy Mediterranean breeze. "They aren't merely toying with necromancy. Their actions will bring about the end of the Deschanels. Worse, it will bridge the door between the dead and the living."

"Only the Quinlans have that power. And we both know they've never... would never... use it for ill."

"Only the Quinlans possess it naturally. Starlight awakeners are an abomination of magic. The bastards of our world. When have you last seen one?"

"Never. I always believed them to be myth."

"Because we wiped them out, Nerys. We struck the few who existed from this Earth, for the damage they could do. The others didn't understand the culling, but they'd never seen the destruction wrought by a starlight awakener, vulnerable to manipulation from the miscreants of the spirit world." He shook his head. "Millennia since we've seen one. How could this be?"

"Who is it?"

"I know not, except that Deschanel blood runs through the creature's veins."

"Do you know who manipulates this starlight awakener? What they want?"

"I know nothing beyond what I've shown you."

"What can I do? How can I help?"

"Stay your course. Find Amelia and Jacob. The Prophecy is the

balm for all these terrible deeds. Others can only attempt to plug the wound temporarily."

"Finn refuses until he has Anasofiya back."

"You cannot, Nerys. A rift grows in the Brotherhood... it is why I come to you only in your dreams. Why Trygve sought you in flesh." Pause. "You know what you must do."

Nerys linked her hand through his as they both gazed out at the cerulean waters. What she wouldn't give to enjoy this peace. "You're no mystic. How did you find my dreams?"

"When you opened your mind to me, you gave me the corridor. Not all know how to follow it."

Nerys turned to face him, but he was gone.

43
ESTELLA

Estella lay restless in bed, mind racing. Her heartbeat had not slowed since she'd witnessed, from the doorway, the figure of her great-grandmother materialize from thin air.

Once the pieces were revealed, she'd never doubted Quillan was a necromancer. This did not prepare her, in any way, for the moment she beheld him summon forth the dead.

Had she doubted he would actually do it? Yes. He was capable, certainly, but also clouded, childish, and impatient. Untested. Untrained. But then Blanche had appeared, and after only a couple attempts. Estella estimated it might take hours. Maybe even several sessions, before Quillan could relax and focus on the task. He had produced a connection so clear and vivid, Estella saw her grandmother before her as if she were a real, fleshly human. And then there was that other thing...

Her great-grandmother had *spoken* to *her*. Or maybe communicated was a better word, because she hadn't articulated through her mouth, but through a link forged with Estella's mind, telepathically. A connection that should have been impossible, under the circumstances.

He is exceedingly powerful, Estella. There is much I must tell you but now is not the time. Once we have achieved our aims, we will have years to catch up.

As she'd spoken to Quillan aloud, surreptitiously Blanche passed instruction to Estella. Words so powerful she'd need time to digest, and decide how to proceed. *He isn't the one, Estella. Your task ahead is a heavy burden, but I would not ask if I didn't think you capable. Do not let him reconnect with Riley.* She repeated the last order three times.

If Quillan heard any of the private exchange he gave no indication. Her great-grandmother then chanced a sly smile in her direction and their private connection was severed.

There is much I must tell you. Ah, this was torture! Estella had waited so long, so many years for this moment, and the connection had been painfully short. Her great-grandmother had things to tell her. Important things, from the sound of it. Things she did not want Quillan to hear.

Do not let him reconnect with Riley.

And what did she mean, *reconnect* with Riley? Had Quillan stopped talking to his brother? What did it even matter! Blanche had never, ever been one to waste words, and she'd used what little time available to repeat a warning about *Riley.*

He is exceedingly powerful, Estella. She had always been so proud of being a Deschanel. For Quillan Sullivan, of that insufferable lawyer clan, to be in the same class as her was really more than she should be expected to bear. So unfair.

But she would bear this insult, because it was the cost of this precious gift that had been given to her tonight. She could never, ever give that up, not willingly. If pretending to tolerate him was the price, she would pay it a thousand times over.

Estella fumbled in the dark for her glass of water. Her hand came in contact with the letterbox instead, and it flew from her nightstand into the wall, crashing to the floor and spilling the contents. She cursed loudly and shook off the covers, switching on the lamp.

As she shoveled letters back in the box, she noticed the chest had broken in the fall. The inside bottom now lifted up. She could have Quillan glue it back down in the morning.

On a closer inspection, she observed the box was not broken at all. A sliver of paper peeked out near the crack. *A false bottom. How quaint!*

Estella glanced around, feeling foolish but nonetheless validated in her instinct she should be alone for this. She unfolded the crumbling paper and skipped to the end. *With loving regard,* Grandpère *Charles*. Dated 1908.

My Dear Ophelia,

It is thus with a heavy heart I appeal to your kind nature, and strong sense of justice and rightness, to plead my case to you, of the real and awful truth. I am painfully conscious you have thus placed the burden of blame upon me for the ruination of this family. While I willingly receive most of that causation, it is for the largest of the crimes I must clear my name, and I must do it to you, the only member of this family with the voice and sense to understand and believe. I plead my case to you, and ask that you hear it with an open mind and heart. This is a dying man's wish.

I must apologize for getting directly to the point but time is not a luxury for this man any longer, and I have much to convey to you in this short window. The Deschanel Curse does not exist. It never has, alas, not in the form you and others believe. Your dear mother, Julianne, did indeed hear those fateful words from your grandmother that night, but they were the words of a grieving and guilty woman who was as much to blame for her daughter's death as I.

Your grandmother and I were close relation. First cousins to be exact. Though you may find this shocking, if you were to go back one generation further, you would see even closer relations. Brothers marrying sisters, as far back as the family keeps records. It fills me with sadness to say this was never an accident. Brigitte and I would have married our own brother and sister, respectively, did we have them. The fact we were merely cousins was a great disappointment to the family who had worked so hard to breed the purest line.

The Deschanels, as you are certainly aware, are a very powerful clan. These powers are not coincidence, nor is chance involved. We were bred this way, for hundreds of years, and it all started with a single relative who possessed more vision and ambition than I've ever had, or been accused of having.

Margarethe Deschanel was born in the early seventeenth century. In her youth, she discovered her unique ability to converse with the dead, and began associating with powerful priests and priestesses, learning about the dark arts. She spent her life trying to discover how to conquer and cheat death, and in the end, had to accept there existed no gratifying answer. There was, however, a way to experience a second life. Her discovery of that knowledge, the moment when she learned of this horrific option, was the spur that started this awful plague upon our family.

It was revealed to Margarethe that she would die, like all mortals must, but could return in a form both immortal and more powerful than anything she had ever imagined—if she could find the proper vessel.

Ophelia, the quest for this vessel is why we are here today. You see, she was told that she could return only through the body of a powerful necromancer. This individual must be of her own flesh and blood, so as to ensure the transformation stuck. As this necromancy trait ran in her own veins, she became obsessed with the idea of breeding the perfect Deschanel, the 'chosen one' who would be powerful enough, and pure enough, to accept her spirit in a state of permanency and thus make her immortal.

Years and years of inbreeding ensued from this one woman's decision. Brother married to sister, cousins when siblings were not available due to plague or illness. A pure line was created and our powers multiplied exponentially, each generation stronger than the last. But the necromancer proved to be a rare type indeed, as only one in fifty years or so would emerge. With each, she attempts possession. Any person too weak to accept her spirit was destroyed in the process. No assailed Deschanel survived her attempts.

Margarethe grew impatient, unwilling to wait half a century to try again, only to fail. Inevitably, her impatience caused her to attempt possession on members of the family who possessed strong skills in other areas—telepathy or telekinesis for example—but each would die, unprepared, and the pile of bodies grew. Margarethe did not care who she destroyed in the wake of her lust for power. She had no love for her family and instead saw everyone as vessels to her goal.

As a child, my parents painted Margarethe as a hero who sought to raise our family to greatness unlike anything the world had seen. There was no greater blessing upon parents than to have their child grow to be the 'chosen one.' Margarethe's daughter Isabelle's last words became a chant passed through the generations, one akin to a Deschanel battle cry: Seduction to sinners. A legacy in splinters. Beware, the myths of midwinter. *The family chose to take this as a warning that they must find a way to endure the evils threatening us, never understanding the evil came from within.*

In my youth, I saw this as not a rallying cry, but a curse. A warning that family would continue to die, over and over, until either a relative strong enough to bear this burden emerged, or someone put an end to it.

It occurred to me, the answer might lay in destroying her pool of resources. If I could thin the Deschanel bloodline, maybe she would be forced to surrender her evil plight. If I stayed in France, in our village, Brigitte and my children would be forced to marry... and their children, and their children's children. The madness would never end, nay, nor the deaths.

I concocted a plan to remove Brigitte and me to the Americas, to Louisiana, where we could seek out greater fortune and profit; build a real empire. It was my deeper desire to separate us from the madness of our family's beliefs and thus create a heritage that could thrive in a healthy way.

Was I guilty of quenching my own greed and thirst for wealth in this process? Yes, I will own that. My disgust at our family ways was matched by my love of money and power. But it was that lust which drove my anger toward Margarethe who'd had her time in flesh and was now looking to steal the time of others. I would stop her madness.

I covertly encouraged your father, Jean, and your uncle Fitz, to marry outside the family. I arranged fine marriages for both. Your grandmother Brigitte was beside herself with fury, believing the New World had dulled their senses; made them bold and insubordinate. Verbally, I raged against their insolence. Silently, I praised it. For their marriages were the first steps toward a new future.

This kept my darling daughter, your Aunt Ophèlie, out of their grasp. I had picked a fine suitor for her, a young man from a family even better off than ours, and her future looked to be filled with promise. But then The War came, and all prospects for matrimony were off the table until it ended. Her intended died fighting for The South, and by the time the war was over, all had changed.

I did not throw her at the Union officers, as your grandmother would have everyone believe. It happened while my back was turned, and though I should have guarded her more vigilantly, once it was done, all hopes of her finding a suitable match were destroyed. Your grandmother was more determined than ever to find a way to match her to one of her brothers. There was even talk of having Jean's marriage annulled when your mother failed to promptly produce a child.

What happened to Ophèlie ruined her chances at a real life, and put her back on the dark path her ancestors had set for her. She had one choice before her now, and Brigitte vowed to find a way to right the wrong created when the boys married freely.

I could not let that happen, my dearest Ophelia. I had not moved my family all the way to Louisiana to see them fall to the same fate as my ancestors. I could not let Brigitte's plans come to fruition. There was only one path I could see clearly. It would seal my ungodly fate for all time, but it might, just might, save my descendants from further pain and sorrow.

It was I who lifted the knife that took the life from my precious Ophèlie. I who snuffed what was left of her broken soul and severed it from this horrible world. I cannot convey to you the sorrow that accompanied this desperate action. It was a father's love crushed by the sight of his daughter's destroyed and broken spirit, a shell of the girl she once was. In ending her life, I did her a great mercy, and also saved our family. I would do it again, if the choice were before me! God help me, but even after years of sleepless nights, I would still make the same choice. I hardly believe anyone else with a mind toward ending this Deschanel madness could have seen a different path.

Brigitte's Curse was no curse after all, but the angry words of a woman who saw her one and only chance of fulfilling her destiny destroyed with the death of her daughter. She did not love Ophèlie the way a mother loves a child, but as a child loves a favored toy. She went to her death in disgrace.

This "curse" has followed our family for many centuries and will continue to follow it until Margarethe gets what she seeks. I pray and hope when the line becomes diluted enough she will give up, but in the depths of my soul I now believe I am wrong. Her years of failure have blinded her, caused her to grow clumsy and full of rage. The death toll grows in France, and will grow in Louisiana. This is our cross to bear, and I know of no way to end it except the deliverance of her wishes. I have reached a point in my sorrow that I would rather see her win and stop this madness, than see further destruction. But as time goes on, I become less hopeful such a person as she needs will ever exist.

You are the only one left to share this with, my granddaughter. I am an old, dying man, and I have kept this story with me all the long days of my life. I am guilty of so many things—greed, disloyalty, being a turncoat, and even filicide, killing my own child—but I needed to set the record straight and give you the story as it is truly, not how everyone would have you believe. Your dear mother, Julianne, was innocent and knew nothing of what went on in that house, the secrets we kept, and so she spread a story she only half-understood. Now you know all of it. I hope you will deign to share it with our descendants so they know what it is they are up against, and the truth of the matter. For me, it is enough I have told you and unburdened my soul.

From here, the story is yours.

With loving regard,

Grandpère *Charles*

In the space below the signature, someone had written in deep-red pen that nearly scratched through the paper: ***LIAR!***

Estella shuddered as the final words trailed from the paper and into her mind. She did not need further evidence or convincing; she believed, without a doubt, Charles' story was true. Her great-grandmother's words, the promise exacted from Estella, now rang with perfect clarity.

Of course this is why everyone died. Why would Brigitte carry a grudge all these years, against ancestors who had nothing to do with Charles and his reprehensible actions? It had never made much sense to Estella that a woman who placed a curse on her husband for destroying the family would proceed in destroying the rest of it for all of time.

She needed to talk to Blanche. Unanswered question after unanswered question piled up. How did Blanche and her ancestors escape this fate? Surely they were as powerful as the other line of Deschanels. And what about the Sullivans? Did they escape it purely because Margarethe didn't know of their bloodline? What were the warnings from Ophelia to Blanche about? Did they have something to do with this shocking revelation from Charles? It was clear from the red marker scribble at the bottom of the letter, Ophelia didn't believe her grandfather's confession. Did Blanche? Did she even know about it?

Blanche seemed to know so much about necromancy. Her vague warnings about Quillan and Riley were even more interesting, with the context of this new information.

Quillan. He was not the chosen one, though Blanche had led him to believe he was. But he'd started the wheel turning, and that made him critical.

Do not let him reconnect with Riley. Estella recalled Riley had been issuing warnings to Quillan about her. Riley did not like Estella, and the reason for this had never interested her much, until now, when his name read like a threat. Could this child ghost have known the outcome of these exercises all along?

Estella's hands shook so hard she dropped the letter, fumbling several times before picking it up. "LIAR!" she read again, harsh red marker that looked gashed into the paper. So much anger. *And ignorance. I no longer have any interest in talking to this weak, naive woman, if she was too blind to see this truth.*

She needed Quillan, so she could make contact with Blanche immediately. She'd have to find a way to distract Quillan so she could have another private conversation with her great-grandmother, without him being the wiser. But where to start, when she had enough questions to fill an entire month?

"*Think*," she hissed, throwing the box and letters on her bed in a heap. What if she could find a way to ask the questions vaguely enough it didn't matter if he heard her or not?

Stop beating around the point, Estella. You know you don't want to tell him, ever. You believe he is the path to the chosen one, and your great-grandmother believes that as well. You not only don't care that this might cost him his life, you're eager to see it done.

Yes, that was the cold truth of it. She didn't love Quillan. How could she love someone so weak and accommodating? Had he stood up to her, challenged her, maybe she could have seen fit to feel something more than pity and disgust for him.

But was she *really* ready to see him die? That was the question she needed to ask herself before she spoke to Blanche and all was revealed.

44
GRACE

Grace Sullivan was born to help people. Early on, she sought out others in need, from abandoned cats to injured mice. Grace was four when her mother died of cancer and her father stepped up, never realizing the resulting care was mutual. Thomas Sullivan, lost without his wife, formed an unlikely bond with Grace based as much in partnership as father to daughter.

Rumors had swarmed the family for years—Sullivans with special abilities. There were those who could move a paperweight across a desk without ever touching it, and some who could close doors from across a room. Thomas dedicated himself to the mission of helping Grace understand who she was, in hopes of eventually learning to control her gifts.

Grace didn't last long in public schools. As a child, she could barely comprehend her rare abilities, let alone control them.

Her first ability surfaced in infancy. On especially hot nights, her parents wouldn't cover her with a blanket, only to return later and find it over her. When hungry, she'd sometimes summon her bottle from across the room, too impatient to await a more traditional delivery. It became clear Grace was a telekinetic, of sorts, but while she could employ the gift in a time of need, she could not control when it happened purely by impulse.

During a playdate, when she was two, the other child took her toy and Grace grew angry. A seemingly invisible force tore the toy from the young assailant, knocking the child over. When Thomas and his wife asked Grace about it later, she shook her head. She didn't do it.

Incidents like this continued to occur throughout her early years, until someone got injured. When a rude teacher pulled Grace by the ears to get her attention, Grace accidentally sent the paper cutter down on that teacher's hand, severing two of her fingers. Grace couldn't be blamed—how could she, when her hands never left her sides?—but Thomas knew his daughter was responsible, even if unintentionally. Thomas, being a mild seer, had also witnessed the cruel teasing from her peers, and inappropriate punishments from authorities. He yanked her out of the system and took on her education, putting his law career in the backseat until she was in college.

Her second ability developed when she started puberty. Grace learned to manipulate the world around her, both tangible and intangible, creating sweeping physical changes. Initially they both assumed it was a factor of her telekinesis, until Thomas discovered, through research, it was a form of magic called conjuring. Once Grace understood she possessed this ability, she often spent hours in her room, bringing forth balls of fire, or rotating orbs of water, spinning them in her hands, enraptured. Until she accidentally flooded the entire downstairs.

The most troubling of Grace's "gifts" was one she did not share with her father. The reason Grace never told her father that her conjuring extended to spirits and ghosts was because she wondered, truly, if she wasn't imagining the whole thing.

The man was not the first ghost she had ever seen. Growing up in New Orleans, it was pretty much a given if you had the sensitivity for it. But he was the first she'd witnessed trying to harm a living creature.

The ghost chased a living man, goading him toward jumping in the river, ending it all. Grace felt that familiar surge of anger and emotion well up in her and the ghost went flying, twisting in the air... like one of her fireballs. The man stopped in his tracks as the ghost spasmed, filled with confusion. He eyed Grace with a greater fear than he had shown toward the bullying ghost, and took off in a sprint before she could say a word.

The specter contorted in anger. Grace's heart thumped wildly. *Spirit elementals are conjurers who can manipulate the entities of the underworld.* She remembered reading this, vaguely, but the words ran heavy through her head as she watched the ghost curse and shout from the spinning ball.

She channeled her focus, pulling her arm back and releasing in one swift, mighty throw. He soared high above the river, nearly all the way across the Mississippi, and when he disappeared from sight, Grace ran home. She ran faster than she had run in her whole life.

Grace never tried that again. For a girl who'd been curious about everything, she was exceedingly *uncurious* about this. She wanted to believe she had imagined it, but Grace had never been prone to excessive fancy.

So when Grace sensed the presence of the spirit in the Claiborne house, the fear gripped her even tighter than the first time. What if it didn't work, and the spirit hurt her, or one of the children? Or Olivia? What if she wasn't strong enough to fight whatever it was?

What if she was wrong?

But she had not been wrong. Though she sensed this spirit was far more powerful than the last, Grace's strength had grown with her. The moment the spirit's particles made contact with her, she saw this was not over. It would come back; it was powerful, and boy, was this spirt *angry.* Angry at Grace for her disruption, but angry at the world as well. The ghost was old, and had survived far worse than Grace's little trick of the hand. In fact, had the spirit been better prepared for Grace, it might have overpowered her.

Well, it will be prepared for me now, Grace thought, as she held Sebastian.

GRACE HAD BEEN PLAYING WITH BOTH OF THE CHILDREN IN THEIR nursery when Stella suddenly leapt and rushed down the stairs. Moments later, Sebastian's eyes rolled back in his head and the convulsions started.

Grace detected another presence in the room: the spirit from before. She—Grace did not know for sure what the gender of the spirit was, but it *felt* like a she—had been back a few times since the initial incident, but only when Grace wasn't present. Her senses had become finely tuned over the years, geared toward subtle changes in environment. She immediately sensed the molecular mass from across the house, but, unlike the first day, chose to do nothing, still trying to determine the best course of action.

This time, the spirit was bold. *She either wants me to detect her, or she doesn't care that I can. In either case, I don't like this one bit.*

A rush filled her chest as the spirit closed in on her. As it drew closer, Sebastian's shaking slowed, then finally ceased.

Despite the malevolent vibe, Grace could not deny that the

spirit *soothed* Sebastian. The young boy had fallen into a deep, fatiguing sleep, whispering in a low, mumbling voice.

"...I'm afraid, Mother... please don't hurt Stella, I love her... please..."

Grace froze in place. This spirit intended to harm Stella? Sebastian called the entity "mother." The only two women the child had ever known as mother—Katja and Olivia—were both still very much alive.

Stella rushed back into the room with her head down, pouting.

Why would anyone want to hurt this child?

Grace realized the spirit had left the room when Stella entered it. "What's wrong, baby girl?" she asked, holding her arms out. Stella fell into them and collapsed.

"Mommy is angry."

"Where is your mommy?" Grace asked, slowly. She was on thin ice, pushing this topic.

"She's here," Stella said, but her voice sounded small, and unsure. *Worried someone will hear. Perhaps her "mother."*

"Where? In the house?" Grace pressed, attempting a gentle touch, understanding one wrong word or gesture would scare Stella into silence.

Stella nodded. She pointed toward the bedroom door.

"Is she in the hallway?" Grace asked. Stella shook her head no. "In another room?" Stella nodded. "Upstairs?" Another nod.

Well, Olivia wasn't home. Katja was locked in a room she never came out of, deep in the basement. "Is your mother still alive, Stella?"

The child's lip trembled and she dropped her head to her chest. Grace reached a hand out to steady her. It was easy to forget, sometimes, that she was only a few months old, when she looked like an eight-year-old. "No," the little girl said finally.

Grace released a long sigh. The confirmation was a relief, in some ways.

"Stella, can she hear us right now?"

"I don't know. I think she's talking to Sebastian."

"Why is she talking to Sebastian?"

Stella looked down and away again, but Grace caught the sadness in her eyes. "He's her favorite now."

Why now? "Does that bother you?"

Stella shrugged. "I guess. I just miss my brother. He doesn't spend time with me anymore now that she keeps taking him away."

A chill shot through Grace's spine. "Where is she taking him?"

Stella shook her head, as if it were painful to explain this to someone who didn't understand. "They aren't actually *going* anywhere. I mean when she talks to us in her secret voice."

Grace thought she was getting closer. Necromancers often spoke with the dead through a different wavelength entirely, undetectable by most people. "Do you know what she's saying to your brother?"

"She doesn't want me to know."

"But you do know, don't you?"

Stella again glanced toward the door. After a long pause, she turned back to Grace. "I can hear them sometimes."

Grace didn't need to be an empath to sense the child's fear and anguish. *Tread carefully.* "You can tell me, Stella. I won't let anything happen to you. I promise."

Tears pooled in Stella's wide blue eyes. Grace's heart leapt, and she prayed, privately, for the answer that would help this girl. "You can't help me. No one can."

"Stella, that's not true. Tell me what's going on, and I'll protect you. We all will."

Stella couldn't be comforted. Her head shook, faster now. "No, once she wants something, no one can stop her. She hurt them all, and none of them stopped her. She said she would never hurt me, but now she's changed her mind and she's turned Sebastian against me too."

"But if she's your mother, why would she hurt you?"

Stella smiled. "She's not my mother, Grace. You know that."

"Of course I know that," Grace said, giving the young girl a smile she didn't quite feel. "But you call her mother."

"She told us to. She said she was our *real* mother, and the only mother that mattered. She said she was the mother of our future, and that we were gonna be famous."

Famous? "Did she say what she was planning to do?"

"Once she's reborn, she'll give us anything we could ever want."

"Re... *born?*" Grace choked the word out, though clarity wouldn't make this any easier to absorb. *She's going to try to come back through the children, and it will no doubt kill them in the process. She's keeping that from them, and pretending it's going to be one big trip to Disneyland.*

That bitch.

Stella's grin faded to a frown. "Now she only cares about Sebastian, though."

Oh, sweetie. That only means Sebastian is in more danger. "Stella, do you trust me?"

"I guess so."

"If I told you we needed to leave, and I promised it was the right thing to do, would you go with me?"

"What about Sebastian?"

He's an innocent child. He doesn't know any better. "We will take Sebastian, too. But I need you to be brave for me, because I'm going to ask you to do something that takes a lot of courage."

Stella looked up at her with big, curious eyes. There *was* trust there, though Grace had not earned it. *Ahh, to be a child again.* "What is it?"

"Remember how you climbed down that huge jungle gym at the park? Remember how careful you were, and how you did so good?" Stella nodded, her big grin returning. "I need you to do that again, but this time by yourself."

"By myself?"

Grace led her over to the window. *I wish there were another way, but there isn't. I can't take her past Greg. It would take too long to convince him, and my gut tells me we don't have that much time.* "I'll tend to your brother, but I need to make sure you're safe and sound first. Look outside." Stella peered out the window, as Grace opened it. "See the top of the roof here? If you climb out on to it, and then walk over to the edge, over there, there is a tree. See it?"

"That's our climbing tree!"

Oh, thank god for small slivers of help. "Yes, that's the one. Can you climb down?"

"I do it all the time!"

"Good girl! I need you to do that for me now. And when you reach the bottom, I want you to walk to the end of the block, sit on the curb, and wait for me. I probably won't be long, but I don't know for sure. Do you have a watch?"

Stella nodded, showing off the pretty pink Timex on her wrist. "If I'm not there in thirty minutes, you need to keep walking in that direction until you get to St. Charles Avenue. Where the streetcars stop, you know? Once you're there, you'll see a small grocery store on the corner, across the street. Go in, ask to use their phone, and call this number." Grace leaned over the child's desk and wrote her Uncle Colin's number on a heart-shaped piece of pink paper. The glittery ink shimmered, and the reality of what she'd gotten herself involved in hit her abruptly.

"Stella," she said, as her voice cracked. *Hold it together. This is the easy part.* "It's going to be okay. I promise."

Stella smiled and crawled through the window. "I know, Gracie. I saw what you did to her last time!"

45
QUILLAN

It was impossible to predict the exact moment a person was destined to snap.

To predict something of this magnitude would mean possessing the foresight, and avoidance, of many terrible, ridiculous decisions. Steps on the path leading you to the moment you perched on the edge of a crumbling cliff, poised to jump.

Oh, for that gift, Quillan thought. To be able to take the knowledge, this brand new, strident insight, and share it with the Quillan of five years ago... even ten, or fifteen. So many years he'd wasted, pining after a person so wretched, treading a path fraught with one embarrassing folly after another. Of course, with the benefit of hindsight, he could admit he'd always known, but ah, how he *knew* it now, how he *experienced* it, like a kick to the gut.

Comprehending this change, how he could love her to the bottom of his soul one day, and loathe her with every inch of that same soul the next, made no logical sense. He couldn't have predicted this, the lack of gradualness. The metal bat of truth had swung for the home run, and knocked it out of the park. Game over.

No specific catalyst was at play. He'd contacted Estella's great-grandmother once again, and spent twenty minutes or so listening to them make meaningless small talk. All rather benign events, in the world of Estella. Afterward, the hug she smothered him in had a touch of genuine warmth.

She began her seduction then, payment for his services, and he'd brushed her aside. Asked for a rain check, and rushed out the door, mumbling something half-coherent about being late for work. He was out the door before he realized it was a Sunday.

His behavior, and more specifically, Estella's fear he might withhold his invaluable gift, led to the first role reversal of their relationship. His phone blew up with her name on the screen, flashing a sickening reminder of a desire which had pervaded him for nearly a lifetime and he now wanted to banish all traces of.

The fog had been lifted. Quillan saw clearly for the first time in his young life. Rather than feeling vindicated, emptiness crept in and put down roots.

Monday came around and Quillan didn't move from his bed. Estella's name lit up his phone, at regular intervals, but for once it was not her name he wanted to see. As for Lauren, it wasn't negligence holding him back from calling her, but the solid weight of depression, which had snuck up as fast as his shift in loyalties.

I'm sorry, Lauren. I'm sorry, Dad. I'm sorry, Leander. I'm sorry, Riley. I'm sorry, I'm sorry, I'm sorry.

Quillan's head felt four times its weight. It may as well have been a lead ball, for all the effort it required even to *think* about lifting it from the pillow. *One leg. Just slide it off the edge. The rest of your body will follow. Come on, buddy. Not so hard.*

When that didn't work, he graduated to self-deprecation. *You've been holding your pee for six hours, you pussy. You really wanna wet yourself? Like a baby? Have fun explaining your midnight laundry crisis to Leander.*

Neither tactic worked, nor the other manipulations he employed. His mind couldn't will his limbs into action, and he added that to the massive tab of failures, ever increasing, never settled.

RILEY SAT AT THE EDGE OF QUILLAN'S BED. THE MATTRESS DIDN'T dimple with his weight, nor did his hand at Quillan's ankle invoke a sensation. "Get up, Quillan."

"Buddy?" Quillan's lips, dry and cracked from staring at his ceiling fan for untold hours, struggled around inadequate questions. "You really here?"

"I'm here, Quillan."

It was his brother's voice, all right, but it wasn't the same.

Quillan scrambled to sit, bursting with the willpower he'd been searching for over the last twenty-four hours. "You scared the hell out of me, Riley! Where have you been?"

"I did as you asked. I left you alone."

"You know I didn't mean it. I mean, you do know that, right? I was mad, but I'd never want you out of my life. Where did you go?"

Riley shrugged, an unassuming gesture that seemed way beyond his seven years. "I went where I always go when you can't see me. Not so bad, I guess, because I had a lot of thinking time, and now I know what I gotta say to you. You don't like to listen to me, but you should. You really, really should."

Quillan propped himself against the headboard. "Look, if it's about Estella, you don't have to say another word. I agree, she's awful, and I don't want to see her again. I still haven't figured out *how* I'm going to completely cut her out of my life, since she has that box of letters, but I… ahh, I don't care, truly. She can have them. Dad already wrote them off as lost. But you're back now, buddy, and that's all that matters. We've got some catching—"

Riley shot forward, landing his Velcroed sneakers on the floor. "Quillan, stop talking. You have to leave. Leave New Orleans and go somewhere else. Somewhere far away, far, far away from Estella and her horrible great-grandmother!"

"Riley, I get it. I'm not going to hang out with her anymore. It's cool. Everything's cool."

"It's not, Quillan, it's not cool. Listen to me, please, *for once*!"

Quillan put his hands forth in surrender. Riley looked as he always did, a seven-year-old still wearing the clothes he'd died in. But the youthfulness he'd maintained through the years had a crack running through it, as if it were a visage he'd worn for Quillan's sake and could no longer be bothered. Perhaps he even wanted him to see the flaw.

"I really wish you'd listened to me before," Riley began. Instead of a tone full of *I told you so,* his words seemed more or less at face value. "If you had, I wouldn't have to do what I am doing now."

"What's that?"

Riley bowed his head. Drew in the weathered sigh of an old man. "The doctors didn't know why I died. But I know, Quillan. I've always known what happened to me, I just couldn't tell you."

Blood rose to the surface of Quillan's entire body. A chill shook through. "But you're gonna tell me now?"

Riley nodded, and wiped away a phantom tear. "Estella's great-grandma isn't a good lady. She's been trying to help the evil witch Margarethe for years. She wants her to come through, because if she does, she'll bring Blanche, too. That's what she tells her anyway, but I don't believe her. She's a liar."

"Who's Margarethe?"

"A Deschanel who lived a long time ago, and didn't wanna die. She did die, because we all have to, but she didn't cross over from... well, from where I go." Riley had the name on his tongue, but seemed hesitant to use it. "Sometimes people stay there because they miss their family, or because they're afraid." He looked away at the last. "She stayed so she could find a necromancer to bring her back."

"That's ridiculous," Quillan replied, less to his brother and more himself. "If necromancers could bring people back, I would have brought you back a long time ago."

"That's 'cuz you're not the kinda necromancer who can do it. Estella thought you were, which is why she didn't dump you like before. But now she knows you're not, and she's going to use you to keep secretly talking to her great-grandma so she can find the real necromancers. Yeah, Quillan, she was talking to her behind your back. You were strong enough for that, but you can't bring Margarethe back. Thank God!"

"So why am I in danger?"

"Blanche was gonna use you to find the starlight awakener. But you dumped Estella, because you got smart, and now Margarethe will try to use you anyway, because you're better than nothing. You're still really strong, you know, even if you're not *starlight awakener* strong. She'll kill you Quillan, like she killed me."

"She..." There it was. After two decades, an answer, and now that Quillan had it, he wished for the comfort of ignorance. The quiet ease in being able to shrug and declare *medical mystery,* which was as frustrating as it was an acceptable answer, in its own way. Broken closure, but closure nonetheless.

What Riley had described was cold-blooded murder.

"Why didn't you tell me?"

"You don't know how badly I wanted to. But there are rules. Getting to hang out and still see our families is a gift, but we aren't alive anymore, and we know things they don't. Things we aren't allowed to share. If we do, we don't get to keep that gift anymore. That's how it works."

Quillan, in a flash of terrible, horrible regret, realized what Riley had done. "Oh, Riley... no..."

"I had no choice, Quillan," Riley said, backing slowly away. His figure, always so clear, never like the ghosts of movies or literature, began to fade. "You think I've been jealous of you, getting to live a life when I couldn't. I'm not though, not really. If I were jealous, I'd let Margarethe get you so I could spend forever with you. But I'm really proud of my big brother, and I wanna see him live a long life. I love you, Quillan, and I'm really, really gonna miss you." Riley smiled sadly, his image flickering in the final moments. "But I'll see you again someday. I love you, big brother."

Riley's form winked from existence before Quillan could say the words back.

He grabbed his wallet, keys, and jacket, leaving without packing a bag.

46
FINNEGAN

Nerys, in that mysterious, maddening way of hers, woke up that morning and declared they could *not* take the ship in Belfast. They must double back, inland, and immediately.

Finn argued the point with her well into the early afternoon. There was nothing for them in Ireland, and everything they were after lay ahead. But as the time neared for their ship to depart, he began to understand he couldn't win this battle. In a human, he would call what possessed her stubbornness, but it was in fact more of an iron resolve. Unmovable, like Thorvald.

He was the only one who bothered questioning *why*; the others instead prepared to follow her blindly, with a level of faith she was still earning with Finn. It wasn't her fault Finn had experienced his share of betrayals and intrigue over the past year, but wariness was his greatest defense. Sometimes, he felt, his only one.

"Okay," he said wearily. "Okay, where, exactly, are we going?"

"We'll know when we get there," she said, obtuse as ever, and disappeared to meditate.

Needing some time for his own mental stability before turning around, moving away from Ana, Finn decided on a jog.

His path took him along the shores of Strangford Lough, an inlet of the Irish Sea. Forbia's route zigzagged in front of him as she explored where her nose took her. Along the shore of the loch, Killyleagh, the small fishing village they'd taken refuge in, reminded him of Summer Island. The quaint ma and pa shops —which shuttered at 5 sharp, closed on weekends—and the slow, languid pace of the town's roughly two thousand inhabitants. A castle towered above the sleeping village, with its fairytale turrets and rough claim to fame for some importance during the reign of King James I.

A half-dozen ships were tethered along the docks, mostly moderate fishing trawlers, meant for the still waters of the loch, not the open sea. Finn's bones ached for *Forbia* with her bulky, ugly construction but heart of pure steel. He could have taken her around the world, had he a mind for it.

Forbia the Younger, his new companion but by no means a replacement—he could not replace his old ship any more than he could replace his new best friend—panted at his heels as he caught up to her.

"I thought I told you to stay back with the others," Finn chided, flashing her a smile from his peripheral.

Forbia quickened, stepping in front of him so swiftly he nearly fell topsy-turvy over her. He stopped, checked his pulse, then knelt before the wolf. "What's up with you, huh?"

Forbia whimpered, looked down, then past Finn.

A tall shadow fell over them both. Finn tensed, then, almost as quickly, drew in a deep breath and rose.

"You're quicker than you used to be," Jon said, between heavy breaths. "Made me work for it. What are you averaging now? Six, seven-minute mile?"

Finn shrugged. "Is everything okay back at the inn?"

"When I left, Anne was reading. The rest are napping, I think."

"Anne." Finn suppressed a snicker. He didn't want to be hateful, or cross. "That a thing now, you two?"

Jon's mouth twisted, a nervous habit, but his eyes brightened at the mention of her name. "I don't know what we are. We have bigger things to worry about right now. When we get home, who knows?" He gestured toward an old stone bench. Finn sat after a reluctant pause.

"You didn't come to talk about your new girlfriend, I take it."

"No," Jon answered. "I came to talk about us."

Finn's laugh rang with angst, sadness, and the tragedy of loss. Of betrayal and wounds still mending. "I don't have the words, or the will."

"Find them, Finn."

Finn snapped his head to the left, blood rising. Forbia sat on his foot, leaning heavily against his legs. He rested his hand on her ruff without thought. "You dare—"

Jon's hand landed on his shoulder. "Please. I did a horrible thing, and I'll repent that action the rest of my life. At the end of my life, I'll be judged by some being, no doubt, and whatever punishment I get, I'll have deserved. But I'm *here* now, Finn. I came to help you, in whatever capacity you need, whether you asked for it or not. There's much I don't understand about the world you live in now. The family you married into is... unique, to put it mildly. But you've embraced it, and so I've tried to do the same."

Finn bit back a hurtful comment about how screwing

around with Anne was a curious way of embracing things. He was surprised to realize he didn't mean it; not the words or the venom. He'd grown weary of this battle. He missed Jon... no, this thought was premature, even if it rang of truth.

He could not put aside all his anger until Ana was in his arms again, safe.

"I'll admit, the Deschanels are still something of a mystery to me too," Finn found himself saying. A relief, to let the words out. He'd been surrounded by Deschanels, or others like them, for so long, he nearly forgot how it felt to belong to the realm of the normal.

Then, he wasn't so normal, was he? Descended from the draoi on his mother's side, and some other supernatural business on his father's. Not knowing for twenty-seven years didn't make it less true.

"How did you do it?" Jon asked. "Fall into this life so easily?"

Finn twisted the gold band on his left ring finger, watching how it took the afternoon light. The distorted reflection of his unshaven face. "I love her. I've loved her since before I met her. You can't love someone halfway. I hear people enumerate things about their spouse they can't stand, and I wonder why they ever married. I love Ana, flaws and all. Maybe I love her *because* of those flaws. Strange family and all. I wouldn't change her, or where she came from, because she wouldn't be the same."

"Maybe that's why I've never had a relationship last," Jon replied. "I can't help seeing people for who I want them to be."

"A cantankerous recluse like you?"

Jon shot him a look. "I prefer the description: strong, silent, debonair gentleman with years of charm hiding far under the surface."

"You say potato, I say asshole." But Finn cracked a smile.

"I guess I'll have to update my online dating profile."

"Don't forget to include how you like long walks on the beach at sunset. Alone."

Jon laughed. "Dad once told me I would end up alone and miserable."

"Dad had the market cornered on compliments."

"He handed them out like million dollar checks," Jon agreed. A gentle breeze passed over them. "Mom would get angry with him, but I could tell she was angry that he'd spoken the words, not that they weren't true."

"Anne is a nice girl, Jon. Not my type, but seeing you together makes a strange sort of sense," Finn said. "I have half a mind to warn her about you."

"She already knows."

"Of course she does. There're no secrets in this family."

"So? You think I'll hurt her?"

Finn watched a group of noisy gulls fight over a decaying fish. Nearby, a fisherman pulled away from the dock. "I have no idea. I never thought you'd hurt me, or Ana, and you did. I know you don't *have* to hurt her. Maybe if you know that, too, you won't."

Jon sat silent for a moment, considering. "I thought she was in love with you."

Finn raised a brow. "She thought so, too. For her sake, I'm glad she got over it."

"Why do you think she came? Really?"

Finn shook his head. "Only she knows her reasons. She had a lot of hatred for Ana, for a long time, and maybe she thinks she owes this to her cousin. Ana doesn't hold grudges, though. She's even forgiven you."

Jon reached down to scratch Forbia behind the ears. Finn noted how differently she reacted to his brother now; no longer wary, but treating him as if he were part of the pack.

"When we find her, I'll give her time before showing myself. I don't want to make this any harder on her."

Finn stood, stretching. It hit him, then, how easily he'd talked to Jon these past minutes, and how he was unable to assess his feelings on the matter. He only knew his blood wasn't running hot, and his pulse had slowed to a normal rate. Peace prevailed, not hatred.

"My greatest fear is that I won't be able to save her. I'll fail, in any number of potential ways, and lose her forever."

The words, aloud, had power. Finn sagged, steadying himself before Jon could.

"Don't let yourself think it, Finn. Not even for a moment. I've never believed in true love, or soul mates, but I've not seen anything like what you have with Ana. Whatever you share has power, Finn. A greater power than any weapon. It might, in fact, *be* your greatest weapon. Bigger than that crazy sword you've been carrying around.

"I believe in you. Everyone on this trip believes in you, or they wouldn't be here. You can do this. You *can*, and you will."

Finn blinked away the forming tears. His glance traveled toward the path. He was ready to run again, for the endorphins to wash through him and leave him feeling confident and ready for whatever waited ahead.

"Thank you," he said, the rest of the sentence trapped in his head, and heart, alongside all the other hurts he'd not yet fully processed. "I'll see you back at the inn."

47
KATJA

Katja sincerely wished she was wrong. In spite of her heightened emotional state, she was still an intelligent girl with her reasoning skills relatively intact. She was prepared to face—in fact, hoping to face—the possibility she was overreacting. But the facts spoke for themselves.

The twins, her children, were fulfilling the ancient prophecy given to Margarethe. Margarethe Deschanel La Napier. This knowledge came by way of the strange, but felicitous, discovery of an out-of-print propaganda pamphlet titled, *La Sorcière de Villeneuve*. A tattered copy sat in an old homestead museum outside Bordeaux, and the curator had been more than happy to email her scans, along with a handful of notes from a contemporary historian.

Margarethe grew up in the agricultural village of Villeneuve-sur-Lot, France, born a very powerful mystic, the daughter of a shaman and illusionist. According to the family tree, as a granddaughter of Claude, the Marquise de Deschanel, son of Aidrik, she was among the third generation of Deschanels after the fated mixing of Empyrean blood. She grew up believing she was destined for great things, and this belief drove her, always.

Margarethe's childhood, however, was filled with grief. She started her life as the fifth child, but by the time she was ten, she was an only, her siblings all fallen to various diseases and ailments. When she was twelve, her father died, and then her mother four years later. The plague took the life of many of her cousins, aunts, and uncles. She watched as her entire village was nearly wiped out. Surrounded by death throughout her entire childhood, it was only natural Margarethe became obsessed with avoiding the fate herself.

In desperate hopes of finding a way to reach her mother, she sought out a powerful necromancer several miles from her village. Through him, she was able to connect with her mother, but this gift didn't come freely. She paid the necromancer by performing various chores around his household and property, moving in with him. Eventually, he claimed her for his bride and they produced a daughter, Isabelle.

Soon, Margarethe also fell ill. The necromancy sessions with her mother grew desperate, insistent. Her mother encouraged her to seek her husband's counsel on the subject of immortality. If Margarethe died, her infant daughter would know nothing of where she came from or what to do with her powers.

Margarethe pleaded with the old necromancer to teach her the secrets of immortality. For many months, he insisted what she asked was impossible to attain. When Margarethe appeared inches from death, his will broke and he shared a tale that had been passed down to him. He could not verify it, but, if true, the story contained the secrets she so desperately sought.

The tale centered on potent necromancers who were not limited to occasional communing with the dead, or fleeting possessions. These necromancers were so powerful they could "awaken the starlight, calling down all the powers of the skies," and form a permanent union with the dead. In that act of fusion, the magic that sealed them together would result in immortality.

The necromancer warned her that no one had ever seen a true starlight awakener; that it was believed to be an old wives' tale, spun by the fires of midwinter. If she tried it with an ordinary necromancer, that person would die. But Margarethe would not heed any of his warnings. All she absorbed was the potential she believed to be true all along: with the right patience, planning, and subject, she would achieve her immortality and bring greatness to her family.

The necromancer came to regret this admission, when Margarethe recovered. As she did, her strength returned tenfold, matched only by her determination to create a family so pure in bloodline, and so great in number, that the odds of creating a starlight awakener would increase with each generation. She birthed an additional ten children, all of whom grew to adulthood. The sons married the daughters, and their sons and daughters married. By her deathbed, she had borne witness to several generations of pure-blooded Deschanels, ready and waiting to help her fulfill her prophecy.

It was through Isabelle, the oldest, second-great granddaughter of Aidrik, that the line continued on through the Deschanels of today. From Isabelle the purity of blood continued, unbroken, until Charles Deschanel murdered his daughter, Ophélie, and stopped the family inbreeding.

Katja couldn't fathom why the twins were born with this special ability. Her research pulled up very little information on starlight awakeners, but the one thing she did find was most interesting, and allayed the one doubt she had in her mind: Even though the twins were close relation, the blood had been diluted by the time they were born. How could they have a higher chance than centuries of brothers and sisters copulating?

The answer Katja found was simple: Contrary to the stories the old necromancer told Margarethe, there was no connection whatsoever between the likeliness of the ability, and close relations. It was, according to what she could find, completely random, with the only contributing factor being that someone in the family must carry the gene. Further research showed that Isabelle, Margarethe's daughter, was not only a necromancer but very likely a starlight awakener in the Deschanel family. It wasn't entirely clear why Margarethe did not attempt to make her return through her daughter. However, it's possible she never had the chance, as Isabelle was burnt at the stake for witchcraft in her middle age.

With evidence Isabelle had been a starlight awakener, and thus scientific knowledge the gene existed in the family, Katja deduced the possibility existed. Coupled with the fact that a defining—and hugely unique—characteristic of starlight awakeners seemed to be their very rapid growth—Isabelle was kept from public eye until her teenage years, for this very reason, according to the pamphlet—the conclusion to Katja was undeniable.

The one element beyond Katja's knowledge was what would happen if Margarethe succeeded in her goal. Immortality, while tempting, was a power the world would not be ready for. It would not only expose the Deschanels to the public, but it could potentially destroy them. Katja would not let the family be abolished. Margarethe had already killed too many Deschanels to number, in her quest for domination. It would end here.

Katja experienced a twinge of sadness at what lay ahead. For her two twin babies, and the third who mercifully died in her womb. She had wanted to love them, and a part of her did, despite all she knew. But all she had to do was remind herself they were not lovable babies, but monsters, and the task ahead didn't seem so bad anymore.

Alain, I guess you were right all along. What we did was an abomination, and this is our price to pay for bringing abominations to this Earth, and this family.

48
OLIVIA

Olivia sat across from Colin in his office. His disposition was far from the welcoming, helpful one of her last visit. He appeared not to have slept in days.

I know the feeling.

Grace had told Olivia there was another necromancer in his family, one by the name of Quillan Sullivan, and she intended to speak with him.

"Is Grace doing okay?" he asked, politely.

"We couldn't ask for a better tutor for the children," Olivia answered, equally amiable. She decided against more small talk and went right to the point. "I need to talk to your nephew, Quillan."

"Well, that, I'm afraid, I cannot help you with," he replied, folding his hands over the desk.

"Why?"

"He's not here."

"As in, not here today, or..."

"No one knows where Quillan has been for the past few days," Colin replied.

When Olivia didn't respond, he expanded on the terse answer. "I don't know where Quillan is, nor does his father, or his best friend, or anyone. He didn't leave a note, didn't take any of his valuables. He's simply gone."

Olivia wavered between anger at this unexpected roadblock, and sorrow for a suffering family. "Do you know who saw him last? Perhaps I could talk to them, and get a sense if they know anything."

Colin shook his head. "We already tried, but you're welcome to it. Either his best friend, Leander, or Lauren. Lauren has the day off. Poor dear feels responsible, which is ridiculous."

"Where can I find them?"

He pulled out a square of paper, a cream, vintage-looking stationary with his name embossed in dark brown at the top, and scribbled the information.

Olivia took it from him. "Leander Broussard... Jasper and Pandora's son?" Colin nodded. "They're my cousins. Strange coincidence."

"Certainly," Colin agreed, but his thoughts were already far away again. Olivia slipped around the side of the desk, kissed the top of his head, and went to find Leander and Lauren.

LEANDER BROUSSARD ANSWERED ON THE SECOND KNOCK. SHE vaguely remembered him voicing opinions at the now-legendary Deschanel Magi meeting where Katja and Alain had shocked the family into further division.

"Olivia," he greeted, with minimal inflection. "He's not here."

"How..." she started to ask. "Of course, you're a telepath.

And I'm not looking for Quillan," she added, remembering to keep her thoughts guarded. "Or I am, but I realize he's been missing for a few days. So I'm looking for—"

"Lauren and me," he finished. Leander studied her. She began to feel keenly uncomfortable when he finally swung the door open and gestured her to come in.

Olivia recognized Lauren as the woman sitting on the couch, though she looked more ragged than she had the last time Olivia had seen her. Her short hair was pulled half-back and frizzy, her skin sallow and free of makeup. Rather than the neatly pressed suit, she wore mismatched sweats that appeared to be from her college days.

"I'm sorry to bother you two," Olivia said. *Hell's bells, could they look any more pathetic? What have I walked into?* "And I wouldn't, if things were not outright desperate at this point."

"You've got some necromancers running around your house," Leander said. "I'm too tired to hear a long story. Sorry." She could smack herself for forgetting to block only *moments* after he'd initially breached her thoughts.

Olivia wouldn't play her hand until she was comfortable with the audience. "The Deschanels haven't had a living necromancer in many, many years."

"Negative," Leander said. "Quillan is one."

"Are you sure?"

"Positive," Lauren chimed in. When she looked at Olivia, her eyes were bloodshot; rimmed in ragged red. "He's been talking to his brother Riley since he was a child. And recently..." Olivia waited for her to say more, but her mind seemed to settle elsewhere.

"Your kids are starlight awakeners? Really, no shit? Are you sure?" Leander asked. How was he getting past her block so easily? Olivia didn't have a chance to answer before he went on. "Wow, yeah. Necromancers. Hard-core necromancers." At her puzzled face he added, "Isn't that why you're here?"

For the first time in her life, Olivia was ashamed at her lack of knowledge on her family's doings. "I'm not familiar with the term. I'd never heard it until Quillan's cousin used it."

"Which one?"

"Grace."

"Ahh."

"She said the twins were starlight awakeners, and if I wanted to know about necromancy, I should talk to Quillan. But I suppose that's not an option at present."

"Where are the twins now?" Leander demanded.

"Safe," Olivia responded, then straightened her blazer. "You're welcome to come back with me, to see for yourselves, but I really need some answers. Something is very, very wrong with the twins and I'm afraid something bad will happen if we don't figure this out."

"Of course we're going back with you," Leander said simply. "But if there are starlight awakeners in your house, they aren't safe there. They're not safe anywhere, once *they* find out."

"They?" Olivia repeated.

"The bitch triplets," Lauren piped up. "Estella, Blanche, and Margarethe."

"Your sister," Olivia said with a glance at Leander. "Blanche and Margarethe?"

"Your blocking is lazy. Fix that, before the wrong person picks up on your thoughts," Leander said, ushering them toward her car. When she gaped at him, he answered her earlier question with, "I'll explain on the drive."

49
ESTELLA

Estella Broussard tapped her manicured nails in annoyance, a staccato percussion against the scarred oak surface of her writing desk. The last month had been one annoyance after another, and it all started with that wretched Quillan Sullivan.

She had always despised him. Weak-minded, shallow, completely uninteresting, and yet somehow he thought himself worthy to stand in her presence. For most of her life she'd managed to shrug him off, but when he came to her with something of value—something that she could not turn away from—what other choice did she have?

What were the odds he would find the one and only thing that could bring her life meaning?

The moment she saw and felt her great-grandmother's presence, Estella's icy heart experienced a surge of warmth and happiness, unlike anything she had known. She was here! The one person who could understand Estella for who she was, was now accessible as long as she kept that flea Quillan around. Surely the universe's idea of a cruel joke.

The contents of the letters between Blanche and her aunt wove a tale so dark even Estella took pause. The warnings, the admonishments. *Don't do it,* Ophelia had begged. *Do not sacrifice your children! It will not end the Curse; it will bring upon us a new one!*

But Blanche refused to heed this advice. She offered sacrifices to Margarethe, hoping one of her own children would be the chosen one. When two failed—*My darling baby boys, Wyatt and Noble,* Blanche had told Estella, as if she hadn't been the one to send them to their graves—Blanche was unwilling to sacrifice more and instead helped Margarethe find other suitable family members. As she did, more died, unable to withstand her ghostly grip. When Quillan came along, both Blanche and Margarethe believed they had found their true chosen one.

They'd been wrong. Quillan, while a strong necromancer, was not a starlight awakener. But for several hours after his final connection, Estella could still converse with Blanche. In that time, Blanche relayed to her not all hope was lost. *Quillan is indeed a powerful necromancer, my child, but he is not the chosen one. Several months ago, two children were born into our family. Twins. These two are the ones we have been waiting for. The starlight awakener.*

Twins? Is she going to occupy them both?

Laughter. *Heavens no, dear. Individually, these two are quite strong. But combined, they are unstoppable.*

Combined?

Child, please at least pretend not to be dense. Yes, combined. Only one will emerge as the starlight awakener. It remains to be seen which one it will be.

What happens to the other?

Estella, I swear I'm beginning to wonder about you. They shall perish, as that is the only way for the other to absorb their powers entirely. We will guide them in this, together. Margarethe will know, when the time comes, which one will emerge as the strongest, and which will surrender their existence for our cause.

But what... cause? Estella halted the remainder of her questions, lest her grandmother sting her further with insults toward her apparent lack of intelligence.

Wait and see. You're our only Earthly connection, dear Estella. You must not fail.

Estella was markedly indifferent about the fate of the children. When her conscience threatened to make an entrance, she swiftly shoved it back in place. But what *did* bother her was the fact her great-grandmother's presence waned, and she felt removed from the center of the forming plans. She was no more than a pawn, though a willing one.

She couldn't eat, or rest, or do anything but fret about the future of this mission. Quillan had disappeared, to the extent not even his family knew where he was. For all she knew, he was dead. While under ordinary circumstances this fact might bring her some measure of delight, he was her only link to her great-grandmother. She loathed that she needed him, but it didn't change the truth of it.

Am I really going to watch them murder these children? She was. She would. Living with her part in it could be sorted out later.

What kind of woman is Blanche that she would sacrifice two of her children for a creature she's never met? For a fate she can't define?

The thoughts were hollow, devoid of any true morality, but rather words any person should ask if placed in such a situation.

She had no answer, either way. If in Blanche's shoes, wouldn't she have done the same?

Estella ignored the pangs of doubt plaguing her, as she

drove toward the Claiborne house. She didn't doubt she would be outnumbered, but once she assessed the situation, there would be no quantity of mortal bodies that could stop what would come next.

Once she gave the signal, Margarethe would sweep in and do the rest.

50
FINNEGAN

The moment the loch disappeared from their rearview, Finn's anxiousness over their intended destination made an appearance. Asking Nerys for anything other than a weather prediction was pointless, and frustrating.

Over two hours they traveled, in relative silence. Jon drove again, while the others gazed out windows at the Irish landscape, breathtaking even under the tense circumstances. Forbia snored softly, content atop the less-neatly piled luggage.

Anne joined Jon in the front, occasionally slipping a hand over his or passing tender glances. Finn couldn't decide if he was wary for Anne, or happy for them both. A combination, most likely. With some, though, not all, or even most, of Finn's anger subsided, he found himself once again concerned for his older brother's happiness and well-being.

Trust was still a far way out. He could love Jon, while approaching him with a careful space between them. One that would grow wider if Ana had the slightest resistance to Jon's presence. Finn would choose her without a moment's hesitation. He'd always choose her.

And Aleksei, his beautiful, kind-hearted son, who slept fitfully against his shoulder. *He won't improve until we're complete again. We're both broken; disconnected. And whatever bootless errand Nerys has us on only brings us further from being whole.*

Nerys called for Jon to slow as they approached a rural village. *Killianshire. Population 950. Since 1339.*

"Killianshire," Anne mused. "Why is that name familiar to me?"

The village boasted a single-lane road, so narrow Jon had to slow to a crawl when entering what passed as their town center. Past supper, no shops were open other than an apothecary, who was in the process of locking up. The street was otherwise quiet, and Finn had the keen sensation of being intruders.

Yeah, but what about this other feeling? Almost a magnetic tug. Like coming home after a long absence.

Some genetic, ancestral pull didn't seem entirely out of the realm of possibility. His mother's family was from Ireland, after all.

Past the center of the village they came upon a cathedral. A towering gothic structure, like so many others in Europe, but this one stood out because its garish size diverged entirely from the modest simplicity present in the rest of Killianshire.

An older man, a priest based on the cassock and collar, stood upon the steps, hands folded patiently across his generously rounded abdomen.

"Pull over here," Nerys directed hastily, in a tone suggesting the thought only just occurred to her.

Jon did as asked, maneuvering the car into the empty lot.

The priest knocked on the double doors of the church, then

descended the stairs, moving in their direction. As he did, the doors opened, and a handful of women exited, following him.

"Stay in the car," Finn instructed his son, planting a brief kiss against his forehead. "You too, Forbia." The dog offered a resigned huff, while Aleksei mumbled unintelligibly as his head fell against the headrest, back to sleep.

Jon and Anne stood facing the strangers, hands linked. Nerys smiled as they approached.

"Duchess Nerys," one of the women, the oldest, droned in a low, gravelly voice. "We are most pleased to renew our acquaintance."

"As I yours, Seara," Nerys replied, affecting a reverent bow. The gesture seemed sincere; whoever stood before the duchess was worthy of her veneration.

"You've brought the heir of Falias?" Seara inquired. The priest reached out to steady her. She leaned forward on a staff carved from some kind of unusual wood. Fair, similar to bamboo, but with lovely dark swirls that shimmered in the fading light.

"Aye," Nerys replied. "Until we arrived, I had no notion this was where we'd end up. Thorvald must have known."

"We've not heard tell of, or seen, Thorvald in many years," one of the younger women said.

"No, but he follows your movements closely. We all do."

"The Dragon Brotherhood," the priest replied. "A conclave which centers around our world, and yet we are not given membership."

"Best to accept the protection for what it is," Nerys suggested with a smile. "Your world is far more peaceful absent the Brotherhood's politics."

"Ahh!" Seara muttered, the wrinkles in her face contorting. She shuffled toward Finn, stretching her shriveled hands upward to his face. "The heir of Falias! A delight indeed."

Finn glanced to Nerys for support. She was smiling, but offered no extraction from the strange old woman groping his cheeks.

Lacking reprieve, Finn patiently allowed the assault, then said, "I'm Finn. This is my brother, Jon, and my cousin by marriage, Anne."

"Oh, I *know* who 'ye are," Seara replied. As she grinned, her face creased to the point her eyes nearly disappeared. "Where, then, is the heir of Murias?"

"Ana is in safekeeping with the Brotherhood," Nerys answered. *A lie,* thought Finn. *Only when she's returned to me will she truly be safe.*

Falias... Murias. Names Finn vaguely remembered from his conversation with Nerys, one filled with proper nouns, people who meant nothing to him at the time. Still meant nothing, though he suspected he was on the verge of finding out.

Finn politely stepped back, removing the old woman's hands from his face. "Why are we here?"

"Finnegan." The younger woman, who'd spoken earlier, stepped forward. Her face rang of familiarity. Or perhaps more that she reminded Finn of someone else, someone who shared her features. "You have many questions. I see them lingering behind your eyes, along with a tempest of emotions. My name is Nora Quinlan, and not long ago I had the pleasure of spending time with my niece Amelia and her husband, Jacob. You're desperate to get your wife back. We can help you, Finnegan. Our guiding purpose has been, and always will be, to protect the heirs. Your son may be half the prophecy, but you and Anasofiya are two of the four heirs."

Finn couldn't explain the dreamy peace that stole over him as Nora spoke. Nor the draw that kept him rooted firmly in the spot. A keen sensation he was returning home.

"Every day we spend without her is a day I come closer to

losing my son," Finn managed, through an unexpectedly choked voice. "I have to find her."

"You will. *We* will," Nora assured. Her voice soothed him, reminiscent of his mother's soft contralto when she sang him to sleep as a child. "There are things you must know, must learn, before you'll be of any help to her. I can guide you, and offer succor to your companions. They are welcome here, as you are. Please, Finnegan. I entreat you to join us."

Forbia, having extricated herself from the car somehow, nuzzled under Nora's outstretched hand. Finn shot the pup a puzzled glance, though his own reaction to Nora had been similar. Placid, searching. Accepting.

"You'll help me find her? That's a promise?"

"Aye, Finnegan." All the strangers' voices came together in a single vow. "We promise."

51
OLIVIA

Traffic on St. Charles was always a pain, but Olivia was positive the fates, or God, or whoever was leading this ship had offered up the worst traffic day of the year when they most needed to get home.

"Estella's thoughts have been all over the place," Leander had said, as they hit every single red light, often stuck for more than one cycle. He'd explained all he'd gleaned from his sister's thoughts, and they were still only halfway home. "She seems pretty certain our dead great-grandmother has asked her to kidnap your twins so Margarethe can do whatever it is she needs to become immortal." When Olivia moaned, Leander threw his hands up. "I never said it didn't sound crazy. Just the messenger here. We were trying to put our heads together and figure this out when you showed up."

Olivia, hard as she tried, could not wrap her head around the insanity of Leander's words. "And this... whatever it is she wants to do... she intends to kill them?"

Leander shrugged from the backseat, a gesture which

seemed more resigned than indifferent. "Seems like murder is a side effect, not a main objective."

"What kind of monster is your sister, that she'd agree to help with this?"

Leander shared a look with Lauren. "Have you ever *met* Estella?"

"I have," Olivia replied, flustered, not sure if she'd met her before or not. "But your father, Jasper, is a decent man." *If a tad strange.* "And Harriett is a lovely girl. And you..."

"I'm hardly a measure of my parents' success at childrearing."

"None of this matters!" Lauren exclaimed from the passenger seat. She bolted forward, turning to face them both. "Something terrible is going to happen. She used Quillan, and now Quillan is gone. He's the only one who might have known about what she planned. We have no idea where he is, or even if he's still..."

"He's alive," Leander assured her, unconvincingly.

"When this is all over, I'm going to look for him," Lauren replied, eyes narrowed. "I wish I had known before, how Estella was playing him, a pawn in this horribleness."

Leander smirked, clearly on the verge of a wisecrack, then stopped himself. "I hope he's deserving of your concern, Lauren."

Olivia slammed her hands across the top of the steering wheel as they missed another green light. "Hell's bells!" She rocked back in her seat, groaning. "Why did I leave my cell phone at home! Leander, let me borrow yours so I can call Greg. Or Grace. They need to get the twins out of there *now*!"

"Mine's dead."

"Heaven's sake! Lauren?"

Lauren flustered about in apology. "We left in such a hurry..."

A wave of lightheadedness rushed over Olivia, likely a result of her savage heart rate. "Sweet Jesus, is the entire universe conspiring against us?"

"Olivia, stay calm. We'll get there," Lauren soothed, but the young lawyer's eyes stayed trained on the traffic ahead.

"Margarethe," Olivia mused. Her hands began to tremble; she gripped the wheel tighter, trying to remember to breathe. In, good. Out, better. "She's been visiting them this whole time. This whole time! Befriending them, playing with them."

"I don't know anything about that," Leander said. "Until last night, I'd avoided listening to Estella's thoughts. Her head is a fucked up place."

"You were worried about Quillan." Lauren reached back and patted his knee. "You thought she might know where he was. Who would have thought you'd learn about all these awful things she was up to."

"Truly, I thought she'd killed him," Leander said in earnest. "Or paid someone to. While she watched. That's more her style."

"I still don't understand," Olivia repeated, frequently. A mantra easier than accepting and fully embracing the horrors ahead.

Leander leaned forward, between the seats. "We recently learned we are descendants of a secret race. Supernatural, immortal superbeings sprung from the fires of Norwegian glaciers. Is necromancy really such a stretch for you?"

Olivia took a sharp intake of air, readied a response, then gripped the wheel tighter. Talking pained her. Everything between where she was, and where the twins were, pained her. Leander's cool, indifferent shell didn't fool her, but it also pained her. Lauren's spastic mumbling, not surprisingly, pained her.

Drive. Only drive. Get there. Drive.

• • •

THEY ARRIVED TO DISCOVER GREG IN A PANIC. HIS FIRST WORDS tumbled out in a rush. "The twins and Katja are missing, and Grace might be dead! Why haven't you been answering your phone, Liv?"

Olivia spun on her husband. "What do you *mean* the twins are missing? And Katja? Did she take them?"

"They're gone. Not here. Didn't leave a note. What do you think I mean?"

"Greg, now is not the time for sarcasm."

"Do I look sarcastic? Do I look like I'm playing?"

"Where's Grace?" Leander interrupted the tense, confused quarrel. "I'm a healer. Not as good as Colleen or Luther, but if I can help, I will."

Greg pointed up the stairs, pacing the room without looking at anyone. "In the twins' room."

"You left her there?" Olivia gasped. Shaking her head, she stopped herself from further accusation. Greg had, clearly, been dealing with the lion's share of the drama before their arrival. "We need to start looking for Kat and the twins. We should split up... yes, we can each start down different blocks and—"

"Liv," Greg interrupted, rushing to her, taking her hands in his. His eyes searched her, pleading. "We can do that. But, honey." He moved his hands to her face, forcing her to meet his gaze. "Honey, there's a quicker way. I know you don't like to do it."

Olivia backed away. Not from him, but from the words. The very idea of what he was suggesting. "Greg... no..."

"It has to be Margarethe," Lauren replied in a haste, rushing forward. "She has them. What Katja has to do with it, I can't guess, but where else could they be than with her?"

"*Who* is Margarethe?" Greg asked.

"Not now," Olivia muttered, dropping her eyes to the floor. Her feet. The carpet. All things which were there in front of her, constants. She could count on them, as she could count on the sun to rise each morning, and the cicadas to sing in the summer. These elements of routine and comfort had stabilized her all throughout her life, shielding her from the erratic nature of her childhood, and the belief anything different was *bad*.

This same belief kept her from using her seer's vision. For years, images only came to her when she couldn't prevent them, an unwanted guest. Now, Greg was asking her to draw upon the part of herself that made her feel abnormal; unwanted.

Not for any old reason, Olivia. He asks for the twins. For children you're raising as your own. Love as your own. You know in your heart they aren't wandering the streets of the Garden District, lost. She has them. That bitch has them. If you don't do this, she'll get her vile wish. By the time you assemble the family to help, it will be too late.

"Liv?" Greg probed, gently.

"Call my mother to come get Rory. And hush, I need silence."

First, she searched for Stella. Her blonde, bouncy curls, and wide, curious eyes. Her high giggles when she played with Sebastian or that other... that awful other.

But neither Stella's face, nor future, presented itself to Olivia.

Sebastian's soft mop of golden hair. His authoritative stance, especially so for a child; the way Olivia sometimes had the temptation to defer to his wisdom. The impish smile, so like Alain, her dear brother, when he was younger and full of mischief.

Olivia locked on to an image. Sebastian. Katja. And... one other. And then another. And another.

Clarity.

Open your eyes.

"I KNOW WHERE SEBASTIAN AND KATJA ARE," OLIVIA PANTED, reaching for her keys before realizing she'd never released them. With a quick glance, she snatched her phone as well. "Greg, stay with Rory until my mother gets here. Then call me, and I'll tell you where to come. Watch for Stella, I couldn't find her. I can't see her. Oh, God, what does that mean?"

"It means Sebastian needs you more," Grace said, appearing on the upstairs landing. "I'm coming with you. And Leander, too."

Olivia would find out later what Grace had been through. What mattered now was they had a destination.

She kissed her husband and fled out the door, cohorts in tow.

52
ESTELLA

Meet me at Vivra sa Vie.

Estella heard the voice in her head as clearly as if it had been spoken by someone standing before her.

Margarethe spoke to her. Estella didn't know *why* she could suddenly communicate with the venerable spirit, but then Margarethe inadvertently provided the answer.

I have the boy. Find the girl. She escaped. Bring her.

So, the presence of Sebastian was enough to bridge the communication. This fascinated Estella, who had so many questions, but was aware this was most definitely not the time. Perhaps later, once Margarethe had come through, and Blanche, they could discuss the details over cocktails. Estella envisioned a future flanked by the two women, her idols, where no one could ever hurt her or mess with her again.

Estella slowed as she drove by the Claiborne house, but didn't stop. Margarethe was clear: the stupid girl had escaped. Estella's final test was finding her in time for everything to fall into place.

She didn't have to wander long. As she neared the end of the block, she noticed a small, blonde girl huddled on the curb, crying. Her arms wrapped around her knees, and she rocked herself back and forth. Another woman, someone kinder than Estella, would have been moved by the sight of this scared waif.

Estella pulled the car over, ignoring the fire hydrant. *Too easy. I am so close to having everything I ever wanted.*

Estella sauntered over to the quivering girl. The child's acute emotions annoyed her, but if she showed it, the child would run. She slapped on her best saccharine smile, an Estella signature, and reached out to touch the sniveling tot.

When the child lifted her head, a surge of white light coursed through Estella, nearly sending her careening into the street. The child's eyes pierced her soul, beseeching, relentlessly penetrating, awakening a dark corner of Estella's heart that had long lay dormant and unused.

What in the hell is happening to me?

Tears slid down her face and on to Estella's hand, a spray of warm liquid gold. Pulsing joy and warmth radiated from Estella's dampened hand down through her arm.

"Who... *are you*?" Estella whispered, unsure of what she was truly asking.

"My name is Stella. I'm afraid," the child answered.

"You don't have to be afraid anymore," Estella assured, in a voice that didn't sound or feel like her own. Not the one she'd lived with her whole life, but it was hers, and it felt more natural and real to her than the previous one. *How is this happening? I love this child. I don't even know her.*

I've never loved anyone.

"Grace said to stay here until the big hand on my watch goes here," the girl relayed. "But Riley says to find Quillan."

Riley! Another new sensation overcame Estella: A sense of purpose, one absent her own self-advancement.

They would find Quillan, and together, she and Quillan would protect this innocent.

The revelation was as clear as anything had ever been to Estella Broussard.

"Does Riley know where Quillan is?" Estella gently probed. "Did he say where we can find him?"

Stella succumbed to her sobs again. Estella took the girl into her arms, deluged with a wave of maternal instinct she would have bet her inheritance didn't exist. But the protective longing was here, and very real. While Estella questioned the origin—were they somehow planted, by this magical child or someone else?—her deeper voice, her very inner self, knew better. This child had stimulated a sense of altruistic purpose in her. She must follow the impulse.

Estella carried her to the car, placing her gently into the backseat. She buckled the girl in, then took her sweater and tucked it in under Stella's chin. *Stella. Estella. It's as if we were born for our fates to intertwine.*

"You're safe now. We will find Quillan, I swear it. If Riley is still talking to you, please beg him to help us. We're going to need it."

Estella flipped the car into gear and spun it around in one wide, arcing turn. She raced toward the highway, but as she merged on to the expressway, she headed in the opposite direction of *Vivra sa Vie*.

53
KATJA

The opportunity to end the Deschanel Curse—for real this time—lay before her. Finally.

Like any scientist worth their salt, Katja had made mistakes along the way. Few great problems were solved without many tests of the variables, and failures were par for the course. She'd been wrong about the path she took Alain down, but she could, nonetheless, feel confident in her approach now. Form a clear hypothesis, identify variables, perform experiment, draw conclusions, rinse, repeat.

Her gut and experience both told her this was it. No more rinsing, no more repeating. This puzzle fit together far more neatly than her last hypothesis, which, she could admit now, was not so much *the* answer as the best option they had at the time.

It had taken so little to convince one of her Guidry cousins to heal her spine when Greg was out on errands with Rory. Why she'd not allowed the repair before was an emotional enigma Katja was not yet ready to analyze. The simple fact was she needed the use of her legs. She needed to be whole again, physically at least.

Katja used only her side-view mirrors on the drive to *Vivra sa Vie*. She couldn't chance a glimpse at Sebastian, who she'd not seen since the week following his birth. Earlier, she'd called through his bedroom door, told him to come down and get in the car. She waited until he settled himself and she heard the seatbelt click, before sliding into the driver's seat, and promptly turned her rearview mirror far to the right, so as not to risk an accidental glance.

Katja watched for gaps in the levee providing a view of the Mississippi. Water had always given her strength. She loved the feeling of surrendering herself to her own natural buoyancy and floating through the soft currents. She used to scare her mother by lying on her back for hours, losing herself in her thoughts. The water over her ears muffling all sounds except the gentle wash of currents created by the pumps.

How courageous she'd been, in planning this! Making the decision to take the lives of her children, in order to save her family. The hours of justification; joy, even. A euphoria only one dedicated to the truth could fully understand.

Whenever sadness threatened, regret for how she now viewed the only children she would ever have, she promptly reminded herself what they were. What they represented. What they had become. And what must now become of them in order to finally stop the Curse that had plagued her family for far too long.

Courage did not require setting eyes on either of the children. On seeing her own bright eyes, or Alain's generous mouth. Her mettle relied on thinking of them as specimens in a petri dish. Organisms under the lens.

Stella, Specimen B, had disappeared before Katja could act, but perhaps the experiment could succeed with only one.

Katja drove, armed with the consolation of her research, ready to do whatever it took to lure this wretched ancestor forth and destroy her, once and for all.

Vivra sa Vie, then, was the only unknown variable. Nothing in her research, or extrapolation of facts, had given her an indication of where Margarethe would attempt her nefarious work.

That she would need to be close to her blood kin, to draw from their underlying strength, seemed a given. *Ophélie* was the solid center of this power. The plantation pulsed with blood memories of a hundred Deschanels, past and present. But Margarethe, that calculating despot, would know better than to go somewhere she could be so easily detected, and perhaps destroyed.

Most Deschanels lived scattered around the Garden District, or Lake District. Too crowded. Too public.

A half-dozen plantations fell under the Deschanel Trust, but most were in the midst of renovation, or open for public consumption.

The plantation of *Vivra sa Vie*, then. A guess as good as any. Owned by Augustus Deschanel, the property in Donaldsonville was used as a country house, or a retreat from the stress of city life. The very same property where Katja's Aunt Elizabeth had taken her life, in the name of the Curse, to save her remaining son. Weather and time had not yet worn away the stains of her choice.

"Where are we *going?* And where's Auntie Livvy?" Sebastian pouted. He'd been so silent up until now, Katja thought.

"Hush."

"Hmph!"

A vision flashed through her mind, of Alain sitting in the seat beside her, their children bickering over a toy in the back. Katja scolding them, and Alain suppressing a smile, telling her children will be children. Katja grinned in spite of herself.

This future was not hers, though. Only a nip at her courage, a nudge to back away from the tough work ahead.

Katja had nothing else to lose. She'd already bartered her soul that night by the lake, in the arms of Alain.

THE PLANTATION STOOD IN RELATIVE QUIET, INVADED ONLY BY THE soft sounds of insects and other small wildlife. No Deschanels here for a retreat, or any other reason, apparently.

Katja stepped out of the car, leaning her back against the door. She reached a hand out, and unlatched Sebastian's door. Closing her eyes, she beckoned him out and forward. "Go. Ahead of me. Don't turn around."

"*Where*, though? Why are you so mean?"

"Just go!"

The boy did as asked, a slouching shuffle ahead of her through gravel, toward the house.

"Around back," she ordered, unsure where the words came from. At least they'd be out of road view.

The child meandered around the house in an exaggerated manner. He stopped and turned to ask a question. Katja immediately barked, "Sebastian, turn around and keep going!"

His name, the one she'd given him herself, one Alain had loved, burned on her tongue. *Dammit. Not again.*

A large man-made lake spanned the majority of the rear property. *Most people don't know your uncle is an avid fisherman,* she recalled her mother saying. *On the rare occasion he takes a day off, he'll charter a boat. Pontchartrain, usually. Catfish, bass. At least until he had that ridiculous lake put in.*

The body of water was so large, the edges fanned out

toward the swampland backing the property. A frog leapt from a rock into the still water with a ringing plop.

"Call your mother, child," Katja ordered.

"But—" Sebastian floundered, caught between a secret and a lie.

"I'm here to help her, kid. Call her. Tell her you're ready. Whatever you do to get her attention."

The young boy grew quiet. Then in a low voice, he said, "She's already here. She's been waiting."

A breeze swept across the surface of the water, catching Katja's hair as it passed through. Unrelated, of course. Margarethe had no such powers, or she'd have used them. But the moment felt pivotal, and pushed Katja to action.

"Margarethe. We're here!" *Do your worst, bitch.*

The oak trees rustled, then came to an unnatural halt. Katja turned toward the sound of feet squishing in mud only to be knocked flat on her back.

The sky ebbed in and out of focus. The layers of clouds went perfectly still, then disappeared entirely.

You birthed a starlight awakener. A voice not her own, not from this time.

That's right. And now I'm giving him to you.

Generous. For your loyalty, you'll live a life such as you could never imagine.

I want nothing except peace for my family.

Where is Stella?

She was already gone when I thwacked the nanny.

Gone where? Estella was to have brought her.

No idea. You're asking the wrong chick.

Peace is fleeing and intangible. I cannot offer you such a thing.

You can. You can cease the plaguing of my family. So my brother can have children someday, and the Deschanels can thrive once again.

You believe, truly, this will grant you peace? You believe me to be the sole proprietor of all ill tidings befalling the Deschanels these past centuries? You know but a pittance.

I ask for nothing more. Whether your absence from our lives does, or does not, bring peace is not your problem. You will have your starlight awakener, but the cost is to leave us the hell alone.

You take after Blanche, though your blood connection to her is thin. She offered me two of her sons, but her requested exchange greatly differed from yours. She wanted me to secure her a vessel of her own. No different from me, as it turned out. But her sons perished. I could have told her they weren't starlight awakeners. Not even necromancers!

But you killed them anyway.

When you have waited as long as I, you'll take what you can get.

You're sure about Sebastian? Katja had her answer long before she'd arrived, but wanted to hear confirmation from the spirit. She had to be sure. Because once Margarethe took root inside Sebastian, Katja would destroy them both, and end the centuries of madness.

Of Sebastian, I have no doubt. I question whether I can achieve the transition without the girl, however.

You can. You must try. Tears burned behind Katja's eyes. She didn't know where they'd come from.

I will. With or without your permission. As you've aided me, though, I feel compelled to remind you that, in performing this act, in finally securing the physical form I've desired for so long, I'll no longer need the Deschanels. The act itself frees you from my attentions. Is there not anything else I can give you?

My life back. Alain back. My desires, and dreams. A restoration of my shattered heart and broken soul. A world where I could love my children. *There's nothing else. Just do it, and be done.*

Katja stumbled, planting one foot into the shallow bank of the lake. The cold startled her, and she whirled as her balance failed.

Sebastian scuffled over, reaching a hand to steady her. Before she could consider the act, Katja took her son's hand in hers, as he pulled her back to dry land.

Katja's mind compelled her to avert her eyes, but her heart could not. His tiny hand, pressed into hers, watching her with Alain's trust-filled gaze. Her flesh and blood, no matter the circumstances surrounding his birth or the truths of his life. She'd denied his existence to protect herself, not him. To shield her heart from the love she didn't believe herself still capable of. Or, maybe more truthfully, feared she could feel for a circumstance she'd created and could not take back.

Sebastian reached forward with his other hand. Before it landed, his chest arced forward, his eyes rolling back to the sky as his body shook, end-to-end. "Mama," he cried in a gurgled whisper, to one woman, or many.

"Sebastian!" Katja snapped him into her arms, shaking him. "Stop! Margarethe, he's not ready!"

The boy ceased convulsing. His eyes rolled forward and focused as his head came down. Mordant, shadowy, like the soul now within him.

Katja moved to pin Sebastian to the muddy ground when his hands shot up to grasp her throat. His lips peeled back in a sneer. Margarethe's lips. "You'll... stop... nothing!" she seethed. A boy's voice and a specter's words.

Katja sputtered as the blood rushed to fill her head. "Let... him..." Her jaw clamped down on her tongue and she whelped in pain.

What have I done? Did I not learn the first time, putting science before love? Facts before reason? He is my son! My flesh and blood.

Whether or not he is the starlight awakener, he is mine, and this bitch can't have him!

She drove her knee into his stomach with a burst of strength, hoping only to render Margarethe's energy temporarily startled, not to damage her son's body. Sebastian sprung forward, landing on his feet with solid dexterity.

"You can't have him," Katja spat, choking to regain use of her throat.

"It was too late for protests the moment you brought him into this world," Margarethe returned, through her son's mouth. "He was born for this, Katja. And since you insist, you'll die for it."

Katja had no weapon at her disposal to fight this being, other than the unexpected, but potently powerful, love for her son. She would get him back, or they would die together. The remainder of the fight left in her beat for Sebastian. "Do it, then!"

As she ran toward them, Sebastian's body remained rooted in place. A wave of something sharp—electricity, acute shock—pierced Katja's chest, sizzling through to her heart, her ribcage, and down into her belly. Back up, rocketing through her scalp, pushing to escape through her eyes. Blinded, Katja reached for her son's hand, but invisible bolts of lightning held her back, burning her up from the inside.

"When you greet your maker, remember, this was your choice," Margarethe said pointedly, through Sebastian's mouth, as she stood over the pulsating form of Katja's near-lifeless body. "You have none to blame but yourself."

Katja witnessed her own hand, reaching up, for Sebastian. Then her eyes closed and the world went dark.

. . .

Orange sun rays over the roof. Buzzing. Cicadas? Her limbs, electric? Pain fixed her in place.

Other voices floated in. Familiar, faraway. No, close. Above her, beside.

Grace Sullivan, the tiny ball of fire she'd not met but heard speak, through furnace grates, or walls.

"Not yours!" Grace cried, straining. Against something. What? Margarethe?

Grace, then, flying back. Backward past Katja and someone else... a man. And Olivia?

Katja's ears rang. She struggled to sit, to speak. She wished to call out to the others, as if they couldn't see her without the words.

She fell into the black again.

Awake. Grace's body radiated in solar colors as she stood engaged in the struggle Katja had started. Katja moved a shoulder, then an arm. Her legs were no use. She flapped her mouth open and closed, to no avail.

"YOU ARE NOT WELCOME HERE!" Grace projected, not her voice, not any human voice, though Katja witnessed the words leave her.

Sebastian—Margarethe—released a feral shriek, overflowing with boiling rage.

The same rage sustained Katja, and kept her heart beating. The walls of darkness, the call to disappear, closed in around her. With all the spirit of the girl she once was, she fought. She would live to see her son survive this.

"Mama!" Sebastian screamed. His own voice.

"Right here, baby boy," Olivia cooed, half-crying, half-screaming. A wind passed by Katja as Olivia rushed to scoop him up.

Right here, baby boy. Katja repeated the words, wishing she could utter them out loud.

Instead, she closed her eyes.

54
COLLEEN

A fish out of water best described Colleen's mood and mindset as she and Luther sat across from her niece, listening to her recap events of the past week.

She straightened her posture, and ran her hands down her pencil skirt, over her crossed legs. "I'd like to be sure I have this correct. You determined I was sufficient counsel on the matter of the twins' rapid growth but did not, at any point, consider I may have assistance to add in the matter of their special powers?"

Olivia folded her hands in her lap and made them the focal point for her ashamed gaze.

"The Magi Collective Council should have been involved in every step of this situation. From the beginning," Luther added, but his steeled scrutiny was aimed at Colleen, not Olivia. "As, however, you are not a member and have never expressed interest in being one, you would not have been aware of the vast resources, knowledge, and history at our disposal."

"You know my feelings on the Collective," Olivia mumbled into her lap. She lifted her head, sniffling. "I only wanted the best for Stella and Sebastian. I never asked for any of this!"

"Your feelings are irrelevant," Luther started in, but Colleen waved a command to halt.

"Olivia has been raised to believe differently than most of us. She took these children on from the goodness of her heart, and embraced them when they proved to have curious futures ahead. We cannot dismiss her goodwill," she said affably.

"Nor is it particularly useful to revisit the past," Colleen went on. "So let us discuss the current situation, as it stands, so that we may produce a plan to move forward with."

Luther grunted and thumbed his newly-developing beard. Nodded.

"Margarethe is gone, though we would be remiss if we believed this to be permanent. She will assuredly return, and when she does, her anger will be a hundredfold more than what it was before. We need to engage the Council immediately to find a suitable trainer for Sebastian. He must master how to block the specter's advances when she returns. This task is of the utmost urgency."

Olivia sniffled again. "We'll protect him, no matter what it takes. We'll do whatever you say."

Colleen reached over and offered a consoling pat. "I know, dear. We've been at cross-intentions in the past, but I have full confidence in the mothering you've given the twins. And will continue to provide, as you assist Katja."

"Child. Singular. The equally pressing matter at hand is that one of the twins is *missing*," Luther reminded them. "We can provide all the training in the world to Sebastian, but if this... *ancestor* finds Stella before we do, all is lost. The damage she might do in an immortal form is unpredictable. This is unprecedented, Colleen. We have nothing with which to compare it."

"Inestimable. We've never dealt with anything on this scale before," Colleen agreed, nodding in a slow, deliberate manner. "But perhaps others have. Contacts I trust outside the family."

Olivia snapped her tear-soaked face back. "There are other families like ours? And you talk to them?"

"Not exactly like ours," Colleen replied with a tight smile. She wanted to offer Olivia more, something substantial to comfort her. The last year had taken every bit of "something more" left in her, though. "You didn't really believe the Deschanels were the only mystical beings on this planet?"

"I never thought about it much," Olivia admitted. She pulled her sweater tight about her, looking as if she desired to disappear within. "We have to get Stella back. My seer abilities are so out of practice. A better seer could determine more, I know it."

"We go straight from here to a Council meeting," Colleen assured her. "There we will procure and engage all needed resources. A trainer, or trainers, for Sebastian. We'll engage the other seers to attempt to determine Estella and Stella's exact whereabouts, thanks to your vision they were together. Perhaps Nicolas can offer his expertise in nested visions. Beyond that, we will need to go outside the family. While Jasper is knowledgeable on the subject of ghosts, he holds no practical experience in the matter. Candlelight talks with Marie Laveau notwithstanding."

Luther stood, buttoning his sport coat. "Jasper will be worried after Estella and Leander, so I'll take on the burden of catching him up. He can help me retrieve the contact list from the vault and begin reaching out."

Colleen exhaled. "Someone should call Patrick Sullivan,

too, about Quillan, though it will be a tough discussion without being able to provide context."

"Tell him the truth. Estella drove him away when she tried to kill him," Olivia said. Her tears had faded to a dazed, hazy sadness. "Unless she actually finished the job."

"On second thought," Colleen said to Luther, as she escorted him to the door, "let's engage the seers first. We may be able to discover something tangible on Quillan's whereabouts and well-being, and that's a far better message for his father."

Luther nodded at them both and left.

"Why would Estella take Stella?" Olivia voiced, after Colleen situated herself to her left, wrapping an arm around her shoulder. "I'm grateful she betrayed her great-grandmother and this Margarethe creature, but why? What could she want with our sweet girl?"

"You'll drive yourself senseless with speculation," Colleen said, massaging Olivia's shoulder and arm. "We can't know until we rally the family, and find her. And we *will* find her, Olivia. We've suffered many setbacks over the years, but this is the first time, in centuries, we've ever had a real answer about what causes our pain. What caused our Curse, something I know you've never believed in but hope that now you can at least consider. To have a cause means an answer exists."

"I should have gone with Leander and Lauren after Estella," Olivia lamented. The last shudder of tears, a small gasp, left her.

"No, darling. Your place is here, with Sebastian and Katja. We will send resources to assist them once we have a direction. Not one stone will go unturned in our search to bring Stella and Quillan back to safety. Or in uncovering the method required to extinguish Margarethe for good."

“How are you so calm?” Olivia asked, eyes wide with obvious, and perhaps envious, incredulity.

Not so long ago, Olivia had voiced a similar question, a barb aimed at Colleen’s heart. Now, she looked at her aunt with a child’s curiosity, and a desire for someone to guide her.

Colleen pressed her head to Olivia’s. “I have no choice, dear. And now, neither do you.”

55
ESTELLA

"Almost there, baby girl," Estella called from the front seat. The child in the back gazed languorously out the window, fixated on the miles of coastline since they'd hit the 101.

"I know," Stella pertly asserted. Estella laughed to herself. Of course Stella knew; she'd been communicating with Riley on the entire journey across country. They were heading toward a quaint Oregon beach community on Riley's direction.

Estella had given significant thought, over more than twenty-five hundred miles, to what she would say to Quillan when she saw him, but none of her ideas seemed adequate. How could she say Stella had changed her? That, in the blink of an eye, in one single moment, this child had moved her heart and mind to a place she did not even know existed?

Quillan knew her. Quillan loved her. He had loved her in spite of everything she'd done to hurt him over the years. He may still love her, even after she tried to have him killed. She counted on this love to keep Stella safe, but what else did his love mean, to her?

She'd directed cruelty toward him for so many years. Laughed at his advances. Mocked him for his persistence. Ridiculed him for every choice he made, for every word out of his mouth. Estella was undoubtedly a different person now; like someone she had known in another life. But cruel Estella was only a few days past, and she could not so easily make up for years of heinous words and actions. She could not expect anyone—least of all Quillan, the one man who had loved her for who she was all along—to believe she had changed.

If she were being completely honest with herself, Estella didn't quite believe it, either. What if this was some bizarre dream, and tomorrow she woke up as herself again? Crazy, but it sounded far more likely than her spontaneously growing a heart and a conscience.

Sociopath, her high school principal had whispered to Estella's father. She wasn't supposed to hear, but telepaths often heard conversations they were not intended to be privy to. She hadn't been offended by the comment; she was inspired. It was a weakness to care too much about others, or to let those feelings consume and guide you. She was proud to love no one but herself. Happy to be self-serving and single-minded toward her own goals.

Estella loves you, and she loves us. She is just going through a phase, she recalled her mother saying to Leander and Harriett. No, it was not a phase, and no, she really did not love them. How could she love her simpering, alcoholic mother? Or her fraud of a father? Her loser brother or idiot sister? They were about as lovable as a mosquito landing on your arm for supper.

And yet… now a dull ache filled her chest when she thought of her mom's long blonde hair and gentle eyes, who yes, loved her spirits and had a flair for drama, but more importantly loved Estella. Her insipid, silly father, with a flawed sense of social decorum, but consistently gracious, to all, no matter their social standing or the width of their wallet. Leander *was* different, but he was also a caring, and kind man. And, now that she was allowing honest introspection, she admitted she'd been determined to hate Harriett from birth. Any female joining the family was a threat to Estella.

She had to approach redemption one step at a time. Quillan waited for her, though he did not know it. Very soon, she would be standing before him and he would be her judge and jury. He would need to decide if she was worthy of him, when not so long ago she had focused on reminding him he was unworthy of her.

56
FINNEGAN

Finn and Nerys sat with Flynn, known to some as Father O'Connor, Seara, and Nora Quinlan, at the wooden table in the cathedral's rectory. Their conversation to this point had consisted of wary glances, and a hesitance regarding who should speak first.

Jon and Anne had taken Aleksandr to the inn, at Finn's request.

"You're safe here," Nerys assured him. "You must believe I'd never bring you anywhere that threatened the safety of your son. Or you."

"Our safety here isn't what's on my mind right now," he replied. His eyes fell on the strangers, traveling the table and back again.

"Speak openly, Finnegan. You're amongst friends. I hope someday you see it that way."

"Excuse me if I've seemed rude in any way," Finn offered, affecting a gracious smile despite his exhaustion. "I'm aware there's a lot on the table, but I can't focus on anything beyond getting my wife back. So, speaking openly, I need to understand why I have a better chance of helping her with your assistance, than without. Otherwise, we're wasting time here."

The three exchanged looks with each other, then with Nerys. Finn disliked her sharing a moment with the others, feeling he'd earned Nerys' alliance squarely after all they'd been through.

"Nerys, I assume, has filled you in on the prophecy? Your role, and Aleksandr's?" Nora asked.

"She's told me about it. But if you want my opinion, ask me after I have Ana back."

More passed looks. Finn shifted one foot toward the door.

"Child, I'm no more interested in your opinion than I am your pretty face," Seara remarked through her heavy wrinkles. "The prophecy exists whether you have one or not."

"What my grandmother means to say," Nora jumped in, "is that the prophecy is real. As real as the trees and the ground under your feet, Finnegan. Your belief will not make it more so, nor will your disbelief dilute it. That you've arrived here is a blessing that cannot be ignored. Until this morning, when Seara received a vision, we did not know who you were. Or Ana, or Aleksandr. We subsisted on faith of your existence."

"Now faith has brought you to our doorstep," Flynn, the priest—Finn, when this was all over, would have to inquire how a druid becomes a Catholic priest—added. "The prophecy is aligning toward fruition, as Morrigan foretold."

"The prophecy is gonna have to hold tight until Ana is safe," Finn said, increasingly annoyed with his need for redundancy. The muscles in his calves tightened, flexed. He was prepared to make a run for it, if they were determined to keep him.

"We said we would help you. A promise we will keep,"

Nora placated, lowering her tone to something gentler. "But you cannot go into this blind."

"That's why Nerys is here. These are *her* buddies we're going to visit." The words held more accusation than he had intended.

"You are, what? Four grown adults, and a child? Against an army?"

"They're our *allies*. Why does everyone assume we'll need to fight folks who are supposed to be on our side?" When no one answered, he turned and directed the question to Nerys. "You've been keeping things from me. You can have your secrets, I don't need them. But if it involves Ana, you must tell me."

Nerys dropped her eyes, then diverted her gaze across the room. "I cannot tell you what I do not know."

"Then tell me what you *do* know."

She sighed. "Only that I have not had regular contact with any of them since you and I left Farjhem. Trygve and Thorvald have sent sparse communications, but they've... defected from the Brotherhood."

Finn blanched. "Defected? Why the hell for?"

"I do not know," Nerys answered. "But I have had no communiqué with anyone still in Agripin's entourage."

"I thought you guys were running this show? What happened to Agripin being your pawn?"

"I told you, I do not know!" Nerys cried, flying forward from her chair. She fled the room, rendering Finn dumbstruck.

"You don't know an ally from an opponent," Flynn summarized, an unnecessary clarification after Nerys' disturbing outburst.

"So, what—are you offering to come with us?" Finn asked the old man.

Father O'Connor leaned forward, laying both hands on the table. "I'm offering to teach you about who you are, Finnegan. About what it means to be a draoi."

The priest placed one hand to his heart. "And how you can use this knowledge to save your wife."

EPILOGUE

For the first few hours, Katja had pressed her face to Sebastian's chest, calmed only by the sound of his persistent heartbeat. The boy, muddled by all he'd been through, didn't resist or ask questions. Eventually, he fell asleep in her arms, succumbing to exhaustion.

She'd told Leander not to heal her, but he hadn't listened. *Sorry,* he'd said, not sorry at all, as he lay his hands on her, restoring her fortitude and physical strength. No healing, though, could repair her fragmented soul.

What had changed? She'd toiled over the question, which seemingly had no answer. She only knew the moment she *had* changed, and that it had been swift and decisive.

The scientist in Katja had perished, to be reborn as a mother.

"We will find your sister," she vowed, whispering the words to a softly snoring Sebastian.

Katja pushed back her guilt. The overwhelming need to blame herself for the problems at hand hadn't waned, but shifted. Her greatest sin—one she would spend all her life atoning for—was forsaking her children.

"Never again," she promised, sealing the words with a kiss on her son's forehead.

Estella knocked on the blue peeling motel door. The Silver Sands Motel didn't call to her finer senses, but it had a dreamy appeal, like all the motels she'd passed along the Oregon coast, on the route to Rockaway Beach.

When there was no answer, she experienced a fleeting panic, wondering if Riley had been wrong, or had somehow led them astray. But then, the door swung open and Quillan stood before her.

His raven hair stuck out haphazardly in all different directions, and his green eyes blazed as he looked into hers. *My god, he's handsome. He's always been handsome, and I've blatantly, rudely overlooked it.*

Quillan reached behind him, into his waistline, then looked behind and around her. *Dear me, he has a gun.* His first instinct seemed to be a sense of being trapped. Estella shook her head, and then reached out to touch his face.

Quillan cringed, but his eyes betrayed him. *He still loves me. He hates himself for it, but he loves me as much as he always has.*

"No one followed us," Estella said. Her voice rang low, lacking her normal coolness. She had never felt less confident in her entire life.

"Us?"

"I brought someone with me. She needs our help." Estella pointed toward the car, where Stella sat patiently in the backseat, still gazing out the window. Estella wondered what she was looking at.

Quillan only nodded. He didn't ask questions, though she

could hear many of them tumbling around in his brain. He was either too tired, or overwhelmed, to voice them.

He opened the door, inviting her in.

She motioned toward the car to let Stella know it would just be a minute. The girl exited the vehicle and meandered to the edge of the parking lot, gazing toward the path leading to the beach.

As Stella stepped inside, she noted the room's disarray: clothes scattered everywhere, to-go containers piled up on the desk next to a new laptop, the box it came in functioning as a second garbage receptacle because his can overflowed.

"You're different," he said finally.

"I am," she replied. There were so many other things Estella wanted to say, and knew she *should* say, but none would roll off her tongue.

"What happened after I left?"

"Everything," Estella said. "A long story. I'll tell you, if you let us stay."

"Why do you want to stay with me?" He sprawled on the bed, leaning back on his hands. He'd taken the gun out of his waist, and it rested on the bed now, taunting her.

In his dirty white t-shirt and running shorts, nothing had ever looked more desirable to Estella in her life.

"I'm not the same person," she choked out. *No, tell him all of it. Tell him how you feel, tell him what happened with Stella, how Riley can communicate still, through starlight awakeners! Tell him!*

"I can see that. Neither am I."

No. She supposed he wasn't. Though she'd detected the love in his eyes, he was not warming to her as he once did. He didn't fall at her feet like a lovesick puppy, and wasn't the slightest bit nervous around her. He seemed a hardened version of the man he once was.

"I came because I wanted to be near you," she said finally. Closer to the truth, and to what she was feeling.

"Get your own room," Quillan said, gesturing toward the door with his gun. "And I'll let you know when I'm ready to talk."

"You trapped me," Finn accused, his words weary. His fight on the matter had fled at the recognition they were walking into a tenuous situation.

"I did no such thing," Nerys countered, recovered from her earlier frenzy. "You know this, but hold on to your anger out of stubbornness. Such a base, human trait."

Finn cracked a smile in spite of his defeated spirit. "You wouldn't be the first to accuse me of leading with stubbornness."

"She would want you to do this," Nerys countered. They both knew whom "she" referenced. "She'll blame herself if you rush in unprepared and get yourself maimed. Or killed. Worse, for Aleksei to fall to harm because you didn't stop to formulate a plan."

Finn sunk into the plush sofa of the inn. "I could murder Agripin. I still might."

"I won't stand in your way," Nerys said, as Nora emerged from the kitchenette with a mug of tea for them both. "And something else to consider, Finnegan, is that Aleksei needs training of his own. The longer he goes without, the more danger he is in."

Finn sighed.

"How long do you think we'll be here?" he asked Nora, as he accepted the teacup with a nod of thanks.

"It has been too long since we've properly trained a draoi,"

Nora answered, considering with a thoughtful expression. "We tried with Jacob, but they fled before we could finish."

"Where did they go, anyway?"

"*When* is a better question."

"Sorry?"

Nerys sat beside him, eyes wide and interest piqued. "You're not suggesting..."

"Aye, I am. Jacob time danced into goddess-only-knows when and where. Untrained, he may not be able to come back. Padraig and Flynn have tried many times to find them, to no avail." Nora looked up. "Perhaps you might be willing to try, Finnegan."

Finn set his tea on the table and stood. "Time travel? I assume that's what you're both making vague references to?"

Both women nodded. "A trait singular to draoi," Nora added. "And thus, one you possess as well. With training."

Finn swallowed. "With training. You want me to—wait, why am I even questioning this? Or questioning anything?" His laughter puzzled them, and Nora asked if he was okay when he fell back on the sofa, doubled over. "Which one of my relatives was a mermaid? Or a centaur? I've always wanted to meet a unicorn."

"Finnegan," Nerys chided with a head shake.

"I believe you," he managed through tear-filled laughs. "I absolutely believe you, and yes, I'll buy your oceanfront property in Arizona." *And if I stop laughing, I'll cry, or punch something, or throw this couch across the room, and I owe it to Ana not to do any of those things.*

"Will you help us?" Nora pressed, nonplussed but determined. "If I'm right, the prophecy binds you to Amelia and Jacob. And if so, once properly instructed, I believe you, and you alone, can find them."

Finn steadied himself long enough to answer. "On one condition."

"Yes, we will devote all our energies to helping you find and retrieve Anasofiya."

"Two conditions," he clarified. His smile puzzled them, he could see, and it ignited something he hadn't felt in a considerable while: fun. Easiness.

"Go on," Nora urged.

Finn looked at Nerys. "While I'm training, you're going to bring Thor and Trygve. They're going to help us. And they're gonna bring their other defector guerrilla buddies. No, this isn't negotiable, Nerys. Stop searching for a rebuttal."

"I'll do what I can," the duchess replied, with a wary gaze. "These are beings older than I. They answer to no one."

Finn locked his eyes to her. "Then let them answer to the heirs of the prophecy."

THE HINTERLAND VEIL EXCERPT

Nicolas Deschanel negotiated the cavernous central hall at The Gardens, his footfalls echoing across a valley of ancient marble. The assuming rows of Corinthian columns, to his left and right, provided both vital supports to this generations-old manor, as well as serving a reminder of its colossal authority.

No matter the number of times he'd traversed the main connector of his aunt's home, Nicolas always paused, momentarily, questioning whether he was headed in the correct direction. Even among the looming Victorians and Greek Revivals of the Garden District, The Gardens felt excessive. Garish, and out of place. As if Zeus had thrust his palace on Mount Olympus down to earth, and it landed in the heart of Uptown New Orleans.

Of course, the Deschanels never did anything halfway. Not architecture, not love. Halfway-loving got Nicolas into this situation. All-the-way, soul-deep love is what brought him to The Gardens, desperate for answers, and as yet unsure if he would ever find them.

Aunt Colleen hadn't hesitated when he called, weeks ago,

asking for help, a weakness until now he'd prided himself on rarely indulging. She had two rooms waiting for him when he showed up with a dazed Mercy on his arm. *Of course, darling, you're welcome to share a room as often as you'd like. I imagine you'll each want your privacy at times, though.*

As with all things that mattered, Colleen was strides ahead, thinking through logistics Nicolas couldn't comprehend because he was so rooted in the terrifying *present.* She'd been right, unsurprisingly. During their tenure at The Gardens, Nicolas and Mercy had slept apart far more than together, a statistic that caused him as much relief as distress.

Nicolas wasn't equipped for this. To love Mercy as he did had changed him. To ease her through an apparent mental breakdown, culminating in her soul-deep belief she carried the child of her god, Emyr, placed him so far from his element he sometimes longed for the easiness of his debaucherous youth.

Not enough for him to turn from Mercy. Adoration turned to affection, eventually to love, and despite his best efforts to fuck it up, he'd breached a critical precipice in his reasoning. He'd committed himself to her, to the bitter end, or the beautiful one... fate deciding.

His lover's delusions seemed a small consequence compared to the other events recently striking the family. The arrival of the necromancer, the starlight awakeners, and the near-fulfillment of the myths of midwinter had thrown every other priority into a tailspin. Three Deschanel Magi Collective Council meetings had been called since he and Mercy arrived. The immediate danger had been tempered, but their crazed ancestor, Margarethe, was still on the run, somewhere, and one of Katja's twins was also missing. Until both could be located, the family remained in peril again.

And when were they not? He couldn't recall a time where talk of the Curse wasn't front and center at every family event.

And now the problem had evolved to include another adversary.

Personally amazed at his willpower to even drag himself to attendance of the Council sessions, Colleen quickly brought him back to reality, finally chastising him for his daydreaming at the end of the massive oaken slab that passed for a table. He'd jokingly asked her once if they imported the thing from the mammoth dining hall at Windsor. She hadn't laughed, but she also hadn't denied it. *You are my eldest brother's only son, and in need of aid, but that does make all your behavior beyond reproach.*

Colleen found him gazing up the double staircase. "Most things, whether it be flora or people, thrive while visiting The Gardens. You've done nothing but wilt, dear nephew."

Nicolas stared down at his shuffling feet, unable to muster the smartass retort she'd always expected from him. "I can't go back to *Ophélie*."

Indeed, he'd done everything to avoid returning, even paying Oz's full attorney salary to reside there and replace him as master until he could sort himself out. His kind best friend had gone as far as pulling his children out of their school, enrolling them in a homeschool program.

He sighed, casting a glance toward the oiled portrait of his grandfather, August. Nicolas often wondered what his grandfather would think of him if he'd lived to see the family now; of all August's grandchildren, only one male had been born bearing the name Deschanel, and Nicolas had done everything in his power, sometimes intentionally, often not, to squander that honor. Bestowing the right of heirdom on Aleksandr had been the closest thing he could muster to a course correction. Hopefully, Ana's son would do better with the privilege than he had.

"A family full of goddamn healers, and not a one can help her."

Colleen rested a hand on his mid-back, and walked with him, steering him toward the rear of the house. "Nicolas, in all my travels and studies, I've met few who could heal a troubled mind. Understand, the ones I *have* met did so by transferring the pain to themselves. You can imagine the sacrifice in such an act."

"Anyone can be bought for the right price," Nicolas grumbled with a sneer he didn't feel. The harsh expression faded to a frown. "You know you can kick us out whenever you want."

His aunt stepped out onto the back porch, as broad as the dining room. "Don't be silly. If I had it my way, my children, my nieces, and nephews, would all be under one roof." She evidently caught his bewilderment in her peripheral. "You're the Deschanel anomaly, Nicolas, craving solitude and isolation. The rest of us feel greater in the presence of more of us. Even when gathering for wakes and funerals, which we've done far too often of late, I draw strength from our masses." Her smile was aimed away, almost separate of the two of them. "I digress. No, my words weren't meant to drive you away. Rather, I was hoping to motivate you. I know you came here seeking answers, but have you found any?"

With a brief hesitation, Nicolas shook his head. "I'm more and more convinced she's gone completely insane. And that, even knowing this, I love her more every day. Doesn't make a damn bit of sense."

"Her state of mind or your feelings for her?"

Nicolas sighed, then half-grinned. "Both."

Colleen nodded toward a plush chaise on the flagstone patio. He sat, and she took the one across from him, sheltered by palmetto and bird of paradise. Autumn was nearly upon them, but the heat hadn't dwindled with the changing season.

"Your ability to love another may be shocking to you, but I've watched you grow from boy to man. Your passions have always run deep, Nicolas. The variable has always been where you chose to swing them."

Nicolas took the glass of sweet tea from Aria, Colleen's head of household, who'd appeared as if on schedule and shrugged. Said nothing.

"As to Mercy's mind... we are still learning about who the Deschanels are, and where we originate," Colleen went on, drawing a sip from her own tumbler. "What it is to be Empyrean, or at least, to share their blood. By all accounts, Mercy's experience of being born Empyrean, dying as one, and being resurrected as human is wholly unique. We can't possibly know what she's going through, or what she's up against, intrinsically and otherwise. And without that knowledge, helping her becomes an exercise in intelligent guesswork and experimentation. Mostly the latter."

"She spends her days resting or praying. It never occurs to her the god who supposedly bestowed on her the next coming of Emyr was the same one who fucking abandoned her in her final moments," Nicolas rattled, not bothering to disguise his bitterness. "I could have expected her coming out of that an atheist, but this?"

"Faith is a powerful, eternal phenomenon," Colleen said. "One that sometimes rides the border of fanaticism and fantasy because throwing your control and life into the hands of something more omnipotent brings tremendous comfort in a world filled with chaos. That same abandonment you speak of, to Mercy, reads like a test from Emyr. She's passed this test and been rewarded. As she sees it."

"And how am I supposed to contend with her ridiculous, thousands-years-old dogma?"

"For starters, never use the word 'ridiculous' to describe another's beliefs."

Nicolas affected the start of an eye roll and stopped. "Fine. And I wouldn't, to her. I haven't. But, you know, a part of me wondered, even knowing it couldn't be possible, if what she believed really happened to her? Who am I to say Emyr didn't knock her up? That's why I brought her here. If anyone could put the sanity caboose on the crazy train, it's you."

Colleen nodded. The soft whir of the outdoor fan kicked in, followed by a fine, cool spray from the misters. They both closed their eyes, breathing in the relief. "While I can't speak to her faith, I've confirmed beyond a doubt she is not with child. Divine or otherwise."

"All right. So she's not pregnant. I'm wilting here, according to you, apparently, whatever that means. I haven't figured out yet how to fix her special variety of insanity. I'm hoping you have a Hail Mary suggestion because I'm at a loss." *Most of all, I can't return to* Ophélie. *My failings as a man, as an heir, start and end there. If I can't fix Mercy, I'm not worthy of the designation.*

"Have you considered stepping out of your comfort zone, and attempting to relate to Mercy on her level?"

"Sorry?"

Colleen set her glass down, crossing her legs. Her manicured hands fell over her knee as she watched him. "Consider the moments in your life when others have tried to convince you of the error of your ways. What was your natural inclination?"

"For them to fuck off."

"Of course, it was," she answered, unruffled by and entirely used to his colorful command of language. "Imagine, instead, if they'd gone along with your mischiefs? Tried to understand and even join you?"

"I can't picture you or any of my other aunts or uncles closing the bars down on Frenchmen with me, but okay. The point?"

"Instead of trying to convince Mercy of her error, why not instead try to see things through her eyes? Connect on her level. Suspend your disbelief, despite the hardship of such an endeavor. See her world."

"Aunt Colleen, she's *crazy*. And I've dated my share of crazies. This one chick I was with for a hot minute created her own ass-backward version of BDSM, but whenever I tried to use the safe word, she'd crack me across the face and scream at me to call her Xena—"

Long sigh. "Nicolas."

He held up his hands. "I'm just saying. I'm no stranger to crazy women, but this is the first one I've ever wanted to *fix*."

"Crazy is often a matter of perspective. To attack a problem, you must understand the source. And yes, that is my medical opinion as well." With a slight start, Colleen checked her watch and stood. "I must return to the hospital, but think about our conversation. You've already committed to the task. Now you need to define it."

Mercy hadn't emerged from her room once that day, a sign he'd come to recognize as her need to be alone in prayer. A rescinded invitation, if her silence was even an invite in the first place.

Nonetheless, Nicolas paused at her doorway. He slipped into the darkened room. The only sounds were an overhead fan and her light, even breaths.

To attack a problem, you must understand the source.

Mercy's face was a canvas of blissful peace, her silver hair —a gift of her resurrection—brushed off her face, cascading down the pillow. A band of it trailed over the bed's edge.

Walking away, as he always had before, whenever the pleasure of learning about another turned to the acceptance of baggage, no longer tempted him.

Yet staying terrified him.

Loving her frightened him.

Suspend your disbelief. See her world.

"I need your help, Mercy. I need you to show me."

Pick up your copy of *The Hinterland Veil* now, and have it ready to curl up at your next reading session!

ALSO BY SARAH M. CRADIT

KINGDOM OF THE WHITE SEA

Kingdom of the White Sea Trilogy

The Kingless Crown

The Broken Realm

The Hidden Kingdom

The Book of All Things

The Raven and the Rush

The Sylvan and the Sand

The Altruist and the Assassin

The Melody and the Master

The Claw and the Crowned

THE SAGA OF CRIMSON & CLOVER

The House of Crimson and Clover Series

The Storm and the Darkness

Shattered

The Illusions of Eventide

Bound

Midnight Dynasty

Asunder

Empire of Shadows

Myths of Midwinter

The Hinterland Veil

The Secrets Amongst the Cypress

Within the Garden of Twilight

House of Dusk, House of Dawn

Midnight Dynasty Series

A Tempest of Discovery

A Storm of Revelations

A Torrent of Deceit

The Seven Series

1970

1972

1973

1974

1975

1976

1980

Vampires of the Merovingi Series

The Island

and more

The Dusk Trilogy

St. Charles at Dusk: The Story of Oz and Adrienne

Flourish: The Story of Anne Fontaine

Banshee: The Story of Giselle Deschanel

Crimson & Clover Stories

Surrender: The Story of Oz and Ana

Shame: The Story of Jonathan St. Andrews

Fire & Ice: The Story of Remy & Fleur

Dark Blessing: The Landry Triplets

Pandora's Box: The Story of Jasper & Pandora

The Menagerie: Oriana's Den of Iniquities

A Band of Heather: The Story of Colleen and Noah

The Ephemeral: The Story of Autumn & Gabriel

Bayou's Edge: The Landry Triplets

For more information, and exciting bonus material, visit www.sarahmcradit.com

EMPYREAN & QUINLAN

EMPYREAN & QUINLANENCYCLOPEDIA

Aanya: A kind and beautiful Empyrean Agripin once loved, but was forbidden from claiming as his duchess her due to her lack of lineage.

Aidrik (Also: Aidrik the Wise): Once a well-respected member of the Eldre Senetat. After Aidrik discovered their true nature, he sliced the Mark of Emyr from his face, freeing him from the Senetat's tethers. He met and saved Anasofiya from death, becoming her evigbond. Lived in a triad with Anasofiya, and her husband Finn, until his death, at the hands of the Senetat.

Aleksandr: Empyrean son of Anasofiya, Finn, and Aidrik. Shy, introspective. Named heir of the Deschanels by Nicolas. A mystic, and time shaper, whose abilities are still surfacing.

Anders: An Empyrean Mercy co-habitated with for a short period of time. She believed him Ascended, but he was, actually, a scout for the Brotherhood, under the direction of Thorvald. His most recent assignment brought him to *Ophélie*, where he is tasked with training and protecting the Brotherhood children.

Arborkinetic: A form of telekinesis involving flora. A strong arborkinetic can command plant life to do their bidding, and some can communicate with plants. Anne Fontaine Deschanel and Duchess Nerys are both arborkinetics.

Ascension (Also: Grand Ascension): The ultimate death and rebirth all Empyreans are promised. It is tied to Emyr's Mark, which is said to come alive when their time is near. Once active, the mark is then supposed to usher them through death and rebirth, into the arms of Emyr. The truth is the mark is simply an infusion of dark magic administered by the Eldre Senetat, from which they control the activation and subsequent death of Empyreans.

Astrid: Brotherhood leader of Ireland and the British Isles, alongside her evigbond, Birger. Birger and Astrid are in the minority in their decision to make peace with Quinlans. They also co-exist peacefully with humans in the nearby villages where they live in a tribe of other similar-minded Empyreans. Many look to them as the moral compass of the Brotherhood. They have one child, Eydis.

Baldur: A sadistic scout for the Senetat who captures Amelia and Jacob, torturing them for information. Is killed by Jacob.

Bestiakinetic: One who can commune with animals. Finnegan becomes a bestiakinetic after being given the Sveising. Yiva and Jorun are also bestiakinetics.

Birger: Brotherhood leader of Ireland and the British Isles, alongside his evigbond, Astrid. Birger and Astrid are in the minority in their decision to make peace with Quinlans. They also co-exist peacefully with humans in the nearby villages where they live in a tribe of other like-minded Empyreans. Many look to them as the moral compass of the Brotherhood. They have one child, Eydis.

Blacksmith: Forger of Ulfberht, and creator of Empyrean Steel.

Bodhran: Goatskin drum used in Quinlan ceremonies.

Brotherhood: See "Dragon Brotherhood, The."

Brother of Emyr (Also: Sister of Emyr): Another way to reference a halfling (or, someone who has both human and Empyrean blood).

Brynja: One of the oldest, original Empyreans. Together with her partner, Einar, they are Brotherhood leaders, residing in Russia. Part of Runa's rebels who escaped after her execution, they are often called, by Runeans, "Adam and Eve."

Child of Man/Men: What Empyreans call humans.

Christiane de Laurent: Aidrik's original evigbond. Human. Lived at the end of the 16th century, as a courtesan of the French court. Wife of Marquise Deschanel, and mother of Claude.

Cianán (Also: Jacob Donnelly): One fourth of the prophecy, descended from the Tuathan tribe of Gorias. He has been reincarnated over thousands of years, with his lover, Cerridwen. Their journey evolves in each lifetime, with the ultimate test being their love bringing them together in their final lifetime, when they have no memory of former lives, thus fulfilling the prophecy. Their child is meant to join with the descendant of Falias and Murias. Jacob is the reincarnated soul of Cianán.

Cerridwen (Also: Amelia Donnelly): One fourth of the prophecy, descended from the Tuathan tribe of Findias. She has been reincarnated over thousands of years, with her lover, Cianán. Their journey evolves in each lifetime, with the ultimate test being their love bringing them together in their final lifetime, thus fulfilling the prophecy. Their child is meant to join with the descendant of Falias and Murias. Amelia is the reincarnated soul of Cerridwen.

Claude Deschanel (Also: Viscount Deschanel): The first halfling Deschanel, being both human and Empyrean. Child of Christiane and Aidrik.

***Crann bethadh*:** Also known as the "Tree of Life," and the center of the Quinlan tribe. It gives life to the tribe, by providing everything they need, from food to shelter. Also a portal between worlds, and the spiritual link to the goddesses.

Crimson Guard: The official guard of the Farjhem, under command of the Senetat. Their uniform consists of blood-red robes.

Cumdach: A lavishly ornamented shrine used in Quinlan ceremonies.

Cyler: Agripin's young, brash second-in-command, and lover. Often shirks orders and goes his own route, though he is known for being excellent with strategy. Is a frequent visitor to Oriana's Menagerie.

Dagr: 7,000 years old. Born without Senetat knowledge, and is one of the Brotherhood leaders, residing in Morocco.

Daughter of Emyr (Also: Son of Emyr): Referencing pure-blooded Empyrean women.

Deschanel Magi Collective: A secret, ancient society, created with the intention of cataloguing all the family's abilities, as well as protecting and preserving the family. Each generation has a Magistrate, the current one being Colleen Deschanel.

Dragon Brotherhood, The: Secret organization of Empyrean rebels. There is no central leader, but instead regional leaders across the world. Some leaders are ready for battle, others content to live in peace.

Dragon Empire, The (Also: Dragon Brotherhood, The): Another name for the wider Dragon Brotherhood.

Draoi: Male Quinlan. It is said these males are sacred, as their occurrence usually portends something important, and prophetic. Draoi are often quite powerful, able to spin wards and time dance. To birth a draoi is to be considered blessed. Male druids often come into their powers when they reach sexual maturity. Attempting to draw from them earlier can sometimes lead to disastrous results. Jacob, Finnegan, Padraig, and Father O'Connor are all draoi.

Drekar: A term of familiarity amongst the Brotherhood. Translates roughly to "dragon."

Duchess Nerys: Nomadic daughter of Grand Emperor Aeron, and sister to Agripin and Oriana. Known for her love of all creatures, and her call to traveling. A bestiakinetic, with loyalties to no one and nothing except peace. Joins forces with the Brotherhood, as she believes they are most likely to achieve that.

Duchess Oriana: Beautiful, wayward daughter of Grand Emperor Aeron, sister to Agripin and Nerys. Known for having a menagerie of human pets, and for her cruelty toward defectors. Is loyal to the Senetat.

Einar: One of the oldest, original Empyreans. Together with his partner, Brynja, they are Brotherhood leaders, residing in Russia. Part of Runa's rebels who escaped after her execution, they are often called, by Runeans, "Adam and Eve."

Eldre Aeslius: One of the nine members of the Eldre Senetat. Following the events at Aidrik's execution, his fate is currently unknown.

Eldre Brutus: Was originally a member of Emperor Elof's privy council, but when he discovered Elof was plotting with rebels, Brutus betrayed and exposed him. The Senetat "Ascended" Elof, giving the crown to his son Aeron. Following the events at Aidrik's execution, his fate is currently unknown.

Eldre Cassian: One of the nine members of the Eldre Senetat. Following the events at Aidrik's execution, his fate is currently unknown.

Eldre Felix: One of the nine members of the Eldre Senetat. Following the events at Aidrik's execution, his fate is currently unknown.

Eldre Lucrecia: One of the nine members of the Eldre Senetat. Following the events at Aidrik's execution, her fate is currently unknown.

Eldre Maxima: One of the nine members of the Eldre Senetat. Has been a secret sympathizer of the Brotherhood for many years, and officially joined their cause following the events at Aidrik's execution.

Eldre Tacita: One of the nine members of the Eldre Senetat. Following the events at Aidrik's execution, her fate is currently unknown.

Eldre Valerius: One of the nine members of the Eldre Senetat. Right hand of Grand Eldre Servius. Following the events at Aidrik's execution, his fate is currently unknown.

Eldre Senetat, The: The ruling government over the Empyrean race. Established many millennia ago, they claim to be blessed by Emyr, and charged with doing His will through enacting and protecting laws. The Senetat grew corrupt with this power, and unknown to most Empyreans, are controlling the fates of all citizens. The creation and installation of Emyr's Mark is the vehicle by which they exact their control.

Empath: The ability to sense feelings, emotions, or sensations in others. There are varying degrees of empaths. Amelia Deschanel is considered the strongest empath in the family. Lucia and Livia are also empaths.

Empyrean (Also: Farværdig): Also known as the Farværdig ("Father's Chosen"), Empyreans are as old as man, and similar genetically, but with several key differences. Where some DNA is dormant in humans, the entire strand is active in Empyreans, giving them special, paranormal abilities, including greater strength and speed, and immortality via perfect cell replication. Their home is Farjhem, in the northern expanses of Norway, but most Empyreans live scattered throughout the world, blending in with men. All Empyreans are born with red hair (which fades to a chromatic silver as they age), and are exceptionally tall. They are also primarily solitary, not subscribing to traditions such as a nuclear family, marriage, or commitment. The exception to this is evigbond. In their early days, they enjoyed a strategic alliance with Quinlans, but, once broken, both races were thrust into strife.

Empyrean Laws: Mandates set by the Eldre Senetat. include regulations around childbirth, mating with humans, and other fundamental freedoms.

Empyrean Steel (Also: Crucible Steel): A rare steel with high carbon content, smelted in a small furnace, and cooled slowly. In swords, it was both strong, and flexible. The technology was not used anywhere else in the world, and was considered better than Damascus Steel, which is the closest point of comparison.

Empyrean traits: Born of fire. Elevated body temperature. Red hair (the redder the strands, the more pure the blood) that takes on silver chromatic hues as they age. When emotions are heightened, they are said to emit an orange glow. Most have pale, smooth skin, and are very tall. All have special telepathic/telekinetic abilities, with some stronger than others. Average lifespan is two thousand years, though it is believed without the mark, an Empyrean could be functionally immortal.

Emyr (Also: Our Father): God, to Empyreans. He is represented by a phoenix, rising from the ashes.

Erikr: Brotherhood resistance leader who led one of the only semi-successful rebel revolutions after Runa's. Was executed in a block of ice. Leader of the Second Runean War, and considered the father of the Dragon Brotherhood, which was formed with the help of Ptolemy I.

Etheric Summoning (Also: Etheric Summoner): More rare than a mystic, an etheric summoner can draw from their greatest weakness and manifest it into a physical strength. Also known as a wraith. Anasofiya is an etheric summoner.

Evigbond: The physical and chemical bonding process that occurs when an Empyrean meets their permanent mate. It is irreversible, and only severed by death. An evigbond between Empyrean and humans is especially potent. Aidrik's first evigbond was Christiane, and his current is Anasofiya. Mercy experienced evigbond with Nicolas, until her "death." Evigbond can occur in two different ways. The first is an uncontrolled, chemical reaction. The second is through consummation.

Eydis: Fifty-year-old daughter of Brotherhood leaders Birger and Astrid. She is halfway to maturity, and emotionally equivalent to a young girl of around nineteen. Wide-eyed, rebellious, but kind-hearted. She sees how in love her parents are because of their evigbond, and is determined to find hers. Her birth accompanied a year of great prosperity for crops in Ireland. Is an illusionist with a specialty in influencing.

Falias: One of the four tribes of the Tuatha Dé Danann. All Quinlans descend from one of these four tribes. The tribe of Falias is mentioned in The Prophecy as such: *A male Quinlan, pure of heart, and a special affinity for animals.* It is not yet known who the subject of this reference is.

Far: Empyrean word for father. Can be used by a child speaking to a parent, or in reference to Our Father, Emyr.

Fardag (Also: Father's Day): Annual Farjhem celebration held in homage to Emyr.

Farjhem: The homeland of the Empyreans. Translated to "Father's Home." Located between two glaciers in northern

Norway, it is not accessible by anyone except Empyreans, or those with Empyrean blood.

Farsengel: The place of law and order in Farjhem, where suspected criminals are sentenced and detained awaiting further punishment. Many stories high, the outside edges contain hundreds of cells, and the inside of the arena has a large stage.

Farskilt: Deep in the bowels of Farjhem, beneath a volcano. "Separated from father." Empyreans are sentenced here for "rehabilitation" when they commit spiritual offenses. Citizens are told that offenders are "reunited with Emyr" and the end of their rehabilitation results in guaranteed Ascension. The reality is they are labor mines, and Empyreans work there until their inevitable starvation and death. The Empyrean equivalent of a prison camp.

Farvann River: (Also: River Farvann): The river flowing through the fjord and glaciers of Farjhem.

Farværdig (Also: Empyrean): See "Empyrean."

Father O'Connor: A draoi descended from the tribe of Gorias, and the man who saved Jacob from tragedy as a youth, sending him to New Orleans. Brother to the tribe elder, Seara. Great-uncle of Amelia.

Feast of Officium Maximus: Once every hundred years, the Scholars graduate their group of fledgling Empyreans into the world. This ceremony, for which many return home, is accompanied by a great celebration.

Findias: One of the four tribes of the Tuatha Dé Danann. All Quinlans descend from one of these four tribes. The tribe of Findias is mentioned in The Prophecy as such: *A female Quinlan, and halfling Empyrean, reincarnated over two-thousand years, originally Cerridwen. Lover of Cianán.* Amelia Jameson Donnelly is the subject of this reference.

First Father: When an Empyrean child has multiple

fathers (via Sveising), the initial father, at conception, is referred to as First Father.

First Runean War: Resistance to the creation of the Eldre Senetat, led by Runa, a warrior who represented the opinions of many Empyreans. Despite her strong supporters, the rebels were destroyed, and Runa publicly executed. Their stunning defeat weakened the resolve of many Empyreans who believed in her cause (henceforth dubbed Runeans by the Senetat), and most went into hiding.

Fledglings: What the Empyrean youth are referred to when they reach the age of spiritual maturity and are released into the wider world.

Forbia: An abandoned Hudson Bay wolf pup discovered and adopted by Finnegan. She becomes his familiar, and he names her Forbia, after his beloved ship he left in Maine.

Galon: A kinsman of Aidrik who was forced into Ascension by the Senetat after he angered them.

Goddess Danu: The goddess and leader of the Tuatha Dé Danann.

Goddess Morrigan: The goddess of divination, and one of the surviving Tuatha, foretold one day that four individuals—one descendant from each original clan—would unite the Empyreans and Quinlans once again. This prophecy was delivered to both a Quinlan and an Empyrean, and said that they would go through nearly two millennia of war and strife before finding peace.

Gorias: One of the four tribes of the Tuatha Dé Danann. All Quinlans descend from one of these four tribes. The tribe of Gorias is mentioned in The Prophecy as such: *A male Quinlan, known as Ciandn (little ancient one), reincarnated with Cerridwen.* Jacob Donnelly is the subject of this reference.

Grand Eldre Servius: The ruling grand eldre of the Senetat for several millennia. Was lesser-ranked at the time of Aidrik's service. Was known for his "scorched earth" policy and for taking the restrictive laws of the Empyrean race to the far extreme. Killed by Anasofiya at the execution of Aidrik.

Grand Emperor Aeron: The last ruling Grand Emperor of Farjhem, and the Empyrean race. Had a reputation for being kind, and benign, but showed no interest in meaningful involvement with his people. Was activated when Agripin spread false rumor of his treason. Agripin then succeeded him as grand emperor.

Grand Emperor Agripin: The current ruling Grand Emperor of Farjhem, and the Empyrean race. Previously Grand Duke Agripin. The only son and oldest child of Aeron and Theda, both deceased. Fought in the Second Runean War, where his distaste for the Senetat was born. Over the years, his love of easy living kept him from taking action, but his partnership with the Brotherhood grew over time. He used Aidrik and Anasofiya as part of his campaign, which results in the burning of Farjhem. Is currently in Trondheim with the rest of the Brotherhood, plotting their next move.

Grand Emperor Elof: Father of Aeron, who succeeded him when he was "activated" for suspected trafficking with the rebels. Betrayed by Eldre Brutus, who was his closest confidante.

Grand Emperor Seti: Ruling emperor of Farjhem at the time the Senetat was created. Supported the Senetat's inception, as he was not interested in being the upholder of laws.

Grand Empress Anasofiya: Born a halfling of the Deschanel clan in New Orleans. Aidrik gave her the Sveising to save her life, which gifted her with more potent versions of her existing abilities, as well as suspected immortality. Married to Finnegan, but evigbond to Aidrik, which created an unorthodox polyamorous triad between them. Mother to Aleksandr, who is the son of both men. Her skill as a resurrection shaman pales in comparison to her most potent ability of all, etheric summoning. She is currently magic-bound by Agripin following the execution of Aidrik, where she destroyed hundreds of Empyreans.

Grand Empress Theda: Mate of Aeron and mother of Agripin. Deceased.

Great Cleansing: Following the creation of the Senetat, Empyreans who refused the mark were sought out and executed. Those who survived were branded Runeans.

Great Commitment (Also: Officium Maximus): The graduation ceremony, once every hundred years, when Empyreans reach their age of maturity and are released from the Scholars' tutelage, out into the world. This ceremony includes the installation of Emyr's Mark, a magical brand in the shape of a phoenix that is said to include a part of Emyr Himself. In reality, it is a device of the Eldre Senetat, as a means to control the Empyreans once they leave Farjhem.

Hakon: Still a fledgling, son of Emperor Aeron through a tryst he had with Hakon's mother. The mother escaped from Farjhem, and she died after birthing Hakon. Trygve took him in, under his wing, in Mongolia. Is a bestiakinetic.

Halfling: Humans with some amount of Empyrean blood/ancestry. A human is considered a halfling even if their Empyrean blood is many generations back.

Holger: Kind and helpful scout of Birger and Astrid, sent to look after Jacob and Amelia.

Illusionist: One who can manipulate the reality of others. Some do this by changing the physical interpretation. Others do this through influence. Markus is an illusionist who can change his appearance. Eydis can influence people to do her bidding.

Inner Voice: Empyreans believe in the concept of an "Inner Voice" guiding them toward their destiny. For Mercy, the Inner

Voice was an illusion crafted by Aidrik, who was guiding her toward safety.

Isabella Deschanel: Daughter of Margarethe and the necromancer. Was the first starlight awakener in the family, raised in secrecy due to her rapid growth. Her life, and eventual burning at the stake for witchcraft, was chronicled in the propaganda pamphlet, *La Sorcière de Villeneuve*. The current Deschanel line descends through her.

Jorun: The Brotherhood leader over South America. Quiet and reclusive, she relates better to creatures on four feet, as a bestiakinetic. Lives apart from the other Empyreans of the region, but looks after them from afar.

Killianshire: A small village in southern Ireland, where Jacob was born and raised. Father O'Connor presides over the cathedral here. The village is Quinlan-friendly.

Kjære: Aidrik's term of endearment for Ana. Translates roughly to "my dear" or "my dearest" in Empyrean.

Leif: The Brotherhood leader over the Caribbean region. Was once a member of the Senetat, but over time grew weary of their hypocrisy. He escaped and became a critical leader amongst the Brotherhood. Can bind the magic of others.

Livia: Born in Spain to an Empyrean mother and human father. Her father had dark olive skin, and her darker skin tone puts her in danger, as no purebred Empyrean has these tones. Is closely guarded under the wing of Thorvald, and has a special bond with Lucia. Empath.

Lucia: Escaped the Scholars when she was still a student, leaving Farjhem without a plan other than the idea of her freedom. Thorvald found her and took her under his wing in Spain, dubbing her *mi belleza*, and fostering her great loyalty. He makes her a scout, and pairs her with Anders. Her most recent assignment took her to *Ophélie* to help train and protect the children of the Brotherhood. Is an empath who can absorb the pain of others without impact to herself.

Margarethe Deschanel: Granddaughter of Claude Deschanel and, therefore, a great-granddaughter of Aidrik. Refused to accept death was the end, and married a famed necromancer, learning his secrets. Upon her death, she was determined to come back, immortal, through a starlight awakener. She pushed her daughter, Isabella, to instruct the family in maintaining pure bloodlines, to increase the chances of a starlight awakener being born into the family. Her attempts to come through non-necromancers and necromancers alike led to many Deschanel deaths over the centuries, which was falsely attributed to the Deschanel Curse. When at last starlight awakeners are born, in the form of Stella and Sebastian, she is prevented from coming through. It is believed she has not given up.

Mark of Emyr (Also: mark, Emyr's Mark): A magical infusion, in the shape of a phoenix, given to all Empyreans at their Great Commitment. The mark is about two inches in diameter, and can be placed anywhere on the body, a choice made by the Empyrean receiving the mark. Empyreans are told the mark includes a part of Emyr Himself, and that when it is time for their Grand Ascension, the mark will call them home to Emyr. In reality, the mark is a sinister plot by the Eldre Senetat, created as a means to control the Empyreans and destroy them.

Marquise Deschanel: Husband of Christiane de Laurent (Aidrik's first human evigbond). He was the First Father of Claude Deschanel, the first Deschanel born with Empyrean blood.

Mercy (Also: Clementyn): Lived three thousand years as an Empyrean who believed in the illusion of Grand Ascension. Piety drove all of her life decisions, often to the point of folly. In her youth, she spent many years with Aidrik, and they did not part on good terms. She found herself crossing paths with Nicolas Deschanel, and when her mark activated, she died but was resurrected by Anasofiya, then becoming human. She currently resides with Nicolas at *Ophélie*.

Mora: Empyrean word for mother.

Murias: One of the four tribes of the Tuatha Dé Danann. All Quinlans descend from one of these four tribes. The tribe of Murias is mentioned in The Prophecy as such: *A female Quinlan, born halfling Empyrean but given far more at maturity.* It is not yet known who the subject of this reference is.

Mystic: Most powerful of all magi, among Empyreans and halflings. Mystics manifest their abilities in different ways. Some are strong healers, others can engage in nested visions, dream suggestion, wards, and other unique traits. All are strong telepaths. Aidrik, Nicolas, Agripin, and Aleksandr are mystics.

Necromancers: Can speak with the dead, though limited to those who have not "crossed over." Quillan is a necromancer.

Nested Vision: A nested vision is an ability only accessible by mystics, wherein the mystic can travel into the mind of another and observe the world through their eyes. The most powerful mystics not only observe, but also control the host. Nicolas Deschanel has newly discovered he is a mystic who can engage in nested visions.

Old Aita: Believed to be the oldest living Empyrean, she is shamed for not having experienced her Grand Ascension. Scholars use her as an example of how not to end up, and as a means of driving fear amongst the fledglings. She is said to have pure white hair.

***Ophélie*:** A plantation on the west bank of the River Road in Louisiana, about an hour from New Orleans. *Ophélie* has been the family seat of the Deschanels for over 200 years, and is passed down through the oldest male in each generation. Nicolas Deschanel, the current heir, has lived there his whole life.

Our Father (Also: Emyr, Our Father of Light, Our Father of Fire): Additional names for Emyr.

Portail: A portal created by a terrakinetic that can send travelers to any point in space.

Quinlans: An ancient line of druidic women, descendants of the Tuatha Dé Danann, and more recently, the Goddess Morrigan. All Quinlans descend from one of the four Tuatha tribes: Findias, Gorias, Falias, and Murias. They believe nature is unconditionally sacred, and that everything is interconnected, and balanced. Their powers are all drawn from nature. They live in secrecy, in protected groves and simplistic structures, all centering around their *crann bethadh*. In their early days, they had a strong alliance with the Empyreans, but that alliance was broken and both races have suffered the consequences. While the Quinlan genetics are passed through the females, in rare cases the male will also manifest. These males are known as draoi, and are more power than the females of the tribe. Most Quinlans keep the Quinlan surname.

Quinlan, Deirdre: Daughter of Seara. Mother of Noah, Nora, Nevina, and Niamh. Grandmother of Amelia. Is the youngest, and so has never taken a strong position of leadership. More of a free spirit, even for a druid. Married Kellan Jameson, a human. Kellan did not know what she was, until after Noah (her youngest) was born. When he threatened to leave, she secreted her daughters away to the tribe. Upon return to fetch her son, she learned Kellan had taken him to New Orleans.

Quinlan, Fiona: Only daughter of Nora. Is young—25—as Nora did not have her until later in life.

Quinlan, Meara: Middle child of Seara, sister of Deirdre and Philomena. Always happy, joyous, but simple-minded. The rest of the tribe closely protects her. Childless, she is not capable of a mutual relationship.

Quinlan, Nevina: Middle daughter of Deirdre, sibling to Nora, Niamh, and Noah. Does not travel outside the tribe. Is worried Jacob and Amelia are too "modern" for the job, and that the goddess waited too long to manifest the prophecy,

Quinlan, Niamh: Youngest daughter of Deirdre, sibling to Nora, Nevina, and Noah. Kind-hearted, and powerful, but often quiet, and whimsical.

Quinlan, Nora: Oldest daughter of Deirdre, sibling to Nevina, Niamh, and Noah. Tapped to take over as leader when the current one passes. Her practical nature makes her a competent leader.

Quinlan, Padraig: A draoi, and husband to Regan. He descends from another tribe of Falias. Trains Jacob, who has newly come into his draoi nature.

Quinlan, Philomena: Oldest child of Seara, sibling to Meara and Deirdre. Bitter to not be her mother's choice as successor. Strong-willed and often quick-tempered, especially now in her old age, which is why Seara did not choose her. Had one son in her youth, and gave him away when he was not a draoi.

Quinlan, Regan: Daughter of Nevina, sister to Kieran. Married to Padraig.

Quinlan, Rosemary: Mother of Enid, and grandmother of Jacob. A member of a tribe of Gorias, she has traveled to Seara's tribe to help with the prophecy.

Quinlan, Seara: Current leader of her tribe. Mother to Philomena, Meara, and Deirdre. Great-grandmother to Amelia. Sister to Flynn. All three of her children were intentionally conceived by men she picked herself, and planned a one-night stand. Has the essence of an oracle, who sees all (the prophecy was passed to her by the last leader). Knows her time is near, and is training her granddaughter, Nora, to take over.

Resurrection Shaman: A healer who is able to resurrect the recently deceased. Resurrection shamans are incredibly rare, and the ability is often volatile. Rarely do subjects come back exactly as they were before death. Anasofiya Deschanel discovers she is a resurrection shaman after Aidrik infuses her with Sveising.

Royal Palace of Farjhem: Residence of the royal family of Farjhem.

Runa: Leader of the minority opposition who rose up when the Senetat was created. Her execution is a symbol of strength for her followers, Runeans. She is often deified amongst her most devout followers. Her uprising is known as the First Runean War.

Runeans: Rebels. Those who oppose the Eldre Senetat are generally lumped together as Runeans (followers of Runa). Secretly, they have organized as the Dragon Brotherhood. Some in the Brotherhood are bloodthirsty and feel a call to action. Others are content to live quietly, off the grid of Empyrean society.

Scholar Saxon: The philosophy Scholar who carried out the execution of Mercy's parents after they were accused of heresy.

Scholars: A group of instructors selected by the Eldre Senetat to oversee the education of all Empyrean children. Their teachings often include propaganda-style support of the Senetat, and a fear-based deterrence of breaking rules. The Scholars spend a hundred years with Empyrean children.

Scholars' Temple: Place of instruction in Farjhem.

Second Runean War: Led by Erikr, the Runeans came together once more, in the spirit of Runa's beliefs, to overthrow the Senetat. As with the first uprising, they were squelched, and Erikr encased in a block of ice. This was the last large uprising of the rebels, who are now scattered and in hiding.

Senetat Sanctuary: Meeting place of the Senetat in Farjhem. Known for being sterile and devoid of any color excepting the crimson of their robes.

Shaman (Also: Healer): Another word for healer. There are varying degrees of shaman in the Deschanel family. Colleen Deschanel is said to be the strongest.

Sindre: Hails from the same Irish village as Birger, Astrid, and Eydis. A young elementalist who can conjure both fire and water, and often employs this skill to the hazard of others.

Skadi (Also: Skadi the Ruthless): The Brotherhood leader of Eastern Europe, residing in Bulgaria. She is known to be ruthless, cutthroat, and volatile to approach. She is remiss in her duties as a leader, in comparison to her peers, but is fiercely protective of her region.

St. Andrews, Finnegan: Husband of Anasofiya, father of Aleksandr. Born and raised in Maine to a normal, magic-free life. At his wedding, he accepted Aidrik's gift of Sveising, to grant him longer life and keener abilities. Recently learned he is descended from the Quinlans, and is a draoi, through this mother's side. Through his father, he is also descended from strong magic. Is a bestiakinetic.

St. Andrews, Ennis: Grandfather of Finnegan, father of Andrew, husband of Fiona. Lives in a protected, secluded clearing in the Scottish Highlands with his wife, who he keeps alive and young through potent magic.

St. Andrews, Fiona: Grandmother of Finnegan, mother of Andrew, wife of Ennis. Lives in a protected, secluded clearing in the Scottish Highlands with Ennis and is kept alive and young through his magic.

Starlight Awakener: An exceptionally rare form of necromancers said to "awaken the starlight," and employ the power of the heavens to occupy the living, and achieve immortality. Margarethe bred the family for centuries in search of a starlight awakener to come back through. Stella and Sebastian are starlight awakeners. Before them, the only known starlight awakener was Isabella.

Stian: A Brotherhood leader who chose Africa as his region because of the strife. He never stays anywhere for long, and is always moving around, helping where he can. As a terrakinetic, he can create a rift in the Earth, allowing a man to leave one place and appear in another, called a portail.

Sveising: DNA fusion unique to Empyreans. It is the process that allows multiple fathers for offspring, as well as the means by which Aidrik is able to save Anasofiya. Sveising can occur through sexual consummation (in the case of creating multiple fathers), but a mystic can also do it without consummation.

Telepath: One who can read the thoughts of others. Rare telepaths can read thoughts over long distances. Very few telepaths can also break a telepathic block. Tristan is a telepath who can reach across long distances and breach blocks.

Telepathic Block: A block employed my magic users to keep telepaths out of their head.

Terrakinetic: The ability to manipulate the spatial elements of Earth to your advantage. Example: a portail. Stian is a terrakinetic.

Thorvald: Brotherhood leader of Spain. He resides in the *Costa del Sol*, where he trains warriors and scouts in preparation for the inevitable war against the Senetat. Also one of the ancients, or earliest Empyreans.

Time Dancing (Also: Time Dancer): A skill unique to draoi. The time dancer can "dance" through time, a form of time traveling, but cannot change the past. Jacob is a time dancer.

Time Shaping (Also Time Shaper): An Empyrean skill that allows the individual to stop time and "reshape" it. The effect can be catastrophic if the caster is untrained, or if time stops for too long. Aleksandr is a time shaper.

Tribe: A group of Quinlans, usually descended from the same Tuatha tribe. All tribes have an elder, and a scribe.

Trygve: A Brotherhood leader, over Mongolia. One of the oldest Empyreans, having also been from the time of Runa, Brynja, and Einar, and has the markings of the ancients: exceptional height, dark red hair. Has one of the larger followings of the leaders. Known to be fair and loyal, but also quick to action and swift to justice.

Tuatha Dé Danann: Descended from Goddess Danu, early deities in Gaelic history, originating in Norway and later settling in Erin (Ireland). Ruled Ireland from 1897-1700 B.C. Many of the tales of faeries stem from their legends. There are four major tribes of Tuatha, each with a unique talisman of power. They hid in *Tir Non Og*, the otherworld, after Milesians drove them out of their lands. They believe strongly in reincarnation. Tuatha were the original druids, though modern day druidism became its own unique thing. The Quinlans descend from the four tribes of the Tuatha.

Ulfberht: A Viking sword produced between 800 and 1000 AD, made from Empyrean Steel (known to Man as Crucible Steel), known for its unusual combination of strength and flexibility. Though man believes this sword was crafted for Vikings, it was, in fact, created by Blacksmith, an ancient Empyrean metallurgist. The technology used to make Ulfberht baffles scientists to this day. Aidrik wielded one of the last of the originals, but gave it to Finnegan prior to his death.

Ward: A magical protection with unclear barriers, most

potent at its center. The ability to create wards came as a result of the alliance between Empyrean and Quinlan, and it was set forth that only an Empyrean (mystic) may create a ward, and only a Quinlan (draoi) can adhere it. Aidrik's ward is one such example, the center of it cast over *Ophélie* where it is most potent, with effects radiating out to protect other relatives. The protection diminishes the further out you go.

Yiva: Brotherhood leader of Southeast Asia, specifically residing in Thailand. Yields a body-length spear and is a powerful bestiakinetic. Known as the "she wolf."

ABOUT THE AUTHOR

Sarah is the USA Today and International Bestselling Author of over forty contemporary and epic fantasy stories, and the creator of the Kingdom of the White Sea and Saga of Crimson & Clover universes.

Born a geek, Sarah spends her time crafting rich and multi-layered worlds, obsessing over history, playing her retribution paladin (and sometimes destruction warlock), and settling provocative Tolkien debates, such as why the Great Eagles are not Gandalf's personal taxi service. Passionate about travel, she's been to over twenty countries collecting sparks of inspiration, and is always planning her next adventure.

Sarah and her husband live in a beautiful corner of SE Pennsylvania with their three tiny benevolent pug dictators.

www.sarahmcradit.com

www.ingramcontent.com/pod-product-compliance
Lightning Source LLC
Chambersburg PA
CBHW020242030826
48979CB00030B/2480/J